HUNTED IN THE SHADOWS

MARY DUBLIN
ANNE KENDSLEY

PRONUNCIATION GUIDE

Aelthorin – [AL-thor-in]

Elysia – [eh-LIHZ-iy-ah]

Marcellus – [Mar-SELL-us]

Nowak – [N-OH-v-ack]

Veloria – [Vuh-LOHR-ee-uh]

Cliff – [Klif]

a ~~delight~~

has sweaty hands

HUNTED
IN THE
SHADOWS

MARY DUBLIN
ANNE KENDSLEY

PRAISE FOR

"IF YOU'RE IN THE MOOD FOR A MAGICAL, FORBIDDEN LOVE ROMANCE WITH A SLOW BURN — THIS IS THE BOOK FOR YOU!
-SHELBY MCFADDEN, BESTSELLING AUTHOR OF THE GROVE HOLLOW SERIES™

"IT HAS TO BE ONE OF THE BEST FANTASY BOOKS I'VE EVER READ. THE BANTER AMONG THEM IS REFRESHING IN A STORY THAT COMBINES THE ETHEREAL BEAUTY OF THE FAIRY FANTASY WORLD WITH THE THREAT OF REAL MONSTERS. IT'S LIKE THE PERFECT COMBINATION OF MURDER, MYSTERY, ROMANCE AND MAGIC."
-JULIA, GOODREADS

"KENDSLEY AND DUBLIN WEAVE A NARRATIVE AS MAGICAL AS THE PROTAGONIST HERSELF – A SPELL-BINDING TALE OF TRUST, DANGER, AND KINSHIP BEYOND BOUNDARIES."
-FABIAN, GOODREADS

"IT'S A WORLD YOU WILL WANT TO STAY IN FOREVER... TO ANYONE MISSING SAM AND DEAN WINCHESTER, FEELS THE PULL OF OLD MAGIC ON THEIR FAIRY SOULS, FEELS THEIR BLOOD POUNDING AT THE THOUGHT OF HUNTING EVIL WITH A SHOTGUN AND A KNIFE, OR EVEN JUST LONGS TO FALL IN LOVE... PICK THIS BOOK UP."
-CORTNIE, GOODREADS

"YOU WILL BE LEFT WANTING MORE."
-JENN, GOODREADS

CONTENT WARNING

This fantasy story includes some content that may be troubling for some readers, including:

Profanity, violence, blood, sexual themes, car accident, conversations around pregnancy, homophobia, alcohol usage, and loss of a parent.

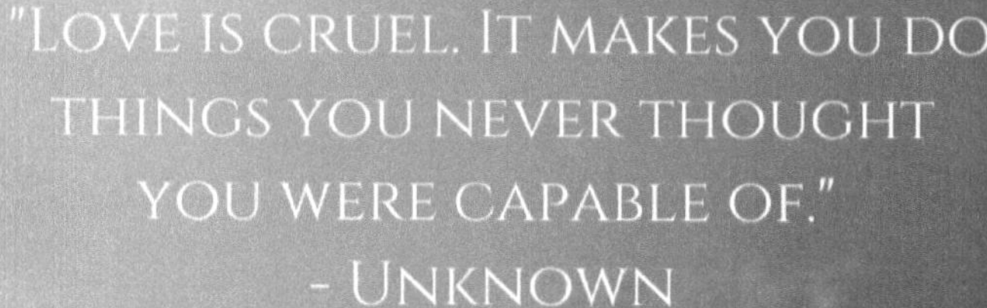
"Love is cruel. It makes you do things you never thought you were capable of."
- Unknown

DEDICATION

For those who have ever felt difficult to love—may you always find the ones who see your worth, even when you can't.

OFFICIAL PLAYLIST & MORE

1
SYLVIA

Vampire blood and stale popcorn smelled just as bad mixed together as I had imagined.

According to Jon and Cliff, Blockbusters like this were the epicenter of human weekends several decades ago. Thanks to the miracle of streaming services, they were now obsolete. This particular Arkansas location had shut its doors nine years prior, but like many places sheltered outside the public eye, it hadn't stayed empty.

Beyond rows of shelves coated in layers of grime and neglect, the musty air was charged with a vampire presence—*only one left,* I thought with tentative relief.

Five had been nesting in the abandoned store when I'd flown in behind Cliff and Jon thirty minutes prior. A small coven, but that didn't mean much when even one vampire could outrun a speeding car and rip a human apart like wet paper.

Unfortunately, I could attest to this personally after only two months of traveling with a pair of hunters.

I struggled to tear my eyes off the headless body Cliff was knelt over. The half-lit glow of the flickering fluorescent lights cast his familiar face into shadow, making him look like he'd emerged from a cautionary fireside tale about hunters. Unnatural, syrupy blood stained the machete gripped in his right hand and smeared across his hands and jeans like molasses. The decapitated head of his kill stared up at me from the faded blue carpet.

"Hey!" Cliff snapped his fingers twice to get my attention. "Don't puke."

"Any other sage advice?" But my attempt at nonchalance couldn't hide that my dinner churned in my stomach.

Three other bodies were strewn across the floor like demented breadcrumbs leading deeper into the store. Each corpse had a gaping blackened hole where its heart used to be, courtesy of an oak stake. An earth fairy would have certainly worked wonders in a vampire hunt, but I made do with ice.

The final vampire's aura made my senses pulse erratically. He was on the move, perhaps harboring more self-preservation than the coven mates who'd been staked and decapitated before his eyes. Rather than make a stand and lash out at the hunters in a vengeful rage, he ducked behind the *Animation* shelves and made a break for the back hallway.

Jon bolted after him from across the store, his stake dripping with dark blood. The weapon was one good strike away from splintering for good. Jon was fast, brimming with adrenaline, but no human was a match for a vampire's speed. I chewed my lip anxiously, once again thinking how this hunt would have been more straightforward if they'd had silver bullets; the hunters' seemingly endless supply had finally been depleted—the last two rounds embedded in the back of the now-headless vampire lying facedown on the carpet. Silver wasn't enough to kill a vampire, but it certainly slowed them down.

I zipped away from Cliff to catch up, pressing my palms together as I whispered a spell. Throwing my hands out, I conjured a shimmering orb that tore across the room. As it made contact with the vampire's back, the light exploded into a burst of crystalline spikes. Many shattered against the unnaturally tough skin, but enough broke through to make him stagger.

Howling, the vampire caught himself against a nearby wall and reached back to wrest the icicles buried in his flesh. Though his back was painted in blood, the wounds were swiftly regenerating.

My attack slowed our target long enough for Jon to close the distance. Without an ounce of hesitation, Jon seized him by the back of the neck and turned him round so they were eye to eye, pinning him against the wall. The stake was a breath above the vampire's chest, ready to plunge.

"Pathetic," the vampire gritted through sharpened teeth. He kicked Jon's six-three frame back like he weighed nothing. He slammed into the adjacent wall, knocking a few faded letters from the *New Releases* sign, along with a shower of old DVD cases.

"Jon!" I half-expected a blaze of pain to shoot through my body to match Jon's, though our Ancient bond had been severed for months. I lunged to assist him, inadvertently putting myself within the vampire's reach.

The monster seized me from the air with his stars-forsaken speed. His blindingly tight grip didn't allow me to draw enough air to scream. If he'd held me any longer, my bones would have caved, but he was still in a frenzy to escape. The world spun as he pitched me away from him, perhaps hoping to break my neck on the central counter.

My wings cramped and my vision was spotty, unable to distinguish up from down. I tried to orient my flight, but I couldn't slow myself—

A shadow engulfed me, and my descent stopped short as I found myself safely in Cliff's hands. He staggered to his feet, breathing heavily.

"Are you okay?" he demanded.

I coughed, blinking away my double vision. "Can I puke now?"

"Not on *me*, that's for damn sure."

From the corner of my eye, I saw Jon scrambling to his feet and kicking aside cases. The vampire vanished into a back room and slammed the door so hard that I thought the building would collapse. That was nothing compared to the Earth-shaking impact of Jon throwing his weight against the door. Amazingly, it didn't budge.

"*Coño*," he growled, pacing in front of the lock.

With a grunt, I pushed myself up and ignored my aching muscles. At least my wings were in working order.

"Maybe we should go around the back," I said, approaching Jon with cautious flight. "He could be running for an exit."

"No time."

Jon instructed me to move back, and when he squared himself in front of the door, I hurriedly gave him space. He delivered a powerful kick near the door handle. The metal squealed in protest. Charging forward, he dealt another blow that might have leveled a tree. The door swung inward with a deafening splinter of wood.

I put a hand over my mouth, eyes wide. *Stars help me, destructiveness shouldn't be this much of a turn-on.* As the dust settled, I shook my head and filed the image away for later. *Focus.*

Jon charged inside—and faltered. I pulled to a sharp hover beside him and drank in the depraved sight before us. What once might've been a break room had been transformed into a human farm. Outdated furnishings had been pushed off to one side, apart from a waist-high shelf that boasted a bulbous TV, the sole source of light. I briefly considered the image on-screen: a movie set in what appeared to be a high school, with young humans chatting in a parking lot.

A line of shackles were crudely hammered into the back wall of the dingy room—six sets. Only one was still occupied.

"One more move and I'll snap her neck," the vampire said between heavy breaths.

He had the one remaining woman clutched to him like a shield, a vice-like grip around her throat. Beneath her ratty tee and jeans, her body was covered in angry, welting bite marks.

"End of the line," Jon said, his voice steadying through shallow breaths. "I'll make it painless for you. Much kinder than the monster who turned you in the first place and ruined your life."

"*Ruined?* Giovanni gave me everything I wanted! Family, power, immortality. I was nothing before I met him. A fucking loser selling printers at Office Depot. But he saw through all of that. He wanted me. He *chose* me!"

Despite his modest appearance—sandy hair, average features, and nondescript clothing—subtle, almost imperceptible nuances in his gaze and posture confirmed the sinister aura radiating off him in waves. He looked entirely human, but that couldn't be further from the truth.

The woman whimpered as the vampire's grip tightened on her throat. Her chained hands scrabbled at his fingers as she gasped for air. She may as well have been clawing at stone.

"Let her go," Jon bit out, all traces of reasoning hardening into resolve.

"I'll raise you one," the vampire said. "Kick the stake over and fuck off. Your little pet and your boyfriend out there, too."

As the movie played on behind me, vivid hues danced across the woman's anguished expression. The lighthearted dialogue and music knotted my stomach.

"*Some asshole paid me to take out this really great girl.*"

"*Is that right?*"

"*Yeah, but I screwed up. I, um, I fell for her.*"

Jon remained rooted, his face etched with steely determination, strategy whirring into place behind his eyes. This wasn't the face of the man I'd spent hours intertwined within the spectral plane. This was the face of a killer.

The vampire gave a soft, throaty laugh. "You think you're strong. Hunters always do. I've seen a few of you, waltzing around like you're God's gift to the world. But humanity is such a fragile concept."

His unassuming features split into a smile that verged on crazed—and I watched in horrified disgust as it morphed into something nightmarish. In near silence, rows of needle-like teeth pushed through his gums, locking into place with a soft, grotesque *click*. My skin screamed for me to run, to *fight*. My body was coiled for action, but I looked urgently to Jon for my cue.

"Do whatever he says," the woman rasped. "Please—go! Get out, he'll kill you all. *Please!*"

I swallowed hard. She wasn't begging for her life—she was trying to save *Jon*. A stranger. I might have surged forward to save her myself if Jon and Cliff hadn't coached better self-control.

"Always a sweetheart, our Veronica," the vampire sneered. Never taking his eyes off of Jon, he intimately brushed his cheek against Veronica's. His teeth grazed his bottom lip like he wanted to add another bite to her collection. "Her blood's on your hands if you don't get the fuck out. I'll take good care of her. Cross my heart."

Jon didn't flinch. "No. You're handing her over."

"I'm not sure you understand how hostage situations work."

To my shock, Jon lowered the stake. "I understand better than you think. How about a trade?" He gestured to me and raised his eyebrows at the vampire.

"Yeah, right," the vampire scoffed, but there was a hint of intrigue in his eyes at the unexpected offer. "She seems pretty loyal."

"You ever seen one? She's like a golden retriever. She'll be loyal to anyone who treats her right. And trains her." Jon raised his free arm toward me, exposing three deep gouges near his wrist. His eyes flickered to me, empty of their usual light. "Heal it. Now."

Either he was creating this ruse on the spot, or he had kept the idea tucked away for an emergency. Whatever the case, my mouth fell open.

Still, I wasn't about to blow it by not playing my part.

Lowering my gaze, I chanted the healing spell and closed the angry red lines on Jon's forearm. The process took only a moment, but judging by how quiet the vampire became, he was truly pausing to consider my usefulness. A healer wouldn't do *him* or his kind much good, but Cliff's journal said that vampires needed to be careful how much they drained from long-term victims. I could increase the longevity of their blood sources. Less missing people meant less hunters breathing down their necks.

"Good girl," Jon said in a low voice that caressed my very soul and made my face flush. It was a wonder I didn't melt. "Now show us how entertaining you can be with your frost. Do the one I like."

Putting on a doe-eyed smile like I wanted nothing more than to please him, I summoned ice between my palms, directing it upward. Mist spread near the ceiling and glittered like diamonds, reflecting the light of the television. Delicate flakes fluttered down, unassuming and beautiful.

Even Veronica, in her delirium, looked enchanted by the impossibility before her eyes. Her slack-jawed expression became taut with a horrified scream when I cultivated the mist and snow into a single stab of ice through the vampire's neck—a precise shot inches from Veronica's face.

The vampire gagged, lurching back and releasing her.

Jon lunged across the room, jammed his oak stake through the monster's heart, and twisted. A strangled, animalistic moan escaped those fanged lips—then, silence. As the vampire's eyes went vacant, the aura of the coven depleted entirely, and I could breathe easier. Jon grit his teeth, shoving the vampire's limp body into the corner, where limbs settled at unnatural angles.

A confusing beat of pride rushed through me as I considered our handiwork—twin spikes of oak and ice protruding from our kill.

As Jon hurriedly picked Veronica's wrist cuffs, he squinted over his shoulder at me. "Your face is red. Are you hurt?"

"I'm fine." Now wasn't the appropriate time to share how uniquely flustering this encounter in the break room had been.

Veronica stared at me, rubbing her freed wrists. "I've gone crazy," she whispered. Her gaze trailed to the vampire's body, then to Jon, eyes brimming with tears. "I've gone crazy, right?"

Jon set a hand on her shoulder to steady her on her feet, gentle near the bite marks as he steadied her. "Not even close. You're almost out of this. You're going to be okay, I promise."

Eyes welling with desperate tears, Veronica leaned hard against him for support and shuddered. Murmuring that she would be home soon, Jon led her to the door, and I followed, leaving behind the corpse and the drone of the television.

The instant we passed the threshold, it occurred to me that we hadn't heard even a word from Cliff. Stopping short beside Jon, I realized *why*.

Back in the main room, Cliff was pinned by his throat against the wall, unable to make a sound.

2
SYLVIA

"They had names, you know." The unfamiliar man with his hand around Cliff's throat was dressed casually like the others—a plain cotton shirt, jeans, and laced boots not dissimilar from the sort Jon and Cliff favored. But when he turned his head to us, an ancient gleam was buried in his cobalt eyes that made my blood run ice-cold. "No matter where I go, your kind comes to annihilate my family."

"Cliff!" I blurted, clapping my hands over my mouth.

His bloodshot green eyes shot to me—a nearly imperceptible shake of his head. "Don't… don't, Sylv."

The tremor in his voice made me queasy. I wasn't sure I had ever heard Cliff this scared before—not since Jon had nearly succumbed to that wound in the Dottage basement.

I watched, helpless, as Cliff's face drained of color in his struggle for air. His towering frame, usually so strong, seemed to wither compared to the man pinning him. His muscles strained as he pulled and clawed, but the hand around his throat only tightened, forcing Cliff's breaths down into ragged gasps. His stake lay on the floor by a shelf, just out of reach.

My stomach bottomed out. Another vampire—but how did I not sense him? Even as I stared right at him, clawing at my senses, I only felt a distant, foul pulsing, easily ignored.

Glamour. It had to be glamour masking his presence. Unlike the fae variation used defensively in Elysia, vampire glamour had a predatory allure that hypnotized victims. But I had sensed every vampire I'd encountered in the last two months, the same as any other ghost or monster.

My only theory was that he must have been uniquely powerful. *Giovanni.* The coven leader who had turned the vampire in the break room—and all the others strewn about the carpet.

"Veronica, get back," Jon said, ushering her into the hallway behind him. She had both hands clasped over her mouth, trembling as she fixed her gaze at the floor as though she couldn't bring herself to directly acknowledge the coven leader.

Jon fixed his gaze back to Giovanni, his jaw set. "A little late to play martyr. Your *family* killed hundreds of innocent people."

The vampire's lips twitched in a smile. "Don't insult me. That's a little modest, don't you think? I don't like to brag about body count, but former slayers *are* the most difficult to put down."

My heart skipped a beat as his words registered.

"You were a hunter?" I croaked.

Giovanni's gaze rested directly on me, glimmering with humor as though he could sense every one of my reeling thoughts. Unbridled arrogance came with his power. I wanted to be vicious, fearless, but I eased a little further back behind Jon.

"Lifetimes ago, I was the most feared witch hunter in Florence," he said, his words drawling with the assurance of a man who had all the time in the world. "A different name, a different man… But that's the trouble with hunters, my dear—always the most at risk of becoming the very creatures they hunt." His sharp smile grew. "Now, I haven't seen a fairy since the days of bathtub gin. Allied with hunters, though… That's a first. Even I wouldn't have stooped so low in my mortal days." He turned his attention back to Cliff. "Curious boys, aren't you?"

Giovanni pressed forward, nostrils flaring as he inhaled deeply against the hollow of Cliff's throat. Cliff's strained expression twitched with revulsion.

"I could smell the neglect on you both from miles away," Giovanni purred. "I've been watching you, same as you've been watching us. A pair of wounded little boys wielding shotguns and stakes because Daddy didn't hug you enough…" He clicked his tongue, shaking his head. The sympathy on his face was unnervingly genuine, his voice dropping into a near-whisper. "I used to take boys just like you under my wing, you know. Boys who didn't have a proper family. We can make our own. You won't be alone again."

"Just eat me, you fucking perv," Cliff gritted out.

"That pretty mouth says 'no', but your eyes say you like it rough. This might be fun for you. Give it a decade or two on the other side of the game—you'll warm up to the idea, same as I did."

Giovanni's jaw rippled, almost like a grimace, and I muscled down a repulsed noise as his set of needle-like fangs emerged, clicking into place. Unlike most vampires, Giovanni had multiple rows—some layered right over the others, like they were competing for space.

The movement seemed to sever some invisible tether on Jon. He surged forward, his bloodstained oak stake gleaming dully in the flickering light.

I caught only a glimpse of Giovanni's sharp, white teeth before they were buried in Cliff's collarbone. A cry stuck in my throat. Jon's roar of anger numbed my hearing. As Cliff bucked and rasped pained curses, the venom weakened him in seconds.

As I raced past Jon's shoulder to attack, Giovanni lifted his head to set his eyes on me, and the world froze to a standstill. His bloodied lips didn't move, yet his words washed over my mind like ink on paper.

"I've been shielding my true nature for your comfort, my dear. You have no idea what you're dealing with. I've walked the Earth since Cortes first got his dick wet in America." I swore his laugh echoed

all around me. *"Look at you. You're ants trying to bring down a mountain."*

And then, he lowered the invisible shield that had so graciously blocked my senses, and his presence flooded me. I wanted to scream, but the sound was too big to escape. Sheer terror pounded through my veins as my senses were rattled by the full scope of his power, and there was absolutely nothing I could do to stop it.

The world swung back into motion, but as Jon closed the distance to Giovanni, I was drowning in the crushing weight of Giovanni's mental assault. I clapped my hands to my head, trying to force the throbbing to subside. I had to be stronger—I couldn't leave Jon alone.

In one swift motion, Giovanni released a weakened Cliff against the wall and lashed an arm out to thwart Jon's advance. A brutal fist closed around the stake before it could impale his heart. The wood splintered, and Giovanni seized Jon by the throat.

"I will enjoy this," Giovanni snarled at Jon, who fought like a rabid dog on a tight leash. The vampire's expression softened into one of sick comfort as he turned to Cliff on the ground. "The bite will heal once you've turned. I'll let you decide whether you want your friend to join you or be your first meal." He chuckled as though he could anticipate the outcome. "Younglings are always so ravenous the first day. Nothing to be ashamed of."

As Giovanni bit down on his own free wrist and drew a stream of crimson, I recalled the notes in Cliff's journal. Vampire transformations required an exchange of blood—much more intentional than werewolves. The bite would weaken him, but a drink from Giovanni's veins would transform him permanently.

I pictured Jon in the basement of the Dottage house, skin hot as the werewolf infection ravaged him. I trembled with thoughts of the terrible things I would do to save either hunter.

I couldn't let the vampire's blood touch Cliff's tongue.

My scream finally emerged in the form of an incantation. I caught a look at Giovanni's face and saw the shock flash through his eyes. Even *he* hadn't been prepared for me to tear through what he had done to me. I flew up near the ceiling—far from his reach—and aimed a spell at his arm. Frost coated his self-inflicted bite, freezing the blood before racing up his shoulder and across his chest. I grit my teeth, unyielding as I whispered the spell over and over.

Giovanni growled up at me, his angelic features melting into a nightmarish scowl. "Your filthy allegiance will be the death of you!"

Even in his weakened state, Cliff spotted the opening. He kicked at the vampire's legs, making Giovanni stumble and loosen his grip on Jon.

"Jon!" Cliff grunted. He grabbed his own fallen stake and tossed it.

Without pausing to catch his breath, Jon snatched the weapon out of the air and drove it through Giovanni's chest, shattering my icy formation like glass. The two of them slammed to the ground, fighting for the upper hand.

The vampire's roar was pure animal, wide eyes hateful and bloodshot. I dove closer, defensive magic coiled up to my shoulders—but as Jon withdrew the stake, there was no need to cast another spell. Giovanni went limp, the agony etched on his face slackening.

Jon snarled, his voice rough in a way I scarcely recognized as he plunged the stake into the heart area a second time. A third. The stake's tip shattered within the corpse, leaving a ragged column of oak in his hand. Silence might have followed, but Jon pulled his machete from its sheath. He raised it high and swung it down over Giovanni's neck, severing head from shoulders.

He spat on the vampire's prone, decapitated body. The display was savage, a far cry from the warm light I loved in him.

No—that light was there. I'd mistaken it for sunlight, but Jon was *lightning.* As frightening as it was beautiful, razing all it touched.

When he yanked the machete blade from the carpet and dismounted the body, I didn't avert my gaze from his. If he was lightning, I would let him burn me over and over.

In seconds, Giovanni's fair skin turned a sickly aged parchment shade. Fissures formed like paint peeling from ancient pottery. And then he crumbled to mere ash—settling like a disgusting snowfall, quiet as a whisper. The chaos dropped into an unnerving silence, leaving only the echoes of our heavy breathing in the stillness.

The remaining vampire corpses littering the floor followed suit—something about being tied to the alpha who turned them, Cliff had once told me. Piles of empty, bloodstained clothes were scattered in their wake. I coughed, flitting back toward the wall Cliff was slumped against. The Blockbuster was cloudy with vampire ash, and it smelled like *shit.* Sulfurous decay hardly added to the bouquet of old movie snacks and bloodshed.

Below me, Cliff coughed raggedly. "I've told you a million times not to stake when my mouth's open!" He spat out ash, glaring half-heartedly at Jon.

"You're welcome," Jon huffed. The rage on his face eased, eyes wide with worry as he studied Cliff. "We need to patch that up, *fast.* Are you feverish yet?"

"I feel great," Cliff said, dragging himself up into a seated position. "I *love* being a human pincushion."

I glided down, catching Jon's eye meaningfully. "I've got him," I murmured, allowing my defensive magic to melt away. Looking between us, Jon gave a nod and murmured his gratitude before pulling himself away to check on Veronica.

Wincing, Cliff tore his shirt further to make his wound accessible to me as I approached him. Tiny pools of blood gathered in the bite's many punctures, trickling steadily down his chest, over his many interlocking tattoos. My head still throbbed from the glamour attack. And *Cliff*—we could have lost him.

I stumbled over the words of the healing incantation, my hands trembling so hard that the magic couldn't form properly.

"Hey," Cliff murmured. I peeked up to find a pained little smirk on his lips. He gestured at the icy formations adorning the inside of the building. "A little over the top, don't you think? You're taking the fun out of the hunt."

A harsh laugh rattled through me. "Any more *fun*, and you would've been tasting blood instead of ash."

"You don't think I'd make a hot vampire?"

"Please. You're enough of a nightmare as is."

Miraculously, our shared chuckle gave me the poise to complete the healing. My handiwork was far from perfect. When I tried to tell Cliff my suspicion that part of his collarbone might still be cracked, he advised me to save my energy and nodded in Veronica's direction. Jon knelt beside her, helping her breathing calm.

"No pressure," Cliff added, softer. "The hospital isn't far."

The hunters never forced me to do anything, but I couldn't bear the idea of letting that poor girl suffer while I had the power to take the pain away.

Jon stayed close behind me like a sentry while I healed Veronica's many bite wounds. Although I doubted she would do anything rash, I was grateful for Jon's watchful stare. His eyes only tore from me long enough to punch in the phone number on his cell to request a cab.

The sight of the fang marks, ranging from weeks-old to hours-old, made my chanted words tight. Veronica stayed quiet other than a few sighs when the freshest wounds faded, but as I finished closing the last few punctures near her wrist, she swallowed hard and drew in a little breath to speak. I braced myself, certain that I would be met with a slew of questions that I'd rather not answer.

"Thank you," she whispered. Relieved tears mixed with the ash on her cheeks. "I forgot what it felt like not to hurt." She still stared like she couldn't believe I was real, but freedom from the utter hell she'd lived through must have superseded all other thoughts.

"I know how you feel," I replied, reminded of the constant ache of a bullet hole in my wing. Except Veronica's captors never had the faintest intention of letting her see sunlight again.

Within ten minutes, headlights pierced the vacant parking lot outside. After looting through a few piles of clothes, the hunters found plenty of cash to cover the fare two times over. Jon pressed the money into Veronica's hands, careful to stay in the shadows when we ventured out the front of the building. I hovered beside Jon at eye-level, mindful of the slow approach of the vehicle.

"You have somewhere safe to go?" Jon asked.

Veronica rubbed her bare arms against the sting of the bitter autumn night. "My brother. He lives across town, not far from my place. He must've worried himself into an ulcer by now. It's been *weeks*."

She attempted a laugh which came out more as a choked wince. My brow knit—I knew the feeling poignantly. It would be some time before that smile came without effort.

Cliff stepped forward, shouldering off his jacket. He draped it around Veronica to quell her shivering. Vampire blood smeared a large portion of the canvas material, but she clung to the sleeves like he'd given her diamonds.

"How can I thank you?" she asked in a thready voice, eyes wide.

Cliff gave her one of those softer smiles that made me melt, exchanging a look with Jon.

"Wait a couple days before you give a statement to the police," Cliff said. "And… maybe you could forget the two handsome devils that came on the scene when you do."

Veronica scanned him up and down, an understanding clench set in her jaw. "What guys?"

Cliff grinned. "Attagirl."

The cab parked at the curb, idling. I cemented myself to Jon's shoulder, silencing my wings to stay hidden. Veronica dove forward to embrace each hunter and paused to regard me—offering a teary smile of gratitude before she ducked away, tearing open the back door of the vehicle and climbing inside.

I became more aware of my heart hammering out a war-beat as ambient stillness took hold, broken only by the rumble of the cab's departure. Its fading tail lights cast a fleeting glow against the damp pavement before turning onto the main road and disappearing into the night.

Relief should have washed over me. We had survived another hunt. We'd saved a woman and perhaps the very soul of this sleepy town.

I cast a look back toward the crime scene, unease licking up my spine. I hadn't sensed the coven leader's presence, and Cliff had nearly lost his life because of it. Were there others I had missed during our stops traveling west?

My fluttering pulse wouldn't slow. What would it cost if it happened again?

Taking wing, I flew ahead of the hunters back into the Blockbuster. Under the weak gray light of the surviving fluorescents, I surveyed the room warily. It was choked in quiet, smoldering with ash and ice.

Jon and Cliff ambled inside behind me, their steps heavy and slow as they scoured the area for any salvageable supplies—which wasn't much.

"Should we call up a cleaner?" Jon asked.

"Nah. Nothing to salvage but dust, and that doesn't go for much," Cliff answered as he rooted through a pile of clothes. "They'd harass us for cash for the trouble, and we can't spare it."

"We should be thorough," I called out, my voice a frightened quiver wrapped in authority. I was too preoccupied to question what a *cleaner* was. "Make sure nothing else is hiding here."

"Relax," Cliff said, pocketing a wristwatch that would likely be added to the hunters' *pawn* stash—whatever that was. "If King Dickhead's ash, so are the rest of his spawn."

"And you know that for sure?" I started back toward the break room, fretful. "*I* didn't know that any monster could cloak their presence from me. Surprises happen."

"Take a breather, will ya?" Cliff called. "Aren't you sore after being chucked across the room? You're lucky that fucker didn't break your wings."

"What?" Jon's voice snapped, bringing forth the image of a lightning crack once more. "Who?"

I sighed and gestured to the break room. "He got hold of me after he threw you into the shelf."

Jon closed the space to me in three quick strides, eyes wide. He reached halfway for me, hesitating as though he might cause more injury. "He put his hands on you?"

"I'm fine," I said with a dismissive chuckle. His stare read me as far too fragile for my liking—even if my arms and ribs throbbed with the promise of impending bruises. A strained smile was the best I could offer him. "Much as I love the murder in your eyes for my sake, there's no one left to kill. Let's give the building one last sweep and say goodbye to it."

Jaw clenched, he conceded—somewhat. "I'll take another look around. Stay here, and stay off your wings."

"Yes, *sir*," I said in a sultry voice that made him flee with color in his cheeks.

Although I remained slightly on edge, an unusual sense of calm permeated the building. In my limited experience, hunts typically ended in a rush to beat police phone calls and escape the evidence of a massacre. Ash stirred in the breeze of the open doors. How long before it could be easily mistaken for the natural dust of abandonment?

Cliff overturned drawer after drawer behind the counter, finding nothing of note. "Wish you could've seen this place in its prime, Sylv. Lots of good memories."

"Prime?" Jon laughed, glancing up from one of the shelves. "This whole chain was on its last legs by the time we were in high school."

"Hey, don't shit on my golden days," Cliff wistfully ran his hand over the surface that had nearly broken my neck. He glanced up at me, eyebrows lifted conspiratorially. "I had a buddy who worked at a Blockbuster, you know. I'd swing by after football games, and he'd hook me up with free candy and let me use the break room."

"For what?" I landed on the counter to heed Jon's order and rest my wings.

Grinning, Cliff rooted behind one of the cabinets. "To nail the head cheerleader, obviously."

"I thought that was the quarterback?" Jon called from across the room.

"Little of this, little of that." Cliff made a thoughtful noise and pried out something from between a drawer and panel. "Hey, check it out—"

He held up a blue and yellow scrap of cardboard for my inspection. It was creased so badly that I could barely discern the lettering: *Blockbuster Membership Card.*

"What's it for?" I asked.

"People used it to check out movies from this place."

"Can I have it?"

"Knock yourself out, kiddo."

I flew up and snatched it from him, too thrilled by my hunting trophy to register my wings' ache of protest.

3

JON

"You're the only person on the planet who's excited to do laundry," Cliff remarked as he pulled our silver Pontiac into the empty laundromat parking lot.

Sylvia gave an insulted scoff from her perch on the dashboard. "On what planet is it weird to be excited about clean clothes?" Crinkling her nose, she pinched the fabric of her embroidered green leggings, which now bore a threadbare hole near the shin.

I couldn't argue with her. With the last two hunts falling unusually close together, we all needed a refresh. We'd even brought our clothes along in the car during the hunt instead of leaving them at the motel room. Our demented list of errands: slay the vampires, then stop at the laundromat.

The late hour was necessary; 1 a.m. usually promised privacy. Despite the proud *24hr Service* sign glowing in the window, no movement came from inside.

Eager as I was to wear clothing that didn't smell like blood and guts, my body ached for bed. Sylvia had healed my open wounds, but there was little she could do to stifle the throbbing aftermath that came from being tossed across a room like a rag doll. I fantasized about a hot shower when we got back to our room at the Briar Inn.

And after…

I stole a glance at Sylvia, tracing the exposed curve of her lower back with my gaze. Adrenaline still thrummed through my veins, funneling my honed focus into a consuming wave of desire.

I hoped she would have the energy to conjure one last spell tonight.

As Cliff and I entered the laundromat laden with duffels and trash bags stuffed with clothes, Sylvia darted off and swiftly located the light switches, flicking half of them off. In our experience, potential customers tended to turn tail if they saw two shady-looking guys inside a dimly lit building.

In the diffused glow that remained, Cliff and I sorted through the chaotic jumble of clothes on one of the lengthy aluminum tables. Sylvia landed with her own sack of garments slung over her shoulder, quick to remark how foreign a human's laundry ritual was compared to Elysia's. I had to remind her that most humans also didn't have to worry about making a *ghoul-tattered* pile in addition to lights and darks.

Cliff and I moved with the ease of muscle memory, lapsing into a comfortable, weary silence. There was the bloodstained pile that needed extra attention, a shredded pile that would be tossed out, and a shredded pile that was salvageable.

Sylvia knelt on the table, dumping her clothes before her. Each piece was an ethereal blend of earthy hues and shadowy gem tones—artfully crafted, impossibly soft to the touch.

Removing blood stains from fabric was a delicate art which she'd picked up decently in our second week on the road. I left a little cap of detergent mixed with hydrogen peroxide beside her so she could scrub off any splotches.

As I pulled my hand away, I eyed the leggings still hugging her curves. The vibrancy of the swirling ivy pattern was dulled by layers of ash and dirt. My brow pinched at the sight, the acrid taste of fear filling my mouth as I noted how tenderly she moved.

She'd been hurt tonight. I hadn't been able to stop it.

There had been close calls in the last eight weeks or so—a ghost shattering windows into deadly shards that could shred her wings, a ghoul's talons coming within a foot of her position midair. But tonight was more—a reckoning. That piece of shit vamp had *touched her,* could have killed her.

I wouldn't let it happen again. No matter the cost.

"You've got the murder eyes again," Sylvia said, drawing me out of my fantasy of crushing my hands around the vampire's windpipe. She peered up at me as she continued her delicate work, a knowing look on her face.

"Sorry," I muttered, then noted how raw her knuckles had become while scrubbing. "Need some help with that one?"

I reached for the stained cloak in her hands, grasping the hem. Sylvia kept hold of the collar, pulling it taut between us.

"Promise you won't rip it like the last one you *helped* me with?" she asked.

My cheeks flushed at the memory, but I shot her a crooked grin. "Trust me, I learned my lesson after you tried to beat me with it."

"You're lucky I was able to cut it down into a shirt." A good-humored smile curved her lips, but she shifted her gaze pleadingly to Cliff after considering her pinkened knuckles. "Sorry, Cliff's better at this stuff. Would you?"

She thrust the cloak toward Cliff, who readily accepted—maybe just to annoy me.

"Not the first time I've been told I'm good with my hands," he said, waggling his eyebrows at her.

"Want to do mine, too?" I pushed my crumpled shirt to him. He deftly swatted it back my way with twice as much force.

"You couldn't pay me to touch your sweaty crap." Cliff dipped a ratty toothbrush in the cleaning solution, the tiny garment draped over his left palm.

"How is mine any worse than yours?" I asked around an affronted laugh.

Sylvia wrinkled her nose at the state of Cliff, then peeled off her creme wrap sweater to reveal a delicate bralette underneath. "Jon has a point. You should throw your shirt in."

Cliff glanced at his front and shrugged. "It's only blood."

"Only? You threaten to gut me for smudging your laptop, but you're unbothered about looking like a *serial killer*?" One of her favorite newfound terms since she began obsessively watching *Dateline*.

Rolling his eyes, Cliff removed his shirt and tossed it into the bloodstained pile. He held his arms out, putting his tattooed torso on full display. "If you're so desperate to see me naked, sweetheart, you could ask nicely."

Looking pleased with herself, Sylvia proceeded to strip off her leggings. She stuffed her clothing into a mesh bag that would keep her items from getting lost within the rest of the laundry.

Heat might have normally risen to my cheeks, but instead, my face drained as I got a better look at her in the low light. Faint bruising caressed her ribs, waist, and thighs. I could already picture how the dark hues would spread and deepen, wrapping her skin until she couldn't find a modicum of comfort.

But she was all smiles as she strode to the edge of the counter and crossed her arms, raising an expectant eyebrow at me. "Now, you."

It took me half a second to stagger back into what she was talking about. I glanced at Cliff, then her—both half-naked. Determined to not be caught off-guard by her brashness for once, I held her stare as I peeled off my undershirt and jeans. She bit her lip to quell giggles, practically bouncing with delight. That little flit in her wings was her biggest tell, though, as if she was physically restraining herself from closing the space between us.

Her gaze followed my collection of scars. She no longer flinched at the sight—not even at the barbed whistler scar beneath my collarbone that had never let go of its sickly gray hue. She looked me up and down like I was someone worth staring at.

"Stop eye-fucking each other," Cliff groused without looking up from his meticulous stain removal. "I'm, like, two feet away."

Sylvia grinned with the promise that our eye-fucking would continue in privacy soon enough, but my smile was half-hearted. I couldn't tell if she was putting on a brave face through the pain for my sake.

By the time the stains were out, she was buzzing eagerly by the washers. Cliff and I loaded up four of the machines, passing detergent between us. I couldn't imagine how we all looked—three serial killers in their underwear doing laundry at 1 a.m.

I held up a bag of coins to Sylvia. "You sure you're up for the responsibility?" I asked.

"Gimme!" She snatched a stack of quarters from the bag and carefully fed each of the machines. She peeked through the final slot as though she could unravel the inner mechanisms' secrets if she squinted hard enough.

Before long, the otherwise quiet laundromat filled with the sounds of churning water and clattering machinery. Cliff and I snickered as Sylvia went from washer to washer, pressing her face against the glass to watch the spinning clothes with utter fascination.

"Laugh all you want," she tossed over her shoulder. "It's beautiful!"

When Cliff became distracted with his phone, I nudged Sylvia's arm to get her attention. She gazed up at me with a hopeful, questioning smile—perhaps hoping I was about to request we start our nighttime fun early.

"Did you ever get a look at his tramp stamp?" I whispered, thumbing in his direction.

Her lips parted, eyes wide. She flew off in a blink.

Seconds later, Cliff's cursing nearly drowned out Sylvia's scream of delight: "It's a *butterfly*!"

4

SYLVIA

Returning with Jon to the spectral plane two months ago had been a horrible, irrevocable mistake. Every minute we were entwined as equals made me more insatiable. Being here with him again now, in this liminal space where only we existed, only deepened that hunger.

I straddled his hips, ignited by the solid feel of him between my legs. The more I touched him, the more I needed. His large hands slid up from my waist, one knotting in my hair. He pulled, and a moan slipped from me.

"Jon," I gasped.

I remembered when his name had been so ordinary on my lips. Now, it was sweet like sugar on my tongue: a blessing, a prayer, this monumental thing.

Jon arched up to catch my parted lips, kissing me like he needed me more than air. I readily returned the fervor, my wings giving an involuntary flutter at the brush of his tongue against mine.

These stolen moments were perfect and golden, quickly be-coming a post-hunt tradition as lingering adrenaline fueled our passion. *Addiction* might be a better word, but I didn't care. Being together like this felt *so fucking good* with the spectral plane providing a private world for us alone. Our sanctuary.

It was hard to believe that this world once housed the Ancients who tormented and drained me. The transcendent landscape was peaceful now, though vast in a way I still couldn't comprehend.

The changing colors of the sky and ground—though distinguishing the two was difficult—created a mesmerizing backdrop.

As I'd spent more time in this place, I had made an effort to make sense of its secrets. The stolen pages of nomadic journals I'd smuggled out of Elysia provided such meager depth. In hundreds of years, only a handful of fairies had ventured to this place. There was no guidemap, no rules. This time, I alone was the pathfinder; I was the one to document my experiences in the spectral realm for generations to come.

If I ever managed to find a place to call home again, that is. Until then, my scrawled notations on blank parchment and annotations to the map Mother had given me rested solely with me.

At times, the plane teased me with images at the edge of my vision—dreams or memories. Sometimes familiar glimpses of willow fronds or hummingbirds. Other times, unfamiliar human structures and flames, like Jon's mind was slowly leaving traces here, too. But whenever I tried to get a better look or point Jon's attention to focus on them, the visions dissolved.

Jon's hands returned to my waist, plucking at the waistband of my leggings. The gentle pressure grounded me, though it lacked tangible warmth in this place. I sat back, arrested by my own happiness that glowed like a kernel of sunlight in my chest.

"What is it?" Jon asked, a slight crease forming between his eyes.

I took my time in answering. I stroked fingertips through his tangle of dark hair, chewing my lip as the action stirred emotion in his face and slowed the feverish beat of his heart.

"Sometimes it stings," I said, "knowing I could have been this happy all this time."

A smile spread on his face—my only warning before Jon's grip tightened, cementing me in place as he effortlessly sat upright.

"Would you like to see what you've been missing?" Jon asked.

My legs were wrapped around his waist, our bodies fused so we were nose to nose. Grinning, I leaned my forehead against his.

"I wish we could have shared revels together," I whispered. "You would have loved the wine. And the company."

Jon made a noise in his throat. "Based on what you've told me about revels, I wouldn't care for them."

"Why?" I blurted, unable to mask the defensive edge to my voice.

His dark gaze devoured me. "If you think I'd want to share you, you're dead wrong, *chula*."

He punctuated this by hoisting me tighter to his front and lowering me onto my back, straddling me, arms caging me in as he leaned down to brush his lips to mine. I forgot to breathe for a few moments, silently delighted by his strength. Even here, he was considerably taller. I felt weightless to him.

The pressure of our friction should have ignited discomfort on my bruises after being throttled during the hunt. The spectral plane masked pain and made even the deepest scars fade. While we were able to explore each other's unmarred bodies with wonder, the aches were always waiting for us when we opened our eyes in the physical world.

Giggling, I brushed the tip of my nose against his. "No one *has* to share at a revel," I said. "There are ways to signal that you're not available for other partners that night."

He looked unconvinced. "Like?"

"Special runes."

His stare darted to my cheek, where a far different rune was etched—the one scar that I could not escape, even here. I dragged my finger over his bare chest, eager for a distraction, and left a cerulean glow in my touch's wake. My face flushed as the symbol took form. This particular set of interwoven swirls signaled a much deeper connection than the casual relationship Jon and I had tentatively agreed upon.

Don't get too attached.

We had promised each other—but he couldn't tell one Fae rune from another.

After peeking down at the mark on his chest, his eyes slid slowly back up to mine and flooded with wicked shadows. "You want me to mark you?" he asked.

The words alone set me aflame. *Fucking stars*—even forever wasn't long enough when Jon said things like *that*. He lowered himself to brush his lips against the side of my neck.

"I'm short on magical runes," he said, breath tickling my pulse. "I'll have to mark you my own way. Would you like that?"

Something between a whimper and a laugh escaped me at the thought of being branded by Jon. *Yes, yes, yes*, I thought, nodding breathlessly. *A thousand times yes.*

A rare, low chuckle spilled from him at my reaction. His thumb applied pressure over the spot his lips had occupied as though preparing me. When he leaned in again, his teeth teased my skin, digging harder and harder. I opened my senses, allowing myself to feel the delectable pinch.

There would be no visible sign of his passion when we awoke in the motel room, making me all the more determined to sink into the moment. This was the only time he allowed himself to be firm with me, to not treat me like something fragile that would shatter under the slightest pressure.

Jon pressed a final, softer kiss to the spot he marked and then pulled back to admire his work. My heart fluttered at the satisfaction on his face. In an instant, he dropped to leave a trail of kisses down my collarbone, between my breasts, and toward my navel. He paused suddenly, going rigid.

"Jon?"

His expression became shadowed as he raised himself slightly to look at my ribs—no doubt remembering the ugly bruises he'd glimpsed when I stripped down at the laundromat. He traced the area with chilling precision.

"Nothing hurts me in here," I purred, pushing myself up on my elbows to kiss him. To my surprise, he jerked back, expression darkening. "Hey. What's wrong?"

Jon searched my face for an unhurried moment before answering. "If we find another case on the way to Aelthorin," he said slowly, "I'd like you to consider staying back from the hunt."

My eyes widened before I could temper my expression. The fact that the request was made out of tenderness softened the blow only slightly.

"We've had this conversation before," I said, determined to keep my voice a sweet murmur despite the outrage flooding me. "I know when to pull back if things get really bad."

"And that low-level vamp still got the jump on you. Got his hands on you."

"He threw *you* across the room just as hard."

"That's—it's different. You know it's different. I can take it."

"You don't get to define how strong I am." The words came out with more of a bite than I'd intended.

Jon faltered, the urgency on his face softening into untethered affection that made me molten.

"Of course not," he murmured. "I wouldn't dare. But I—" After struggling to string together the right words, Jon sighed through his nose, shifting his weight to one arm so he could sweep a lock of my hair off my face. His fingertips were warm, his touch drugging. "I don't want to lose you. There's just something about you, Sylv. I couldn't bear it."

Focusing on *anything* was hard with the pleasant weight of his body over mine, my own body demanding to arch into him, to claim him.

"What happened to *don't get too attached*?" I teased—though the shared mantra at the beginning of our time together felt age-old now.

"Guess I fucked up," Jon said, brushing my jaw.

I let my eyes fall shut, leaning into his hand. It was so gentle, so tender, I almost forgot how dangerous he could truly be. I was glad my days of being prey were long behind me—because that look on Jon's face would surely lure me into letting my guard down.

In the recesses of my mind, his request for my safety stirred uneasily, but the matter could be dealt with another time. He would come to his senses when the veil of lust and adrenaline wore off.

I smiled coyly up at him, eager to distract from a potential argument. "What exactly is it about me? Enlighten me."

Eyes darkening in the way that made my stomach flip, Jon leaned down.

"You're brave. And kind. And dangerous." He punctuated each word with a kiss, trailing over the intricate lace of my bralette.

"And pretty?" I prompted.

"Beautiful." Jon's lips brushed the traitor mark on my cheek. "*Eres tan hermosa como las estrellas.*"

A delighted giggle spilled out of me, heart fluttering as his lips stole mine again. "I love when you say nice things to me in Spanish. I'm going to assume that was nice, at least."

A familiar thrill rushed through me as we entwined. Sometimes, our time together still felt unreal, like Jon would always be this myth just out of reach. This rush rekindled the memory of our first return to the spectral realm—the dizzying, almost unbearable anticipation as we shared our second kiss. That deceptively innocent brush of lips flooded me with something electric and dangerous, making me ravenous. Out of all my partners, none had ever made me feel so reckless, so *alive*.

I didn't have to wonder if Jon felt the magnetic pull—the one that tugged us toward something we shouldn't want but couldn't resist. I saw it in his eyes. We shared the same wild hunger. We were both twisted in the same way.

I gripped his shoulders, feeling the hard-earned muscle on him. Though reality shifted from blink to blink, the solidity of Jon's body pressed over mine was constant. I could feel his hunger, his aching care for me in every move he made.

He slipped a hand beneath me and massaged between my wings—a trick he'd learned early on in our time together. His mouth stretched into a smile against my neck when I rewarded him with a pleased moan, the sensitive skin hugging my wings coming alive under his touch. The spectral plane glowed blindingly bright in response to my ecstasy, forcing my eyes to squeeze shut. When I peeked past Jon's shoulder, the sky and ground shimmered with shooting stars, bright hues of pink and cerulean swirling together. They bled together like watercolors, the air abuzz with silent magic that raised hairs on the back of my neck.

Jon and I broke apart to observe the spectral realm shifting around us. He collapsed beside me, and I cuddled up against him to lay my head on his chest. The miraculous display settled, but brilliant sparks still streaked in and out of sight.

"Sorry," I said sheepishly. With each visit, this plane seemed to root deeper into the connection with my mind and heart—for better or worse.

He stayed quiet for a few seconds, the warm brown of his eyes mixing with the manifested colors as he drank it all in. "Don't apologize—it's *you*. The most beautiful things about you." He rubbed my arm up and down.

My throat went tight. I had one job in this arrangement—*don't fall for the lethal hunter you'll have to leave.*

I shifted nervously against him, tucking hair behind my ear. "Jon, do you believe in soul bonds?" My voice was unusually soft and restrained as I absently traced another rune across his chest.

He turned his head, studying me. "I don't know. I never really thought about it."

"It's just another old Elysian story," I said. "The concept of this invisible golden thread of starlight tied between two souls—unbreakable, always pulling them together, even when it defies all logic. A thread that spans through all time, all distance. Like somehow… the stars intend that they should meet."

"Sounds like destiny," he mused. "That can be dangerous if you're not careful."

A deflection. Good—that was good. One of us had to be strong enough to keep lines drawn.

I let my tracing fingers drift to his throat, easing my vulnerable query into a purr. "Oh, I see. Still afraid of me?"

Jon put his hand over mine, making me marvel at how his hand encompassed my own. He applied a firm pressure to his throat with my hand, shooting me a soft, sinful smile. I was suddenly grateful he usually saved these grins for me, so that no one else would know how it made him glow like a benevolent god—the corners of his eyes crinkling, the dimples that flashed.

"I've *always* known there was a chance you'd be the death of me, Sylv."

I kissed him for that, crushing our lips together. The spectral plane colors pulsated with every taste of his skin, glistening corals and golds nearly blinding us. When a bright shape arced particularly close to us, I drew off him to observe it. The display was beautiful—not quite fairy magic, but familiar in a strange sort of way. Like a building storm cloud made of light, it ebbed and flowed in a gentle, snaking pattern above and below us.

"I can barely wrap my head around how much you affect this place. It's incredible," Jon said, though I felt him grip me to his side tighter—perhaps the small dizziness he seemed to experience here from time to time, now that I knew heights unsettled him.

"It's you, too," I pointed out, thinking of the flashes of his mind I'd seen in the distance. Maybe if he was more intentional about his influence, the images would be less unsettling. "I'd love to see you try."

He frowned. "Try what?"

I waved my hand at the luminance my passion had conjured. "Taking control."

"I don't know the first thing about wielding magic." There was an edge to his voice. "I doubt I could make it change, anyway."

I groaned, nuzzling his jaw. "Do you *always* have to be such a human? Come on—just try. I could get back on top of you, if you think that'd help motivate you."

He snorted, then fell silent. I glanced up to see a look of concentration shadowing his face. A thrill of surprise ran through me when the soft colors around us were flooded with cool shades of veridian and blue. For a single second, our influence seemed to mingle in perfect harmony. The sight filled me with excitement, but Jon gave a small gasp—one of alarm.

Sudden, vicious clouds roiled on the horizon, fast-approaching. I sat up, glimpsing the house on fire in the distance, much closer than I'd ever seen.

"Jon—" I covered my mouth when I spotted blood trickling out of his nose. That never happened this soon. "Oh, no."

He sat up halfway with a frown, touching the blood. Without waiting, I chanted the spell to drag us back to reality.

In an instant, we both woke with sharp intakes of breath, lying side by side on Jon's bed in the motel room in Holly Grove, Arkansas.

I sat up on the pillow, blinking hard to make out the red numbers on the alarm clock: *1:54 a.m.* Our time in the spectral plane had felt like half an hour at least, yet only two minutes had passed here. Adjusting back to real-world sensation was still jarring. My ribs ached. My wings were sore. But most painful was the familiar pang of disappointment at losing our equal stature.

I flew up as Jon fumbled for a tissue. Nothing else translated from the spectral plane back with us, but his nosebleeds were real. It happened every time we visited the plane together—Jon left exhausted, a small trickle of blood marking his right nostril. Tissues were always at the ready near his pillow for that reason. He normally bounced back within the hour, but it was hard to shake my guilt that I was left unaffected.

Still, we both agreed that lightheadedness was a small price to pay for the moments we stole together in our secret sanctuary.

"You good?" I asked as Jon sat against the headboard with his head tilted back, the tissue pressed to his nose.

He gave a noncommittal grunt and a thumbs up, but the anxious knot in my gut was not appeased. Having our session cut so abruptly was unusual. I suspected his attempt to alter the spectral landscape must have taxed his human capacity. My flight drooped a little when I recalled that *look* he'd had on his face—like he'd been afraid of his own ability to control the strange magic there. *Unnatural.*

Bile rose in me. Two months ago, he might've said the very same thing about *me.*

The bleeding tapered off a few minutes later. Jon tossed the crumpled tissue into the bin between the beds, posture straightening where he leaned against the pillows and headboard. A fragile sense of relief took hold of the room as he caught his breath.

"I think I broke our sanctuary," he announced with a self-deprecating chuckle.

"You did not," I huffed, rolling my eyes. I fluttered down to sit on his bent knee—one of my many favorite perches. "It was only your first try, anyway. Don't be a baby."

Eager to keep that hungry look in Jon's eyes—and take both our minds off the dark turn in the spectral plane—I rubbed the side of my neck and shot him a vixen's wide smile.

"I swear I can still feel it," I murmured. I tapped the spot. "Right... *here.*"

Fuck, it was worth it just to see that sinful sort of pride flash over his face. Jon cupped his hand behind me, his thumb brushing that sensitive spot between my wings.

"Next time, I'll mark you hard enough it comes back with you," he said.

I shivered. "I'll have to hold you to that."

My gaze fell to the patch of earth that lay on the bedspread beside Jon. My outline of the spectral rune was still there, intact. We were lucky that we didn't need to lay on the ground outside to activate the spell—a pile of dirt poured from a plastic bag worked perfectly fine to satisfy the spell's demand for contact with the earth. If Jon wasn't so sapped from our visits, I would have begged to reactivate the rune immediately.

The neighboring bed was empty. Cliff had departed to the nearest bar shortly after donning freshly laundered clothes. Maybe he found someone else to go home with for the night. Good—he deserved to enjoy himself after a hunt.

I glanced back to Jon, who was tracing the spot on his arm I had healed during tonight's hunt. It was barely visible now—just smooth skin with a faint hairline shimmer under the lamplight—but he kept staring at it with a faraway look in his eyes and his face carved into an expression I couldn't quite read. My stomach sank when I remembered his plea for me to sit out from future hunts. Was he still imagining how I'd been injured? Angry with me for refusing his request?

I studied him, feeling the familiar tug between the intimacy of what I knew so well of him and the shadows of what I didn't—depths I might never reach, no matter how I tried. His five years on me both thrilled me and unsettled me at times, a reminder of everything he had seen, everything he carried. He had already been hunting malevolent spirits for a year when I was first learning how to control my affinity.

"Hey—it's your turn, isn't it?" I asked, breaking the silence.

Jon groaned out a laugh. "Not this again."

"Come on, you love it."

"I *tolerate* it."

"Liar. You wouldn't keep playing if you didn't like it," I countered, breaking into a grin.

He didn't need to question what I meant. A game of sorts had taken shape between us in past weeks, where we shared memories based on simple prompts to uncover more about each other. The game was for his sake, really. Now that I no longer had to keep secrets from him, I could babble endlessly about my life. Jon, though… He had a harder time opening up.

Nonetheless, his eyes lightened at the change of subject. "Give me a prompt, then."

"Candy," I said without hesitation.

He rolled his eyes, settling against the headboard. "Nope. Anything I say is gonna end with you demanding sweets."

"I do *not* demand. I ask very politely." I pouted, hugging one leg close and dropping my chin to my knee in thought. "Fine. Tell me more about your restaurant. You said if you ever gave up hunting, you'd open one."

"That's a big *if*, remember?" Jon said.

"Even still," I urged. Determined though he was to bury it, I saw the tiny gleam surface in his eyes.

Jon cast his gaze toward the window, where patterned curtains concealed our view of the sleeping city. "It'd be hard. Barely fifty bucks to my name and a high school drop-out to boot." He puffed out a sigh. "Not to mention, any standard background check will reveal my prolonged visit to the psych ward. Even getting a job washing dishes could be a longshot."

"Put logic to rest for now," I said. "Say you get the money somehow, and your restaurant is open. What would it be like?"

Slowly, his expression unknitted. "It wouldn't need to be a big place. I always picture something cozy. Something that could feel like home. I could give some of my family's recipes fresh life."

"Like *tostones*?" I asked, hoping I wasn't butchering the pronunciation.

Jon beamed at me. "Right. And *lechón asado*—though, you wouldn't miss that one."

"Meat?"

He nodded. "But the seasoning… It's fucking unreal, Sylv. Garlic and citrus and spice. Especially if we had a professional cooking it," Jon said, clicking his tongue. A pause drew out, his voice taking a softer decibel. "I'd always make sure we had a room curtained off in the back, just for friends and family. They'd never have to pay a dime."

My gaze lowered, tracing the familiar map of scars on his chest and arms. Some were faint, barely noticeable. Others were still discolored like the skin would never fully heal—and I had tried my hand at it more than once. But only master healers could unwind such deep scars; it was a particularly advanced magic that my secondary affinity simply couldn't offer.

His body was a story—though, I couldn't tell if it was a legend or a tragedy yet. A particularly discolored scar was nestled below his collarbone. Victory scarcely came without a cost. Not for the first time, I wondered what Jon might've been if life hadn't turned him into a weapon.

I let myself sink into his happy fantasy, tried to picture his remaining family gathered around a special table at the restaurant. I imagined faces for the members he had mentioned—adding a few extra cousins and uncles he may have omitted. I pictured Jon *happy*, with that wide smile that made me weak in the knees.

Curiously, I found it difficult to insert myself into the scene, but I was too well-versed in daydreaming to let that barricade me. I muscled through the feeling of being uninvited in my own reverie. And then I was sauntering into the restaurant, as human as any of them, colorful skirts dancing around my heels. His family was thrilled to see me, and Jon swept me into his arms in front of everyone—

"That's beautiful," I said.

Jon chuckled, the sound low and callous. "It doesn't mean anything. It's just a nice thought."

"Of course it does!" I blurted.

The heavy look he gave me made me sucked the air from my lungs. "We both know hunters don't get endings like that. I'll just be lucky if I get a little peace before one of these bastards does me in someday."

I blinked, his bluntness slicing through the lingering warmth of my daydream.

"You don't have to believe that," I offered. "If memory serves, you've been wrong before."

I lifted a brow, attempting to goad another laugh out of him. Instead, I watched walls go up behind his eyes. Jon looked back down at his healed forearm, rubbing it.

"I can't just walk away. If I stop, people will die," he said. "Innocent people. Families. How could I live with myself for that? There's too much out there."

I let the heaviness settle for a moment, refolding my wings at my back. "People will always need someone. Why does it have to be *you*?"

"Sylv, you know why."

I recoiled slightly because I knew those shadows in his eyes, how his grief so often curdled into anger. I knew about the countless nights he had tossed through nightmares, trying to forget his father's voice when he knew it wasn't really his father anymore.

Staring at him, it hit me like a blow; nothing else would ever be enough. Jon would never be satisfied—no tally of victories enough to sate his conscience.

I was raised to believe that bad things happened sometimes to make room for something new, something better. But sitting here with him, both of us adrift without our families, I couldn't bring myself to voice any sage optimism. It would feel hollow and insincere. We had each other, but I hesitate to assume he felt the same comfort in that fact. We were temporary. I was a lost cause.

"I just wish you could have a beautiful end," I murmured. "You deserve that."

"Yeah, me too," Jon conceded.

As his gaze softened on me, growing pensive, I couldn't help but feel a seed of hope despite it all. Maybe he could still defy his fate—with or without me by his side. The thought stirred something raw in me, an ache that made my chest tight.

Aching to hold onto *him*.

The reality stung more than I liked to admit, knowing that my place in Jon's future was as much of a fantasy as any far-fetched dream. If he *did* build another life for himself someday, I would certainly not be a part of it. I never minded rotating partners with Damian, moving person to person between revels. But suddenly, the image of another woman at Jon's side made me heat—stealing *my* daydream.

"Would you remember me if you *did* ever make it out of hunting?" I asked.

"I'll try to keep you straight out of the dozens of fairies that have saved my life," Jon answered, deadpan.

He was trying to get a laugh out of me, but that possessive beast in my chest was restless, had me reaching for my sheathed dagger at my hip. I gave it a little flip, the way Cliff had taught me, and I was proud when my fingers caught the handle instead of the blade. "Would it help if I left something behind?"

Jon's breath stilled, his brows pulled together as I slowly twirled the blade in my hand. "Like what?"

"A symbol," I said, studying his bare torso to pick my place. "So anyone who comes next will know you were *mine* once." The idea possessed me. I'd never once considered it before, but now I could hardly breathe for my anticipation.

Jon's answering smile was caught between surprise and heat. "You want to mark *me*," he breathed.

I hovered by his right shoulder, meeting his gaze as I set the tip of my blade to his sun-kissed skin. "Yes," I all but growled.

I could feel his pulse quicken, but he didn't pull away. He stayed still, *waiting*.

I held my breath, hesitating for a moment before plunging my dagger into his skin. There was more resistance than I expected, and I heard Jon suck in a sharp breath. I glanced at his face—his eyes shut like this was a delicious kind of pain, a kind to be savored. And it was mine to give.

His blood ran over my knuckles in thin streams. Jon didn't breathe a word of protest as I carved the Fae rune over the strong slope of his shoulder—interlocking circles and delicate swirls, a brutal approximation of the one I had given him in the spectral plane. Teenagers playfully designated this marking for their *beloved*, but the sentiment seemed to take a more potent translation as it seeped blood.

It went against every instinct not to immediately conjure spell-work to heal Jon. *No*—not this time. When it did heal, slowly and painstakingly, the symbol would scar over, and my mark would join the story of scars on his body. With him always. My heart leapt to my throat. It was more beautiful than I'd imagined.

I heard a soft breath escape Jon, and I nearly flinched—pulled out of my reverie to gauge his expression.

"You know," he said, gingerly brushing a finger over the fresh cuts. "You're just as twisted as I am."

The shadowed half-smile on his face nearly undid me.

I studied the dagger in my hand, a soft chuckle drawn out of me. "I don't mind being a freak if it's with you," I said.

5
SYLVIA

Just a second longer…

The gem shard's aura pulsed under my touch, teeming with wordless promises. I stood perfectly still on the bathroom counter, allowing myself five—no, *ten*—more breaths with the amethyst in my hands. I held the last breath for an extra beat, then tucked the gemstone under the freshly cleaned clothes in the box that held my personal effects.

Even then, the reassurance of power teased me. I wished there was a way to shut it off. A little piece like that wasn't nearly enough to fuel a transformation spell. Yet, it found its way into my hands any time I came to freshen up.

I closed my box pointedly and turned to the mirror. Late morning sunlight streamed through the tiny window reflecting behind me.

The traitor brand was stark black on my cheek. Somehow, the sight was becoming familiar, though the dark circles under my eyes made the rune less prominent. Between that and the bruising along my body, I was a mess. I'd given in to two hours of sleep, then lied to Jon that I'd gotten far more. He was out getting coffee. Although I couldn't stand the taste, I considered choking some down to wake myself up.

I adjusted the snowflake necklace at my hip. There was a chip in the corner of the charm that I hadn't noticed until now. I traced every detail of the weathered plastic groove with my finger. I couldn't be sure if the damage came from our many moves between motels or when I'd dropped it between seats during a drive. The clasp had become less secure over the weeks as well. I swallowed guilt for not taking better care of Jon's gift; at least the damage was the consequence of being well-traveled.

After combing through my hair one final time, I peeked out of the bathroom. Jon's bag was already packed on the bed, prepared for travel. Perhaps there was time for me to search the room once more. I'd made it a habit to scour our motel rooms for treasures to add to my stash. The other night, I'd found a button under Cliff's bed and an earring with a missing gem behind the dresser. Not my most interesting haul, but better than the dead roaches from the previous place.

I hovered at the threshold, a spark blossoming as I caught sight of Cliff. Considering his late night, he shouldn't have been out of bed this early. Still in his undershirt and a pair of navy joggers, he was hunched over his laptop—a mug of motel coffee in his right hand and entirely too absorbed to notice me.

He was practically handing me the perfect opportunity to inflict some innocent revenge.

Throughout our journey, both hunters had been extremely supportive of my desire to continue training—to challenge myself. With the number of hunts that intercepted our route, honing my skills was a necessity. *Survival of the fittest* was one of the most apt human expressions I adopted.

But truthfully, I trained for myself. To quiet that incessant, gnawing voice in my chest that no longer settled for the naive girl who had fled Elysia.

Cliff coached me, advising workout regimens—both physical and magical—and sparring with me when we could spare the time. His instruction was harsh, pushing me to my very limits. Sometimes, I resented the ache in my muscles the day after a grueling session.

Despite this, I kept my whining to a minimum; the results were certainly there. I not only felt stronger, I noticed the difference. My belongings were becoming easier to carry. I could perform twenty-five pushups instead of a painful ten. My spellwork, too—I could switch spells in quicker succession, not stumbling over the ancient Fae. Conjured ice lasted hours if I reinforced it.

Jon helped me train, too, but he was admittedly less effective overall, given how *distractible* he became with me. On a rare occasion—my favorites—Jon and I would abandon training altogether and simply find a place in the forest to lie under the autumn sun and talk for hours.

Watching Cliff take a sip of coffee, I whispered a spell under my breath. I kept my magic in the shadow of the doorway, shaping the swirling frost into a javelin shape with a soft *chiiink*. The rotating weapon was about the length of a human forearm with dulled tips that would little more than bruise when it found its mark. And, with any luck, it would scare the shit out of Cliff.

When he set the mug down, I thrust my hands out and sent the ice whistling forward.

Cliff ducked—*easily*. The projectile flew over his shoulder and smashed through the front window.

I winced at the explosion of glass. *Shit.*

"Good morning to you, too," Cliff said, glancing at me with a lift of his brows.

Jaw slack, I glided across the room until I hovered over the table.

"You saw me?" I didn't bother to hide the childish deflation in my voice.

"Heard you. I know the sound of your wings."

Chilling yet oddly flattering.

"I can patch it with ice," I said, looking at the torn curtains that now fluttered from the jagged hole behind them. "Maybe the motel staff won't notice until we're on the road."

Cliff waved a hand. "Trust me, this place has seen far worse. If you're gonna kick yourself about anything, do it for being so obvious. I've seen grizzly bears with more stealth."

"You fucking liar," I said, sending a small burst of frost at his chest. "I just need to practice on someone who's not a paranoid freak."

Cliff smirked. "Hey, in our line of work, that's a compliment."

I folded my arms, glancing from the shards of glass littering the carpet to scan Cliff's athletic frame.

"How was last night?" I asked.

"Good. Real good. How was your trip to pornstar coma-land?" He peered at me over the rim of his mug.

I huffed, rolling my eyes to the heavens.

"You know if you just came and visited just *once*, you would understand," I said, dropping down to sit on the open edge of his laptop.

He scoffed. "I've seen you guys passed out with that pile of dirt too many times to count. It's creepy as shit."

I chewed my lip. His tone wasn't cruel, but it gave me pause all the same—as it always did.

From the moment we peeled away from Elysia, hiding trysts with Jon to the spectral plane had been impossible—tentative ventures that became quickly a routine indulgence. Cliff knew from the start. Aside from dry remarks, he never outright objected, but I saw the dark look he shot at Jon's back sometimes. A guarded disapproval that we all deftly evaded discussing—that I was wrong for Jon. That *we* were wrong, some unique abomination in the landscape of their lives.

Too often, I considered whether Cliff was right.

"I know Jon talks to you about it. Don't you ever wonder what it's like?" I doubled down, batting my eyes at him. "Why won't you come see me there?"

"I think I just made my case. Why would you want *me* there, anyway?" He lifted an accusatory eyebrow.

"I don't know. Curiosity?"

He chuckled softly, in that decibel like velvet sandpaper. "*Curiosity*," Cliff echoed, shaking his head as he tipped my chin up. "Sweetheart, you'll just have to get me out of your system another way."

He grinned as I shoved his hand away, my cheeks burning.

"By vomiting?" I offered sweetly.

I tucked unruly locks of hair behind my ears and debated again on asking for a sip of coffee. But Jon would be back soon, hopefully with something less bitter than the cheap brand that the Briar Inn stocked.

In his absence, the faint pulsing of my gemstone shard seemed to call out to me from across the room. Until I could use it as I wanted, its aura was a mocking lullaby. But I could do *something*.

I flew to the table, tapping on Cliff's smartphone where it lay facedown beside the laptop.

"May I?" I asked.

He unlocked it. Not that I needed him to—but he was unaware I had peeked at him typing his passcode three weeks ago.

"Candy Crush?" Cliff asked.

"More important than that," I scoffed.

He returned his attention to the laptop. Glancing at it, I realized a video had been quietly droning in the background. It wasn't what usually held his attention—typically, I could expect to find him combing through grisly news reports of bizarre dismemberments or missing persons that led to a new case. And on more than one occasion, rewatching old episodes of *Xena: Warrior Princess*.

This was nothing like those; the screen displayed a video of a chamber filled with people sitting in tidy rows. Somehow, it held Cliff's attention raptly.

On his phone, I pulled up the search engine. My palms danced over the digital keyboard with muscle memory, painstakingly scouring the local news for any reports of nature miraculously blooming out of season or wildlife acting out of character—the most common telltale signs of a charged gemstone in the area.

To my surprise, there were several nearly identical entries below mine that had been entered only a few days prior.

> *unusual plant blooms in fall*
> *strange animal behavior in Arkansas*
> *unexplained occurrences nature near me*
> *things acting fucking insane for no reason*

I peeked up at Cliff, my heart aching. If he hadn't been so absorbed in his video, I would have sprung up to embrace him. For all his grumblings about my obsession to change forms, he was trying to help me.

After several minutes of fruitless research, the familiar leaden weight of disappointment set in. I rocked back on my heels, sighing. More of the same: *absolutely nothing*. Every hopeful report on a possible gemstone so far had led us nowhere on our meandering journey west. Empty caverns, boring meadows, and nothing but more miles on the car to show for it.

Maybe the next leg of the journey west would finally offer a stroke of luck.

Abandoning the phone, I rose into the air and circled around to see what Cliff was watching. Still the same video: the screen showed a vast number of humans dressed in robes. One by one, young men and women walked up to the stage and shook hands with important-looking people wearing the most peculiar hats.

"Is this a ritual?" I whispered.

Cliff exhaled through his nose, stifling a smile. "It's a livestream from May. I found out my kid sister graduated college with honors. They're almost to the *E*'s now. They'll call her name soon, and she'll walk across the stage here."

"Ah." I did the math in my head, trying to remember the human-named months. This video was at least half a year old.

Cliff peeled his eyes off the screen to study me for a second. "You gonna ask me what college is?"

I smiled at him knowingly. "You look so excited to explain it to me, anyway."

"I oughta make you guess," Cliff muttered with a little laugh. "It's a place humans go to learn and prepare for the job they want after high school. Graduation means they passed all their classes and didn't get so plastered that they slept with the dean's daughter."

"Personal experience?" I asked.

"Friend of a friend."

I cringed a little inside. *Stars*—of course that hadn't been him. He'd been busy being disowned by his family and hunting his first spirit with Jon when other students were progressing toward that milestone.

"It reminds me of affinity ceremonies back home. It happens much younger, closer to ten or twelve summers, but we do a far better job making it festive."

He snorted. "Not like they can set off fireworks in an auditorium."

"The affinity ceremony takes place *underground*, and it still looks more exciting," I insisted. "It's one of the many festivities during Midsummer. Special foods are prepared to honor the children who found their affinity since the previous summer. The affinities welcome new members into their cohort by creating a spectacle."

"Let me guess. Lightning strikes? Wildfires?"

I swooped closer to elbow his neck. "Nothing that draws unwanted human attention, obviously. Air affinities make objects dance above everyone's heads—scarves, goblets, wine, that sort of thing. Water fairies make the dining hall sparkle with floating streams. Oh, the earth displays are a favorite. They make flowers and mushrooms sprout right out of the ceiling—it smells *amazing*." I glanced wistfully at the cracked plaster overhead.

"What about ice?"

"It's been a couple years since we've had a new ice affinity, but last time, we made these huge, glittering ice sculptures all around the hall. They didn't melt for days and days."

My mind wandered to my own affinity ceremony—my acceptance into the ice cohort. More than anything, I pictured the pride in my father's eyes as I raced toward him across the chamber.

I cleared my throat. "Hazel was disappointed that she didn't find her affinity before the ceremony this summer. Chances are, she'll find it before the next. Even if she doesn't, that's alright. She's still on the younger side."

Cliff's pause was noticeably heavy. Before he could say anything, he stiffened, his attention back on the screen.

The voice in the laptop said, "*Anna Grace Everett, graduated with a bachelor's degree in environmental science, summa cum laude.*"

A pretty blonde girl with the same green eyes as Cliff filled the screen. She strode onto the stage as people cheered from the crowd. Finding the camera, she waved both hands overhead, soaking up the attention with a good-natured grin.

"Environmental science," Cliff said. "Always a tree-hugger, that one. You'd probably get along with her." He swallowed hard, pausing the video on another close-up of her face. He stared like he was memorizing it. "Can't believe how grown up she is—twenty-three years old now. Feels like last week she was little enough to squeeze under the couch when we were playing hide and seek."

Truth be told, I could hardly wrap my head around Anna being older than me. Any time Cliff spoke of her, I pictured a child like Hazel.

"And how old are you again?" I asked with tentative levity. "Forty?"

"Twenty-seven, you little shit."

I chewed my lip. In two months of gently prying about Cliff's past, I learned that his mother had once convinced him he was allergic to gluten and that he'd briefly had a pet snake when he was eight. Nothing more. Jon was slow to open up, but Cliff was a fortress.

"I've seen her name in your phone contacts," I said. "Have you gotten in touch with her lately?"

Cliff bristled, voice sharpening. "What have I told you about digging into my phone?"

"I was trying to call Jon, and *Anna* just happens to appear at the top of your contacts list."

"Tell that to the last three hookups you texted back for me. That chick from Tennessee calls me once a week asking if I still think about her in the shower—thank you so much for *that*."

Pushing the laughter from my voice, I said, "You didn't answer my question."

He blew out a sigh. "Guess Blockbuster got me nostalgic yesterday. Figured it wouldn't hurt to check what Anna's been up to," he muttered. "Looks like she's still under Dad's thumb since she went to the university he always wanted us to go to. I'm not gonna bother her. It's enough to know that she's doing alright."

"Is it?" I murmured. "I would give anything to be able to pick up the phone and call Hazel right now if I could."

Cliff leaned back in his seat so I received the full effect of his crooked smile. It was a kind of cocky, well-meaning grin that could disarm anyone. I had to remind myself that he was a master of misdirection to keep from smiling back. I had seen this deceptively simple move work many times on others.

Enough to see the flicker in his eyes that came with it, the faint clench to his jaw.

"Sylv, I'm *fine*. We finally iced that vampire nest, basically saved the city, and hey—bonus—none of us died in the process. It's been a good end to the week, and you're being a buzzkill."

I huffed, shaking my head. "Come on, that '*I'm fine*' garbage doesn't work with me anymore. It's not a crime to talk about her, if you wanted to." The hum of my beating wings felt deafening as I dropped my voice lower, gentler. "Anna didn't hurt you the way the rest of your family did, right?"

A ripple of tension set through Cliff's frame, but I felt bold, desperate not to lose my grasp on this shred of his past. I glanced at his neck, where his pulse was pounding.

"No," Cliff said after a second. "She was barely fourteen. Just a kid."

His gaze set on the cell phone like it was burning an acidic hole in the table. When he spoke again, his voice was fragile and gravelly—scarcely recognizable from its usual commanding resonance.

"It's been *years*, Sylv. A long fucking time. If she can get past talking to a dead man, she'll think I ran out on her—or worse."

"You don't know that," I offered.

"And you do?" He rubbed his eyes with his palms. "I wouldn't know what to say."

"Maybe start by saying you're proud of her. I mean—anyone who knows you could see that."

He sucked air through his teeth. "That's not enough."

"Come on—you could sweet talk a rock into buying gravel. Trust yourself."

I angled my hover into a graceful arc toward his phone. No sooner had I landed and swiped my palm over the touchscreen, Cliff snatched it out of my reach.

"This isn't your goddamn business, okay?" Cliff said, the sudden punch behind each word making me jump. "Fuck off about this. Who cares?"

He shut the laptop with a harsh *snap* and started to rise from his seat. I acted on a half-formed thought—*stay*—and thrust my palms out to conjure a spell. Ice connected to his wrist, creating a thick cuff that sealed against the tabletop. Cliff's eyes glimmered with surprise as they shot to me. He attempted to free himself with several vicious tugs before it became clear my ice was too thick.

"Cuffing people to tables now?" he grumbled, dropping back into the chair. "Dick move, Sylv."

I drew in a shaky breath—bracing myself. "I know you don't like to talk about what happened with your family—"

"And yet here we are," Cliff drawled.

Pulling to a hover, I folded my arms over my chest and glared at him. "I'm done with your walls and your fucking secrets and you constantly shutting me out. If you want to brood alone, fine. But don't pretend like no one cares."

My heart pounded the moment the words fled my mouth, each coming out sharper than intended. I rarely raised my voice at Cliff like this, and now our eyes caught and my nerves buzzed. What if I had impulsively crossed a line I couldn't return from?

But he didn't look upset—in fact, the corners of Cliff's mouth indented like he could be convinced to smile.

"You yell a lot when you care," Cliff said. "Kinda starting to think it's your thing."

I eased back in the air, giving him space. "Don't you think your sister at least deserves a chance to hear the truth?" I asked softly.

"Just drop it," he cut in, the anger draining from his voice. "Now's not the time."

"Then, when?"

"I dunno, maybe never. It's goddamn better that way. What's your deal about this, anyway?"

I paused, looking inward. The sharp sting wasn't entirely his doing. I hugged myself, rubbing a spot of freckles on my arm.

"I just had to say goodbye to every family member and friend I've ever known, and you've got the chance—even if it's just a *chance*—to have a sister again. I guess I'm jealous."

Cliff's pause drew out heavily. When I looked up, his expression was unnervingly... not *fucking annoyed* at me.

"You wanna talk about it?" he asked.

I raised my eyebrows sharply, giving him a moment to recant the offer. "You're really going soft on me, aren't you? Do I get a hug, too?"

Cliff smirked, but to my immense surprise, he doubled down. His studious gaze raked me up and down, and I felt rooted in midair. All at once, I was back in the Elysian forest, meeting his wide-eyed stare in the night as the Elder declared my banishment from the only home I had ever known.

"You're doing a good job working through some heavy shit," Cliff murmured. "And if, I dunno, it's *too* heavy..."

"I'm fine," I answered quickly.

Cliff let out a low, skeptical scoff. "Bullshit. You're going to hit me with that after bitching at me for the same thing?"

I placed a hand over my heart. "Fairies aren't known to lie."

"Guess you're a trailblazer, then," Cliff muttered.

"Well, I suppose I could open up a bit if you give your sister a call."

Cliff's jaw feathered. "Not happening." He leaned forward, rapping his knuckles on the table. "Now, you gonna let me out, or is this some new kink for you?"

"Don't rule it out." I landed on the table, running a hand over the thick, icy cuff. Then I looked up at him through my lashes. "Why the hurry? You have somewhere to be?"

Taking wing again, I backed away in the air.

He glared at me, rising halfway, only to be caught by the cuff. "Sylv..."

I couldn't deny there was some level of thrill to this, observing a powerful hunter rendered helpless by my magic. Part of me wanted to see how far he'd go to free himself—drag the table in pursuit of me, or perhaps attempt to break off a chunk of the wood that held the cuff.

Cliff tugged again, his anger useless to him as his voice rose. "Let me out of this goddamn thing, or—"

The door lock clicked open, interrupting us. The relief on Cliff's face was plain as Jon entered the motel room with a drink carrier in one hand—and my wayward ice javelin in the other. He paused in the doorway, looking between us.

"Everything okay?" he asked slowly.

I shrugged. "Of course. Why do you ask?"

"Routine question when I find Cliff stuck to a table next to a shattered window."

"We were training," I said innocently. "I was just about to free him." Waving my hands, I made the cuff vanish.

Cliff yanked his wrist to his chest and held it protectively like I might change my mind. I thought he might curse me out, but I swore there was a hint of begrudging pride aimed at me beneath the annoyance.

"Just a spontaneous workout," Cliff told him. "No psychopath behavior here."

Jon caught my gaze knowingly as he shut the door with his back. He lobbed my icy blade back toward me. I whispered a spell in sync, the magic cradling the ice in midair and dismantling it into a freezing mist that fizzled out as I stretched my palms apart.

"Well, as long as there's no psychopath behavior," Jon scoffed. He set down the drink and brown paper to-go bag. "Maybe let's ease up on breaking shit."

"I can't," I joked dryly, sweeping a hand from my collarbone down my leg. "It's the price of the warrior's physique you see before you. I'm simply growing too powerful."

Jon melted into a chuckle, the kind of boyish grin that came more often lately, like he had bottled sunlight in him.

Following the delicious scents wafting off the drinks, I brightened. "They had hot chocolate?"

Jon frowned. "You didn't want black coffee?"

He uncapped a frothy drink topped with whipped cream and chocolate shavings, and my grievances died on my lips.

"Don't even joke about that," I mumbled.

Before long, I was sitting contentedly at the edge of the tabletop with a warm, fairy-sized mug in my hands. I cast a mild cooling spell to keep it from burning my tongue—years of practice that I had perfected with tea. As I thought about scooping up a refill, I considered the mug in my grasp. It had been among the supplies that mother had thoughtfully provided before I fled with the hunters.

My heart twisted the way it always did when I thought of her.

"Aelthorin's just days away now, isn't it?" I asked.

Jon couldn't quite look at me. "There's that possible haunting in Kansas we're monitoring, but yeah—the spot in Colorado marked on your map is a straight shot from here."

His eyes cut to Cliff, who seemed to mirror the unreadable expression.

"What aren't you telling me?" I asked. "I don't have the patience to sit through another one of your silent, brooding conversations."

Cliff set down the sandwich Jon had brought for him. "We need to head south for a supply run first."

"Oh." Yet another delay on our journey west. I racked my brain, thinking of last night's brutal hunt. The *click* of Jon's gun as it pulled against an empty chamber. "Is it the silver?"

Jon nodded. "We're cleaned out of ammo. Besides my knives—" He tapped his jacket, where the twin blades rested against his chest, "we have nothing. Between that nasty wraith and the nest here in Holly Grove, it drained us."

I set my mug in my lap, letting out a measured breath. "So if we run into so much as a runty ghoul on the road…"

"We're toast," Cliff finished for me, his voice thick as he took another bite of his sandwich.

"Every day we go without restocking is a huge risk," Jon tacked on, pushing a hand back through his hair. "But there's a hunters' outpost not too far from here. It won't delay us more than a day or two."

He shot me a small, reassuring smile, but a beat of uncertainty seized me all the same. I had delicately traced an approximation of our path toward Aelthorin on my map. The line zigged and zagged with car troubles, time-sensitive hunts, even my own fruitless detours for potential gemstone locations. At this rate, it'd be another month before we reached the mountains if the same patterns persisted.

Were Mother and Hazel waiting for me already? I couldn't see how it was possible for them to reach Aelthorin, but Mother had seemed so *sure* that we would reunite soon. My guilt deepened at the truth that I didn't hate this prolonged time with Jon and Cliff.

For all I knew, my family was worried sick about me while I was foolishly opening myself up to Jon and taking in whatever fragile pieces of his heart he offered.

"I imagine there will be other hunters. Any chance they'll be thrilled to see me?" I remarked, smirking as I observed the boys' reactions closely.

"You won't be anywhere near that place," Jon said firmly. "We go way back with the marshal of this location. Cain will get us what we need quickly, and we'll be back on the road."

I frowned, drumming my fingers against my mug while images raced through my mind. An entire facility dedicated to the nightmares I had been warned about since I was a child.

"Are there other locations? These… outposts?" I asked, trying to suppress the visible chill snaking down my spine at the thought. Dozens, perhaps hundreds of hunters, all gathered in one spot. Something told me the vast majority wouldn't share Jon and Cliff's disposition toward my kind.

"It's nothing you need to worry about," Cliff cut in. "But yeah. There's about a dozen stateside. Most of 'em specialize in what their territory needs. Tracking, witch-warding, rare artifacts…"

"And this one?"

Cliff hesitated, glancing at Jon. "Louisiana's outpost specializes in training."

I forced a smile, but it was tight, suffocating. *Training*. Somehow that term was more visceral than any armory. Men and women being forged into killers, set to eliminate all non-humans. Turning boys like Jon and Cliff into living weapons.

I pretended to sip on my empty mug, sighing through my nose. "Well, we can't have you fighting the next vampire nest with toothpicks—even if I'm there to save your asses. Again."

"When did you get so cocky?" Cliff asked, chuckling through the diffused tension.

"When I realized how badly you needed me around."

A new kind of melancholy strain rippled from my statement, especially when Jon and I briefly locked eyes. We shared silent questions that neither of us knew how to answer.

I owed it to my family to reach Aelthorin as soon as possible. I should be among my own kind again, not traipsing around with hunters. But the longer I stayed, the harder it was for me to picture settling into a village for good. It would mean parting ways with Jon—likely forever. With each passing day, the mental image of saying goodbye became foggier.

More than ever, I found myself regretting our safe plunges into the spectral realm. Every visit only made my forbidden wanting grow.

Yet, it was a mistake I would willingly make over and over.

6
JON

Sylvia had, thankfully, come to understand that she shouldn't fly in front of the driver's side of the car while she was admiring the landscape. I could hear her flitting around in the back seat, unable to settle on which window held the most interesting view. I was envious in a way; it would be nice to stretch my legs without sacrificing the efficiency of our drive time.

We had left the dense forests of the Ozarks seven hours behind us. Sylvia surely noticed our surroundings flattening; expansive fields ribboned with creeks stretching out on either side of the road as we drove deeper into Louisiana marshes, the setting sun reflected golden on the water.

"Uh, guys?" she called out from the backseat. Notching down the music, I twisted around to see her perched at the back passenger window, tapping the glass. "Shouldn't we be taking care of that? That field is swarming with kelpies!"

"Horses," I corrected, suppressing a bemused smile at the reminder that Sylvia knew more of monsters than ordinary animals from her limited studies in Elysia. "They're totally harmless. All they'll do is eat the grass out there and shit. Most people love them."

"Herds of anything are rarely *harmless*," Sylvia muttered, a pinch in her expression. "But I suppose I'll trust your judgement."

She looked between me and the field once more before spreading her wings and looping gracefully back to the other side.

"We gotta make a side trip to a zoo sometime so she can see a giraffe," Cliff remarked under his breath, grinning ear to ear. "She'll lose her fucking mind."

I snickered as I imagined her pretty face contorting into utter shock as she followed the length of the animal's long neck. I indulged further, picturing Sylvia lighting up as we encountered more impressive landscapes as we journeyed west: rolling hills, wide-open skies, and eventually, the alpine meadows and foothills of the Rocky Mountains. I could practically hear her awed gasp in my ear and see the flush in her freckled cheeks.

But the more we saw, the less time we would have together.

Leaving her was inevitable—it was *right*. But I wasn't in the mood to dwell. As it was, Sylvia's presence was surreal. This beautiful, ethereal creature chose *me*.

I never understood how some people softened at the edges and let someone in without flinching, without fear. I'd long since resigned myself to the easy routine of one night stands and the detachment of fleeting hunting partners; no expectations, no strings, sometimes not even names. Entanglement without feeling was simpler, even preferable at times. Solitude fit snugly, familiar like a well-worn glove.

But Sylvia—she knew how to pry open my carefully laid armor with a grace that made my chest ache—gentler than any woman had ever been to me. The vulnerability chafed sometimes, if only for a moment. Even as I was drawn into her, I knew I couldn't keep her, which only reminded me of why I'd built those damn walls up in the first place.

I had to let her go.

Storm clouds gathered on the horizon, casting a shadow over the already darkening road ahead, as though mirroring my surly train of thought. I hoped it would pass quickly; we were only an hour out from our destination. Not that I was keen on arriving. If there were any other outposts within range, we wouldn't be headed anywhere near this place. Too many memories. Too much risk. The Underground in New York or the Nevada Outpost were much further drives—too risky to be undersupplied that long and unfair to Sylvia to stretch our journey longer than we already had.

After another minute, Sylvia found a perch by my window. A faint wince crossed her face as she folded her wings. She must have been particularly sore to finally settle. Her yawn seemed to stretch out forever. Any concerns I voiced would be brushed off, but I studied the exposed line of her navel. The bruising was stark against her fair skin, though mostly hidden by her elegant, earth-colored wrap sweater. At least she was resting now.

"Jon, can I ask you something?" Sylvia said.

The half-lidded look she swept over my body caught my attention. "Fire away."

She arched her back, a coy smile curving her lips that matched the fox-like sparkle in her eyes. "Now that you know I'm not a vicious creature of the night… Is the spark of excitement between us gone?"

I huffed out a chuckle, forcing my tone into a deadpan drawl. "It's funny you ask because yes—it is. Not a spark in sight."

A playful pout flashed over her face. With a flick of her wings, she was airborne—landing on my shoulder.

"Maybe I'll show you more of my tricks, then," she breathed. "One. By. One."

I felt her soft body press deliberately against the sensitive skin of my neck as she stretched out an arm to tap my throat in three spots to punctuate her words, fingertips so cold that it was almost painful. I moistened my lips, but my mind was abruptly blank, and I could only manage a pathetic little exhale. The fact that this kind of thing worked on me was almost embarrassing. *Jesus,* what was wrong with me?

Sylvia's musical chuckle sounded to my right as she pressed her hand over my fluttering pulse. "I can feel your heart racing. It's out of control."

The car made a sudden swerve, and Sylvia was knocked into the air with a yelp. Catching herself in a hover, she glared at Cliff.

"If you give him another boner, I'm throwing you out the window," Cliff said, pulling a hand off the wheel to stab a finger in her direction. "I'm not kidding this time."

The memory alone made me avert my gaze guiltily, but Sylvia made only a growl of irritation as she returned to sit by my window. "We've been driving for ages. How do you expect me to keep to myself for *eight hours*?"

"Well, it's less than *one* now, you little freak. You're almost out of the woods. Are all fairies this horny?"

"Feeling left out?" Sylvia batted her eyes at him.

Cliff ignored her and turned up the music.

She shared a comfortable grin with me, one that lingered as she settled into her perch. "Your playlists are getting stale," she called over to Cliff. "Can you play 'Rocket Man' again?"

Forcing a neutral smile, I cringed internally. The first time she belted along off-key to Elton John was adorable. The seventh time was downright grating, though I'd cut off a finger before telling her that.

"Nope," Cliff blessedly interjected. "Guns N' Roses until we get there."

She huffed. "It sounds so angry. How can you stand it?"

An argument might have occupied the rest of the trip if my phone didn't start ringing. As I pulled it up, the incoming video call made my eyes widen, and I realized—*fuck*, it was the first Saturday of the month. Usually, I made sure that I could answer this call privately, but there was nowhere to go.

"Jon?" Sylvia cocked her head up at me, frowning. "Are you alright?"

I swallowed hard. If I ignored the call, I'd have to wait another month—maybe even longer. Fixing Sylvia with the calmest look I could manage, I said, "Stay there until I hang up. It's a video call."

Her eyes swam with questions, but she nodded.

Straightening, I held my phone in front of my face and tried to block out Cliff and Sylvia's heavy silence. When I accepted the call, I smiled as though I didn't spend most of my time trying not to fall apart.

"*Hola, Tia,*" I said, reaching over to lower the radio volume. "We're on the road—sorry about the noise."

Tia Sonia sighed with relief. "*Mijito,* I thought you weren't going to answer! How are you? How's work?"

"Same old." I rolled my eyes. "Heading to Michigan to meet with a client."

"*Ay,* why can't they send you closer to home? There are plenty of factories right here."

"*Claro que sí, pero* they're trying to reach more of the Midwest. I'll come around to visit when I can. Promise." I focused on the screen, shame heaping onto me as Sylvia witnessed how easily I lied through my teeth. I cleared my throat. "Mom's there? She's talking today?"

"*Sí,* the nurses said she had a rough night, but we've been having a nice late lunch together." She gave me a meaningful smile, then looked past the camera. "Ivette. *Es tu hijo. ¿Quieres saludar?*"

"Jon?" Mom's voice wavered. "*Dámelo.*"

My throat tightened when her face filled the screen. Dark eyes, wavy black hair that had gone dull over the years. Still, when she found me on the screen and her expression lit up, she was the most beautiful person to have ever existed. She had been too unwell the past couple months to be cleared for visitors at the hospital. Now, her grin was like a medicine I didn't realize I'd been deprived of.

"Mom," I said, fighting to keep my tone light and casual. "*¿Qué tal?*"

She grimaced dramatically. "*Estoy llena.* You know your tia always brings too much food. You should come have some."

I hesitated, unsure if she was joking or not—it was always hard to tell. So I shrugged. "Maybe I can come around for Christmas. I'll make you *pasteles.* How does that sound?"

Her eyes hardened a little. "Why can't you come now?"

"I'm on the road, *Mama.* Working."

That didn't make her any less agitated. "Always working," she muttered. "At least let me talk to your dad. Adam?" Her voice rose suddenly. "Adam? Are you driving?"

My heart sank. "No, Mom—Dad's not driving."

She blinked. "Let me talk to him."

"Sorry, he—he can't."

I knew by her expression that she was too far gone. The sudden stillness, the blank stare. Tia Sonia saw it, too. She murmured delicately for Mom to say goodbye and hand the phone back.

"No." Mom's voice dropped to a whisper, jerking back.

Tia Sonia made a soft noise of comfort. "Ivette—"

"No!" Mom screamed. "No, no, no!" Each word was like a punch. "Where's Adam? Where is he?"

The phone was yanked away, the video going dark. "*Mijito,* we'll catch up later—she'll be okay. *No te preocupes.*"

In the background, I could hear orderlies trying to get Mom under control. And then, the call ended. The car plunged into silence.

"Sometimes a short call is better, yeah?" Cliff remarked after a weighty pause. He reached over and clapped my shoulder, the gruff motion somewhat easing my lingering sense of fragility.

I muttered my agreement, shoving my phone into my jeans pocket. She had remembered my name the last three calls. That was something, at least.

"They think I'm a sales rep for a machinery company," I said, glancing at Sylvia to answer the burning question she was too kind to ask. "It's just… easier this way."

As the rhythmic hum of the engine carried on, Sylvia flew back to my shoulder, nuzzling up against my neck like a touch-starved kitten.

"Hey—I'm fine, Sylv," I said, an affectionate smile pulling at my lips.

"Everybody knows 'fine' is the worst answer," reproached her dulcet voice in my ear.

Jesus, she was cute. I reached up to rub her side, burying the stab of pain that tightened my throat—the pain of wondering where I would be right now, what my life would be like if my father had never been possessed by that fucking spirit.

Why me? Nearly a decade had passed, and the question had lost none of its acrid sting.

In the distance, thunder rolled viciously. A flicker of lightning cut through the black clouds. Sylvia tensed up against me, cursing softly.

Cliff cursed much less softly, side-eying her perch with equal parts concern and irritation.

"This oughta be a peaceful drive," he muttered.

He tossed a look at me, well-versed with Sylvia's fear of thunder, even if he didn't know the reason behind it. I tightened my hold on her as raindrops splattered onto the windshield, a gradual drumming that became a roar. She was shivering against me, her easygoing demeanor sapping like a switch had been flipped. No matter how she tried to shake her terrible childhood memory, that single moment had etched itself into her very being.

Thick clouds ate away the golden light of dusk, steeping us in a darkness that belonged to a far later hour. A few miles in, the car's headlights struggled to pierce more than a yard ahead of us.

I frowned, noting through the lashing windshield wipers that the land on either side of us was already waterlogged.

"Damn it!" Cliff tapped the brakes, sending me lurching forward in my seat to narrowly avoid a collision with the minivan swerving in front of us.

I squinted through the heavy droplets of the passenger's side window. The minivan sat in the emergency lane, winking hazard lights like dying fireflies. It vanished in the storm's embrace, leaving us the sole vehicle on the road.

Another crackle of thunder rattled the sky. The pinpricks of Sylvia's fingers dug into my neck.

Her breathing huffed irregularly as she fought to find her voice. "Can't we head back and wait out the storm? Why go toward it when that other car was in a rush to get away?"

"Don't worry about it," Cliff said, eyes set forward. "I know what I'm doing. Just hang tight."

The next thunderous crash lasted even longer, like several rumbles rolled into one.

Sylvia shuddered. "Cliff—"

"Let me focus."

"Cliff, *please*." *Mierda*, she sounded close to tears.

"I've driven through plenty of storms," he said wearily. "Trust me."

Rain pelted the car, filling Sylvia's answering silence. The thick, inky darkness beyond the headlight beams was barely visible, but I caught glimpses of trees beginning to crowd near the road. They did little to protect us, only creating more shadows. If I recalled correctly from our previous trips to the outpost, our path was little more than a strip of land cutting through the swamps by this point.

Before long, the wipers did jackshit to keep the road in view. As Sylvia trembled against me, my mind filled with images of the car missing a turn and plunging into the swamp.

"Hey," I said evenly. "We might be better off pulling off to the side and waiting this out."

Cliff grunted. "Hell no—we'll get flooded if we sit around. The quickest way out of this is through it."

"It's two against one," Sylvia snapped.

Judging by the set of his jaw, Cliff was doing everything in his power not to snap back. "It's not a vote," he muttered. "Close your eyes, cover your ears, whatever you gotta do."

Another beat of silence. Then Sylvia flinched dramatically—without thunder or lightning this time. "What was *that*?" she uttered.

"What?" I asked.

"There—through the window. There was something in the water."

Narrowing my eyes at the glass, I wondered how the hell she could discern anything except torrential rain and scraggly vegetation. "I don't see anything," I said.

I meant to soothe her, but intention meant nothing when another streak of lightning filled the sky. The promise of another thunderclap put her over the edge.

"I *saw* it! I felt it—"

Her voice tapered off when the thunder hit. Her skin suddenly felt bitingly cold against my neck. I pulled her in front of me, rubbing her upper arm with my thumb. She was almost painful to touch, but I couldn't bring myself to let go. She buried her face in her hands, shoulders heaving.

"I'm here, Sylv," I whispered, bringing her closer and cupping my hands to block out the downpour. "I've got you. We're safe."

She gave a little nod, head down.

Soothing her worked for all of five minutes—until there was a crash of thunder that shook the entire car. Cliff and I cursed in unison, and Sylvia shrieked. As she hyperventilated, a crackling sound caught my ear. My eyes widened when I peeked up from her to find *ice* crawling onto the passenger-side window.

"Sylv—hey, *hey*, you're alright," I breathed, watching with wide eyes as the frost spread. My hands were freezing cold.

"What the fuck?" Cliff barked. Ice had started spider-webbing from the corner of the windshield. "Get your shit together, Sylv! I can't see through your fucking ice!"

"I'm trying!" she cried back viciously.

"Whatever you're trying's not working!"

"Don't yell at her!" I snapped at Cliff.

"I'm just trying to get us there in one piece."

The air in the car was so frigid that our exclamations were visible puffs. My fingers were growing numb.

"I—I told you we shouldn't be here!" Sylvia cut back at Cliff.

"We'll be fine if you just—"

A vicious *CRACK* sounded ahead of us, and the headlights caught the flash of a huge branch falling directly into our path. The tires squealed as Cliff swerved. I pulled Sylvia close against me as weightlessness flipped my stomach. A brief but brilliant pain exploded behind my eyes before the world went dark.

I was wading through fog. My head throbbed with pain, the pungent tang of burnt rubber making me choke on my next breath.

"Oh, thank the stars—you're breathing. Jon? Jon, wake up!"

Through my daze, I heard her voice: melodic even in her stringent urgency.

With great effort, I moved my lips. "Sylvia?"

Scraps of sensation pulled me back to consciousness, little by little: the seat belt cutting across my chest, rain drumming on the windows, the hissing gurgle of cold water seeping against my boots.

Wait—*water?*

A frustrated flit of wings preceded another twinge of pain—a lock of my hair being sharply tugged. Groaning, I opened my eyes. Sylvia darted back as I reached up to gingerly brush the tender spot on my head where I must've slammed it against the window. No nausea or crippling dizziness, all limbs responding without numbness. It seemed I had made it through without a concussion, at least.

The windshield bore a menacing crack, a spiderweb of fissures obscuring our view beyond. Frigid night air seeped through the glass, mingling with relentless rainwater as the storm battered on outside. Beside me, Cliff was fumbling to unbuckle himself with a groan. Sylvia flew to him, summoning a cerulean glow to her skin. Her ethereal light danced around the car's interior, and a jolt of shock hit me as I registered our precarious angle.

Half the vehicle was submerged in the swamp.

"What hurts?" Sylvia demanded an inch from Cliff's face.

"M'fine," he hissed, brushing her away—urging her to land. "Get out of the air."

"You could have hit your head, you idiot," she said in a wavering voice. "You probably *did!*"

Cliff's jaw set. "Your wings are gonna get drenched, and then what? You plan on swimming out of here?"

He gestured at a dry spot on the dash, mostly devoid of glass shards. Sylvia wavered, then did as he said.

Sluggishly, I unbuckled and tested my range of movement. Then Sylvia gave a sharp gasp, patting down her waist and leggings. I went still, studying her posture for any sign of injury as she felt around her waist. *Fuck*, she could have been…

"Are you hurt?" I asked.

"Barely even dizzy. You caught me," Sylvia said, searching around distractedly. She sighed, her eyes swimming with almost-tears as they darted from me to Cliff to the pitch-black forest waiting outside. "It's just—I can't find the necklace you gave me. The clasp must've finally given up. Damn it. But never mind that now—we can't stay here."

Armed with what meager supplies we kept in the glovebox, Cliff and I climbed out of the car. The water hit up to my knees, sinking into my jeans uncomfortably. Sylvia tucked herself against my neck, seeing as her wings were useless in the deluge. I couldn't tell if she was shivering from shock or cold, and I hated that I couldn't do more to assuage her discomfort.

Eyeing the car's position lodged between two waterlogged mangroves at the base of the sloping road, I supposed the fact that we were alive was its own comfort.

Every step sloshed as I joined Cliff at the back of the car. As he produced a flashlight and began pocketing a small arsenal, I pulled out my cell phone.

"No signal," I said, squinting at the phone screen. "*Puñeta.* We'll have to walk to the next town to get a tow. I think it's six miles."

My fingers quickly lost purchase on the wet glass, making it unusable. I tucked it away again, swallowing a shout of frustration.

"We can just follow the road, right?" Sylvia said, her voice still rife with nerves. I wanted so badly to hold her, but my soaked hands wouldn't be of any help.

Cliff passed a couple of handguns to me, expression taut. "Genius," he said under his breath.

I shot him a reproachful glare as I tucked the weapons away safely. Sylvia had done nothing to deserve his temper, but I conceded to the shiver of shock that lay beneath his coarse tone.

Cliff's flashlight flickered as we rummaged through the trunk. He cursed, hitting the handle. This earned a few more moments of dim illumination before the batteries went out altogether, and darkness plunged around us. The drum of the freezing rain seemed to intensify as we willed our eyes to adjust, feeling blindly for the most crucial supplies.

A faint whisper came by my ear—and then a soft cerulean light blossomed. We stopped short, craning our necks; the glow Sylvia's had conjured to her skin had detached into a fae light. The orb hung brightly over our heads, illuminating a five-foot radius around us. It brought the rippling water and moss-laden trees around us into focus—along with the supplies.

"Thanks," Cliff muttered, locating two working flashlights in the clutter of our belongings. He tucked them both into a backpack with the other weapons and slung it over his shoulder.

"Not a problem," Sylvia responded just as snippily.

Cliff straightened, his green eyes flashing at her in the peculiar light. "If you're gonna be like this all night—"

"*Me?*" I felt Sylvia gesture widely at the torrential downpour. "We wouldn't have had an issue if you hadn't insisted on plowing through. But that's what you do best, isn't it?"

A whip of lightning split the sky above us, followed by a monstrous roll of thunder. Sylvia's snarl tapered into a whimper of fear, and she curled against me to ground herself. Cliff's gaze hardened on her, like this was condemning.

"The *issue* is you can't control yourself. If you were an actual hunter, you'd be a goddamn liability," he gritted out.

"Enough. Lay the hell off her," I snapped.

Silence stretched following my words, like all the air had been sucked from the clearing. I shot a withering glare at Cliff. He faltered as our eyes met, the anger fleeing his expression as he glanced back at Sylvia, then to me again. I couldn't see her face, but a new tension radiated off her in waves.

"Let's focus on getting the hell out of here," I voiced firmly.

Cliff swept a hand through his hair, the cropped blond strands damp and plastered messily against his forehead. He nodded wordlessly, pulling a black tarp over the remainder of our arsenal and reaching up to slam the trunk shut. With each of us burdened with a bag, we had the essentials that we couldn't risk being flooded with water.

We turned, and Sylvia's fae light followed our movements as we gathered our bearings. Finding the slope of the road, we started forward. The mud sucked at my boots with every step, slowing our progress to a miserable trudge.

"You have the energy to keep that up?" I asked Sylvia, nodding at the light. I tried to keep my tone level, but I swore she could hear the protective thoughts swirling in the back of my head.

"Do you have to ask every time?" She sounded so weary. "It's not a difficult spell. I won't melt from the effort. When we get to the next town, obviously I'll—"

A sudden lurch in the water jolted through the darkness—*behind us*.

I whipped around, my heart pounding. Cliff already had a small blade in his hands, scanning the shadows. The water's surface was jarred by the constant rain, making it nearly impossible to discern the source of the movement.

"Fucking stars, it's—something's—" Sylvia stammered, her voice coming out in short, urgent bursts.

My blood went cold. Any comforting notion of a wild animal moving through the storm vanished; Sylvia's sense for non-human creatures was never wrong.

A faint collection of bubbles gurgled up from beneath the tossing tide. Sylvia's pale blue light couldn't penetrate the depths. I staggered back in the water a few steps, my mind conjuring images of bony hands seizing my ankles and dragging me down, down—

A shadow surged beneath the water, zagging toward the submerged wreckage of the Pontiac, perhaps for cover. At the same instant, Sylvia gave a harsh cry, and a gale of ice shot through the blackness. The frost connected like a bullet, crackling as it spread a thick layer of ice over the water, three feet in diameter.

We stood, waiting for the mysterious presence to retaliate. Cliff and I looked behind us, mindful of every crackling branch. It wasn't uncommon for monsters to travel in packs. As I made a slow circle of my position, I began to form a contingency for how to protect Sylvia's life while her wings were soaked. She couldn't fly, which meant she couldn't leave my side. *Fuck.*

A tense minute passed, with only the faint roll of thunder and the steady drum of rain mingling with our heavy breathing.

Finally, Sylvia slumped against me, a rush of air escaping her. "It's gone—whatever it was."

Mild relief washed over me. Not for the first time, I wished I shared her supernatural sense for the mere comfort of confirming that we were alone again in the marsh.

"Rougarou?" I asked, my stomach knotting at the very idea of facing the haggard, werewolf-like creature in this state. I exchanged a harrowed look with Cliff, who seemed to share my mixture of relief and persisting dread.

Rougarous were smaller than their urban counterparts, but what they lacked in size, they accommodated with speed and savagery. I'd heard of a family of hunters in the South who had devoted themselves to keeping Rougarou numbers in check over the last two decades. Still, it wouldn't be out of the realm of belief that some poor soul had been taken victim to the curse.

"I don't think so," Sylvia said. "I mean, I can't be sure. It felt like… glamour. Almost like *fae* glamour. But—that's impossible. No one would be able to fly in this weather. They'd drown in minutes."

Still, uncertainty lilted in her voice like she wasn't quite convinced. She moved her fae light higher, scanning the web of tree branches overhead, curtained by swathes of moss that swayed in the urgent breeze. I half expected to see dozens of tiny, winged silhouettes peering down at us like dark sentinels where her light touched.

But like the water, the branches were vacant. The emptiness began to feel like a mockery, raising hairs on my arms that refused to quell.

I peered all around us, paying special attention to the submerged section of the car, where something could easily take refuge out of sight. I pulled out my flashlight to sweep a second beam over the rain-pelted water, but nothing stirred.

"Let's go," Cliff's voice carried over the storm. "No need to sit around and wait for it to get desperate."

Sylvia put up no word of protest, still scanning the unsettling gaps of inky darkness that lay beyond the glow of her spellwork.

7

JON

After a miserable half hour, the trees became less crowded, but the road was a nightmare to follow under the rising water. For all I knew, we had veered in the wrong direction. Even between our flashlights and Sylvia's glow, we could only discern more darkness ahead of us.

We all nearly jumped out of our skin when my beam caught faded white boards and a colorful glint of stained glass.

"Fucking finally," Cliff groaned. "We can wait out the storm." He trudged forward without waiting to see if we would follow.

"A house?" Sylvia's detached light grew dimmer by the minute. "What if someone lives there?"

"It's not a house," I said. "But there could be squatters, especially in this weather."

However, ordinary humans were the least of my worries, especially with the scare we'd gotten outside the wreck. I strained my senses, scouring the clearing around the church for signs of something more sinister out here with us. There was no tell-tale stench of decay, no trace of mutilated animals… Of course, the damn storm could have washed away any lingering odors.

Judging by the church's architecture, the lone building was sixty years old at most, but corrosion had reduced it to a husk. Ivy and lichen crawled over the crooked steeple that jutted accusingly toward the heavens. Peeling white paint exposed cracked gray boards beneath, and the arched windows were stained with grime and graffiti. Some windows were missing entire panes of glass, leaving them to gape like empty eye sockets as we approached.

I vaulted up the stairs behind Cliff, each step making the old wood shriek. Up close, the neglect of the structure was more pronounced: wild grasses pushed up through the rotting floorboards, and the sign beside the entrance was too faded to read. The door was locked, but it took no more than a firm shove to force it through the warped frame. A thick wave of musty silence welcomed us as we stepped inside.

"Smells like ass in here," I remarked under my breath, nudging the door shut behind us. Still, a shiver of ease kissed down my spine at the sudden relief from the pelting rain.

Sylvia reduced her fae light once we were safely inside, draining the ethereal blue from the aging building. Dust danced in the beam of my flashlight as I swept the room. We stood in the remains of a lobby. The partition wall was reduced to a skeleton of support beams, revealing a cavernous room lined with dusty pews. The distant drip of water disrupted the otherwise stagnant air that made it feel like the whole place was holding its breath, frozen in a moment of time.

Gravel and glass crunched under our boots as we moved inward. I grunted, nearly tripping over a candle holder in pieces just beyond the threshold to the next room. The likeness of the prophet engraved was in the bronze, weathered beyond recognition. I kicked it aside, trying to temper my expression as I eyed the shadows.

Although my jacket was heavy with a small arsenal of iron and silver, the distinct lack of my favored sawed-off shotgun left me feeling exposed. It was too conspicuous for a sleepy Louisiana town, too large to stow in my bag. Last we'd been to Cypress Hollow, local civilians had welcomed visiting strangers with open arms, but I doubted they'd extend the same hospitality if we came waltzing in brandishing machetes and scoped weapons.

My fingers twitched as I dwelled on everything left behind in that patch of swamp.

Cálmate, I told myself. We'd been in far worse pinches before. There was no need to feed the rooting fear in my gut.

I idled by the doorway and reached for my shoulder, brushing Sylvia's side. Her cropped sweater and leggings felt like they were frozen to her delicate body. My heart lurched at the thought of her limited belongings getting ruined or lost out there in the wreck. I couldn't shake the pain in her voice when she'd lost track of her snowflake charm.

"How are you holding up?" I asked.

She gave my neck a reassuring pet. "You act like it's my first time being stranded in a terrifying swamp in the dead of night," she simpered, drawing a chuckle out of me. "I'll be better after a hot bath, but I'll pull through for now. *No tengo mierda.*"

My heart stuttered as it always did when she spoke Spanish—broken as it was. There was something otherworldly and undeniably *hot* about hearing my second language on her perfect lips.

But this particular mispronunciation had me sharing a slow smile with Cliff.

"What?" The purr of Sylvia's voice rose to a snap when Cliff and I snickered.

"Look, that's adorable," Cliff said. The irritation in his voice had softened gradually during our long trek, and he now shot Sylvia a crooked smile. "But you just told him you don't have *shit.* You meant *no tengo miedo.*"

Sylvia made an indignant noise that tapered into confusion. "How do you know that?" she demanded.

He glanced back over his shoulder, smirking. "What? Ten years with this guy, and you don't think I picked up a few things? *Me has hecho daño.*"

I could imagine the expression on Sylvia's face—the pinch of her lips as she pouted in thought. "Bathroom?"

"That would be *baño*," I said.

"Ugh." And that was her rolling her eyes.

Her waterlogged wings tickled my neck as they tried to shake themselves dry. She might have attempted flight if it weren't for the flash of lightning through one of the broken windows. Even I flinched in tandem with her yelp when a bolt illuminated the silhouette of a person outside.

"Just a statue," I assured after blinking a few times. The image in the billowing grass stayed etched in my mind's eye—a crumbling woman in flowing robes, arms outstretched as though awaiting an embrace.

We moved away from the shattered windows, inadvertently herded closer to the altar. Tattered bedding, food wrappers, and empty bottles between the pews pointed to squatters, but the makeshift camp looked like it hadn't been touched in ages.

Sylvia breathed in sharply. "There's something about this place," she said in a softer voice.

"What?" I asked, my voice a whisper.

"Like… something *used* to be here. A bad memory."

My flashlight beam swept over the crumbling pews. A few of them were shoved about haphazardly, splintered in some places. Upon closer inspection, I found a couple of bullets lodged into one of the backrests.

"Places like these are prime real estate for hauntings," Cliff muttered. "But with the outpost so close, nothing around here can stay haunted for long."

Legs aching, I lowered myself into the sturdiest-looking pew up front. "You're sure it's gone—whatever was here?" I asked Sylvia.

"It feels like a smudge of sorts, like a handprint on glass. Nothing more." In her brief silence, I had to wonder if I was feeling the same thing as her—that unsettling heaviness in the air. "I've been feeling it lately after you've killed a monster."

"Sounds like your senses are getting sharper," Cliff called over from where he was rifling through a stained chest of drawers in the left alcove. "Good girl. Keep it up."

"Tell that to the vampire king that snuck up on me," she muttered in reply. Managing a short flight, Sylvia perched on the backrest across from me. As she combed her fingers through her hair, wringing out the tiniest droplets. "Whatever I felt by the car definitely wasn't a memory, though."

The mere mention of the close encounter added another layer of tension to her face. I studied her, noting the circles under her eyes—which she had been diligently trying to hide from me lately.

"How'd you sleep last night?" I asked.

Her pout was reproachful, but she averted her eyes like she'd been caught. "I'm wide awake, Jon. I *know* I sensed something out there."

"I believe you, it's just—" I sighed, wishing I could ease every sign of stress from her features. "You look like you're burning the candle at both ends. You have for days."

She looked ready to soften, but another flash of lightning accompanied the muted drumming of the rain. She went rigid, fists clenched in her lap to weather the answering crash of thunder. The illumination cast a fleeting pattern of colors on the walls as the light refracted through the intricate windows.

"You're sure you don't wanna hide until it passes?" I asked. It wouldn't have been the first time a coat pocket or sheltered space had served as a panic room for her.

Sylvia shot me a hard look, shaking her head. Frustration laced her voice like thorns, but not directed at me. "I'm not under the willow anymore, and I'm tired of hiding," she said. "I should be better than this by now."

My jaw feathered. Sometimes, I saw too much of myself in her. Sylvia had voiced embarrassment over her panic attacks more than once, but soft assurances from Cliff and I fell short when it wasn't *us* she needed to prove something to. Though, I was sure his callous remark earlier hadn't helped.

"We all have our blind spots," I said. "If we were at a high altitude, you know I'd be worse off."

"Damn straight." Cliff's voice was further away now, his athletic frame barely visible as he rifled through a pile of rubble behind the altar. "Remember that time we had to take out that ghoul in a high rise? Thought you were gonna hurl when it went out on the fire escape."

He chuckled to himself as though he could sense how I paled at the memory. Sylvia shot him a grateful look—seeming to take the shift in his tone as a signal that his anger was not lasting. She sighed, cupped her hands in front of her, and gathered a shimmering orb of ice between her palms. The cool breeze of the magic caressed my face as she stretched the substance—somehow both liquid and solid—into different shapes. She settled on a small double-sided spear before pushing her palms together and ousting the magic like a snuffed candle.

"Father used to tell me stories about Fae warriors from long ago. Ones who lived hundreds of years ago, their days filled with danger and excitement." Her smile turned bitter. "Living in Elysia, you can understand why I clung to those stories so ferociously. I lived through those heroes like a second life when I was a child."

"Like Karolyn the Gilded?" I ventured.

The corner of her mouth lifted. "Good memory."

Sylvia had readily latched onto this legend and shared it with me our first week on our journey west: a fairy who had supposedly used gem magic to change forms into various animals, even stealing the likeness of other fairies temporarily. Fitting, considering our joint quest to find Sylvia an equally capable stone.

"She's an obvious favorite of mine," Sylvia said, giving a little toss of her hair. "But most fairies don't see it that way. She was a little cutthroat, and trying to use deception to steal the crown became her legacy above all her other feats."

"Royalty?" I quirked a brow, recalling the Elysian governance Sylvia had explained. A few of those assholes I'd seen with my own eyes.

"Apparently, her coup is part of how my village eventually moved to the council of Elders." Sylvia shrugged, some of the light dimming from her eyes at the very mention of them—the people who had banished her. It didn't escape me that while she cared for me—for both of us—her decision to stay with us was made under extreme duress.

"There are so many others, though," she went on, brightening. She stretched her legs out, wings fanning in sync with the motion. "Heroes that became legends in the stars, like Edin the Valiant. Father loved him—another gem scavenger of old. I think Father was jealous of the prestige scavengers used to get. The story goes that Edin used gem magic to protect his village, somewhere far off where streams and mountains cut through vast red trees. His greatest tale of bravery—the one all the children cared about, anyway—was when he was supposedly trapped in a cave with a wolf for three days. Only his magic and wits to protect him."

"Hell of a bedtime story," I scoffed.

Sylvia grinned, shaking her head. Her gaze was distant, torn between me and that cozy hearth room under the willow she had described so often.

"He conquered it against all odds. Some thought him immortal, but he ultimately sacrificed his life for his closest friend. Another reason Edin's name is synonymous with courage and kindness.

That's his legacy." Sylvia fell quiet, her eyes dropping to her lap. "And my legacy? Crying like a child at every thunderstorm that passes."

My smile dropped away, the bitter tone in her voice cutting like poison. "Sylv—"

"It's true," she insisted, voice hardening. "I can't shake the feeling that I should be better by now. Like… maybe it's time for me to stop being afraid. I should be something to be feared. It's safer that way."

My lips pulled into a mournful smile as I felt torn between protecting her from every dark corner of the world or admiring the hell out of her, because *that's my girl.*

I leaned my arms on my knees, pinning her with a look until she met my gaze, a flicker of uncertainty crossing her face. "You may be the bravest person I've ever known."

"I don't see it that way," Sylvia snorted, but there was a threadiness there—that sacred trust she reserved for me.

"Then, I'll help you see." I gave her a once-over, my certainty pushing a brighter smile onto my face. "Give it time, I think you'll have no shortage of legends in every corner of the country about you."

A wash of satisfaction softening the anxious lines on Sylvia's face. "I look forward to hearing them. But I know how hunters exaggerate. How can I trust a word you'll say?"

I let my voice drop to a conspiratorial whisper, leaning closer. "You can't. I'm extremely biased."

Despite the gusting wind rattling the wooden walls, she and I shared a soft laugh. Seeming to wrestle herself into a new train of thought, Sylvia leaned back on her seat and craned her neck to study our surroundings.

She gestured at one of the intact stained-glass windows, where there was a depiction of an angel. "I've never seen such colorful panes. It makes the lightning a little less horrifying, I suppose."

I shined my flashlight where she pointed, illuminating the figure and its glorious feathery wings. Sylvia's eyes lit up at how the beam sent refractions of color across the rest of the room. She looked down at her hands, marveling at the light dancing across her skin. For the first time since the storm had begun, a breathless grin brightened her features as she wiggled her fingers. In the moment I was studying her, I forgot I was cold and soaked to the bone.

Sylvia looked up at me, grin faltering as she studied me. "What bothers you so much about this place?" she asked in that gentle tone that read far too deeply. "You look ready to bolt, but I know for a *fact* you've seen worse than a few creepy statues."

"Just because hunts tend to take us to rotting buildings doesn't mean I *like* it," I deflected, lifting my eyebrows at her.

Sylvia rolled her eyes, her smirk flickering with transparent disappointment. *Don't hide from me,* her gaze pleaded. That chafing feeling panged me again—the relentless prying at the careful walls I maintained. She deserved more, and I resigned even as my throat closed around the words.

"The last time I was inside a church, my family was still intact." I exhaled through my nose, pushing a hand back through my wet hair to sweep stray locks off my face. "I really never minded going; it was tradition. But after everything that happened to us… The evil I've seen thrust onto so many others—good people, *innocent* people…"

I trailed off, my chest tight. I still remembered some of the faces, and my pulse raced. For every life Cliff and I had saved over the years, there were ten others who had suffered a brutal, unjust fate. We hadn't been enough—hadn't been fast enough.

"I can't help but feel cheated," I finished softly, pinching my shoulders in a tight, dismissive shrug. "There's nothing out there listening to our pleas. So it's up to us to carry out what we want to happen."

Sylvia's expression knit thoughtfully as she eyed the vacant out-line of a cross between windows. She lifted her hands and whis-pered a spell, conjuring another fae light—golden this time—to replace the one that had faded. I watched the glow's trajectory as she sent it soaring toward the ceiling with a flick of her wrist.

Her magic was a reflection of *her*, and I was beginning to understand how to decode it. The shimmering orb, a little larger than my palm, bore a steady light, suggesting that she was re-covering from the initial shock of the accident. It never ceased to amaze me how resilient she was for someone so delicate, even if much of it came from sheer stubbornness of will. The added light fixture illuminated more of the windows, spreading a warm hue over some of the peeling walls.

"Well, the stars brought you to me," she said, almost shy as she faced me again. "So I wouldn't rule out hope entirely that *nothing* is listening."

The corner of my lips lifted. She was wrong, but her idealism painted color into the world.

"The stars couldn't give us a less violent way to cross paths?" I asked. Though our first encounter at Dottage mansion felt like another life now, the image of her terrified expression was etched into my mind like glass. More than once in the last few weeks alone, she had brought up our use of *that damn box* with icy bitterness.

But now, she laughed.

"How could it be any other way? Look at you," Sylvia said. "All you boys do is raise hell wherever you go. And besides, who are mere mortals to question the cosmos?"

I grinned gamely, leaning my arms on my knees as I leveled my gaze closer to her. "Give me names, I'm more than happy to rattle the stars for you."

Her drooping wings gave a flutter as my words washed over her. "Jon, don't give me filthy thoughts during a thunderstorm. It's confusing to sort through," she breathed out.

"What? I didn't do anything."

"You know exactly what you're doing! With your stupid, wet hair and that tone in your voice…"

I flicked my gaze over her. She had a point about the wetness; her hair hung in tight crimson ringlets just above her shoulders, and her sodden clothes clung to every curve, leaving very little to the imagination. A few scant droplets still lingered on her exposed shoulders and navel—and my single, consuming thought was how much I wanted to kiss them off of her body. Maybe ease a few of those bruises with some warmth.

Jesus, I was such a freak.

But now that we'd started, I couldn't bring myself to stop. "It's not too late to admit that I'm too much for you," I challenged, letting my voice dip lower.

That familiar spark of wildness crept onto her face. Slowly, she leaned forward to match my smoldering gaze—unafraid.

"No. I'll have you, violence and all," she said. "I already tried to push you from my mind a million times before—and look where that got me."

I felt my heart give a very physical ache in my chest. *Fuck,* the hold she had on me. If we found that gemstone, I would never let her go.

Not human, screamed the voice in the back of my mind. *She's not human.*

But lately, it didn't seem to matter anymore. Not like it should've.

"Hey, pornstars. Take a break from being gross and check this out," Cliff interrupted, approaching us with his arms full.

Sylvia scowled as we broke apart. If she weren't so miserable and soaked, I had a feeling she would have doubled-down and closed the distance to me just to spite Cliff.

"Here, hold this." He handed me a small, leatherbound book so that he could focus on inspecting the kerosene lamp in his other hand.

I wrinkled my nose, thumbing through the worn pages. "What is this?"

"Definitely bound in human skin and inked with blood," Cliff said chipperly.

Gagging, I dropped the book to the floor and kicked it across the aisle—eliciting another booming laugh from Cliff.

"Looks like a circle of druids planted their flag in this place sometime ago," Cliff said, sobering as he fiddled with his lighter. He glanced at the book, then nodded in Sylvia's direction. "No wonder you're feeling echoes or whatever. It's like they had a checklist for making it freaky. Drawn full of cryptic symbols? Check. List of the impure? Double check."

Sylvia's fae light overhead dimmed to nothing, as though frightened away in sync with her grimace. "Fucking stars," she muttered.

"And," Cliff said, his voice low and laced with something conspiratorial, "you gotta see what I found at the back of the closet." He paused for effect, letting the words linger in the air as a boyish excitement crept over his expression. "*A secret room.* Flashlight batteries are dying, so I couldn't get a good look at it."

I puffed out a coarse laugh. "What're you hoping for more—treasure, or a sacrificial altar?"

"Fifty-fifty." The lamp finally ignited, setting Cliff's intrigued expression into eerie shadows as he backpedaled. "You coming, or what?"

With her wings finally dry enough to sustain flight, Sylvia took the air and led the way after the glow of Cliff's lamp.

The moment I stepped through the closet door, I had half a mind to request another warm, glowing light from Sylvia.

A wide opening sat at the far end of the closet, and when I passed the threshold to descend a short flight of steps, I knew at once that this area had been tended to much more recently. The sleek handrails and solid stairs were nothing like the rustic architecture that druids favored.

This belonged to something entirely different, and the main attraction awaiting us at the bottom of the stairs was in ruins.

"What the fuck?" I muttered as I emerged into a basement.

The cages caught my eye first. Half melted criss-crossed bars lined the walls, looking eerily similar to how rabbits were enclosed in test labs.

Then, there were the scorch marks crawling along the warped walls. Apparently, this place had been reinforced enough to keep the fire from spreading, but the items within hadn't been flameproof. Ashes were scattered along the ground, nearly everything burnt to a crisp.

"You think the fire was set on purpose to cover up whatever was going on here?" Cliff mused, kneeling to sift through a pile of ashes with his free hand.

"Maybe," I said, frowning as I scanned every corner with my eyes. "Whatever equipment was in here, it looks expensive. I find it hard to believe they'd blow it up like that. Something must've gone wrong."

A large metal workbench was the most discernible thing besides the cages, and even that was warped from the heat. Tools were melted to the surface, and portable chargers to power the equipment were completely busted—all of it unusable now.

There didn't appear to be a corpse in sight—human or otherwise—which was somehow more unsettling than if there *had* been one.

"Hey, look at this." I delicately pulled a scrap of charred paper from a pile of ash under the workbench.

Cliff brought the lamp over. No more than a word or two could be read from the sheet, but a logo at the top was visible enough. A circular emblem in the vague shape of an *E*. The sight of it felt strangely corporate and out of place in a church this old. But it appeared perfectly at home in this ruined, high-tech basement.

"Am I crazy, or does this look like an invoice?" Cliff said, squinting at the ruined lines of text beneath. "Or an order form?"

"Beats me—it's falling apart just from being moved."

A small voice came from the entrance. "They're iron."

I didn't realize until then that Sylvia hadn't moved far from the door. I turned my flashlight in her direction, careful not to blind her. She was paler than before, staring at the metal bars. I thought about teasing her to ease the tension—but that look on her face was not to be toyed with.

"Sylv?" I murmured, taking a step toward her.

She flinched like I'd startled her, tearing her eyes away from the cages. "Why iron? What was in them?"

Her implication sent a chill down my spine. Of course her mind would go there. I couldn't blame her.

"Hey—whatever happened, it's long gone now," I said. "Chances are, this place was some kind of below-board lab. Druids are known to use animals in their rituals. Whoever came in here and replaced the druids… maybe they got curious about the magicked animals and wanted to study them."

That didn't seem to make Sylvia feel all that better—and I couldn't say my theory convinced me, either.

Even as Cliff and I gave the basement one more sweep, she remained firmly by the stairs. With no other clues as to what we had discovered, I snapped a photo of the scrap of paper I'd found. No doubt it would disintegrate if I pocketed it.

Back upstairs, we settled around the kerosene lamp. Sylvia was especially close to it, basking in its warmth. The next fae light she conjured was even stronger than the last, casting away most of the shadows in the vast chamber. She still flinched at the thunder, but gradually, the claps came further apart.

Squinting at the window, I waited for another flash of lightning that never came.

The rain was finally letting up.

The sole mechanic shop in town—Gulf Care Auto—wouldn't open until seven in the morning. At least the tow service number from the diner hostess was useful. I strode back into the diner, still damp from the thirty-minute walk from the church. The rain had been on and off, but the brutality had waned.

The diner was a grungy but classic establishment that hadn't changed since the last time I'd been here. Colorful neon and 1960s decor clung to the past, and the same could be said for the few patrons who occupied the tables.

I slid back into my seat at our corner booth. "We'll need to get a room to stay overnight," I announced, remembering the flickering vacancy sign we'd passed down the street.

"Figured as much," Cliff said. "Well, I guess it could be worse. We're lucky the mechanic's open on a Sunday morning, and this town only pads thirty minutes onto the drive into the outpost."

Sylvia wrinkled her nose at me from behind the dessert menu on the table. "You're not talking about that Top Star Motel we passed, are you? That place looked filthy."

I shot her a dry smile. "You'd rather stay at the church? It'd be free, at least."

Grimacing, she shook her head. The flicker of horror in her eyes no doubt reflected what we'd seen in the basement. "It's only for one night," she conceded. "As long as it has hot water and a place to dry off."

As I watched her shiver, a pang of concern fluttered in my chest. I patted myself down again for something, *anything* that could warm her up. In the fourth jacket pocket I checked, my fingers brushed a scrap of flannel I'd missed earlier buried under a box of bullets. *Perfect.*

"Hey—I found your blanket," I said, grinning as delight exploded across Sylvia's face.

I wiggled the scrap free, pleased to find it had been largely protected from the rain. She had sawed herself a square from my blue plaid shirt with her dagger in our second week traveling together. She'd thought I wouldn't notice the gaping, eight-inch piece missing from the garment, and was relieved when I voiced how endearing it was when I inevitably found out. After ensuring the few other diner patrons were invested in their meals, I draped the flannel around Sylvia's shoulders securely.

She practically purred, nuzzling the fabric under her chin. "Thank you. I thought we'd lost it back there."

"If you lose sensation in your fingers, speak up," I said, my frown setting back into place.

"I promise not to freeze to death. Focus on *food*, Jon. I'm starving." Sylvia leaned to the side, tracking movement behind me. She scooted to the right, urgently scanning the menu propped before her again. I braced myself; Sylvia's desire to sample as many human foods as she could en route to Aelthorin had her ordering food like a career athlete coming off a grueling triathlon.

Even still, I did a double take at Sylvia's request, which included two full desserts. Before I could protest further, the waitress returned. Sylvia ducked back into hiding as I ordered enough food to feed a small army. I heard faint, excited wing flutters as

I confirmed the desserts in particular—a hot fudge sundae and a slice of apple pie.

The waitress raised a brow when Cliff tacked his order onto the end of mine, her lips pursing as her pen scratched against its pad. She looked to be mid-thirties, with smudged winged eyeliner and an air of boredom that suggested she was weary of the small population. She'd been eyeing Cliff and I like fresh water in a wasteland since we walked inside, and I took full advantage, flashing her a toothy smile to soften the blow of the unusual order.

She departed without comment, a little pinch between her brows.

Relaxing, I sipped at the beer set before me and cast another look around the room. The smell of fresh coffee and fried food mingled with the humid bayou air outside, evoking a unique sense of nostalgia. The peeling paint and faded memorabilia on the walls looked untouched, as though no time at all had passed since our last visit to the southernmost hunter's outpost.

"Place hasn't changed much in two years, has it?" Cliff said, following my sweeping gaze. "Hey, I wonder if my quarter's still jammed in the jukebox."

The machine was tucked in the corner just behind our booth, buttons worn from decades of use. The yellowed catalog behind the domed glass boasted classic rock and country—and some old favorites Cliff and I still blasted in the car on occasion.

Cliff sighed as he peeled off his sodden jacket, folding around the weapons lodged in its pockets before dropping it on the cracked vinyl booth beside his bag.

"How many times have you been here?" Sylvia asked, shifting carefully into the light.

"Too many to count," I said. "Tammy had us spend three months training at the outpost when we first hit the road, too."

"Your mentor, right?" Sylvia asked. "She was a hunter, too?"

"Yeah—and more vicious than you'd think for a mom of four," Cliff said. "Tammy put us on the right track bringing us here, but it was three months of hell."

"It's kind of a baptism by blood," I tacked on. "She rented us a room from the marshal at the time, and had us in the Pit four days a week for hours, putting us against practice targets."

Sylvia's brows knit together. "Monsters. Your mentor threw you in a cage with—"

"*Weakened* monsters," I cut in. "But yeah. It's where a lot of recruits figure out if they're cut out for this. Nearly broke my nose in my first wraith fight with the other newbloods, but... We pulled through. Tammy was a good coach. A good friend when the rest of the world had turned their back on us. She got us on our feet until she was satisfied we wouldn't get killed the moment we walked into the next demented spirit. When she left, we started branching out."

Sylvia nodded like she was adjusting to a sour taste in her mouth. "Like training an affinity. Do all hunters end up learning here?"

"Not all, but many."

She frowned, looking between us. "What happens to those who don't cut it?"

I shrugged. "Some become cleaners. Hunters pay them to ensure no trace is left after a particularly gruesome hunt—especially when working with covens or packs."

"And... the ones who don't make it as hunters or cleaners?" Sylvia pried.

"We've got archivists and medics, but..." I gave her a hard look. "Some guys don't make it out of that first fight at the outpost at all. It's not a perfect system."

Sylvia swallowed, nodding with grim understanding.

"It's not just training, though. It's a community, you know?" Cliff said, taking a pull from his beer. "Even if half the guys are assholes, there's some good people too. Real hero material."

"Except *you*," Sylvia teased.

"Watch it. I actually met the best lay of my life around these parts, so I can't knock it entirely."

My insides soured, but I tried to keep my expression neutral. "You can't mean Gwen," I said.

Cliff shrugged, but there was no mistaking that wistful gaze washing over him. He wore it only for *her*, as long as I'd known him.

I softened my next words with a dry chuckle. "I think you're forgetting how you two ended up screaming at each other at least twice a week towards the end."

"Yeah. We broke up at least a dozen times in this place," Cliff said, glancing around the diner with a fond look.

"Was she a hunter, too?" Sylvia asked.

"A damn good one." Cliff's eyes went distant. "A good fucking shot. *Almost* as good as me."

"I've got the scar to prove it," I muttered.

"Hey, it was a misunderstanding," Cliff said.

Sylvia huffed at that, but her smile was teasing. "A good shot. No wonder you had it bad for her."

"For a while," Cliff said, shrugging.

"Wait, did *she* end it?" Sylvia's jaw dropped. "Okay, whose heart do I have to freeze? Say the word." She slammed her palm on the table, sending a delicate line of frost toward Cliff. He seized his beer before the spell could touch it.

"Killing, Sylv? Don't you think that's a little extreme?" Cliff shot her a scathing look for all of five seconds that had her stammering before he broke into a wide smile. "I'm just kidding."

They shared a laugh, and I found myself chuckling along with them.

"You have to tell me more about her," Sylvia said eagerly.

Cliff's amused smile turned tight. "Fun fact—no, I don't."

"Seriously? I hear every detail down to the thread count of the sheets about others, but—"

"There's nothing to tell," Cliff cut in. "She was good in bed, good with a gun, end of story."

Sylvia looked at me questioningly, and I gave my head a small shake. She frowned but held her tongue.

I cleared my throat. "The guy on the line for the towing company mentioned that the mechanic has a car lot, too. Chances are, we'll need a replacement. The price of repairing the damage might not be worth it."

Sylvia looked down, guilt etched on her face.

"It wasn't going to last much longer, anyway," I assured her.

Rather than bring Cliff's mood further down, the change of subject actually perked him up a little. "It's been years since we upgraded. Man, I'd kill for a sexier car. Imagine being behind the wheel of a Thunderbird again—or a vintage Impala. *Those* are sexy cars."

"Is it normal for humans to be sexually attracted to machinery?" Sylvia piped up.

"The way you freak out every time you see a new lamp, maybe you shouldn't be talking," Cliff scoffed.

I glanced around the other booth to make sure our conversation hadn't turned any heads. The few other patrons remained invested in their own quiet meals, and the waitress was cackling at something in the kitchen hallway, the faint smell of cigarette smoke wafting back.

As I relaxed, the glint of the unused spoon laying on the table caught my eye. Before I could think twice, I slipped it into the inner pocket of my jacket, the slight weight against my chest. I didn't need it—I wouldn't even remember it tomorrow, but it appeased that gnawing spark in me that demanded to be fed.

Cliff watched me, shaking his head with a bored sort of smile. He'd seen me pilfer far worse, but sometimes, I still flushed with shame that he didn't share the same compulsion.

"How much cash do we have left?" I asked, dodging Sylvia's curious stare.

"Starting to look bleak," Cliff sighed. "The nest egg's gotten us this far, but it won't get us much further at this rate."

Sylvia's curious stare drilled into the two of us. Not for the first time, she said, "Money's weird." She jabbed the price listed at the bottom of the dessert menu. "Trading makes much more sense. Or better yet, why not just *give* someone what they need because they need it and you don't?"

Cliff chuckled. "The hunter's outpost is all about bartering. Probably not as glamorous as your little village, though." He smirked at her. "What was it? A blueberry for a comb?" When Sylvia didn't respond with anything more than flushed cheeks, his mouth dropped open. "Wait, it *was?*"

"As though trading guns and money is any better," Sylvia grumbled, lifting her chin to pointedly ignore Cliff while he fought back another laugh.

Thankfully, the food arrived, and Sylvia was forced to duck back into hiding before anything more could be said about the outpost.

No way she was going anywhere near that cesspool.

We all fell quiet for a time, eating ravenously to make up for the long, soggy walk. The only words exchanged were occasional offers between Cliff and Sylvia, who were trading bites of food from each other's plates. He even poured her a cap of beer—proof that he wasn't holding a grudge over their shouting match in the car.

I took advantage of the peace, pulling out my phone to do some research on the area. I couldn't forget Sylvia's frightened insistence that there had been something unnatural in the water—not once, but *twice*. Giovanni may have slipped past her senses, but she had never been wrong when she *did* feel something.

"Jon," Sylvia said through her mouthful. "You *have* to try this!" She held up half a fry drenched in hot fudge sauce.

Ignoring Cliff's perturbed expression, I accepted her offering. It wasn't her most outlandish food combination—that prize went to her peanut butter and pickle sandwich from last week.

"Check it out," I said, turning my phone toward her. "Looks like there's a few fairy legends in the area. Maybe you were right about the glamour. It's definitely worth looking into."

She paused her attempt to slather another fry with whipped cream. "What have you found?" I almost wished I'd let her finish eating—her voice tightened.

"I'll need to dig some more, but there's stories about encounters in the swamps in the early to mid-1800s. About two hundred years ago," I added when her expression went blank. "After that period, the legends taper off."

"What kind of encounters?" she asked tentatively.

"They're pretty vague so far. Stories about glowing lights in the woods. Travelers being led astray and never being seen again. Most people chalk them up to gator attacks. There's a few mentions of 'the Fair Folk', though. Some urban legends."

"Maybe there's a village here, obscured from humans," she said, glancing up at the rain-streaked window with a distant expression. "Like Elysia."

Cliff made a face, reaching for his drink. "Swamp fairies sound like a fucking nightmare, not gonna lie."

8

SYLVIA

When we set out the next morning, the sun was barely a sliver on the horizon, casting a faint golden glow over the town of Cypress Hollow. The air was thick with remnants of last night's storm. A heavy fog hung low, shrouding everything in a ghostly mist so dense that I could scarcely discern the outlines of the buildings we passed. If not for the low sounds of the waking city—the faint clink of silverware, the hum of large vehicles, muted chatter behind curtained windows—I could have believed we were entirely alone.

Though Halloween had been over a week ago, there were still neglected remnants of the celebration scattered through the city—a jovial purple and green clown figurine posed on a balcony, a cluster of flickering skull-shaped lights above a door frame, a faded poster announcing a parade slicked to a light post.

My mind still buzzed with all that I had seen of the holiday when we had cut into Tennessee to take out a vicious spirit—the revelry, the costumes, the lavish sweets, and ample drinks. A part of me wondered what this city had looked like in the peak of it all or whether we were far better off not inviting any added spirit activity to this historic area.

Moisture from the damp air condensed on my wings, bringing with it a ripple of irritation. Flying was one of my greatest joys, yet a damn nuisance when the area was *wet*. My wings had taken all night to completely dry. Between that and the soreness from the other night's hunt, I was fighting twice as hard to keep my flight at a level pace. Despite the autumn breeze pushing through the tangle of trees that intersected weathered buildings, sweat beaded beneath my hooded knit top.

I smelled the auto shop before I saw the yellowed sign stabbing the air—the salty scent of wet earth and the metallic tang of what I'd learned to be gasoline. Gulf Auto Care sat on a secluded lot near the outskirts of town, where paved roads became gravel and the marsh began to reclaim civilization in swathes of unruly vegetation. As I landed on the chain link fence to catch my breath, I swore I was looking at a forgotten relic—the weathered two-story building, a couple of sturdy garages nestled beside it, stood in the shadow of massive, gnarled oaks draped with moss that drifted like locks of hair in every gust of wind.

One of the garages was open, giving view to a couple of sleek, well-kept cars that drew Cliff's eye immediately. He whistled low under his breath. "Is that a fucking *Challenger*? Who keeps classics exposed like that?"

"Idiots," Jon agreed, a little smile tugging on his lips. "Or someone who likes to show off their trophies."

The lot was a maze of cars, parked across the dirt lot in front and gathered behind a chain link fence that wrapped around the back of the garages. I squinted—*too damn tired for this*—unsure how we'd pick our battered 1972 Pontiac from the mix. Jon and Cliff pushed toward the back, empty duffle bags slung over their shoulders. With a groan, I spread my wings and flew to catch up.

"*Stars,* is everyone in this town out of a vehicle right now?" I grumbled when I was back between them.

I tried to read their faces. Did they have even a kernel of the anticipation and anxiety that was making my palms sweat? We'd have a hell of a time trying to explain ourselves to the owner if we were caught breaking in. This little adventure was a risky move, but it was even riskier to leave the veritable armory that remained in the trunk. If any sane human found that kind of firepower, they'd call the authorities in a heartbeat.

With a little murmur, Cliff broke ahead of Jon and I like he could hear the car calling to him by name. Following him, I saw that his instincts were correct—our car was parked near the front of the fenced-off lot.

Cliff produced a lockpick like it was a bodily function, and before I could fully register his movements, the padlock clicked open. The thick chain wound between the fence slithered to the ground in a defeated heap.

Pushing inside, Cliff threw a grin over his shoulder at Jon. "How long did it take me to pick that?"

"Wasn't timing you," Jon scoffed.

He winked, drawing an eye-roll out of Jon. "Of course you weren't."

As we drew closer to the car, the knot in my stomach clenched. It was hardly a wonder I hadn't noticed the car from further away; the damage from the accident had left it scarcely recognizable. Once sleek contours were now marred by dents and scratches. The hood was crumpled like paper. An echo of fright shot through me—the crippling panic of seeing Jon slumped in the passenger's seat, wondering if he would wake up.

"Can they fix it?" I asked, hoping I sounded less anxious than I was.

"Fat chance in a town like this." Cliff brushed a hand over the battered silver paint, his striking features etched with grief that cut through me. I'd seen how hard he and Jon worked on keeping this car running like it was a living creature. He glanced up at me as he rounded toward the trunk. "We'll see. I'll take a look under the hood and see what's not completely fucked."

"Can I fly in and check the engine?" I asked, eyeing the crunched hood. I doubted this would be like other times he'd guided me through checking the engine for loose or damaged parts, but it felt wrong not to offer. Guilt churned through me for distracting him with ice before the wreck, even if I still firmly believed he should have swallowed his pride and pulled off the road. "I'll be able to see it better than you—just tell me what to look for."

"Don't even think about it," Jon chimed in. "You'll slash up your wings in that mess."

Cliff softened at the disappointment on my face. "I'll finish teaching you all about fuel injectors when we're not dealing with a death trap. Capiche?"

I nodded, forcing a smile. When he looked away, I studied his face for any sign of lingering resentment. *A goddamn liability.* Words either spat carelessly under duress, or—

Or he'd meant it.

As the hunters rummaged for the spare set of keys they'd kept, I wondered if I could at least search the front seats for my snowflake necklace. When they popped the trunk, however, my attention was drawn to a familiar buzz of energy.

"The gemstone," I blurted as I wheeled around to the back of the car. "It's in my bag. Can—can you give it to me?"

Jon located the sliver of amethyst after digging through my belongings. He gave me a curiously meaningful look as he handed it off to me. I swallowed hard, wondering if its power would be too tempting if I started carrying it regularly.

But I settled my resolve and nodded at Jon. "After that strange feeling by the wreck, I—"

Before I could finish, the early morning stillness was shattered by a scuffle of movement. Footsteps beat against the ground. A *bark.*

I tensed, whipping my head around to find the source. There was no tingle of a monster's presence, but—

A blur of fur shot out from between cars, lunging for Jon.

In an instant, I was back in the Dottage basement. Decaying jaws snapped in the dim light, ripping into Jon's flesh. His face would soon pale with infection, and then, the voices—*the voices.*

A guttural "*no!*" clawed up my throat. They couldn't have me again. Couldn't have *him.* Mist shrouded my hands, stolen from the saturated air. Jagged icicles took form, ready to plunge through skin and bone, ready to end this before it started—

"Stop, hey!" Cliff's voice snapped me back to the present as he waved a hand in front of me. "It's fine, Sylv—just a golden retriever."

Breathing heavily, I saw Jon stumble back against a nearby pickup truck as the silky-haired dog hopped up on its hind legs and shoved its muddy front paws enthusiastically against him. Jon used one hand to hold it back, but it bounced up again in determination to lick his face. Even as I lowered my hands, I couldn't consolidate the riotous terror pounding through my veins with Jon's growing grin.

Steadying my breath, I tucked the gem shard into my pocket. I tentatively flew closer, managing a weak laugh as the dog whimpered for affection and wagged its tail so hard that its whole body swayed. "Pet it before it eats you alive."

The dog's excitement drew the attention of at least three more dogs who observed with interest. A few others snoozed under the trees indifferently. I spotted the sharp eyes of a couple of cats peeking out from beneath ruined vehicles.

"Strays?" Jon straightened, placating the golden retriever by stroking its head.

"They've got collars," Cliff said. "Gotta belong to the owner. Looks like they're shitty at being guard dogs. We should get on with it before they start barking, though." He searched the ground, then knelt to grab a chewed-up rubber ball from the dirt. With a sharp whistle, he drew the golden retriever's attention and tossed the ball into the maze of vehicles.

At once, the golden retriever bounded off with a few other dogs scrambling after.

The hunters hurriedly popped open the trunk and began sorting. I wrinkled my nose at the scent of stagnant rainwater that pooled within, though it hardly seemed to bother them. They worked as one, exchanging no more than a word or two as they decided what to stuff into the duffel bags and what to conceal deeper in the trunk.

No less than a minute passed before the golden retriever galloped back. It dropped the ball by the hunters and nosed Jon's leg, whining insistently. Jon sighed and reached for the ball, but I beat him to it. With a whispered spell, I conjured a small gale of ice and aimed it downward to send the ball spinning across the lot. Three dogs bolted after it.

"I'll keep them busy," I said, meeting Jon's surprised look with a grin. I flexed one arm. "Call if you need me to carry anything."

He scoffed. "Stay close."

The dogs were a bit brighter than I thought, seeming to make the connection that I was the one moving the ball when I shouted my spells and used exaggerated gestures. Whenever one dog would catch the ball, they would bring it back and drop it under my hovering shadow.

"Hazel would love you," I sighed before sending the ball a few dozen feet away, rolling beneath several cars.

Eyeing the vehicles, I noted that not all of them were in ruins. Perhaps Jon and Cliff could have one of those. My stomach churned as I wondered if I'd hurt their chances of affording a car by ordering multiple desserts last night.

Don't be silly. A hot fudge sundae can't cost as much as a car.

I recalled Jon deftly swiping silverware from the table last night and tucking it into his coat. Perhaps his skills extended to cars, too. Surely the owner wouldn't notice *one* missing in this labyrinth.

As I flew deeper into the maze of vehicles and oaks, my musings came to a halt when I found myself mere feet away from the chain link fence that circled the property. Peeking out from behind curtains of moss, I found the two-story building tantalizingly close, slightly obscured by fog. It was different than the Dottage mansion—smaller, for one thing. But there were signs of life that hadn't been present outside of Alice's home. Wicker furniture sat on the porch, surrounded by a plethora of more chew toys. Stairs on the side of the building led up to another entrance on the second floor, the balcony crowded with potted plants that would make even the most seasoned earth affinity jealous.

Itching for a closer look, I flew past the moss. Scrambling paws and a whimper came from below, drawing my attention down to the returned ball.

Chuckling, I was about to send it bouncing away from the fence when I heard a gasp.

Goosebumps prickled up the back of my neck when I laid eyes on a human woman mere feet away. I'd flown right into her path from behind the tree, eye-level with her.

She staggered two steps back, dropping what she held in her hands. The ceramic bowls shattered on the ground, sending kibble over the gravel. The sound may as well have been an explosion in the peaceful lot. Distantly, I heard Jon and Cliff call my name in alarm. The dogs, oblivious of any trouble, excitedly clambered for the fallen food among the shards.

The human woman snapped out of her shock, trying to block them. "No, no—get! *Get!* You'll cut yourselves!"

Without thinking, I shouted my spell to launch the ball toward the house. The woman yelped in alarm, but it did the trick—the golden retriever went sprinting to find its toy, and its friends followed.

Eyes wide, the woman brought her stare back to me, pressing a hand over her chest. "You were… playing with them?" she breathed.

Monsters were one thing. Victims were another. But she was neither, and my carefully curated instincts grinded to a halt. She was perhaps a few summers older than me, with dark brown skin and a dozen black braids that cascaded to the middle of her back. Her eyes were darker than Jon's, and though she was stunned, a gentle awe lay buried beneath her confusion.

Even so, I jolted back an inch when she took a tentative step closer.

"No, wait—don't be afraid—please," she said in a soft, stammering voice. "Please don't go."

One hand slowly lifted toward me, and all I could do was gape.

I scarcely registered the rustling leaves behind me until her eyes flicked from me and bugged wide.

"*Hey*! Don't touch her!" Cliff's voice was like a gunshot slicing the air.

My mind raced to catch up. Cliff materialized between us, his body like a wall of protection.

Naturally, the woman screamed.

She frantically dug for her pockets, whipping out a folded knife. Her fingers trembled against the polished wood handle. Before she could unfurl the blade, Cliff swatted it out of her hands to send it clattering into the dead leaves several yards away. I winced a little, touching the dagger sheathed at my hip. My first encounter with the hunters was perpetually fresh in my mind: scrambling to reach my weapon lying on the dusty floor, out of reach. Outmatched.

"Take it easy. I can explain." Cliff held up his hands, his stare placating now that she was unarmed. "No one's gonna hurt you."

The woman was coiled like a spring, shifting her weight from foot to foot while her hands folded into fists. Her gaze darted between the knife and Cliff's imposing stance—then back to me, like she was trying to piece together how the hell the two of us fit together.

Cliff inched closer, hands still raised like he was soothing a skittish deer. "How 'bout I take you down the street for a cup of coffee and we can talk through it all, huh? I'll throw in some of those little beignets with the sugar on top. My treat. Just give us a chance to—"

His words cut off as the woman sprang forward, a fist aimed at his face. Cliff dodged. She lunged again with a cry. He ducked with the same frustrating ease.

"C'mon, don't do this," Cliff said.

With her next swing, he caught her wrist and held fast. She jerked in his grip, expression twisting.

"Let go of me!" she spat.

The woman was quite tall—nearly as tall as Cliff—but her frame was willowy, no match for his warrior's physique.

"Sylv!" Jon's voice carried across the yard, accompanied by crunching footsteps.

I turned, flying lower to meet him as he sprinted to us. His gaze roved me wildly, assessing the scene and demanding silent questions.

I was seen, a voice screamed in the back of my mind. "I'm fine, but—"

The door to the second floor burst open, and another woman appeared on the landing. She was petite, warm bronze skin contrasting against mint green pajamas. Her hastily laced boots and raven hair pushed back in a messy bun matched the wild look on her face.

"Hannah!" she screamed, bolting down the steps.

She was halfway down when I noticed the gun in her hands.

Jon inhaled sharply beside me. "Oh, fuck me," he muttered. "Of *course.*"

But when I read his face, his urgency had been replaced by a resignation I didn't understand. He stayed rooted in place, even as the newcomer seized the back of Cliff's jacket and wrenched him backward. The first woman—*Hannah*—bolted to the foot of the stairs, watching with alarm as Cliff twisted free of his attacker. He moved like he had been anticipating a gun pointed at his face, jarring her grip with a harsh twist of her arm. She cried out, and the weapon slipped from her grasp and into his own.

The new woman had none of Hannah's frantic aim. Her movements were precise, powerful. She lashed out with her elbow, connecting with Cliff's stomach with force enough to make me flinch from ten feet away. Cliff swallowed a curse and grabbed the collar of her silken top, pushing her up against the chain link fence to pin her. The barrel of the gun pressed to her stomach felt like overkill with how he towered over her—he had to have at least a full foot on her in height.

Silence crackled across the lot as Cliff drank in her fierce, ground-down expression. Shock flickered over his face. No—*recognition.*

"Gwen?" he breathed.

His grip on the gun slackened—the woman noticed, too. With brutal precision, she drove her knee into his groin. Cliff's eyes widened in agony as he doubled over, a guttural groan escaping his lips. In one swift motion, she seized the gun from his lax grip and spun to face him, leveling the barrel at Cliff's head.

"What the fuck are you doing here, Cliff?" Gwen barked.

Cliff heaved like he might vomit, but his panting words were laced with spite. "Would've—taken my chances—walking across the country if—I knew you ran the shop."

"It's my girlfriend's shop, you idiot." She bared her teeth and shoved the gun closer to his head. "Who sent you after her?"

He glared between her and the gun's barrel. "No one." A wheeze weakened his voice as he managed to straighten. "I was defending a friend."

"Oh, bullshit. Like your freakishly tall attack dog needs a—" She stiffened when she glanced in Jon's direction and found *me* hovering beside him.

All at once, my racing mind caught up with the familiarity of her name. *Heartbreaker* Gwen. *Hunter* Gwen. And as I watched her hands tighten on the gun and turn toward me, I remembered—*impeccable marksman* Gwen. I shuddered but didn't dare budge so much as a finger. One wrong move and a bullet might say hello to my body instead of just my wing.

Jon stepped in front of me without hesitation. "Sylvia's not a threat," he said evenly. His hand tensed toward his pocket, prepared to introduce another weapon to the mix. "But if you don't move that gun off her, we're gonna have a problem that we can't come back from."

Gwen laughed coldly. "We cleared the point of no return years ago, Nowak."

"Would you put the gun down?" Cliff snapped.

"No!" When I peeked over Jon's shoulder, I saw that she'd rounded the weapon back on Cliff like she was trying to assess who was the greater threat between them. "You break onto our property with that little fucking monster, attack my girl, and you expect me to just bend over for you?"

"It's a misunderstanding!" Hannah blurted. She still looked shaken as she drifted away from the stairs. She held up her hands, glancing placatingly from face to face. "Look—whatever the hell is going on, let's talk it over inside before the whole town sees you two waving guns around like it's the Fourth of July."

"Coffee?" Hannah entered the dining area with a steaming pot. It shook slightly in her trembling hands. Cliff leaned back in his chair with crossed arms and eyed her like she'd just offered freshly brewed poison. She laughed tightly at his reaction. "It's locally sourced."

"There's a roastery here?" Jon asked. From my perch on his shoulder, I felt a sliver of his tension ease. His eagerness coaxed a faint smile to my lips.

"Right off Heritage Avenue," Hannah said. "The owner's a friend of my brother. They've been open a little over a year now, and we were so worried about people being too attached to the national chains to give it a chance, but wouldn't you know it, they've got a line out the door every morning. It's nice to see more young businesses thriving in this little pocket of the world, don't you think?"

She spoke rapidly, her hand trembling as she finished filling the mugs. Jon took no more than a sip before she blurted, "How is it?"

"Really good," Jon said without an ounce of pretense. "Am I tasting chicory?"

He made an effort to brighten his expression—a peace offering if I ever saw one.

It worked—Hannah smiled. "You know your coffee."

"I worked at a shop in high school. I can appreciate a good blend. I'm a little rusty with making anything that doesn't come from a packet, though."

I didn't have to guess why Jon's time at the coffee shop ended. The thought of him in that psychiatric ward, robbed of every great and small joy, made me too cold inside to bear.

Hannah offered a little smile to Cliff and pushed his mug closer. "You sure you won't give it a try? Come on, I'm sorry for almost stabbing you."

He remained stoic. "Keep your *sorry*. You didn't come close."

Her cowed expression tempted me to apologize on Cliff's behalf, but she hurried back into the kitchen before I could work up the nerve. Even with only the three of us at the table now, a heavy beat of silence shrouded the room.

I nudged Jon's neck with my elbow. "Why so tense?" I peeked at the archway that led into the kitchen, where Hannah busied herself in front of the stove and murmured to Gwen beside her. "If you thought Gwen was plotting to kill me, you'd give me a fair warning, right?"

Little fucking monster. I couldn't shake those words.

"She would've tried by now." His chuckle was taut. "I'm just not used to you being out in the open with other people this long. It's getting under my skin."

"Oh, *right.*" I waited until he took another sip of coffee before adding. "You prefer me to be your dirty little secret." He nearly sputtered out his sip while I giggled unabashedly.

After a beat, Jon recovered, his tone lowering to a tantalizing decibel. "Actually, yeah. I like that no one else but me knows you like I do. I want to keep it that way."

Just like that, I was back in the spectral plane in my mind—imagining what he could do to me there. What he *wanted* to do.

Color flooded my cheeks. "I think I'll mark your other shoulder for that one."

Cliff hissed to Jon's right, but for once, his annoyance wasn't aimed at us. He pulled back in his seat to peer under the table. A roaming cat with a patchwork of orange and black fur had taken a particular interest in his leg, rubbing insistently. He cursed, nudging it gently with his boot in a fruitless attempt to shoo it away.

I fought a grin as he was uncharacteristically incensed by the second cat that leaped onto the table. It deftly padded gray paws between mugs of coffee, squinting golden eyes in my direction.

I eagerly stretched a hand, but the cat was more interested in sniffing Cliff's sleeve.

"Don't laugh," Cliff grumbled.

I bit my lip. "It's hard not to."

"*Try.*"

"But I thought you loved animals," I said as he scooped the cat up like a sack of flour.

"Yeah, but I also love breathing without sneezing every two seconds. I'm allergic to—" Two rapid sneezes cut through the sentence. He sighed, gesturing with the cat. "To *these.*"

He set it on the floor, eliciting a chirp of outrage from the cat. It glared over its shoulder at him, then promptly bathed where it had been handled.

My bottled laughter finally spilled out of me. "I can't believe I used to be scared of you."

"I can fix that." Cliff arched an eyebrow, fixing me with a look that would've sent a chill down my spine a few months ago.

"I'm afraid it's too late. You're adorable."

Cliff opened his mouth to retort—only to bury another sneeze into his elbow.

I scanned the room, grateful I didn't share his affliction. The animals were an unexpected delight in this shocking turn in our morning. Even with Gwen and Hannah in the kitchen, the cozy dining room was alive with activity—paws scuffling, water bowls clinking, and the occasional bark from outside. A sleek black cat sat on the windowsill, basking in the early morning sunshine. A plump white and gray cat was curled up on an armchair, watching us with half-lidded eyes from across the room. Two dogs, a golden retriever and a small terrier, lay on the carpeted floor with tails thumping as they tracked the food in the next room.

My guard threatened to lower. This place held a sense of *home*, like the building itself wanted to wrap me in a hug and welcome me in.

"Gwen! You got a spray bottle or something?" Cliff called. The orange and black cat beneath the table wove against his ankles again, more demanding. "Your cat thinks I'm a scratching post."

Dodging the eager dogs, Gwen returned. She set a carton of creamer on the table and scooped the cat into her arms.

"Good girl, Artemis," she crooned, pressing a kiss between its ears. "Helping mommy push out the unwelcome visitors quicker."

The sunlight streaming through the window skimmed Gwen's face as she paced the room, highlighting her skin's golden undertones. Her eyes were gently angled at the corners and framed by thick, natural lashes. Her raven hair, pulled back in a simple style, would have hit just below her shoulders in soft waves. Though her smile seemed like a rare gift, it lit up her features with a warmth that was both girlish and feline. When she wasn't calling me a monster, she was undeniably beautiful.

My heart ached a little as I glanced at Cliff. Gwen was effortlessly agile in ways that complemented his warrior's physique. Her curves were slight where he was sharp and defined.

They would have been striking together, side by side.

Jon muttered something in Spanish I couldn't quite make out—though I was *fairly* certain it was a profanity—his eyes narrowed in Gwen's direction. "We're hardly here by choice," he said louder. "Once the car's back in working order, we'll be gone."

Gwen eyed him with peculiar caution and set the cat on the carpet. She took a seat at the table across from Cliff. "You two really haven't changed, have you?" Her voice dropped lower, almost pitying. "Still the same cycle of self-destruction and violence, isn't it?"

The bitter tension rifting between them made my stomach twist—though I wouldn't let them see it. I couldn't. Hunters lived brutal lives; making enemies was inevitable. I just hadn't anticipated having *breakfast* with one of them.

Hannah returned with a basket of muffins, seeming to force herself down into a seat beside Gwen. For a moment, Hannah seemed unsure of what to do with her arms—folding them, then resting them on her lap—until Gwen stopped her fidgeting by taking her hand and gently squeezing it on the table.

I watched how Hannah's eyes nervously settled on Jon and Cliff seated directly across from her. "I know they're intimidating, but they're not so bad once you get to know them," I said.

Jon cleared his throat delicately and whispered under his breath. "I don't think it's us, Sylv."

I would have protested, but then I realized her eyes were actually locked on *me*. And it was no wonder. Other humans who'd seen me were hardly shaken by the sight of a fairy after coming face to face with a bloodthirsty monster.

Hannah took a deep breath. "So, you're still real. You can all see her, right?" Her laugh was taut. "Fairies are *real*."

"More than that, sweetheart." Cliff turned pointedly to Gwen. "You seriously didn't tell her?"

"There was no need. I'm retired," she answered sharply, releasing Hannah's hand so she could fold her arms over her chest.

Cliff's mouth dropped open. "*Retired*? What—for how long?"

Gwen's gaze flickered to Hannah guiltily. "Six months. She wasn't supposed to get mixed up in any of it. Why am I not surprised *you'd* be the ones to come along and screw things up?"

Tearing her eyes away from me, Hannah gave Gwen a hurt pout. "What were you thinking—keeping this from me?"

"I told you I used to hunt," Gwen mumbled.

"Obviously I thought you meant, like, deer! Not vampires and werewolves! Should I be grateful I didn't find one of *those* playing fetch with the dogs instead?"

I squirmed. All three of us may have trespassed, but I suddenly felt like the worst offender. "Should I wait outside?"

"*No*," everyone other than Gwen said at once.

"It's fine, honey," Hannah said, offering the same small smile she'd given me outside. "This is a lot to take in, but I'll cope." She stared for another beat like she could force herself to get used to my existence. "I like your tattoo, by the way."

My hand leaped to my cheek, words failing me for a moment.

"Thanks," I bit out, combing my hair to curtain the black mark—because it was easier than saying, *it was branded onto me by force to permanently ostracize me from my people.*

Hannah stood, scooping up her emptied coffee mug. "The omelets should be about done. We've got ham and bacon."

"Sylv's vegetarian," Cliff announced, though I had never seen him look so pleased about it.

Although Hannah's expression puckered, she didn't recoil this time. "The muffins should be safe enough. Is there anything else I can get you, Sylvia?"

I hesitated—the way she inserted my name felt curiously similar to how Jon calmed victims by saying theirs. *Manufacturing a sense of connection*, he called it. Still, Hannah seemed sincere.

"Strawberries, if you have them," I answered.

Hannah gave me a small smile—as though both awestruck and amused that I had requested something so mundane and not some celestial recipe dipped in shimmering blue goo.

"I'll see what I can rustle up," she said. With that, she vanished back into the kitchen.

Gwen leaned halfway across the table to glower at Cliff. "I should put a knife to your throat, the way you keep talking to her. You jumped her, and now she's making you breakfast, for fuck's sake."

"I never minded your hands at my throat. But that would ruin this lovely…" Cliff grimaced as he rubbed the trailing edge of the lace tablecloth between his fingers. "What is this, a giant doily?"

Jon tugged the basket of muffins toward him. He picked up a blueberry one and gave it a brief inspection before tearing off a piece to offer it to me. We dug in hungrily, sharing a delighted glance as the distinct buttery sweetness hit our tongues. After weeks of shadowing a hunter's life, I quickly learned to cherish the rare gift of a home-cooked meal. Notes of cinnamon carried on the next bite, and for a moment, I was sitting in the Elysian kitchen corridors, sneaking extra tarts with Damian and Kyra.

That's not your home anymore. The harsh voice at the back of my head pulled me back, then grounded me in comfortable numbness. *Don't waste your tears on people who wouldn't do the same.*

Gwen took a long gulp of coffee, moving her guarded stare between Jon and Cliff over the brim of her mug. "If no one sent you, what the hell are you doing in Cypress Hollow?" she asked. "Is it a hunt? Those black-eyed demon kids aren't back, are they?"

"Supply run," Cliff said. "Barely got enough silver on us to buy a lap dance, and you know the bayou outpost is the prime place to stock up. Had to make do without any bullets while taking out a vamp coven the other night."

Somehow, that was enough. The wavering panic in Gwen's face melted into a weary sort of understanding. "You've faced worse odds than that."

"A couple of dead men walking shouldn't be giving fate the finger any more than we already do, right?" Cliff offered a good-natured smirk—until he saw Jon reaching for a second muffin. With a betrayed double-take, Cliff tugged the basket away. He glared toward Hannah's distant movements in the kitchen as though we had agreed to sell enemy propaganda.

Jon shot him a look—a resounding *what the hell?*

"Don't eat her muffins!" Cliff hissed under his breath like it was obvious. "Whose side are you on?"

I pouted at him—those seconds had been for *me*, too. Still, I bit my tongue and followed Jon's lead on treading carefully with… whatever the hell *this* was.

Gwen rolled her eyes at the exchange. "Jesus, I forgot how territorial you can be."

"Don't flatter yourself." Cliff shot her a look that could strip paint.

Jon waited until Cliff wasn't looking before pilfering a second muffin. Without breaking his conversational posture, he discreetly tore off another piece, and I flew down to snatch it. I mouthed *thank you*, lifting my eyebrows conspiratorially as we both took cautious bites like children sneaking sweets after curfew.

A cruel smirk touched Gwen's full lips as she leaned back, studying Cliff. "You look good, I'll give you that. Still drowning your emotional constipation in the bottle?"

Cliff's smile was downright icy, his gaze roving over the crowded bookshelves and reusable grocery bags neatly tucked by the door. "Says the woman who's one glass of chardonnay from being some housewife cliché. What happened to you?"

Her eyes flashed—this had struck deep. "The same fucking argument. Retiring isn't giving up, you know. You can make a difference without violence."

"Next time I cross paths with a werewolf, I'll be sure to invite it to the block party."

"You're talking mad shit for someone who's buddying up with a non-human. Are you insane?"

Their combined stares drifted toward me, making me squirm uncomfortably, dodging eye contact. I would have preferred to eat in peace, away from the ex-lovers' quarrel, but I brushed crumbs from my hands and eased forward to hover over the table.

"I may not be human, but I'm not a monster, either," I cut in over Cliff's retort. "And I'm not here to cause trouble. They're just helping me travel west."

"A hitchhiking fairy," Gwen scoffed, turning dubious eyes to the boys. "You realize their M.O. is glamour and deceit, right? No offense," she tacked on, sparing me a hasty glance.

"She saved my life," Jon said. I became aware of his shadow darkening over me protectively.

"So, it's a bargain."

"*So*, you can shut up about her," Cliff said. "She's not glamouring us. End of story."

Gwen arched her brow. "Now I've seen it all," she muttered.

I was almost relieved when Hannah returned, arms laden with a skillet and a colorful bowl.

"Careful, love," she said with a tight laugh as she served up four omelets and set one in front of Gwen. "There's all kinds of local legends about having to be polite to the Fair Folk, you know."

I looked over my shoulder, my gaze catching Jon's in a brief, unspoken exchange. The dark gleam that had surfaced there perfectly mirrored my own curiosity. I turned back to Hannah, trying to school my desperate hope that those vague legends Jon had scoured online weren't just whispers of the past.

"My threshold for rudeness must be high, seeing as I haven't cursed Cliff yet," I said. "What sort of legends have you heard?"

A playful, conspiratorial look crossed Hannah's face as she took her seat, looking around the table. "Half the folks in town will tell you they've seen flickering orbs of light over the bayou—especially on cloudless nights. My Tante Halle swore up and down that she saw them herself, dancing where the moonlight touched the water." She smiled as she spoke, warmth bleeding into her voice that had me leaning forward. "Rumor was, if you got caught watching, they would lure you in and entice you to wander off the path. If you strayed too far, you'd be lost to the swamp forever."

Gwen chuckled dryly. "Fairies wouldn't flaunt their presence so openly. Correct me if I'm wrong." Her gaze cut to me for confirmation.

A beat of surprise rippled through our side of the table, and her expression fell as she realized her mistake.

"You've seen fairies before?" Jon asked, leaning in. "When? *Where?*"

Gwen gave him a funny look. "You didn't hear about it? There was an incident some two years back. A fairy triggered a trap in the swamp. Outpost residents caught it and kept it caged under archivist study for months off-site, studying it until—" She stopped short, eyes cutting to me. Her jaw feathered, and I got the strange feeling that she was appraising me.

"It didn't end well," she finished, quieter. "People got hurt. Rumor has it that the off-site location was burned, and the fairy went with it."

My head spun. More fairies entangled with hunters. That dank room beneath the old church flashed through my mind's eye—the smell of charred wood and ash stinging my nose at the memory. At least that place was done for, abandoned.

"Are there any being held captive now?" I asked, my voice thready and harsh. My heart pounded in my ears. "Anywhere else?"

"I dunno about *now*," Gwen said. "I've kept my distance since calling it quits half a year ago. Didn't like the way things were headed."

I turned, trying to read Jon and Cliff's stony expressions, but they were inscrutable. All I could think of now were those weakened monsters that hunters trained with in that enclosure—*the Pit.*

Was it possible my own kind were among them? The thought twisted my gut like an iron dagger.

No—I wouldn't let myself imagine it.

Jon broke the heavy silence, shifting his attention to Hannah. "What can you tell us about the car?"

Hannah gave him a nervous smile. "Oh, uh—it's probably fucked."

"No shit," Cliff muttered.

She ignored him. "You're probably better off selling it for scrap, but I may have a gutted model or two that could have the parts you need to get it back up and running. I'll see what I can find and get back to you with a quote."

"How long will that take?" I asked, feeling another prickle of guilt. Another indefinite delay. More time before I fulfilled my promise to Mother.

"A day or two, maybe."

"What about a loaner car?" Cliff asked, jutting his chin toward the window that framed the view of the auto lot below.

Hannah chewed, regarding the three of us thoughtfully. A furrow pulled between her eyes. "Don't take this the wrong way, but you look like you could use a break."

Cliff chuckled darkly. "We're not really the vacationing type."

Hannah's lips quirked up at the corner, shooting Gwen a knowing look. "Where have I heard that before? Yeah, I've got a couple in the back I can spare. Do what you gotta do."

Jon sighed with relief. "That'd be great, thank you. We can hit the outpost and stock up in the meantime."

Gwen rubbed between her eyes, sighing audibly. "Guess I'm going with you, then."

"What?" Hannah straightened sharply, her fork clattering onto the plate. The golden retriever padded over, snuffling the ground for a fallen bit of egg.

"Sorry, did I miss the part where someone invited you?" Cliff demanded.

"Well, good luck finding your way there without me," Gwen said. "They rerouted the road about a year ago—you'll go in circles if you don't know what you're doing. A few too many lost hikers and monsters with vendettas found their way there."

Cliff took a beat, studying her intently. Slowly, he smiled. "Oh, I get it."

"I can guarantee you don't."

Cliff folded his arms on the table, cocking his head to the side as if goading some shared secret out of her. "You're still worried about me."

Gwen let out a short, stunned laugh. "For fuck's sake…"

"It's alright, you don't have to say it. But gotta admit, I can't blame you."

"The sooner you're done there, the sooner you're gone, right?" Gwen asked. She seemed to savor the way his crooked grin froze.

Lips pressed into a thin line, Hannah touched Gwen's arm gingerly. "Honey, can't you just give them directions?"

"It's not that simple. Things have gotten more complicated with the new management taking over. These two may be idiots, but I don't want their blood on my hands, either."

Jon straightened. "New management? Cain isn't the outpost marshal anymore?"

Clicking his tongue, Cliff shook his head. "Don't tell me he finally kicked the bucket—I liked that guy."

"Don't get weepy—Cain's still around, as far as I know, but he got talked into handing the keys over. Some cleaner showed up and flashed a bunch of cash to invest in upgrades for the outpost. All of a sudden, he wasn't just some cleaner anymore. He started calling the shots."

Cliff's expression darkened. "Who is this guy?"

"Goes by Rhett."

Fresh tension seized the breakfast table.

"Rhett *Iverson?*" Jon questioned.

Gwen narrowed her eyes, then nodded. "Why, you know him?"

Jon and Cliff groaned in unison, and I recalled the two of them griping now and again about some hunts gone wrong. The name *Rhett* had come up once or twice—and I suddenly remembered why.

"Wait," I piped up, looking between the boys. "Is this the prowler incident guy? Is he the reason why you won't hunt with anyone else?"

Cliff nodded. "It was a few years ago… A short while after you ditched us, actually—" This he aimed at Gwen, whose eyes went wide with outrage.

"That's not what—I didn't mean—" Gwen started.

"Don't interrupt. So we got looped into this hunt with a couple of cleaners looking to kill this prowler," Cliff went on, turning his attention between Hannah and I. "These things need to be burned to keep them from reanimating. Simple enough, but these guys—Rhett and Jameson—they wanted extra hands. Especially Rhett. Turns out his friendly attitude was all because he found a client willing to pay for anything he could salvage."

"He didn't bother to tell us he was after the prowler's eyes because he didn't want to split the payout," Jon said, pushing a hand through his hair. "So when the time came to burn the corpse, he said he'd handle it. Instead, he tried to knock us out and ran off with the head to remove the eyes. Next thing we knew, the body was back on its feet and slashing its way toward us."

Cliff shook his head. "He was pissed when we got the upper hand—looked like he wanted to kill us both then and there. But he was smart enough to know we'd cave his chest in if he tried it."

"And *that's* who's in charge now?" I asked, looking at Gwen in alarm.

She rubbed between her eyes again, giving a half-hearted shrug. "Money talks. He brought along updated security and some new systems that are helping the outpost make bank. That's what rubbed me the wrong way—it isn't about targeting the monsters causing the most bloodshed anymore. It's all about collecting what's most valuable."

Hannah shuddered. "That doesn't sound like any place you need to be," she told Gwen pleadingly.

"I know what I'm doing. I'll just get them as far as they need. As much as I try to be a heartless bitch, I'm still a work in progress." She shared a chuckle with Hannah, interlacing their fingers together. "Hey—you wouldn't want your new customers to bite it before they have a chance to pay you, right?"

Hannah kissed the back of Gwen's hand, giving it a firm squeeze. "Text me every five minutes, you hear me? And at least finish your breakfast before you head out."

I looked between the muffins and fresh fruit laid out on the table. Anxiety had suddenly ruined any appetite I'd had. But this venture was absolutely necessary—we needed that silver.

Cliff idly watched Gwen, who picked at her omelet meticulously. He lifted his eyebrows, shooting Hannah a humorless smile. "She likes her eggs scrambled, by the way."

Gwen stood, jabbing her finger at the door. "Out. You're eating on the porch, asshole."

9
JON

"Do me a favor and *please* tell your sidekick to stop staring at me," Gwen snapped from the backseat.

Sylvia scrambled off my headrest and perched by the window. "Does she have to sit right behind you?" she grumbled. "What if she pulls a weapon?"

"You don't have to worry," I said, not bothering to lower my voice. "If she wanted to off me, she'd want to watch the life leave my eyes."

"I'm more interested in the *sound* you'd make, actually," Gwen replied dryly.

Sylvia huffed, fidgeting as she turned her gaze outside. The marsh was different in the daylight, though very little sun could penetrate the fronds and the moss. The crowded trees and mucky paths were familiar in ways I preferred to forget. I'd slogged through this mud when I was barely eighteen, second-hand clothes hanging off my lanky frame while a veteran hunter barked at me to keep up. Their damn monopoly on quality silver brought us back to their door dozens of times over the years, but unshakeable heaviness always rose within me. Tammy may have spent a lot of time in these parts, but most other outposts didn't carry the same unsettling reputation.

My eyes fell back to Sylvia at the thought of Tammy, and I was almost relieved to hear Gwen behind us again.

"Slow down here—see that sign on the tree?" Gwen asked.

A metal plate drilled into the bark declared: *PRIVATE RE-SEARCH FACILITY. TRESPASSERS WILL BE PROSE-CUTED.*

"Yeah. One of the guide marks," Cliff said.

She shook her head. "It's got a new layer of security. See that trip wire up ahead? Releases toxic mist."

Cliff scoffed in disbelief. "Oh, so they're melting civilians for wandering too close these days? Can't say I'm surprised, with that asshole in charge."

"It's harmless to humans," Gwen said too casually. "But it's a cocktail of silver, bronze, and iron. If you take the car over the tripwire, the bulk of the fumes will come through the A/C."

Sylvia kept her face pointed toward the window, seemingly calm, but I could see her reflection. Her eyes were wide, lips slightly parted at the imagined horror of her flesh bubbling and melting away.

I resisted the urge to coddle her with an assurance that she was safe. It would be a lie, anyway. She should have stayed behind at the shop. "Any way around?" I asked Gwen.

"Not unless you want to drown this car, too," she said wryly. "It's a single-use mechanism. Park here for a second while I trigger it. If you give it a minute, the mist should dissipate enough to be safe."

"*Should*," Sylvia echoed hollowly. "Lovely."

Cliff eased the borrowed green Accord to a stop, the tires crunching over the fallen leaves. He and Gwen stepped out, the humid air scented with moss and earth. He hovered close as Gwen knelt at the base of a towering oak, her fingers deftly tracing the nearly invisible wire. She looked up, meeting Cliff's eyes briefly. I couldn't hear what she said, but Cliff shook his head, even as her fingers pulled—triggering the device.

Clouds of mist sprayed from the branches above, the hidden devices coming to life with harrowing precision. I glanced at

Sylvia, but she didn't flinch. She stared vacantly as the mist rained and swirled directly around the space our car would have occupied if we'd continued driving forward.

"At least a wandering fairy wouldn't accidentally pull a tripwire that close to the ground," she murmured.

"You're right," I said readily, trying not to imagine what a brutal way to go that would be—agonizing and humiliating.

Finally, the mist sputtered out and faded, leaving a faintly metallic stench. Gwen stood, brushing dirt off her black jeans. Dropping the limp wire, she returned to the car.

"Let's go," she called over her shoulder.

After scanning the muddy path ahead, Cliff followed and climbed back behind the wheel. He glanced Sylvia's way before turning to confirm with Gwen. "You're sure it's safe now?"

"I can sense it," Sylvia announced before Gwen could answer. "It's settled into the ground—not the air."

Cliff took the car at a crawl nonetheless, waiting until we'd passed the hidden devices entirely before moving at a normal pace. We drove for another twenty minutes, evading two more defense automations as the car bounced over the increasingly uneven ground. Some obstacles we recognized. Others were new—brought to our attention by our backseat driver.

It was with a little bitterness I had to admit Gwen was actually pulling her weight. If she'd wanted, she could have taken us over the tripwire without warning and claimed ignorance when Sylvia started shrieking in pain.

This deep into the marshland, sunlight became even sparser behind the towering trees, each cloaked by a mossy curtain. The faint lights of the outpost were noticeable at once—a sight that made my heart lurch. A vast stretch of water stood between us at the cluster of buildings down in the distance.

The tires struggled against the mud until we reached a spot where the earth became too soft to drive over. Cliff pulled off the paved road, parking the car under the shade of a gnarled oak.

The four of us exited the car, and I paused with a mouthful of rancid air to take in the sight. We were too far away to make out any movement on the massive, dilapidated structure.

"It smells like a fish died eating another fish out here," Sylvia complained, wrinkling her nose.

Cliff snorted. "If you saw the inside of this place, you'd *wish* that was what you were smelling."

Sylvia frowned, looking back at me with a shiver. "I swear I can sense the captive monsters even from here. Aren't they supposed to be weakened? How do you know some of them haven't gotten loose from that… What did you call it—*the Pit?*"

"You know better than most how paranoid hunters are," I said, the corner of my lips lifting in a self-deprecating smile. "Nothing gets in or out without them noticing."

But even I could feel the unsettling quiet here—birdsong swallowed up.

Gwen crossed her arms and leaned against the car. "For all the extra tripwires they invested in, doesn't look like they've reinforced the bridge." She grimaced at the wooden walkway that stretched over the bayou before us. Rainwater drifted along far below in the swamp, carrying twigs and muck and God knew what else. "This is as far as I take you. You have fun, boys."

"You're not coming?" Sylvia asked.

"Hell no. You think I spent six months cutting ties just to get roped back in? Keep my name out of your mouth while you're in there. I started a rumor that a ghoul got the better of me in Texas. The less of these fucks know I exist, the better."

Sylvia narrowed her eyes. "Why would you practically live in the outpost's backyard, then?"

"You're the last one who should be questioning lifestyle choices, Tinker Bell."

"My lifestyle choices these days have involved saving *humans*, you know," she snapped, flying closer to me and Cliff. Her shoulders squared with a sense of duty. "Can we get this over with? My skin's about to crawl off my bones just from breathing the air out here."

I shared a look with Cliff, lips pressed into a thin line. He averted his gaze to the outpost in the distance, ignoring my silent plea to be the bad guy and break the news. Sighing, I braced myself. "Stay with Gwen, Sylv. Someone's gotta make sure she doesn't leave us stranded."

"*What?*" Her eyes widened with instant outrage. "You want me to babysit?"

Once again, I wished I'd insisted that she stay behind at the shop—where she would be safe in the company of Hannah and a pack of docile animals.

"Yes," I said, matching the hard edge in her voice. "I'm not stupid enough to invite you into a hunters' outpost—especially one with updated security measures. You're lucky I let you come this close."

The humid air cooled slightly. "*Let* me?"

"You know what I mean," I pushed on, faltering at the sting of betrayal in her glare. "Dozens of hunters from across the country set up shop here for weeks at a time—"

"I heard you before," she cut in, sighing as she raked her hands through her hair. "I get it. I just hope you know what you're asking of me. To sit here, helpless, wondering if you're alright. You *know* there was something by the car wreck. What if there are more of them—whatever they are?"

Her voice strangled off, her eyes darting between Cliff and me, swimming with shadow. I knew that look well, but it was arresting to see it on *her*—that crippling fear of being the one thing standing between a loved one and their demise.

I stepped closer and reached out to brush her hand resting at her side—to provide even a shred of comfort. "I'm not asking you to like it. I'm asking you to trust me."

Avoiding my touch, she flew in an arc out of reach and alighted on a branch overhead. "Don't make me wait too long."

"Half an hour, tops," I said.

Pulling a gun from the waistband of his jeans, Cliff tossed it to Gwen. "Just in case. You remember how to use it?"

She smoothly caught the weapon and cradled it in her hands, scoffing. "If that's your way of volunteering to be target practice, I'm game."

"As tempting as that sounds, I'll have to rain check," Cliff said, a smirk pulling at his lips. "Think of it as payment."

His gaze briefly flickered up to where Sylvia sulked, and he added under his breath, "Keep an eye on her."

Gwen shooed us off with the barrel of the handgun. "Yeah, yeah. Hurry up, would you? I'm not giving up my whole Sunday for this. Just—" She faltered, swallowing the words back as her gaze rested on Cliff. "Be careful. Idiot or not, Iverson's got this place by the balls."

Cliff cocked his head to the side, sweeping a glance over her. "You keep trying to convince yourself you're not carrying a torch for me."

"If you get yourself killed, this will take twice as long," Gwen returned.

She and I locked gazes, and the faint glimmer of warmth drained out of her eyes. It became obvious that any concern rooted in Gwen did not extend to me, with the weight of unspoken words hanging between us. Memories glimmered behind her steely, kohl-rimmed eyes, promising that she hadn't forgiven me for what had happened to Luke.

Not that I needed her forgiveness. Not then, not now.

I glanced toward Sylvia, suddenly arrested by the awful thought that she might not be entirely safe with Gwen—not when I had made it clear she meant something to me.

"Stand down, Nowak," Gwen muttered, following my flighty gaze. "I'm not gonna lay a finger on her."

"If you try, it's not me you'll need to worry about," I replied, eyeing Sylvia's perch in the branches above us. A cryptic smile played on my lips and seemed to rouse Sylvia slightly, even though her pretty features remained a taut mask of wary concern.

When I turned, empty duffles slung over my shoulder, Sylvia didn't say a word.

Cliff and I set off along the bridge, beginning the long trek to the outpost. The wooden planks, dark and perpetually damp, creaked under our weight. I slowed my stride and glanced at the brackish water below. The bridge was elevated twenty feet—a drop that made my stomach churn, even if I'd crossed these planks enough times to avoid the trick ones. The unsteadiness of the bridge was yet another method of deterring wanderers, but one of these days, the precaution was bound to backfire. I white-knuckled the railing, watching algae drift in the gentle tide.

The bridge gave a sudden, jarring tremor. I glared as Cliff passed me with deliberately heavy strides.

"Really?" I barked, irritation mingling with my queasiness.

His laugh echoed across the marsh. "Afraid of a swim?"

"Asshole." But the word lacked its usual bite. Amid the old wounds surfacing and the persistent uncertainty, falling into stride beside Cliff brought a peculiar comfort. He'd been right here with me the first time I'd crossed this bridge, and against all odds, he was still by my side now.

The marshlands stretched in all directions, the mist oddly thick for the warm morning. The stillness unsettled me; the croaking of frogs, the birds calling out, the distant splash of wildlife moving in the water—none of it was here the way it should have been. When I glanced back the way we'd come, I could scarcely make out the bank against the haggard tree line. The car wasn't visible at all.

"Sylv will come around," Cliff said, following my gaze. "I'm sure she'll cool off before you guys get your freak on again tonight."

I snorted in protest, but worry overtook embarrassment. "I hope so. Still, I'd rather her be upset about staying behind than having her see that place. If she saw the Pit for herself…" I pushed the image from my mind. "She might look at me different. Dunno if I could bear that."

"You're overthinking it. After keeping her in a box for two nights, I doubt much is gonna shake the way she looks at you."

He said it nonchalantly, but dammit, my heart stuttered. I felt like a teenager dying for more detail—*How exactly does she look at me? What have you noticed? Has she told you anything?* If going down this road distracted me from looking at the water below, I supposed it was worth a shot.

"Maybe you're right." I hesitated. "The other night, in the spectral realm—"

Cliff groaned over me. "Spare me the slutty details, please."

"Keep your shirt on." I shouldered him, my grin flickering as I pictured Sylvia's earnest expression peering up at me, her scarlet hair fanned over my shoulder. "Do you believe in soul bonds?"

He stopped in his tracks. "What?"

"A soul bond. Or something to that effect, anyway." Heat rushed to my face as his bewildered stare bore into me. "Like maybe… some people are just *made* to find each other on some cosmic level, you know?"

"Holy fuck. You spend two months with a fairy, and now you're talking like you walked out of a John Hughes movie. Who *are* you?"

Gripping the sturdiest part of the railing, I came to a stop and cast my gaze over the rippling, dark water. "I know it sounds insane—believe me, I know. But I've had this tug inside me since I met her. Lately, it's… It's hard to ignore."

"You sure that's your upstairs brain talking?" Cliff asked, quirking a brow.

I conceded a smirk at that, but my heart was pounding. Sylvia's face was seared in my mind like a brand—*my addiction*. As real as the mark she'd carved into my shoulder.

"You, of all people, know how much sleep I've lost over what happened," I said. "Losing my dad. Losing *everything*. I mean, why us? Why were we the ones to be burned with all of this?"

I faced him with a hard, pleading look as the memories resurfaced—family photos splintering, beloved kitchen wallpaper curling away under the heat of the roaring flames, Cliff's unyielding grip on my arm as he peeled me away from the wreckage, from my father's corpse. I dropped my stare, shuddering.

Sobering up, Cliff followed my gaze to the water, where the idle ripples distorted our vague reflections. I quelled the memory of acrid smoke with the smell of cinnamon and rain—*her* scent.

"Sometimes I wonder if *she* is the reason," I said, finally ejecting my point. "Maybe everything I went through—all that loss, all that suffering—it was all leading me to *her*. Like we were meant to meet even if…"

Even if she's not like us, our shared silence echoed.

Cliff's gruff voice softened with a level of concern that toed the line between insulting and comforting. "Jon, I get it. I do. After the fucked up shit we went through…" He shook his head. "But

I think the truth is worse than any kind of fate or destiny bullshit. Sometimes, people just suffer."

"You don't understand," I muttered. He couldn't register that look on Sylvia's face when she spoke of her lost father. I knew that vacant, mournful stare—because it was like looking at myself. Cliff hadn't met someone whose soul seemed tailor-made for his.

"I understand more than you think," he replied quietly. "But this? With *her*? You may as well be trying to hold onto a ghost."

I peeled myself away from the railing and readjusted my grip on the bags slung over my shoulder. I'd been broken for so long. There was no way to explain how badly I wanted to feel whole again—even if grasping at something intangible was the only way to do it.

"Hey—you're listening to me, right?" Cliff called after me.

I shrugged, forcing my thoughts into the here and now—onto one step in front of the other. "Of course," I said. "You're right. It's only a temporary thing. What else could it be?"

Cliff fell back into stride, eyes narrowing on me.

"But let's be honest here—you're clearly jaded because of Gwen," I added.

He cursed under his breath, jaw feathering. "Can't believe she retired," he muttered, taking the bait. "Such bullshit."

His disdain made me falter, a thread of guilt tugging from my chest as I thought about the daydream I'd woven with Sylvia where I retired and started a new life. Even if I'd callously shut down her suggestion of making it a reality, entertaining the fantasy felt traitorous with Cliff beside me.

"And the fact that she left us in the middle of the night has nothing to do with it?" I prodded.

"Ancient history."

"Clearly." I wasn't cruel enough to remind him of his foul mood and excessive drinking that followed her sudden absence that fateful morning. "Come on, you can't be shocked after how much she was pulling away toward the end. There's no rule about staying in it for life. Maybe this is a good thing."

"Seriously? She was one of the best in the game. What a waste."

I scoffed, unable to mask my venom to spare him. "She was *decent* at best."

"She got the run on *you*."

"One time," I muttered.

"And you still have your panties in a twist over it."

"She *shot* me!"

"It barely grazed you," Cliff said breezily.

I rolled my eyes. "Fuck, you're insufferable when she's around. And look—I stand by what I said. None of us sign a damn contract when we start hunting. Her heart clearly wasn't in it even years ago. Let her live a normal life without policing her."

From the corner of my eye, I sensed Cliff's dark look—a questioning one. We'd been down this path years ago when he'd slammed the door behind him hard enough to make that shitty Iowa motel rattle. I never thought *I'd* be the one poised to run, though—even if it was just a distant daydream.

"There's never a normal life after touching this world," Cliff said with finality. "You know that. And the *real* point is, she moved on too quickly from me."

"It's been five years at least, Cliff."

"Please—it takes a *lifetime* to get me out of your system." His insufferable smile turned considering as he gave me another look over his shoulder. "You know, she might've been jealous as fuck if I had shown up at her door with a tall brunet on my arm…"

I scoffed out a harsh laugh. "She wouldn't have believed it for a second."

"What, you don't think I can pull someone as *incredible* as you?"

"I've seen you pull."

His smirk returned. "Yeah, you have. Come on, aside from being covered in blood every other night, you'd date me, right?"

"Even if I swung that way, you're not my type."

The walkway abruptly stopped rattling when Cliff stopped dead in his tracks. I walked past him without a second glance.

"How the hell am I not your type?" Cliff snapped. "I'm everyone's type!"

"What's the big deal? You're not even into me."

"That's beside the point! What's your type, then, tough guy?"

"I don't know, man." I glanced back, assessing him as he caught up. Gripping the railing tightly, I assured myself we weren't far from the end. "You're shorter than me, for one thing."

"Oh—*two inches*, you bastard. Try again."

"I'd need someone more rugged." I couldn't fight a grin at his outraged scoff. I was only sad Sylvia was missing it. "But who can be tender with me, too, you know?"

"Fuck off, I can be tender!"

"And you fly off the handle at the drop of a hat. You're literally screaming at me for no reason!"

A blur of gray and brown fur suddenly darted in front of us, dropping from the tangle of branches overhead. Cursing, Cliff staggered back into me. I shoved him off, a coil of anxiety surfacing at the thought of our combined weight splintering the rotted wood, careening off the sharp drop—

A squirrel skittered up to the railing at waist level, bushy tail twitching. *Not this again.* Cliff gripped my jacket with one hand. The other whipped his handgun from its thigh holster so quickly that I struggled to track the movement.

I groaned. "Come on, don't shoot it."

"You know these fuckers have it out for me! Ever since Virginia. It's a curse. I *know* it's a curse." His aim was centered with deadly precision on the squirrel's tiny, furry skull.

"We *don't* know that." I stepped in his path to push the gun down. He leaned to the side to lock gazes with it over my shoulder as the squirrel chittered. It stared back at him, glossy eyes vacant.

"Come on." I pushed Cliff forward, leaving the squirrel behind us. Cliff flinched as it gave a shrill squeak, but when nothing further happened, he flipped the safety back on his gun and tucked it out of sight.

"Whatever. Like I was saying—you wouldn't stand a chance with me," Cliff went on, salvaging his dignity with a sweep of his hand through his dark blond hair.

My smile dropped into a grimace. "Dude—"

"You'd wake up in a hospital bed."

"You wish," I scoffed.

A beat passed between us as I tried not to think about it. Tried not to picture—

"Are you blushing?" Cliff demanded.

"Nope. Don't even try to make this about anything other than your vanity."

"You *are*." Cliff chuckled fondly at my expense. "Lightweight."

The last stretch of the boards bridging us to solid ground grew narrower, slick with moisture. This area was sturdier, swaying less with each lap of water against the poles that vanished into the depths. The outpost rose as a single-story fortress from the water, the air heavy with the scent of decay and something sharp and metallic. The weather-beaten wood of the structure had turned smooth from years of harsh weather and the rough hands of hunters. Old—but impossible to infiltrate. The wood was reinforced with iron and steel at every opening.

Abandoned supplies lined the railings surrounding the outpost—cages, nets, assorted hunting gear. I lifted a brow at the sight of a crossbow protruding from a canvas bag.

We approached a few hunters who idled outside the entrance, smoking and talking. Their conversation quelled, and they eyed us with a mixture of curiosity and suspicion. Any lost hikers who'd trespassed this far would certainly turn tail upon seeing even one of these guys. One of them, a burly man with a salt-and-pepper beard and a missing tooth, chuckled as we passed.

"Hey, pretty boy," he called out, nodding at the gun holstered on Cliff's thigh. "Know how to use that thing?"

Cliff kept his gaze fixed ahead with militant focus, even when the jeers turned vulgar—though admirable in their colorful description. I pushed them from earshot as the bouncer peeled away from the shadows of the entryway to stop us before the final walkway leading to the building. He was a monolith of a man, likely pushing seven feet tall. I was generally one of the tallest people in any given room; lifting my chin to meet his appraising stare felt strange.

"State your business," he rasped, voice coarse from years of chain-smoking.

"Just a couple of researchers collecting data," Cliff said casually.

"Who's your coordinator?" The bouncer asked, providing the second half of the pass phrase.

"Tammy Gordon," I answered.

With a quiet *shiiink*, he withdrew a machete from his belt. "Follow me."

As we trailed behind him along the walkway, I braced myself for what had to come next, but a glint from above distracted me. Nestled discreetly under the weathered wood overhang was a sleek camera pointed in our direction, its modern casing a harsh contrast to its surroundings. The state-of-the-art security measure proved Gwen's claim about the upgrades.

A chittering hiss came from within a stack of crates near the door. Leathery wings and clawed hands poked through the slats. Ahools. They were often mistaken for bats, though they could grow to be much bigger.

Strange—they normally avoided humans unless provoked, and they weren't native to this area to begin with. I'd heard about the versatility of their wing hide, though, and had no doubt these people were delaying the kill until the little beasts were fully matured.

Something else thudded, water sloshing. I jerked my attention back down, noting that one of the luggage-sized crates near the edge of the wrap-around walkway was a tank. A creature surged back and forth inside, palms beating on the glass. White-blonde hair drifted around a slender face. The hollows of her cheeks were pronounced, and her large eyes were flooded with unnatural blackness like the dead of night.

"A siren?" I breathed.

I'd never been able to observe one openly. No one could—not without being glamoured into a watery grave. A siren's captivating eyes were just as dangerous as those razor-sharp teeth. This one appeared to be in a bizarre state of in-between—part decay with hints of beauty meant to lure unwitting victims into diving after her.

She made a pitiful crooning noise.

"Dumb bitch," the bouncer buttered. He stormed over and pounded a fist on top of the grimy glass case. "How many times have I told you to keep your mouth shut?"

The siren gave a waterlogged screech, covering her eyes with taloned hands. The bouncer pounded again, smirking as she curled up at the very bottom with animal disdain twisting her pretty features. He sauntered back to us.

"Don't worry, boys. She can try, but we keep her half-starved. Too weak to hypnotize a damn frog."

That pleading, frightened look on her face didn't bring any sense of comfort. Sylvia's face flashed through my mind's eye.

"What are you going to do with her?" I asked.

"She'll be shipped off soon enough. Something about breaking down her blood for medicine—bullshit, if you ask me. They're paying top dollar for us to keep her breathing, though."

"Who's they?" Cliff questioned, stealing a glance at the siren with uncertainty that mirrored my own.

"Hell if I know—ask the marshal if you wanna outbid for her." The bouncer positioned himself before us and grunted, gesturing for us to hold out our arms. "Test of humanity. Roll up your sleeves."

I exchanged a look with Cliff as we complied. Code phrases could only get us *near* the door. The process of actually getting through was far less pleasant. The bouncer's machete glinted in the hazy sunlight.

Clearing my throat, I said, "Last time we came by, it was a smaller knife."

He seized my wrist, wrenching my arm out. "Don't be a pussy."

I gritted my teeth, but the incision was surprisingly delicate. The silver blade drew a narrow line of blood across my forearm. Next, he produced an iron bar to press firmly over my skin. The bouncer gave Cliff the same treatment. No acrid, smoldering effects followed, nor any of the general agonized symptoms that would be drawn out of a monster.

The bouncer wiped the blade on his shirt and sank into a chair by the door that looked barely capable of supporting his weight. "Go on," he grunted.

I pulled open the thick, iron-banded door and stepped inside.

"Okay, I thought that was gonna be way worse," Cliff murmured under his breath. He tapped off a quick strip of gauze before handing me the roll.

"Dude, right?" I said, sharing a small laugh. I rolled the sleeve of my khaki green shirt back down after covering the wound. "Tiny back there has a delicate touch."

"*Tender* enough for you?" he sneered.

I pretended to consider it. "Almost."

"Bastard." Cliff elbowed past me. "Let's lock down that silver first."

We paused shortly after the door shut behind us, taking in the unfamiliar layout of the outpost. While there were still hunting trophies in abundance, the usual stalls and tables were nowhere to be seen.

"Where the hell are the weapons?" Cliff muttered as we strolled further inside. The floor was made of the same dark wood as before, scuffed by countless boots.

"Maybe they moved their supplies to one of the rooms." I noted the four doorways along the wall that branched off into other spaces, but they were shut tight. The only other exterior door led to the side outdoor area which housed the Pit.

Despite the lack of ammunition and weapons for sale, there was more energy about the common area than I'd ever witnessed. There appeared to be more archivists and strategists present than before, consulting groups of hunters with maps and diagrams. The most familiar sights were the shooting range and the bar—the latter of which was unusually empty.

As for the shooting range in the far corner, a row of four hunters were taking aim at moving targets. Cliff looked longingly in that direction before tearing his gaze away. There was no time.

"Even the fucking community supply cache is gone," Cliff said. "What the hell is this place for, then?"

I had no answer for him, surveying the common area again slowly. Activity by a stack of crates along the wall caught my attention. For a hopeful second, I thought they might hold the cache—until I saw a group of people packing unusual items inside.

Nudging Cliff to follow, I approached them casually. A foul smell surrounded the area—chemicals used for taxidermy. I caught a glimpse of werewolf pelts and polished horns, which were typically sold off as practical wares for hunters. But I also noticed spiked tentacles, ugly mounted ghoul heads, and a full basilisk statue poised in mid-strike.

"Need something?" one of the men at work snapped at me. He looked too slight to be a hunter—maybe an archivist.

"Just curious," I said. "We haven't been around in a good couple years. Where's all this going?"

He narrowed his eyes. "Classified. Take it up with the marshal."

I had to clench my jaw to keep from pressing. Too much push-back could land us in hot water with the usual crowd that ran around this place. I thought about pressing my luck and asking where the supplies were kept—particularly the silver, but Cliff elbowed me.

"Hey—is that Cain out there?"

Following where he pointed, I saw movement through one of the windows. Sure enough, Cain was outside the Pit with a newblood—a young man with dark hair. If Gwen was to be believed, Cain wasn't the marshal anymore, but surely he could still snag us some silver.

As we passed through the doors, I couldn't help but thorough-ly examine the Pit. The massive, circular chain-link cage was suspended over the wooden walkways over the murky bayou. Although it had been reinforced and patched many times over the years, it looked almost the same as when I'd first stepped into it. The iron and silver chains hanging from the domed ceiling were a new touch, though.

A fairly small creature was curled up on the concrete base.

Cliff gave a low whistle. "What do you think? A familiar? An alp?"

"Hard to say when it's calm," I murmured back. At first glance, the creature looked like a dog—unusually large, but the sort of lovable mutt that should have been found dozing on a living room rug.

I scanned the area, curious of what other creatures might be entering the Pit sometime soon. Slight movement caught my eye from around the corner of the building. Surrounded by heaps of garbage, a seemingly human person was tied to a stake, hands behind his back. His blond head was lowered, and the air seemed to shimmer around his skin—burning in the overcast sunlight. I was surprised that they would keep a vampire around to this point of weakness; he wouldn't be much good for training in the Pit.

"You've got to be prepared for any of its forms," Cain was saying to the newblood. "Tell me—what are the signs that it's about to shift?"

"It'll pause, but only briefly," the young man answered with an eagerness that should have been saved for a university classroom. "Striking mid-shift is the best way to take it out—"

"And if there's no time to strike?" Cain said.

"Take the opportunity to get out of range and assess the new threat it turned into."

Cliff sauntered forward to interrupt. "And you might wanna be prepared for your mind to go blank the moment you step in there. Takes time before you start thinking clearly in the heat of a fight."

Cain's weathered face split into a grin. "Well! The Appalachian Reapers finally grace us with their presence. Here I thought some ghoul or other got the better of you boys."

"The Appalachian Reapers?" The young hunter was slack-jawed. "Seriously?" He cast furtive glances between us, eyes flicking down searchingly.

I chuckled. "I'm guessing you heard the rumor that one of us cut off a hand to use as bait?"

The kid's face flushed. "I-I mean—I didn't *believe* it or any-thing."

"You'll learn soon enough, Brandon," Cain said. "Most assholes in the business like mixing their information with whiskey." He gave Cliff and me a fond smirk. "But the truth's nothing to sneeze at. Two men against a pack of feral whistlers out in the belly of the mountains, protecting a pregnant civilian while they were at it. Should've been torn to pieces by all accounts. Hunts like that are once in a lifetime, boys."

Brandon continued to gape, starstruck. "It's an honor to meet you," he stammered.

If we had the time, I wouldn't have minded sitting down with a beer so Cliff and I could regale Brandon with further detail—especially about how the woman hadn't just been expecting. She'd been in the throes of labor pains, and I'd muffled her raw screams into my jacket to avoid being detected by the whistlers crawling in the forest around us.

"You just keep that weapon raised, kid," Cliff said.

Brandon chuckled self-consciously. "Easy for you to say! Is it true you nailed twelve of those whistlers with headshots while it was practically pitch black out there?" His eyes flickered not-so-subtly to a tattoo that peeked out from under Cliff's collar.

Cliff pulled at his shirt and angled his head to reveal the full design—skeletal antlers inked in a delicate circle on the right side of his neck to commemorate the hunt. Brandon inhaled a reverent gasp.

"Missed plenty of shots out there, too, but lucky we were stocked up," Cliff said, then turned pointedly to Cain. "Speaking of—can you clue us in about what the hell happened to the supply cache? And the silver vendors?"

Cain waved a dismissive hand, perhaps to distract from the discomfort lining his face. "New systems got put in place, I'm sure you've heard. Not much I can do about it, seeing as I'm not the marshal anymore."

"Can't you just sell it to us?" I asked.

"Supplies like that aren't sold anymore. They're earned. Provide for the outpost, and the outpost provides for you."

"Sounds like you handed the place off to a cult leader," Cliff scoffed. "Seriously—*Rhett Iverson*? That crazy-eyed bastard shouldn't be in charge of a McDonald's, let alone an operation like this."

A burly hunter approached—one of the Pit keepers. "You heading in there, or what?" he directed at Brandon. "Bets closed five minutes ago—they're getting antsy." Behind him, at least a dozen other outpost denizens surrounded the Pit in anticipation. The bookie leaned against a stack of crates, counting a wad of cash.

When Brandon paled, Cain clapped his shoulder. "Keep your wits about you. Understand, boy? Remember, you can call it off at any time, and one of the keepers'll subdue the beast."

Nodding shakily, Brandon tugged at a cord around his neck, rubbing a set of beads between his fingers. He froze when he noticed me watching.

"Good luck charm?" I questioned.

He cleared his throat. "My sister got it for me from some tourist trap in NOLA. I know it doesn't do anything, but…"

"Hey, I get it," I said, flashing the azabache bracelet on my wrist. "Some things just make us feel safer."

Brandon straightened, bearing more confidence as he headed for the Pit door. It was strangely detached from the buzz of energy in the air—the understanding that hunters, cleaners, and archivists alike had bet money on how long he'd last before getting maimed or calling it quits. The kid looked so scrawny. I could hardly believe Cliff and I were just like him, once upon a time.

If we made it, so could he.

He circled the sleeping dog slowly while spectators jeered at him to attack. Brandon started to ease forward, only to lose his nerve and back off. I had no doubt Cain had trained him thoroughly, but that didn't change the fact that he was too young and nervous to initiate the fight. If Tammy were in Cain's place, she would have been barking orders for Brandon to take control, to *strike*.

"We saw some crates being packed in the building," I said, drawing Cain's attention away from the nonexistent battle. "Where are they being shipped?"

Huffing, Cain shook his head. "I don't know all the details."

"Why?" Cliff cut in. "You ran this place for—how many years? Decades? Why wouldn't you want to get all the information you can about what comes next for it?"

"What do you want me to say? I'm old, boys! I was ready to pass the mantle, and the new marshal assured me that the bounties and supplies are going to a good cause."

"But how do you know for sure if you can't say what cause it's going toward?" I pressed.

"Look around you, boys!" Cain gestured widely. "You ever seen this place more lively? We can afford better supplies, better protection. Hell, hunters can actually make a living around here now, thanks to the marshal. I'm not one to look a gift horse in the mouth—not at my age."

One of the spectators viciously clanged on the chain-link exterior of the Pit, finally rousing the dog. It lifted its head to find that Brandon had invaded its enclosure. At once, the beast was on its feet, hackles raised and teeth bared.

"Strike, boy!" Cain shouted. "Before it changes!"

Brandon looked cemented to where he stood for all of three seconds. Then he gave a war cry and lunged. Before he reached the dog, its fur shivered, and it grew in size. In the blink of an eye, a bear had taken the place of the dog, rising onto its hind legs to tower over the kid.

A massive paw swung, catching Brandon square in the chest and sending him onto his ass, blade skittering out of reach. He howled in pain, clutching his front as crimson seeped through his fingers.

"Get him out!" I shouted.

But the head Pit keeper at the door shook his head. "*He* needs to call it."

Brandon was in no state to call anything. He scrambled back in a panic as the bear loped for him. He made a valiant attempt to dodge, but it was no use. The monster caught Brandon's hand in its jaw first. His ear-splitting shriek made my nerves stand on end.

"The fuck are they waiting for!" Cliff growled, stalking forward to grab one of the cattle prods leaning against the Pit. Cain and I followed his lead, but I had the sick feeling we were too late.

Blood spilled over the already-stained concrete floor of the Pit. Bits of Brandon's mangled hand and arm lay scattered in several directions. Cliff elbowed past jeering spectators to get in reach of the bear. He managed to get a good jab at the creature's flank, but it jolted out of reach of all three of us—taking Brandon with it.

The bear had caught the kid's shoulder in its jaws. Jerking back, it sent Brandon down on his back and braced a paw on his body, spasming its head side to side until there was a sickening pop—followed by a wet ripping sound.

Brandon's scream drowned out the roar of the small crowd.

Finally, the other Pit keepers set to work. They strategically surrounded the chain link enclosure, lunging cattle prods through the fence with well-placed strikes to make the bear retreat. No one seemed keen on trying to remove the severed arm from its jaws.

I didn't realize Brandon had stopped screaming until I saw him being dragged from the Pit—fully shocked into silence, gaze distant.

"*Pinches pendejos*," I muttered, regrouping with Cliff and Cain. "That alp wasn't weakened enough. Putting a kid alone up against a monster like that?" I gave Cain a hard look. "Is that part of the new *system*?"

"It hadn't shifted into a fucking bear before, I'll tell you that," Cain sighed. "Excuse me, boys—I need to be with him in the medic's room."

He looked almost relieved at the excuse to end our conversation. He disappeared past a group of bettors arguing with the bookie about technicalities and payouts. I couldn't banish my own memories of the dismembered revenant I'd been pitted against five days in a row when I was Brandon's age. Many had bet against me, not bothering to hide their disappointment when I emerged victorious day after day.

If Brandon pulled through, at least I could rest assured he wouldn't be fighting any more monsters.

"Poor kid," Cliff murmured as we abandoned our cattle prods where we'd found them. "They made sure the alps were half-dead before pitting us against them, didn't they?"

I heaved a sigh. "Nothing's right about this place—not that there ever was. But this is different." I glanced in the direction Cain had vanished. "If there was anyone around here who could tell us what the hell is going on, it's him."

"Maybe if we root around, we can scrounge up some silver and be gone before they know it," Cliff said dubiously.

As much as I wanted to get the hell out of this place and return to Sylvia, I hesitated. "If there's a demand for specialty non-human parts, it's worth looking into. Do you really buy that these things are going to a good cause?"

"It's bullshit," Cliff agreed as we circled back around the Pit. "But if Cain's keeping his mouth shut about it, what are the chances we can get any of these assholes to clue us in?"

I came to a sudden stop as I caught another glimpse behind the back of the building—the captive burning slowly in the sunlight. As my eyes flicked toward Cliff, I found that he had followed my gaze, expression thoughtful. He and I shared a look.

"Looks hungry," I muttered.

Cliff casually picked up one of Brandon's severed fingers from the gore that sprayed along the edge of the Pit. "You don't say?"

10
SYLVIA

s the seconds crawled by, I realized I had no way to tell the time. Had I already become so reliant on human technology? Then again, the sun and shadows were no help with the density of the foliage.

Hesitantly, I peeked down at Gwen. "How long has it been?"

She scoffed, glancing at her watch. "Less than twenty minutes."

Hugging my knees, I slumped against a thick twig that branched from my perch. I kept a careful eye on the ground below, feeling like I was keeping company with a prowling wildcat. I bristled when Gwen finally moved, but all she did was pull out a cigarette and light it.

Her eyes flicked up and met my stare. "I don't suppose you want a hit of this?"

Wrinkling my nose at the smell, I shook my head and thanked the stars that Jon and Cliff didn't partake in the habit.

"Right." Gwen took a generous drag and sighed. "You're probably more of a Fruity Pebble flavored vape kinda girl."

I couldn't begin to puzzle out half of those words, but I supposed it was an insult. No wonder she and Cliff had been so involved with each other—and fell apart spectacularly.

Whatever edge Gwen was trying to take off, the cigarette wasn't doing it. She grumbled something under her breath about it being fucking gross outside and it wasn't even noon. I had to agree, given how much I had to flick my wings to keep dew from collecting on the membrane. Murmuring a familiar spell, I summoned coolness to the humid air for a small reprieve. Reluctantly, I extended the enchantment's reach toward the car.

Gwen stiffened at the change and narrowed her eyes up at me. "I suppose you want my mortal soul in exchange for the A/C?"

"No. I've got my own." I draped myself along the branch and folded my arms under my chin, offering a tentative smile. "But I wouldn't mind a dog…"

"Not happening." Surprisingly, she chuckled before surveying the area and relaxing again. We settled into comfortable silence for nearly a minute until she asked, "So, what's the deal with you and Jon?"

No preamble, no benefit of the doubt. I was beginning to understand that was just Gwen's way, but I stumbled over my words nonetheless and felt increasingly stupid as the seconds stretched. I couldn't describe something that I hadn't defined for myself. Even though I'd had plenty of time over the past weeks to settle on an answer, the truth eluded me.

How could I describe the way he looked at me with those tender brown eyes? The way I recognized him by scent alone? How he laid his head on my lap in the spectral plane and we talked for hours like nothing else mattered? Whatever Jon and I had… it was fragile, temporary, brilliant—like a star burning itself out as it streaked across the sky.

"We're… friends," I said.

Gwen laughed throatily around her cigarette. "So much for fairies being master deceivers. You two whisper like preteens at your first co-ed party."

My lips thinned. I didn't need to explain myself to any-one—least of all, an ex-hunter with no intention of aiding us beyond a single outing.

"I don't know what to call it," I answered anyway. "It feels good."

"How long?"

"Two moon cycles—I mean, months now."

Gwen gave a low, impressed whistle. "Well, whatever it is, that's gotta be Jon's longest record in years—maybe ever. Even for a hunter, the man was like a goddamn revolving door for a while."

"He's nomadic. They *both* are," I replied with a shrug. "Commitments are damn near impossible."

Hurt flickered over her expression as though I'd slapped her. It was the same wide-eyed look she'd worn when Cliff had accused her of leaving. Gnawing curiosity mingled with guilt. I was scrambling for an apology when Gwen sighed, giving a reluctant nod.

"Yeah, you've got that right. Hard to live such a brutal life and keep it secret from your partner." She scanned me up and down, the corners of her red lips twitching in a small smirk. "When you're *part* of the secret, I guess that's a little easier on Nowak's sorry excuse for a conscience."

I arched a brow. "Don't tell me you're upset that I got to him before you could?"

"Hell, no." Gwen cringed. "He always scared me."

"*Jon?*" I laughed.

Comparing the two hunters, I found it difficult to believe Cliff hadn't been the one to scare her straight. With his commanding voice and readiness to act without hesitation—shoot first and ask questions later—seemed far more likely to scare Gwen straight.

But maybe she had seen straight through all that from the start.

Gwen's face darkened, watching me with a renewed scrutiny. "You've seen him hunt, haven't you?"

Yes—with more fascination than I cared to admit. Goosebumps rose on my arms at the mere memory of the feral look in his eyes the moment before a kill.

He was pure lightning. *Strike, strike, strike.*

"You've been face to face with literal nightmares," I said slowly. "I find it hard to believe another hunter has you in knots like this."

The flicker in her gaze roared into a fire, and her effort to douse it only amplified the goosebumps running up my arms. My goading smile dropped away, replaced by a growing chill.

"What did he do?" I asked, brow knitting as I tried to read past her expression.

Gwen's gaze darted to the ground, then back up, her ruby lips pressed in a thin line. Wind swept through the woods, tousling my hair and making me flex my wings to maintain balance. Her tension put me on edge. I struggled to reconcile Jon's gentle, curious smile with whatever visage had clearly shaken another hunter to her core. Every piece of history I'd drawn out of Jon had felt like a victory up until now. I was struck by the awareness that I'd only scratched the surface, and the gaps in Jon's history suddenly seemed like dark, gaping maws.

"Let's just say he's not as noble as you're trying to paint him," she gritted out.

"You have no idea how much he tortures himself," I snapped. "He doesn't need someone like you around to drag him down further."

"You don't know shit about him."

"Enlighten me, then." I kept my tone cool, but my wings gave an involuntary twitch. I was grateful Gwen didn't seem to note the indication of the tension coiling inside me.

She let out a sharp laugh—though I didn't miss the way her breath caught and turned shallow. "I'm not spilling my guts to a fucking fairy," she bit out.

The word *fairy* landed like a slap. Outrage bubbled to life inside me like claws raking beneath my skin.

"Fine. Keep your festering wound to yourself," I said, venom seeping into my tone. "Don't expect me to beg to hear whatever moral high ground you think you have."

Gwen's jaw tightened, her free hand flexing and curling into a fist as though resisting the urge to reach for her weapons, to lash out.

"He killed Luke!" she snarled, her voice splintering.

I flinched, the name hitting me hard. I pushed myself up, sitting straight. "Luke?"

Gwen dragged a hand through her pulled-back hair. "My friend. Nowak used him—a fellow hunter—like a fucking worm on a hook to lure at a shapeshifter on the Pacific Coast." She prowled closer to my branch, eyes wet as she jabbed a finger in my direction. "He'd do the same to me to finish a job. To anyone—even you."

Shock rippled through me, cold and vicious. I couldn't picture it—I *wouldn't*. Jon was a warrior, not a mindless killer. He was gentle and kind in ways that still astonished me day after day.

"I don't believe you," I said, hating the betrayal of my thready voice.

"Ask him yourself since he's got such a soft spot for you," Gwen shot back. "Or better yet, corner him in a no-win situation and see what he does."

"Here's another idea." I leaned my arms on my knees. "We leave you here and you can walk back to your shop."

She gave a dark chuckle, rolling her eyes. Some of her hackles lowered, but I didn't miss the odd touch of worry that sat behind her irritation. "You can think I'm a bitch. Frankly, I don't give a shit. You seem like a decent person—wings and all—and I'm just trying to save you some grief. Maybe your life. Jon Nowak is *dangerous,* and I can't think of a single time that mixing humans and non-humans didn't end in disaster."

"You've heard of others?" I seized the chance to change the subject, pushing off the dark images that crept into my mind—Jon, binding another man as a living sacrifice.

"It's more common than people think," Gwen said, sighing heavily. "Hunters fall for ghosts they're supposed to send off. Vamps convince regular civilians that they can have a star-crossed romance. You can imagine how that ends."

No need to imagine. One of the nightmares in my rotation included a vivid image of Nolan opening his arms to a monstrous Lily, only to have his throat ripped out, blood spurting across a lupine muzzle.

"As though *humans* are any less messy on their own." I raised my eyebrows accusingly at her. "I'm shocked, frankly, that you and Cliff haven't strangled each other yet. Hard to picture you together."

Gwen snorted, but I swore the faintest hint of fondness lay buried under the ire. "Believe it or not, he was even more of an idiot when we met."

"Impossible," I said airily. "Do tell."

The jab earned a half smile. "We were so young—barely old enough to retire the fake IDs and walk into the bar like we owned the place. He and Nowak got into some stupid fight not long after they hit the road together. Cliff says he couldn't stand Nowak's bitching anymore. Personally, I think Cliff was looking for an excuse to call it quits and make his own way in the world. Had his bags packed and everything. But Tammy convinced him to back me up on a hunt."

Tammy. That name again. The boys always seemed to change the subject shortly after she was brought up. A small sting came; even an estranged hunting partner knew all about the mysterious woman.

They're hiding something, hissed a voice in the back of my head. *You know there's something they're not telling you and you're too much of a coward to ask why.*

"How long were the boys apart?" I asked, coaxing my paranoia to quiet.

"Couple months, at most. I thought they both would've ate it by now, but they're not a bad team when they have their heads out of their asses."

An understatement if I'd ever heard one.

Not for the first time, I wondered what Cliff would do with himself if Jon abandoned hunting. I was afraid of what answer I would receive if I posed the question to Gwen, so I pivoted. "Is Hannah the reason you retired for good?"

Gwen raised the cigarette to her lips, taking a long, deliberate drag. She glanced at her watch, giving an impatient huff as she glanced toward the outpost.

Her dark eyes drifted back at me, narrowed in thought, and I was struck again by the fierce quality of her beauty. Her black hair, woven into a single braid, gleamed faintly in the hazy daylight. She was stunning in the way a polished blade was beautiful—captivating but dangerous when you drew too close. When Gwen exhaled, a bitter-smelling cloud of smoke hung in the air.

"Didn't think *retirement* was in my vocabulary," she admitted, the edge to her gaze softening. "I was hunting a wraith, and the wraith was hunting her. She was oblivious. I swear, if that thing had knocked right on her door, she would have offered it a place to crash for the night." Her lips pulled into a wider smile, shaking her head.

"I didn't mean to start talking to her—it just sort of happened. Then when I found out that she…" Gwen trailed off, glancing at me. "Doesn't matter. Even when I bagged the wraith, I just didn't feel right leaving her alone with a hunter outpost a few miles away."

I frowned. "Why would a human have to worry about hunters?"

Gwen stared in the direction of the rickety wooden bridge that stretched across the water like it might lunge toward her. "I've got a protective streak, as it turns out. Only takes one asshole to cause trouble, right? But it was impossible to convince her to move away from her family."

"You stuck around for her," I murmured.

She gave one resolute nod. "I told her I'd lost my job—which wasn't a total lie. She invited me to stay until I was back on my feet. Became a running joke between us—because days turned into weeks, and then months. Hannah never said a word to urge me out. Somewhere along the way, I woke up one morning, and it felt like home."

I couldn't quell the rush of warmth in my chest as I pictured Jon doing the same for me. Giving up hunting, letting us find *home* in each other's arms.

Gwen scoffed. "What's with the dopey smile?"

"Nothing. Just curious." I descended to a lower branch, trying to catch her gaze. "How hard was it to let go of the hunting life?" My heart fluttered uncertainly as I thought about how adamant Jon's stance had been on never changing. "So few humans know about monsters. Even fewer are cut out for hunting them. Did you feel… I don't know, guilty about settling down?"

A touch of defensiveness flickered on her face as though I was being accusatory. But perhaps that was what made her answer. "I realized I could do more for Hannah than just save her from a monster. There was a space in her home, and she was ready to fill it."

I let the idea sink in, thinking about how swiftly and fiercely she had come to rescue Hannah from Cliff. But it was more than that—their hands reaching for each other's at the breakfast table and Hannah's worry over Gwen accompanying us here.

"Have you texted her that you're still alive?" I asked.

Rolling her eyes, she dug her phone out of her pocket and tapped out a one-handed message.

A *ping* indicated an immediate response—and Gwen's face softened to a degree I didn't think possible. Which was what possessed me to say, "You're lucky to have found each other."

Gwen stowed her phone and gave me an unreadable look—except I had seen it on Jon and Cliff's faces many times by this point. It was an analytical stare meant to unearth thoughts that even I wasn't aware I was thinking.

"You think he'll settle down for you?" she questioned in a tone that wasn't entirely cruel but stung all the same.

I averted my eyes. "I didn't say that."

"You're really cock-drunk for him, aren't you? What's got him so whipped for *you*? You got something on him?" Gwen dropped the spent cigarette to put it out under her boot. "Or is it the other way around? Just oughta clue you in—I know a bullet hole when I see one."

I snapped my wings shut, fingers digging into the branch that held me. "That's got nothing to do with it. Jon didn't—" I stopped short, mulling over how to explain our macabre first days. "He saved my life. He took a werewolf bite to protect me—and the rest of that damn city."

For the first time, true shock washed over her. "He… That should have killed him. Or turned him. How the hell is he alive?"

"Well, I—" I faltered, looking down at my hands. Though no magic coursed through my palms, the moment I'd touched Jon's wound was forever seared into my mind. That sacred, fated contact between us. The thought of heavily charged magic drew my attention to the pulse of the gem shard in my pocket. I closed my fingers around it as though I could choke its aura. "I couldn't let him die."

"You healed him," Gwen breathed, letting out a rush of air. "Now *that* makes sense. See, Hannah would call Nowak a burdened soul. But me—I'd just call him a sorry bastard who can't tell the difference between love and guilt. Once he considers his debt paid, he'll leave you high and dry."

"Fuck you." The words leapt from my mouth without a single pause to consider their consequence—along with a hard line of frost that cut through the air.

I had conjured the magic impulsively, barely feeling my lips move around the spell. The glistening icicle whistled well past Gwen's head, and I swiftly released the shard in my pocket, but the damage was done. I'd shown aggression toward her, just like any monster she'd ever hunted. Renewed tension crackled in the air between us as she regarded me cautiously.

Jon makes me feel alive, I wanted to snarl at her. *That's worth everything to me. Every single risk.*

Another voice surfaced in my mind—a new, sickening caution. *Even if he's killed an innocent?* The question cut like a jagged blade, stinging in its uncertainty.

I tensed, prepared for Gwen to reach for her weapon in retaliation. The familiar, crushing hand of anxiety—the tiny hope in my chest that I would see Jon and Cliff emerging from the misty path at this opportune moment—was only a brief companion this time. In its place, a smoldering determination surfaced. I had hunted werewolves and ghosts alongside seasoned hunters. My magic endurance was stronger every time I trained, my spells more elaborate, the duration focused and sustained. And now, I carried a shard to amplify it all.

If she hurt me, I would make her regret it tenfold.

The silence settled heavily as the last flecks of frost fluttered to the ground. Gwen's face was set in an inscrutable expression as she sized me up. Her fingers twitched closer to her hip, where the handgun Cliff had loaned her was tucked away. I could feel her indecision warring within.

"I had hope for your kind. Thought you might be different than the other bastards out there," Gwen said. "Now? I know better."

A long, gut-wrenching scream split through the air, drawing us apart. I took flight immediately, conjuring defensive spellwork to both palms. The sound came again, clawing its way through the trees—from the direction of the outpost. The faint roar of other voices followed, inspiring a sickening dread to squeeze my chest.

Jon. Cliff.

I flew to the edge of the dilapidated walkway, scanning the horizon. The misty silhouette of the buildings in the distance had not changed, but *something* had happened.

"Relax," Gwen's voice came directly below me, and I turned to see she had followed me to observe. "It's probably just some skirmish. There's always some kind of bullshit going on between a few trigger-happy assholes."

Her tone was so readily dismissive, it ignited something feral in me. "That didn't sound like a *skirmish*. Someone's hurt." I faced her, my heart drumming. That dread persisted at the edges of my senses, pulsing. If something happened to Jon and Cliff because I didn't act—

"I'm going after them," I announced, steeling my resolve.

"*Jesus*, you're a little martyr, aren't you? I told you, it's *nothing—*"

"I didn't ask you to come with me."

I started forward, only to have Gwen step into my path. "Your scary boyfriend told you to stay put," she reminded me in a heavy breath.

"And you always do what you're told?" I asked, my cold smirk a silent challenge.

The scream had turned into a faint sob, carrying across the water. I strained to make out any familiar tones, a trace of Jon or

Cliff's voice in the distant chaos. My mind raced with possibilities, each darker and more dreadful than the last.

There could be more than weakened monsters housed here. There could be other fairies out there. Or even—

My eyes slid back to Gwen, my insides churning.

A trap.

"Did you set them up?" I asked, my voice a hoarse thread.

"What? No!" Gwen's eyes widened, and she recoiled a step back. But I was done listening. I strengthened my spellwork, frost climbing up my arms, mist clouding behind me that made leaves crackle and freeze on the ground.

"Get out of my way," I said.

"Sunshine, you've got to fucking reel it in."

I didn't have time for this. If something had gone wrong, Jon and Cliff didn't have the luxury of waiting.

I struck, aiming for the ground. In an instant, Gwen's boots were frozen to the earth and ice was crawling up to her knees. As she cried in outrage, I halted the spell and didn't dare turn back to look at her. She was locked in place—at least long enough to buy me time. I bolted across the water, trying to tune out her pleading shrieks.

"Come back! Sylvia, you don't know what the fuck you're doing! They'll kill you!"

Dodging past waterlogged trees, I sailed over the stream—avoiding the direct path of the bridge to ensure I didn't come across another hunter. My nerves stood further on end as I approached the outpost. The minimal hours of sleep and the moisture in the air left me winded far too soon. I paused to catch my breath, wings heavy as I surveyed my surroundings.

The building was far bigger than I thought, sporting only one entry point out front that I could see. I glimpsed movement through the grimy windows—hunters milling about like menacing shadows. Could I fight them all off if they already got the jump on Jon and Cliff? It seemed so reasonable at the time, but now I cursed the boys under my breath for making me stay behind and cursed myself even worse for allowing it.

For all I knew, they had been killed ten minutes ago.

The thought set me in motion again. Idle traps, nets, and chains were strewn about the wrap-around walkway, setting my teeth on edge. I had no doubt that this fortress was crawling with iron, but the unmistakable sensation of a *monster* nearby absorbed the entire attention of my senses.

The commotion I'd heard from across the bridge wasn't quite as raucous, but a group of voices still came from around the side of the building. I flitted as close as I dared, perching on a branch to observe. My stomach churned as I caught sight of a giant chain-link dome.

The Pit.

It was two stories high, a jagged patchwork of metal, barbed wire, and a half-dozen other reinforcements. A creature lay inside, gulping down what I could only assume were human remains. Deep crimson pooled in streaks across the concrete floor of the enclosure, gleaming under the sun. The beast resembled a large wildcat, but its bear-like ears and paws told me this was a shapeshifting creature between forms.

My people didn't have a name for this creature, but I had seen sketches in one of Cliff's journals—*alps*. Meticulous ink and graphite drawings had depicted silvery eyes within uncanny forms of various animals—dogs too large for their form, eagles halfway transformed into serpents, and massive predatory felines like this one.

Muscling through my nausea, I refocused on the surroundings of the Pit. At least a dozen humans were gathered around the cage, amicably talking with each other. One of the men scooped up a rock to pelt at the creature. The alp rose to lunge against the cage, only to hiss in pain when another man jabbed it with a band of silver to sear its flesh. Laughter rose through the air, making my blood heat.

The creature itself deserved little sympathy, but the hunters' glee was barbaric and cruel, serving no noble purpose. Perhaps Elysian legends about hunters had been entirely right, and Jon and Cliff were merely the exception to the rule.

You've seen him hunt, haven't you?

I shooed away Gwen's words. Jon wouldn't stoop to such behavior. He and Cliff killed monsters swiftly. They didn't wait around to grin at the pain they inflicted or relish their trophies.

Still, I searched the hunters' faces, their forms. Jon and Cliff weren't among them. I bit down on panic and tried to remember what the boys were wearing as I glanced at the dark scraps of fabric strewn about the floor of the Pit.

I couldn't be sure. I needed to search the inside of the building.

Snapping my wings into motion, I considered my options. To my dismay, the fortress was practically airtight, even for me. The side entrance beside the Pit had constant activity, and I couldn't squeeze through a crack in the reinforced windows.

I came to the harrowing conclusion that the only way inside was through the front door. There was less activity there, less eyes. Humans didn't tend to pay much mind to things they could confuse with a dragonfly. The sun was brightening through the haze, but that meant I didn't need my glow to see. I could fly right over their heads or under their noses, if I was careful enough.

A hulking human sat by the door, occasionally looking up from the machete he was sharpening to chime in conversation with a few others that leaned against the entryway railing. In a twisted way, they reminded me of Ayden and the Entry Watch outside Elysia, vigilantly monitoring the entrance.

Perching on the gutter, I watched the heavy mist for any sign of movement. From here, I could look down at the top of the hulking man's balding head and the profiles of his companions.

To them, I would be nothing more than a fluttering leaf if they looked up.

But the walkway remained empty. As the minutes ticked on, my heart began to pound anew. The muffled chatter and movement from inside made the walls vibrate, mocking my anxious waiting. My plan hinged on the door opening. But no one was coming.

Fucking stars.

I steadied my breath, mopping sweat from my face with the draped hood of my wrap blouse. Cliff's voice suddenly snapped in my memory, *"You hyperventilate, you're fucked. Understood? That's not an option."*

His lessons on patience didn't account for this situation. There had to be an opening somewhere. The hunters who maintained this establishment couldn't possibly account for the sturdiness of every wooden board in such humid conditions. As I paced the gutter, searching for a gap between the top of the wall and the roof, something shiny over the door caught my eye. Months ago, it would have been nothing more than a nameless human gadget. Now, I knew a security camera when I saw one.

I'd flown right past it. *Fuck. Fuck!*

Darting away to avoid the camera's eye, I found myself dangerously close to the guards in my beeline to reach the crates piled near the edge of the walkway.

I landed on the boarded ground, certain I was out of the hunters' and camera's sight. Perhaps my way inside was lower to the ground, anyway. If I could find a path under the floorboards… I wrinkled my nose at the thought, but I was too desperate to truly care about having to wade through muck.

As I made my careful way around the crates, several creatures moved within. My senses clicked. It felt unnervingly similar to what I'd experienced after the car wreck. Muted but *there*. Swallowing hard, I searched for the source, determined to not be caught off guard.

One of the crates was not a crate at all but a tank of water. The edges were reinforced with bronze. I inched closer to the grimy glass and nearly screamed when a face appeared on the other side. I covered my mouth, eyes wide as the monster and I regarded each other.

A siren.

She looked young. Malnourished. Terrified. And though her eyes were drenched in darkness, eerie in every way, the creature's expression lit up at the sight of me. Perhaps she thought a meal had wandered into her grasp.

She pressed her hands against the tank. *"Mistress. I found you. You're here."*

I gasped. Her mouth hadn't moved, but I could hear her voice in my head, clear as day. The sensation reminded me far too much of the Ancients, and that alone tempted me to move on and ignore her. But I stayed rooted in place. *Mistress?*

"What do you mean you found me?" I breathed.

"They plan to strip my flesh, to steal my bones and scales and blood." The siren made a mournful humming noise.

A voice roared from above. "Shut the fuck up!" The tank rattled as a hunter on the other side kicked it.

The siren regarded me desperately.

"Free me," she said in her silent voice.

I shuddered. "You… You drown people," I whispered. "Innocent people. You eat them."

The siren shook her head, face twisting into desperation. *"My tribe's creed prevents seeking man prey without provocation. Have mercy, Mistress. I want to go home."*

She might be lying. Or she might not.

But my heart lurched. I saw far too much of myself in her, and I couldn't stop thinking—who were these hunters protecting through these barbarous torture methods? *Who?*

I couldn't stop the first spread of ice that emanated from me. My spellwork webbed up the glass, beginning at the corner and spreading fast. There was a split second when I could have reeled it in, but *stars*, I couldn't make myself do it. Instead, I lifted my hands, magic pulsing bright beneath my skin, and let it pour out unchecked. I froze the side of the tank facing me, obscuring my view of the siren. I couldn't see her anymore—just the thick reflection of my own spellwork over the grimy glass.

Even when the crackling ice broke the quiet, drawing a hunter's startled voice, I didn't stop. I couldn't.

I stepped out of the way just before giving a final thrust—a blow that shattered the frozen glass with a deafening crack. Water exploded from the tank. I veered away, but a wave slammed into me and stole my breath, splattering my wings. I landed hard on my back, my view of the sky swimming in doubles. The siren spilled out and clawed into the narrow gap between the walkway and the main building, vanishing into the brackish depths.

Commotion exploded behind me, shouts amounting to "*What the fuck was that?*" ringing out.

I pushed myself up and tried to fly, desperate, groaning—but my wings clung to my wet skin, heavy and sodden. *Useless.*

A shudder wracked me—painfully aware of how exposed I was as I scrambled for cover on foot. The crates around the shattered tank were shoved aside and nearly smashed into me. I threw myself out of the way, but it wasn't enough. In my desperate dive, I found myself staggering face to face with a hunter scanning the deck—two guns raised. His eyes locked on me.

"Sweet Jesus in Heaven…" A half-burned cigarette fell from his mouth.

"What is it?" a voice demanded from behind him.

"It's—I think it's a fucking fairy! Get the iron!"

He stowed one gun to free his hand and lunged for me.

I was grounded, but I still had my magic. I could survive this. And for once, the moisture in the air was on my side.

I shouted the offensive spell, sending a flurry of razor-sharp icicles behind me as I bolted in the other direction. Pierced flesh squelched, followed by a shout of pain.

As I sprinted, I was struck by the distance to the nearest cluster of trees. *Too far.* There was no foliage to hide behind—only the open walkway and the unforgiving water dozens of feet below.

I cursed, crashing to my knees as my foot caught on a gap in the old wood. As I scrambled to stand, I heard the front doors fly open. More hunters were coming.

I managed three more steps before a hand caught me around the middle. My wings screamed in agony, crumpled against my back. My ribs threatened to shatter under the tremendous pressure.

"Got it!" It was the cruel voice of the machete-wielding guard, the one who had kicked the siren's tank.

There was no time to hesitate, to consider mercy. If I didn't act *now*, I'd die. Somehow, a clarity gripped me despite my heart pounding like a drum in my ears. Rather than pull ice from the air, I focused under the man's skin. Blood vessels froze and shredded within his fingers, his palm, then burst through his skin in pinkened crystals.

His howling curse deafened me as he spiked me back onto the boards.

Fresh agony erupted through me. Every breath hurt. I turned onto my hands and knees and crawled toward the edge of the walkway. I couldn't run anymore—I needed to jump. Drowning was a kinder fate than being at the hands of hunters, but perhaps I could still save myself. My fingers gripped the edge of a board. If I could freeze the water into the right shape, I could slide down and get under the walkway, race back to the trees on a frozen platform. I could get out of sight—

Amidst the hunter still screaming about his forever-ruined hand, I couldn't react to another approaching until it was too late.

Something slammed around me.

I tried to draw in a full breath, tried to form the words to shred this hunter's hand, too. I plunged my hand into my pocket for the gem shard. With that added magic, I could go further—I could freeze him solid from the inside out.

But gravity tipped, and I was forced to grit my teeth together to keep from biting my tongue in half. When my world righted itself, I found a small wooden floor beneath me. A clanging sound rattled my senses.

Bars. They had caged me.

As I tried to summon the gem's magic to free myself, I felt as though my soul was being ripped to shreds. Doubling over, I gasped in agony. The wooden bottom of the cage gritted against my knees. The enchanted cold on my skin was gone, snuffed out like a choked flame.

The world blurred. With each attempted spell, I felt emptier. I reached for the bars but stopped short when I became aware of the crackling heat billowing from it.

Iron.

11
JON

The commotion in the Pit ebbed into the steady hum of the swamp as we made our way behind the main building, though the faint echoes still carried—sharp clinks of metal on metal and occasional bursts of shouting. The alp had shifted into the form of a panther, its sleek body coiled with fury as it viciously lunged at the hunters who subdued it from the other side of the cage.

The familiar cocktail of brackish water and old wood clung to the walkway, but as we approached the captive vampire, a new smell began to weigh in the air. The stench of flesh and decay, along with something more bitter—like vinegar, cloying and foul.

The vampire's clothes hung off it in shreds, leaving much of its skin exposed to sunlight. He groaned in his throat as we stepped closer, something that might have been a growl if he were at full strength.

Cliff whistled low under his breath. "I'm not gonna sugarcoat it. Your modeling days are long gone."

"Isn't the entertainment over *there* riveting enough for you?" the vampire rasped. "Leave me be."

I glanced behind us to ensure that the building and crates were obscuring us enough from view. I spotted a glimpse of metal—a single machete that was kept nearby for security or torment. When I fixed my eyes back on the vampire, I noted the fear beneath that half-hearted snarl on his face. Good—maybe we could count on some cooperation.

"We're looking for some information," I said, cutting to the chase. At any moment, someone could round the corner. "How long have you been out here?"

The vampire's gaunt face twisted with disgust, and he offered no response. I watched him carefully—how his eyes darted rapidly, the faint tremors of reaction to sounds too subtle for me to catch. Tortured or not, his enhanced senses were obviously unbroken.

"You must see and hear plenty," I insisted. "The shipments of monster remnants that are circulating through this place—where are they going? Who's the buyer?"

"I smell the ash of my kin on you," the vampire said in a low voice. A long, rasping inhale followed. "Centuries old. A lineage destroyed. Why should I tell you anything?"

"Your *kin* was keeping a human farm," Cliff scoffed. "Pretty pathetic that a centuries-old lineage was reduced to holing up in a Blockbuster. If you ask me, we did them a favor."

The pinched expression on the vampire's face flickered with curiosity, and I could see the question he wanted to ask. I seized the opportunity to keep him invested, and more importantly— *talking*.

"Does the name *Giovanni* ring a bell?" I asked.

A sharp breath rattled through the vampire. He looked between us slowly, a glint in his eyes. Mourning, but also a hint of relief. "That name takes me back. Giovanni was always a bit of an arrogant prick—but generous. I've never seen anyone more willing to give someone the shirt off his own back."

I rolled my eyes. The vampire's withered lips twitched in what might've been a smirk, savoring my obvious disgust. "I suppose there is dignity in being staked—a kinder fate than this," he said, grimacing at the cut of sunlight across his scabbed torso. He looked between Cliff and me, sunken eyes moving slowly. A wariness surfaced, as though he struggled to comprehend that Giovanni was truly gone. "You really killed the alpha?"

"We're not interested in keeping prisoners," Cliff said.

Sickening familiarity jolted through me. Hadn't we told Sylvia something similar when we held her captive, demanding answers? I swallowed the memory, forced myself not to match the fear on the vampire's face to Sylvia's. This was nothing like that.

"If you help us out," Cliff went on, "we're a little nicer than the average asshole around here. How 'bout a chew toy in exchange for some info?" He held up the severed finger.

The vampire's eyes widened, his jaw going slack as a drop of blood plodded onto the wooden ground. His breathing came quicker, and he straightened, pulling against his restraints as though he had no other choice. His eyes, filled with new life, snapped between us and the finger.

"I haven't heard very much," he choked out.

"Keep your voice down," I said, drawing as close as I dared. "What *have* you heard? Where are the crates going, and who's paying for them?"

"Different locations. Some for their rarity. Some for—for study. Experimentation, if you ask me." He looked desperately at the severed finger. "That's all I know."

Cliff lifted an eyebrow—a mocking expression that didn't quite match the alarm sparkling through his intense gaze. One of our tried and true tactics for wheedling out information: making the mark feel all the more isolated.

"Experimentation?" Cliff asked, forcing down a chuckle. "You think some fucking scientists are playing with monster parts?"

"Don't act so surprised," the vampire snapped, his gaze hardening. "You hunters—always acting like humanity is above such atrocities. Perfectly ordinary humans took no issue with experimenting on their own kind during the Second World War, so long as they were born on different soil. I saw it with my own eyes."

This gave me pause. Looking at this haggard, sore-covered creature, it was hard to imagine the man he had once been so many years ago. Perhaps a soldier on the front lines, serving his country. There was something tragic, seeing where his road had ultimately led him.

The vampire's gaze turned distant, but as another drop of blood hit the boards, he snarled and pulled feverishly against his restraints. "They come at night," he panted, somewhat desperately. "Uniformed. Armored vehicles. That's all I've seen—I swear to you."

Additional needle-like teeth were filling his mouth. His groans were on the verge of becoming animalistic bellows. I elbowed Cliff to give the vampire his prize, hoping that would shut him up.

Cliff tossed the finger, and the vampire devoured it whole—an anguished, sorry sight.

The vampire slumped, shoulders heaving with relieved breaths. His calm lasted for about five seconds before he snapped his head back up, eyes wide. He strained against the silver chains, making them clank.

"*More*," he growled under his breath. Then his voice rose. "I need more!"

Cliff seized the vampire's rotting scalp, jerking his head forward. "Tell us what else you know, and we'll get you more."

But the vampire was too far gone to listen. He snarled with bloodlust, fighting his restraints with a fervor that couldn't be stopped by any promise. He made a vicious pass at Cliff's arm, who recoiled from range.

I reached back and grabbed one of the machetes atop the crate.

"There's nothing more we can get from him—not like this," I said, exchanging a look with Cliff.

Lunging forward, I decapitated the vampire with one clean swing.

In the sudden silence that followed, I found myself imagining if Sylvia were with us—wondered what she would truly think. Even she would have had to agree that a swift death was kinder than a torturous end under the sunlight.

"I was going to use that, you idiot," a voice snapped from behind.

The familiar drawl sent a chill down my spine, and before I whirled to face him, I knew I'd be looking at a man who'd nearly handed us into a painful end.

Rhett Iverson stood a few feet away. His livid stare faltered into surprise. I saw the memories hit him, too: fir trees lined by silvery moonlight, the acrid smell of smoldering skin, flames casting our faces in flickering hues.

Cliff braced in unison beside me. My grip tightened on the machete.

Somehow, the grin that spread on Rhett's face was more alarming than his ire. He smoothed a hand through his tousled chestnut hair, chuckling. "Well, I was wondering when I'd see you two around here. You know that vamp wasn't going anywhere, right? What a waste."

He stepped closer, cocking his head to observe the slow roll of the decapitated head along the wooden slates. I flicked my gaze over him, noting how Rhett's lean frame bore more muscle now—no longer the scrawny young man we'd once known. He sported a cropped beard that framed his face well, and his clothes looked clean and new.

"Didn't look like you were getting much use out of him with all the junk back here," I muttered.

"You'd be surprised how often I get a line on someone looking for a still-breathing vamp," Rhett said with a shrug. His gaze drifted back toward the vampire's corpse, appraising what remained.

"Yeah? How much are they going for these days?" Cliff asked. "Up there with prowler eyes?"

The jab made Rhett's sharp blue eyes tighten around the edges, but he managed a strained laugh. "Come on, guys, you're not still hung up on ancient history, are you? No hard feelings."

"Hard feelings?" Cliff looked about five seconds away from decking him. "You fucked us, Rhett. You nearly got us *killed* for a damn payout."

"Did I? Or did I just make the best of a tight situation?" Rhett pursed his lips, a faux-innocent sneer. "Come on, I thought you guys could handle it! I mean, look at you. Alive and well and violent as ever. Clearly, I was right."

He motioned at us with a sweeping gesture—a movement which brought a small iron pin on his collar to my attention. All my time hunting, I had only ever seen it on Cain.

"They really made you marshal?" I said, not bothering to mask my flat disdain.

Rhett flashed me a bright smile. "The people have spoken."

"Did they?" Cliff folded his arms over his chest. "Last I checked, you couldn't shoot a deer if it was standing right in front of you, but now you're in charge of an entire outpost?"

Rhett laughed, the sound echoing across the waterlogged cypress forest around us. He strode over to take a seat against a steel drum with a weathered *Hazardous Material Storage* sticker peeling on its side. He propped one foot on the side of the vampire's severed head, rocking it slightly.

"Look, Goldilocks, I may not be on your level with the world-class sharpshooting, but I do know how to run a business," Rhett said.

"This isn't a business," I cut in.

"It is now." There was an edge to Rhett's voice that made me pause—some of the irreverence replaced by something sharp and cold. Still, he kept a lazy smile on his face as he jutted his chin toward the weathered wood and steel of the outpost looming behind us. "What do you think of the place?"

"You mean the restrictions fucking up our day?" Cliff asked.

Behind Rhett, I spotted movement in the window. Three men—what looked like two hunters and an archivist—were idling by the grimy glass. They busied themselves with a map laid out on a table, but I didn't miss the way their eyes flickered towards us periodically—keeping tabs on their marshal. Rhett may have come outside unaccompanied, but he certainly wasn't alone.

"Think of it as opportunities," Rhett answered placatingly. "Welcome to the concept of *commerce*. You realize the fine people of this outpost can actually get paid for their work now? On top of that, I got more specialized medics on site—you can get cleared to take one along with you if you're put on a riskier hunt. Hell, I even snagged a couple of attorneys who help hunters out of legal mess with the local law if they get sloppy taking out a target."

"In return for what?" I scoffed. "Hunters do what we do to help people, not to make a quick buck for a con artist."

Rhett snorted. "Oh, please. I hate to break it to you guys, but not everyone shares your little white knight fantasy. Half of these people would sell out their own grandma for a six-pack." He paused, lifting his eyebrows at us expectantly. "This is your cue to say '*thank you, Rhett*' if it's not too much to ask."

I rolled my eyes, blood heating. "Get fucked."

Realizing I was clutching the weapon in my hand with a white-knuckle grip, I hesitantly set the dripping machete back on a crate—though I stayed within reach. I tried to keep my tone even.

"You've got an investor," I said, letting the accusation hang in the air. "Someone's helping you."

Rhett heaved a long sigh, like this was the most tedious conversation he'd had all week. "People need things, I provide things. That's Econ-101, big guy."

"You're a snake," I growled.

"You trash my product and insult me? Not gonna lie, starting to hurt my feelings a little bit." Rhett kicked the vampire head, where it wobbled an uneven path along the walkway until it halted against another steel barrel.

Cliff stepped closer, looming over Rhett's seated position. "Where's it all going? The siren, the vampire, the monster parts—who are you selling to?"

"Not that I can go into much detail—but *some* of it does go to a very good cause. I'd be happy to bring you into the fold—show you what it's all about. We could use someone with your skills, Everett."

"Shove it," Cliff said, expression darkening.

"I'm serious. I've heard the stories of what you're capable of, and…" Rhett paused to let out a whistle. "You have no idea what a partnership between us could do for you. Besides, we both know you've done worse for less."

"At least I don't need to buy people to stand beside me," Cliff snapped. "I didn't come here to have my ass kissed. We need a restock on silver, and we'll be on our way."

Rhett straightened off the steel barrel, his amicable tone sharpening into something authoritative. "Well, the way things work around here, you're not getting what you want until you contribute to the outpost."

I clenched my teeth. I hated this. I hated needing *anything* from this smug bastard. Even being in the same space with him made my skin crawl.

"What, is this a country club now?" I said. "We have to pay dues?"

"It means doing what I say," Rhett drawled. "Silver's a hot commodity. I can't just go handing it out to every pair of moody drifters that pass through. But relax—it's nothing you won't enjoy."

Fishing into his pocket, he pulled out a folded piece of paper—I caught a glimpse of a list. It looked like it had been printed on letterhead, with some sort of green insignia at the top. I didn't get a long enough look to tell for sure, but I *swore* I'd seen that strange E-shaped logo—the same symbol that had been littered about the abandoned lab in that church basement.

"Our benefactors have particular requests," Rhett said, scanning it. "Lucky for you, the current bounties should be simple enough for seasoned hunters like you."

My gaze followed the list back to his pocket, and the subsequent look I shared with Cliff needed no words. He'd seen what I had—and we had to get our hands on it.

Cliff drew an aggravated breath and started forward to brush past Rhett toward the main hall. "We're not doing your grocery shopping, you psycho."

Rhett moved to block him—as I had anticipated. "Everett, hang on. You'll want to hear me out."

"Because that worked out so well last time?" Cliff scoffed.

Rhett sighed, rolling his eyes. "Okay, yes, I'll admit that I may have *slightly* overstepped with the whole using you as bait thing. But this is different strokes completely, trust me. Now… I can give you everything you've ever wanted."

Cliff's smirk was sharp enough to gut a person. "And here I thought you didn't swing that way. Do me a favor and buy me a drink first."

For the first time, Rhett's smirk vanished altogether. He turned red, eyes flying open wide, and *finally*, I caught a glimpse of the unhinged young man who'd been with us on that prowler hunt.

"Watch it," Rhett gritted out, his voice low and restrained.

Cliff's chuckle was a cruel sound. "Oh, right—I forgot you're too busy fucking your mom, aren't you?"

Rhett lunged, shoving Cliff against the wooden railing, his fists knotted in the fabric of Cliff's plaid shirt.

We hadn't gathered much about Rhett's family when we'd first met him, but we knew enough to know most of the money he scraped together back then mostly went to taking care of his mother back in Georgia. And, of course, rumors followed through hunter circles—the kind that twisted into something uncomfortable over the years. Something about Rhett doting a little too much, a little too *close*.

Judging by how Rhett's jaw ticked, it was still raw enough to strike a chord—and Cliff had hit it dead-on.

"Don't talk about her," Rhett seethed. "Don't you fucking talk about my mother. You're still valuable, Everett—even if someone puts a few holes in you first. Am I clear?"

For a moment, Cliff's cocky mask slipped and true confusion clouded his expression. "Valuable to who?"

I shoved between them, slipping two fingers into Rhett's pocket as I pushed him back.

"Hey!" I barked. "That's enough—get off him. We'll pick up silver elsewhere."

I transferred the folded list into my jacket in the same breath. Grabbing Cliff's shoulder as though I'd have to physically steer him away, we rounded the corner.

"Don't fucking walk away from me!" Rhett shouted, his quick stride snapped on the wood behind us.

We barely passed the threshold of the main building when commotion came from the other side of the hall. At first, I worried that Rhett had remotely raised some sort of silent alarm to sic the rest of the outpost officers on us in retaliation, but he shoved right past us to investigate the growing crowd.

The main entrance was swarming with people trying to glimpse what was happening.

"Rhett!" Another hunter intercepted him in front of us, his breaths heavy and eyes wide. "Your siren—it got away."

"What?" Rhett bolted toward the commotion, seeming to forget us entirely.

As he muscled toward the front, another figure forced into the hall, shoving against the growing crowd's flow. I squinted, momentarily bewildered. The person was so short, I briefly mistook them for a child.

Then I got a good look at her face—*Gwen*. Her eyes locked onto mine, and even from a distance, her wild desperation was visible. A faint ringing filled my ears as Cliff and I ran to meet her halfway.

Sylvia. Where's Sylvia?

"What happened?" Cliff asked, grasping her shoulders as she came to an unsteady stop.

Gwen breathlessly gaped at us, looking lost for words. Flecks of ice caked Gwen's ankles and combat boots.

I stepped closer, setting my shadow over her. "What did you do? Where is she?"

"She—" Gwen carefully scanned the distance between us and the lingering hunters in the building. She lowered her voice, eyes swimming with apology that made me sick to my stomach. "I couldn't stop her."

It started with a shout at the door—"A winged creature has been captured!"

The words split me open. Word traveled like wildfire, igniting the two dozen hunters piling outside. The female creature had been on the offensive—set the siren free, obliterated the bouncer's hand into a bloody stump.

Panic set into me like a knife in my chest. I shot a frantic look at Cliff, whose wide eyes mirrored my dread.

They were taking her to the Pit.

Gwen's presence reeked of betrayal, but I would deal with her later. We burst back through the side door with the stragglers, and chaos hit us like a wall. The crowd flooded the rickety walkway around the Pit, passing money around, betting on which monster would best the other—the fairy or the alp.

Some of the onlookers were awestruck, jaws hanging open as one of the keepers unlocked the Pit, wielding a small cage and a cattle prod. Like us, they'd thought fairies were a drunkard's myth. It would be safer for them to believe that. Now Sylvia was fighting for her life like a goddamn sideshow attraction.

"Twenty against the fairy?" A woman decked in denim and fighting leathers waved a sweaty bill toward me.

"Fuck yourself," I answered reflexively, not slowing my path.

"Damn. Suit yourself, asshole."

My vision tunneled on the portable cage that Pit keeper was boasting—obscured as more bodies circled the domed enclosure, eager for the best view.

Cliff grabbed the collar of a gangly hunter pressed against the fencing and yanked him out of the way. The man protested colorfully but cowed at the icy glare Cliff sent back at him. I shoved in beside Cliff. My height proved an advantage; the hunter to my right sized me up irately before settling for grumbling and setting his eyes back on the center of the Pit. Begrudgingly, I allowed space for Gwen to peer between us.

The crowd erupted as the keeper emptied the small cage—and Sylvia tumbled into view, landing on her hands and knees. Her iridescent wings twitched, flinging off drops of water, and her bare arms trembled as she pushed herself up. That carrier cage had iron bars. She hadn't been burned, but I could see how the proximity alone had affected her.

"Sylvia said she hunted with you these past months," Gwen said.

"And?" I asked tersely.

The keeper left Sylvia there on the bloodstained ground, striding over to the alp crouched defensively on the other side. It had reverted back to dog form—muzzle still red. The keeper jabbed the alp once with the cattle prod, riling it up. The dog's growl morphed into a hiss as it transformed before our eyes into the form of a lynx.

"Maybe that's a good thing," Gwen replied in a tense breath.

The keeper dodged the snapping jaws with experienced reflexes—beating the feline muzzle away with the prod. As the blow registered, the feline form flattened and coiled into that of a massive cobra. Its hood flared wide, forked tongue tasting the air rapidly. For the first time, the monster noted that the keeper was not the only thing inside the enclosure with it. The keeper retreated, casting a wary look at Sylvia as he passed. He exited, barring the door behind to join his clamoring colleagues on the other side.

"Settle your bets, boys!" he roared.

The air was thick with the smell of old blood and sweat and money changing hands. My entire world centered on Sylvia as she got to her feet. It was to my benefit that every other asshole here was gaping just as abjectly. I was frozen—my instinct to charge in and rescue her would out us all. We would have two dozen weapons on us the second I had Sylvia in my hands. I liked our odds against half of them, maybe—but these were trained killers.

"What the hell happened?" I snapped at Gwen, glancing down at her ice-ridden boots. "What did you do to her?"

Gwen's face twisted with outrage—and a flicker of fear. "Nothing!"

"Right. Should I just take your word?"

"Fucking nothing happened, I swear! Either you bagged a girl as paranoid as you, or you taught her everything she knows, Nowak."

"It's just an alp," Cliff cut in, nodding toward the furry mass inside the cage. "One thing in our favor. She has a chance." He wove his fingers through the chain link fencing, tugging. Searching for a weakness.

I desperately tried to catch Sylvia's gaze—if only to reassure her that I was there, that she wasn't alone, that we were going to get her out of there somehow. She flicked more water off her wings as she got to her feet and looked all around at the enclosure—the barbed wire and chains and deafening, hateful jeers. The cobra hissed, slithering curiously toward her. Sylvia jumped five feet into the air, giving a strangled yelp. Hunters around us laughed.

She threw her hands up, and though her mouth moved with words I couldn't make out, I realized she wasn't casting magic. She was trying to quell the creature, to sweet-talk it into submission.

After a few upward snaps, the monster shivered into another form. Its forked tongue and bared fangs morphed into a razor-sharp beak. Feathers erupted around its body, sprouting wings and talons in the space of a breath. The sight of a hawk had never inspired terror in me until now—even with the excitement roaring around me, I heard Sylvia's horrified scream clear as a bell.

My knees threatened to give in as she flew higher, dodging the chains that hung from the ceiling. As the hawk flapped toward her, she threw out a gale of icicles that snuffed out too quickly. The monster was deterred only long enough for Sylvia to dart to the other side of the enclosure.

Fuck. The proximity to the iron walls was fizzling her magic out. She'd have to put herself closer to the center to fight, exposing herself. I nearly opened my mouth to bark out the advice, only to see her catch onto the idea herself.

A few bodies away, Rhett's voice carried over the roar of onlookers. "You fucking morons. Do you have any idea how much fairy blood is worth? That alp's gonna rip her apart and leave nothing behind!"

"We couldn't just leave her out," someone protested. "Look what she did to Russell's hand!"

Rhett rounded on the man who'd spoken, donned in dark, practical clothes that blended into the marshy woods around us. He staggered a step back as Rhett's icy gaze settled on him with an unnerving weight.

"First of all, Austin, you have the intelligence and personality of a used tampon, and everybody here knows it," Rhett said. "Second—if you *ever* toss a fairy into the Pit without consulting me first, I will personally feed you this alp one piece at a time."

Austin paled, his gaze flighty even as he tried to maintain a semblance of dignity. "Yes, of course. Sorry."

Rhett shoved past him, gripping the chainlink dome to watch Sylvia.

For a single second, I thought that could be the ticket to saving her. If preserving her parts was reason enough to stop this circus act, I'd have a better chance of saving her.

But one of the Pit keepers nodded towards Rhett. "Doubt a little thing like that will get ripped apart. It'll probably be swallowed whole."

Rhett's gaze barely flicked to acknowledge him. "As long as I can slice open the alp's stomach before she's digested, I'll get what I need. My client's gonna be pissed about the siren, but a fairy's more than a worthy replacement."

My fingers dug into the chain link, itching to rip out his tongue and shut him up forever.

Cliff grabbed my shoulder, stealing my attention. "Cover me. No one's looking our way, right?" he pulled out his gun and discreetly checked its magazine. "I can make the shot, take it out before it gets to her."

"It's moving quick," Gwen muttered. "What if you hit her?"

He smirked tightly. "Remember who you're talking to?"

"They'll know it was you," she snapped.

The crowd erupted with new noise—some with disappointment and outrage, others with awe. I put a hand over Cliff's wrists to make him lower his gun. "Wait."

Although Sylvia had been herded to the middle of the enclosure, she was anything but helpless. She shot volley after volley, hitting her mark almost every time. The few stray bursts of spellwork felt intentional as they smashed against the Pit's walls and sent some of the more vicious audience members skittering back to avoid shards.

Most of the hunters seethed at the collateral attack, but a heavily tattooed hunter beside me chuckled and elbowed me. "Adorable little thing, isn't it?"

Sylvia zipped aside to avoid the hawk's trajectory, but there was no need. It careened toward the ground with a pained screech, wings blooming with black blood. She didn't relent, not even when the creature weakly began to change again. The alp collapsed, motionless, a bizarre cross between a hawk and an alligator.

"Yeah, adorable," I muttered in response, stifling a proud smile.

Another roar rippled through the spectators as bets were lost and won—judging by the disproportionate anger, hardly anyone expected Sylvia to still be breathing. I observed Sylvia with a beat of pride. She stayed hovering over the alp, tearing her eyes away only once she was sure it was dead. Her shoulders rose and fell with frantic pants. She turned slowly, clearly searching the crowd, but she was facing the wrong way.

"Maybe they'll keep her in there like the alp," I whispered to Cliff, tentative hope blooming. These people liked having something to gawk at. Something to train with. After everyone had their fill of staring, we could figure out how to free her without getting caught.

"Okay, enough fucking around," Rhett said, glaring impatiently at one of the Pit keepers. "Open the door."

Shit. Fuck.

Rhett pulled an iron blade from his jacket, making my blood run cold.

"Wait—I can do it, Rhett," Austin staggered forward, patting the weapons holstered across his person.

"I need this thing intact," Rhett said, barely sparing him a look. "The wings alone are gonna buy you folks a new building—and then some. I don't need your butterfingers fucking that up."

I glanced at Sylvia. Her flight faltered like she might collapse right there in midair as the door rattled, but instead, she shot upward. Her frantic path took her around the top of the dome in search of an escape that she would never find.

But I could change that.

I forced my way forward. "Wait! I'll do it!"

Rhett cast a bored look at me over his shoulder. "Stay out of this, Nowak. You've made it clear you're not interested in playing ball with me."

"You saw what she did to your guy. You really wanna risk losing a hand for this?" I demanded, fixing Rhett with a blazing look.

"And you do?" Rhett lifted his eyebrows. A few other hunters echoed his incredulous chuckle.

I pressed forward, easing away from the other hunters surrounding the door. "How many of these creatures have you squared off with head-to-head?"

He scoffed. "I could ask you the same."

"We took out a nest in Wyoming," Cliff said, appearing behind me.

A lie tinged with truth. It unsettled me to think what had come of Elysia after our departure.

"Get us some iron," I insisted. "Cliff and I can snuff her out with no more than a burn here or there. She'll be intact, wings and all."

Rhett narrowed his eyes. "A whole nest, huh?"

I tried to steady my breathing, knowing that I was too eager, too emotional. And he was trying to figure out *why*.

When Rhett hesitated in thought, Cliff tacked on, "C'mon, what happened to us being assets?"

A slow smile grew on Rhett's face as he looked between us. "Tradition says no more than one at a time in the Pit. That's one I can't help but agree with. Better decide quickly." Then he shouted over his shoulder for someone to bring out an iron weapon—no blades or bullets allowed, lest I damage my target too much.

A heavy hand clapped my shoulder. Cliff spun me to face him.

"You don't have to do this," Cliff said under his breath, giving me an intense stare—a look that promised he was just as willing to put himself on the line to bring Sylvia home.

"Watch my back," I said.

"Nowak." Gwen appeared from behind Cliff, giving a small shake of her head. "What the hell are you gonna do?"

I scowled at her. "Whatever I have to."

Giving Rhett a meaningful look, I stepped forward—this time, there was no resistance. Two Pit keepers stripped me of my weapons and handed me an iron bar. Rhett smiled at me, leaning in close.

"I always thought you were the wildcard hunter between the two of you," he said in a conspiratorial whisper. "Prove me wrong, yeah? I don't want a drop of that bitch's blood gone to waste. And hey—maybe I'll throw in that silver you're after if you do this right."

I took a shuddering breath—hating the smell of him, how he reeked of salt and cologne and bloodlust.

"Touch me again," I said. "And I'll cave your head in before hers."

His face paled slightly. "Easy, Nowak. Save that spirit for the Pit." Rhett pulled away, sauntering toward the bookie to observe the newest round of cash bets.

One of the Pit keepers unwound the heavy iron chains and lifted the thick wooden blocker from the door. The door swung open into the dimly lit holding walkway, flooding the air with the stale tang of the alp's blood. A fine mesh of steel netting separated me from the fighting ring's inner dome—the last fragile barrier between me and what I had to do. My hand closed around the iron bar, gritty and cold against my palm. The sharp, metallic tang of anticipation flooded my mouth as I willed my feet to move.

"Hurry inside before it gets any ideas about flying out," someone growled near me.

I stepped in, leaving the roaring crowd at my back. The door clanged shut and locked behind me at once.

It wouldn't open again until one of us was dead.

12
SYLVIA

There was enough iron present here to massacre all of Elysia—perhaps a dozen fae villages.

Its sharp aura clouded my senses and made thinking difficult. My wings ached from prolonged flight, but I didn't have the luxury of landing to gather myself. Not if I wanted to survive.

Dodging around the dangling chains that wound through the peak of the dome, I searched the circumference for the seventh time. Surely there was a hole somewhere in the patchwork of materials, a sloppy gap someone neglected to reinforce with iron. None of the gaps were quite large enough to squeeze through without the risk of burning myself. Try as I might, I couldn't summon magic this close to the fencing to do any targeted damage to the enclosure. Even the gem shard's power was unresponsive when I plunged my hand into my pocket.

Begrudgingly, I acknowledged that the barbarians below me had done a very good job building this damn cage.

The evidence of past prisoners was written all around me—scorch residue, faint claw marks, caked blood disguised as rust. Spots in the metal had been torn away and rebuilt smarter. I couldn't fathom how many creatures had died in here, teaching a new lesson to these brutes about monster containment each time.

And now, I was the latest lesson.

Swiping panicked tears—*no, I wouldn't cry like a damn child*—I noted the fresh blood splattered on me. Bright crimson spotted my hands, my clothes. Surely not mine, and not from the near-black puddle surrounding the alp. Perhaps the blood belonged to the hunter who'd grabbed me near the entrance. If he lost function of that hand forever, I hoped he would remember me—how I was not the fragile creature I appeared.

A dozen feet below, the crowd of hunters roared with renewed fervor—twenty bloodthirsty cheers overlapping and making my ears ring.

Three figures gathered at the doorway. The heavy chains sealing the Pit clanged as they were unwound. I balled my fists at my side, bracing myself. Whoever they sent in to finish me off, I would do the same to *his* hand, too. I would leave him with nothing but ragged, frozen stumps.

If he doesn't kill you first, a demented voice rang in the back of my head.

Finally, the door creaked open, and a hulking figure filled the frame. He was easily one of the tallest humans present. Dark hair was swept off a handsome face, brows furrowing over earth-colored eyes that methodically surveyed his surroundings. He appeared to carry only a slender bar of iron as a weapon, but I knew that powerful frame was capable of great damage unaided.

"*Jon,*" I breathed, unable to believe my eyes.

He was *here*. He'd come for me.

The door slammed shut, locking audibly with a metallic scrape. I couldn't make sense of that part. Whatever the hell was happening, I wanted to face it from the safety of Jon's hands.

Choking back a sob of relief, I started toward him, only to stop short.

Why is he looking at me like that?

Someone rapped a beer can against the side of the fence near Jon. "We don't got all day here, kid. Move your ass!"

I glanced behind me to see if Jon's glower was aimed at someone else. When I faced him again, he was removing his jacket. He tossed it aside and picked up the iron rod, weighing it. His knuckles went white with devastating clarity as he secured his grip—hands that had brushed my cheek like I was a delicate treasure. Right now, I could only remember how those same hands had beheaded a vampire leader as easily as slicing an apple.

He looked so cold, yet mournful as he looked up at me, stepping closer. He didn't look like *my* Jon. I recoiled from his approach.

What's happening? I begged silently with my eyes. Jon's gaze was an unreadable storm of emotion. I couldn't pluck an answer out of the dozens churning there.

I surveyed the ravenous crowd once more. The money passing hands again, the hungry eyes. I tried to spot Cliff, but I still couldn't make him out in the chaos. I hoped he was safe.

Jon circled my position from the ground with predatory grace, careful to avoid the deformed carcass. He came to a pause just beneath me while the shouts rose to a deafening volume.

Cheering for him.

The fragile seed of hope in my chest broke. Jon wasn't here to save me. He was here to kill me.

No. I was out of my mind. He had to be pulling some kind of ruse, but the thought of what he must have in mind was unspeakable. I would not feed these monsters' bloodlust. I would not put on a show for them. There had to be another way. Jon couldn't simply free me, but surely he couldn't be blamed if I simply found a way out.

I pointedly stayed out of range, flitting higher over his head in another maddening search.

The crowd was displeased. A glint caught my eye, sailing over my head. A brown bottle shattered on the dome. Glass rained. Choking on a scream, I drove to avoid the shards. A few stray bits nicked my arms and wings.

Before I could make sense of how far down I'd flown, Jon caught me by my legs. My vision blurred as he swung me down and pinned me to a wooden crate near the door. Splinters dug into my back and wings.

I struggled, clawing at his hand. The jeering was closer, too deafening to allow me to think straight. And Jon looked just like one of them, glaring down at me with that dark gleam while his hand gripped me tighter than it should—*just like in training*. I wiggled uselessly, wondering if this was part of the ruse. I couldn't tell anymore.

If I was wrong, if he wasn't acting, my bones were going to snap in his loveless grasp.

"Jon," I gasped, and he squeezed me tighter, silencing me.

My eyes swiveled madly. There were beers in many hands. Liquid I could use. The swamp water below was too faint, too far away through the iron. But from this close... those glass bottles could save me.

Fight back.

I snapped my attention back to Jon, unsure if he had said it aloud or if it was only in my head.

The iron bar he slowly moved toward me was certainly real. The crowd roared with every inch it drew nearer to my skin. I whipped my hands up and conjured a powerful thrust of frigid air, knocking Jon back.

His grip relinquished me as he slammed into the wall, making the Pit rattle and clang.

In my mad scramble into the air, I could only think of protecting myself. Even in my panic, the hours of training surfaced like a lifeline. I conjured a wall of ice to thwart his approach as he grunted back to his feet. I wouldn't be able to maintain it for long—even with the humidity and terror-driven magic, there was only so much strength coursing through me.

The crowd gave another nasty cheer as Jon shattered the ice wall with his iron bar. He stalked toward me precisely the way he approached a monster—a serpent ready to strike with bite after bite until its prey was dead.

But in the heat of my retaliation, his expression wasn't quite so composed anymore. Something broke through the unreadable stare locked on me, and it wasn't malice or bloodlust.

Terror. Grief. Desperation.

This wasn't a man who hated me but one who cared for me beyond words, beyond reason.

And now I couldn't shake the awful thought that arrived with the realization—what if he accepted there was no possible way for me to leave this outpost alive? What if this was his last kindness toward me—a swift mercy kill to ensure that none of these other hunters tortured me to death?

His expression darkened once more as he recomposed himself.

Corner him in a no-win situation and see what he does.

He charged, swinging the rod in a wide arc. I zipped past it safely, but the proximity to the toxic metal made me all the more lightheaded. There was no time to recover. He swung again, this time far too close.

Upon his third swing, I focused my attention on the beer behind me. Liquid spurted from two bottles, coming together in a javelin aimed for Jon's face. He staggered, just as startled by my aim as I was. The discolored ice barely whistled past his head, shattering into the side of the cage and making a number of hunters curse and scatter.

Jon touched his face, interrupting a smooth line of blood that trickled from where my attack grazed him.

Stars, I wanted to heal him. I wanted to beg for his forgiveness.

But his expression hadn't changed, those empty, predator eyes fixed on me like he would not rest until I was nothing but a corpse at his feet. Everything about him drew me back to that night in Dottage, when he was but a hulking shadow hellbent on killing me for daring to exist.

Jon Nowak is dangerous.

So was I.

With a cry, I conjured another three beer javelins. Hunters shouted their ire, glass shattering as they dropped their bottles in alarm. Jon swung the iron, decimating two spears. He caught the third in his hand. Blood pooled between his fingers. He threw my weapon back at me—and missed.

I took control and redirected it before the ice could break against the cage. While he dodged, I couldn't help but wonder how he missed me by such a wide margin—was it because he had no intention of hurting me, or because the splintered ice in his palm threw off his aim?

Fuck, there had to be a way out of this alive—if I could only untangle his intentions. I flew back up, desperate for a breather. I conjured an icy shield over my head in case another beer bottle was tossed at the dome.

Below, I finally caught sight of Cliff. I'd recognize his chiseled profile and dark gold hair anywhere. He was weaving through the churning crowd, his eyes locked on me. I tried to read his face, to find some kind of answer there, but—

Something lurched at me from the corner of my eye. Iron. *Chains!*

I ducked just in time and saw Jon grabbing one of the chains, pulling hard. The connected ones at the top near me swayed and jumped, shattering the veil of ice over my head. One slammed into my knees—thank the stars for my ankle-length trousers that protected me from an agonizing burn—and sent me hurtling downward.

I gathered my bearings, only to see the *entire fucking crate* flying at me. With a shriek, I flew out of its path, flinching my hands to my ears as it exploded into splintered wood against the fence. *He isn't holding back,* I thought, tasting wood dust in my mouth.

He had herded me within three feet of him near the center of the Pit—the close quarters he needed to gain the upper hand.

Fuck him. The thought lashed through my mind, and before I knew what I was doing, my hands were poised at heart level, fingers steepled for a spell. Frost surged from my fingertips, spreading across the ground beneath Jon's feet, turning it into a slick, icy trap. My lips moved faster than my thoughts, weaving a spell to liquify the trap. I balled my fists and swung them to my sides, jerking Jon forward with a sudden, brutal force. He went sprawling, his rod clattering beside him.

That's for throwing a fucking crate at me.

"Get up, you pussy!" Someone in the crowd beat their fist against the fence. "Use the iron on her!"

Jon groaned as he pried himself up, sporting a busted lip and a gash cutting through the sleeve of his black tee. One of the nails in the deck had caught him badly. But he was on his feet with speed I couldn't decide was relieving or terrifying—and lunged for me again, the slender rod grasped in his left hand. Jon's hand closed around my legs. *Fuck*—I'd drawn too close.

I shouted a spell, summoning a spike of discolored ice between his boots. Jon cursed, releasing me to evade it. As he circled me, I focused on his footing. I had seen him fight dozens of times—I knew how he moved. I could match him blow for blow.

I shifted my focus down to his boots, an idea taking hold. I channeled all my magic at the deck, frost crawling up the leather, up to his ankles, crackling as I laid it thicker and thicker. Jon's eyes widened, and for a moment, I felt a pang of remorse. I didn't want to fight him.

Jon kicked free of the ice building on his left boot, but the right one caught. His stance wavered, cemented where he stood. I refocused on the left again, fastening that one, too. This strategy had held Gwen in the woods, and maybe it would save my life now.

Spots danced in my vision, briefly making my magic flicker and falter. I was teetering toward magic exhaustion. He knew it as well as me—I could read it in those smoldering brown eyes. I grit my teeth, conjuring a slender blade of ice from the structure at his feet, guiding it at an angle toward his throat. I let it move slowly, let panic build on his face. It was horrible that a piece of me purred at the sight of his fear. The most intimidating hunter I'd ever met, the terror of Elysian legends, dominated at my own hands.

Jon's gaze snapped up, and he wound back, hurling the iron bar straight at me.

"Fuck!" I screamed, my heart pounding as I swooped my flight low. Air rushed against my hair as it narrowly avoided the spot I'd occupied moments ago.

CRACK.

Jon was stronger than Gwen—without more reinforcement to the spellwork, my ice couldn't hold him nearly as long. The ice shattered with a deafening series of cracks as he broke free, like a thousand glass shards exploding. One of the thicker pieces slammed into my stomach, knocking the wind from my lungs.

As I flitted back up to gain control of my flight, cold metal grazed my shoulder—the end of a low-hanging chain.

An agony that was not of this world tore through me like wild-fire and stole my senses. My vision blurred. Jon's hand wrapped around my waist and pulled me out of the air.

I was on my back, pinned under his palm on the damp wood. The pressure was not crushing but frightening all the same. The gem shard pulsed in my pocket, but I couldn't hope to reach it now. I struggled to pull in a full breath as Jon knelt over me, our wide eyes locking.

It was over.

The iron bar hovered excruciatingly close to my chest, pre-pared to deliver the same soul-sucking pain that throbbed through my shoulder. Even the crowd fell into murmurs of anticipation. Looking him straight in the face, I desperately attempted to summon ice, to rip his hands apart if I must. But I couldn't. Not with the iron brushing against my blouse.

Jon's heavy breaths became visible puffs. I couldn't create searingly cold gales or icicles, but the air was freezing, clouding our world. He blinked hard as if in realization.

"*Missed*," he whispered.

I grimaced, staring up at him without comprehension.

"*Missed*." His voice was rougher, like an order.

Was he seriously mocking my missed shots right before he dealt the final blow?

Then, it hit me—*mist*.

I could hide us. I forced power behind what remained of my magic, teetering on the edge of consciousness as my iron wound burned in protest. The cloudiness thickened around us, obscuring our surroundings until it was just us two.

He inched the iron toward my exposed navel. My breathing turned to whimpers. In my feverish exhaustion, I was certain he wanted to kill me in private. Perhaps it served me right for not listening to him about staying away. I could only hope he would do it quickly and spare me the agony of the iron's burn.

But there were worse fates than dying at the hands of a man I loved.

The word split my mind—beautifully, painfully bright.

Loved.

I wish I could have told him, even if it changed nothing. A breathless sob shook through me, and something in Jon's expression broke as he read mine. He swallowed hard. The hand pinning me twitched.

He couldn't do it, I realized. *But he had to.* I gave the feeblest nod of permission. If he didn't kill me, we'd both die at the hands of those bloodthirsty onlookers.

His grip shifted, covering my arms and legs. Raising the bar high over his head, he brought it down.

I flinched.

But the pain never came. I turned my head to find the end of the iron rod grinding into the boards beside me.

I met his eyes, a conspiring sort of look filling them. He raised his eyebrows expectantly.

And I did my part—I screamed. It was the easiest thing I'd ever done. I shrieked my lungs raw, releasing every drop of fear and fury that had found a home in my bones since being captured.

My voice tapered off, followed by my magic. I fell still.

13
JON

The crowd exploded with cheers and hollers and vicious boos. Apparently, some people had a little more faith in Sylvia after seeing her annihilate the alp. Hell, if it weren't for the iron, I had no doubt that she *could* have killed me.

She was a patchwork of blood and scrapes that I didn't have time to assess as the mist faded. The image of her lying there, flushed and unmoving, made my heartbeat stagger.

"Sylv?" I breathed, quiet as possible.

The tiniest dip of her chin assured me. She was good. *Too fucking good.*

I snatched her up in a single hand, cradling her wings carefully before closing her up out of sight. Thrusting my fist triumphantly, I gave the onlookers what they wanted. I tossed the iron bar against the cage, making it clatter noisily. Sylvia flinched at the sound. I held her close to my chest, boots crunching over glass and blood as I stepped over the alp's body, sweeping up my jacket as I went.

Just a little longer, cariño.

The Pit keeper flung the door open, and I was praised with claps on the back as I exited. I sidestepped, pointedly dodging curious stares. No one could fault me for keeping my kill hidden—she was a rare prize, after all.

From the corner of my eye, I could see Cliff collecting money from bets and hurrying over with Gwen. His cheekbones were flushed—more breathless than I'd seen him in years.

"Weapons," I said flatly to the hunters who had searched me. I stuffed my leather jacket over one arm and reached out expectantly.

"Now, hang on a minute. I'd like my merchandise first." Rhett materialized beside me, clapping my shoulder. I grit my teeth against the sting of my open wound. "*Please,*" he added, a wolfish smile tugging at his lips.

"I said I'd kill her without a scratch. Didn't say anything about taking your offer." I lurched back from his touch, turning back to the young man who was clutching my knives and handgun with white knuckles. "Weapons, *now.*"

The snap of my voice made the younger man flinch—he couldn't have been more than twenty-three at most, with that wispy attempt at a beard clinging to his jaw. He looked around the others, to Rhett, and then back to me, a quiver in his voice.

"Listen, man," he said. "I know who you are, and it's an honor to meet you, but I—I'm just following orders."

I ducked closer, near enough to feel the shaky pull of his breaths. "Move," I growled.

The younger hunter staggered back a step, but he looked over my shoulder to Rhett, cowing for instruction. Gritting my teeth hard enough to feel it in my jaw, I turned back to face him, too.

"I earned the trophy," I said. "I fought for it through blood. That's the rule."

"I hate to pull the *outpost marshal* card, but…" Rhett sucked through his teeth—a mocking motion that gave me fantasies of smashing his face against the domed wall of the Pit. His eyes flickered to my closed fist. "There are some new rules. That thing set loose a damn good catch. You got any idea how rare it is to find a siren wandering alone? Especially one that young? I'm owed compensation."

"That's got nothing to do with me," I snapped.

The dull roar of the onlookers seemed to dim. That stupid half-smile on Rhett's face faltered like it was now a plaster replica of the real thing. I'd seen this unsettling coil in him before when we'd ordered him at gunpoint to stand back while we burned the prowler's corpse. His eyes were his tell—fiery, yet cold and tracking every move like a mantis ready to strike.

"You know, I have a good sense of humor but my client's not as good-natured as me." Each word dripped with that veil of Southern charm—poison hiding in honey.

"Unfortunately for you," I growled. "We don't give a shit."

Out of the corner of my eye, two other hunters—a man and a woman—stepped into the walkway, blocking any path toward the bridge.

"Just give me the body, Nowak. I'd hate to add yours to the bill. Really, it would tear me up." Rhett took a beat to look me over. His appraisal made my skin crawl. "Though… Bones of an *Appalachian Reaper* might make a mighty fine talisman to some folk. You boys are probably worth a fortune thanks to that shitty story."

I grimaced, shooting him a look for the comment. I swore I felt Sylvia flinch against my palm, too. Rhett stepped closer, one hand pushing his jacket aside to rest the handle of a 9mm tucked in the waistband of his jeans.

"I'm going to ask nicely just one more time, Nowak," he said, placing his other hand on my shoulder. "Give me the body, or you can kiss that silver goodbye."

He was too close to Sylvia. Too close with that *goddamn smirk*. "Get your fucking hand off—"

CRACK.

A gunshot sliced through the air, close enough to graze the fabric of Rhett's outstretched sleeve and leave a shallow, bloody smear in its wake before it tore through a crate of supplies.

Everything stopped.

Rhett froze, eyes flashing to the side to find the offender. I didn't have to look to know who had fired.

"Touch him again," Cliff's voice cut through the tension, "and I won't miss next time."

Cliff shoved through the crowd to put himself between Rhett and me, Gwen pressed close to his side. Her borrowed handgun was drawn, clutched in a low position between both hands. The faint ripple of surprise that she was defending us, not working against us, ebbed through me.

Rhett's chuckle chilled me as he glanced between us—a stark contrast to the rage building behind his eyes. "You two are adorable. I mean, *wow*. Points for entertainment value. I'll let you keep the wings, how's that sound?"

He silently gestured for a hunter behind us to move in toward me. Cliff raised his arm and fired off a round that clipped the man's shoulder. The hunter cursed, staggering back while others began murmuring, gazes shifting between Cliff and me with both wariness and rage.

Turning back to Rhett, Cliff matched the cold smile point for point. "How about you suck my dick?"

Gwen snorted, and I caught Rhett's glare shift toward her before sweeping over the hunters around him—as though her laughter might be contagious.

Rhett stared at him for a long moment, a vein twitching in his forehead like a sick beacon. "You know, I feel bad for your father," he ground out, his drawl stripped of its trademark charm. "God gave him one son, and *this* is what he got."

The corner of Rhett's mouth lifted in cruel victory. Red flooded my vision as Cliff's face went blank. The words had cut deep—as though Rhett had known precisely which strings to tug at to clip beneath Cliff's armor. Then, Cliff snapped—moving with brutal speed.

Rhett met his blow like he'd expected it, seizing Cliff's left hand and twisting hard. The gun dropped with a hard thump on the walkway. Another hunter—a burly man with a cropped beard—stepped in to aid Rhett, clasping Cliff's arm in place to restrain him. In the same instant, another hunter took Gwen's shoulders, pulling her back. She cursed and bucked but was no match to outmaneuver him hand-to-hand.

"You make an enemy of me, you make an enemy out of everyone here," Rhett said in a low voice, angling his head to meet Cliff's seething gaze.

"I'll take my chances if it means I get to beat your hick face into the ground," Cliff replied, strained. His eyes skimmed the hunters around us, making note of which hands were tensed toward weapons—and the man who held Gwen. Our gazes caught briefly, but I struggled to make sense of the glimmer buried beneath his gaze. I was all too aware of Sylvia's fragile body in my grasp and how outnumbered we were.

"You know, if you were so desperate for my help, you'd have known one thing about me," Cliff said, straining against the men's grasp.

Rhett rolled his eyes, and for a moment, I thought he'd shoot Cliff on the spot. "And what's that?"

Cliff's smile widened into something sinister in its ease. "I'm not left-handed."

Gwen drove her heel into her captor's shin with vicious precision. He buckled with a shout of pain, his grip loosening just enough for her to twist free and toss her weapon to Cliff. He caught the gun deftly in his right hand, slamming the butt of it into Rhett's skull with a sickening *crack* of bone against metal. Rhett slumped onto his side.

Twisting with a shout of effort, Cliff broke free from the other man restraining his left side. He chased this with a brutal kick that sent the man sprawling against the railing. The barrier splintered under his weight with a crunch of wood, leaving the hunter to plummet into the swamp below with a startled scream.

"Jon!" Without breaking his stride, Cliff kicked his fallen gun to me. It skidded across the wooden planks, and I dove to snatch it up with a swift, desperate motion. The cold weight of it was grounding as I pulled it into my grasp.

Though Rhett was still dazed, barely able to peel himself off the ground, it was clear his authority was not a bluff. The two dozen hunters that had been cheering for me mere minutes before were now ready to apprehend me for crossing their marshal.

I couldn't let them get near—not with Sylvia in my grasp.

I shared a brief look with Cliff, who gave the smallest nod. *Run.* He'd hold them off as long as he could.

I turned and bolted, my boots hammering on the walkway. Years of hunting had honed my reflexes—I dodged a swing and ducked through an opening between bodies—but even during the most dire hunts, I rarely had such precious cargo in my grasp. I could feel the air pressing in on me as people lunged for me, only for them to grunt and go down as a bullet clipped a shoulder or leg. Cliff was clearing my path.

Another man seized my wounded shoulder, trying to pull me back. The pain alone nearly sent me off balance. I threw my elbow back, connecting with his nose and jaw. Something warm spurted, spraying my tee—and then I was free.

Rounding the corner of the main hall, I pressed myself against the wall and opened my other hand. Sylvia was ashen, eyes wide with terror.

"Can you fly?" I demanded. The chaos was seconds from catching up to us—yelling, gunshots, wood splintering.

Sylvia's voice was a choked sob, tearing at my heart. "Yes."

I spared a glance over my shoulder. "Get back to the clearing. Go!"

She hesitated, an argument on her lips. Then, with a snap of her wings opening, she bolted—flying for the tree line, a blur too quick for my eyes to track.

My breaths came easier, watching her vanish into the golden haze. *Safe.*

And not a moment too soon, as the sound of the remaining attackers caught up. Cliff backed around the corner, firing a deafening shot. Then, *click*—the sound of an empty chamber. He muttered under his breath as he ejected the spent magazine with a grace that was almost clinical. He slammed the fresh one home with a satisfying snap. Standard steel bullets. Maybe they wouldn't kill a monster, but it would certainly stop these fuckers.

"Where's Gwen?" I asked, adjusting my grip on the semi-automatic in my right hand. Judging by the weight, it had maybe five or six shots left in the chamber. Not great, but it would have to do.

Cliff's eyes snapped behind me and widened. I pivoted to see the flash of movement through the reinforced window. *Fuck*—a few of the hunters had gone through the interior to cut us off at the entrance. The main door flew open, a man and woman filling the doorway. I raised my gun, planting my feet with a deliberate movement.

"We don't have to do this," I said, even as tension built in my trigger finger.

The woman's expression twisted with betrayal rather than rage. I tried to place her, but at a brief glance, nothing seemed familiar.

"You think you're above the marshal because you've got a good kill streak?" she snarled. "You were supposed to be *with* us. Have you lost your minds?"

You don't understand, I wanted to snap back. My eyes cut briefly to the dock to my right, jutting into the water with steel-lined crates secured by cutting-edge locks.

Maybe they *did* understand—it was possible half these people knew Rhett was selling out everything hunters had stood for, piece by piece. Maybe they just didn't care, and profit was more appealing than standing on principles.

She adjusted her grip on the pistol between her hands. The man beside her tensed, mirroring her practiced body language. Even a stand-off would be a victory for them, if they could delay us long enough for Rhett or the others to catch up.

A cry tore from behind us, shrill and wild. I snapped my head toward the sound, but before I could make sense of it, something small—something *fast*—blurred past right past me. Gwen threw herself at the man on the right. He cursed, seizing her under the arms to throw her off. She landed like it was a dance—graceful, almost beautiful in her steady movements. Gwen spun, kicking up from the ground to the back of the man's knees. He staggered forward, and she leapt onto his back, arms locked around his throat.

The female hunter spun her weapon onto Gwen, only to falter. Rage flickered with shock. "What the fuck? *Gwen?* I thought you were dead."

More footsteps pounded behind us. Three more men. Cliff turned on them, his movements defensive and calculated as he held them at bay.

I fired off a round, catching the female hunter's shoulder and making her stagger away with a scream of pain.

As the male assailant lost consciousness from Gwen's grip, she sprang from his body, letting it slump to the ground, and caught the woman in the stomach with her boot. Even seeping blood from the superficial gun wound, the woman wasn't going down without a fight. Her surprise that Gwen had miraculously resurrected clearly didn't supersede her survival instincts. She caught Gwen's knee with a brutal kick that sent her down. I charged forward, but Gwen was back on her feet. She tackled the woman's legs and wrestled the gun from her grasp, swinging the handle down to the back of her head with a sharp *crack*.

The female hunter went limp, sprawled across the wooden planks.

Breathing heavily, Gwen dismounted, her skin gleaming from exertion. For a slight thing, I had to admit she was damn impressive.

"You're bleeding," I said, eyeing a streak of crimson on her cheek when she brushed past me. It looked like a fingernail scrape—like someone had clawed at her face.

"You wanna kiss it better or get out of here?" Gwen asked, not looking back at me.

I jogged behind her, using Cliff's cover to start across the bridge. Gunshots had turned to blows—fists and elbows connecting in a blur beside the shattered remnants of the siren's tank. But more men were coming, and even Cliff couldn't hold them off forever.

Then, I saw him—the younger hunter who'd been holding onto my weapons. He cut through the chaos, eyes locked on me with abject panic.

Gwen started toward him, only to stagger back as a warning shot exploded near her boots. She fell hard on her side, her gun sailing from her grasp. It skittered across the damp wood before ultimately dropping off the side, vanishing with a hollow splash into the swamp.

Fuck.

"Not another move!" the young hunter barked. "I'll shoot you next time. I swear I will."

He stepped fully into our path, his face pale and set with determination.

"You really wanna follow orders from a guy like Iverson?" I took a menacing step closer, noticing how the kid's grip on the gun—*my gun*, I realized—began to shake. "A guy who'd sell out his own people for the right price? You're nothing to him."

I took another step toward him. I kept my weapon lowered, silently offering a peaceful stalemate.

"You don't know anything," the kid snapped. Fear wavered beneath the ambition in his gaze as he sized me up. He straightened instinctively, trying to close the gap, but the inches I had on him wasn't lost on either of us.

I let a small, cruel smile touch my lips. "You heard him earlier, didn't you? You're a *joke* to him."

This struck a chord. He readjusted his grip on the gun with a growl of outrage, knuckles white as he leveled a shot at my chest. The space between us had shrunk to just two feet—close enough to smell the clammy sweat on him.

"For the record, I meant what I said before. It really was nice meeting you," he said. "But even the Appalachian Reapers aren't immortal. I'm sorry, but I have to do this."

I didn't think, didn't give him time to react. My body moved on instinct, closing the remaining distance between us in a fluid motion. I shot out my free hand, thrusting the gun away and twisting his wrist until I heard the snap of tendons. The weapon slipped from his grasp, landing between our feet on the ground, but I didn't ease up.

I grabbed his jacket, swinging him into the railing with enough force to rattle the wood. His breath left him in a surprised burst. My hand plunged into his inner pockets, rooting around for the familiar weight of my silver blades and the box of ammo he'd been withholding at Rhett's command.

The young man spluttered broken pleas, all bravado evaporated in my unforgiving grasp. His wide eyes darted to my weapons. He thought I was going to kill him. I could—but pity stirred through my rage.

"Nice meeting you, too," I said before hauling him over the railing into the water.

I hurriedly helped Gwen to her feet, pressing my knives into her hands. "Can you use those?" I asked.

"They're perfect. I can stab *both* of you at the same time when we get out," she said, glancing up at me with a begrudging... was it gratitude? Admiration? Whatever it was flickered out as Cliff stepped onto the bridge—followed by a trio of seasoned hunters.

A silver-haired hunter in the middle kept his shotgun trained on Cliff, as did the two men flanking him. I didn't blame them. Back near the Pit, a dozen hunters were either unconscious or still tending to wounds Cliff had inflicted. Lucky for them, he was showing remarkable restraint. He could massacre them all, but then every hunter in the country would be on our asses by sunset.

"Lower your weapons, *now*," the silver-haired hunter growled. "If the marshal hadn't ordered you boys to be captured alive, you'd be dead where you stand."

Cliff didn't waver.

The lead hunter chuckled, revealing tobacco-stained teeth behind the untamed beard. "Son, you need to know when you're outnumbered. If you shoot me, my boys will have that pretty face turned into Swiss cheese in seconds." His eyes narrowed, that smile widening into something certain. "You won't do it."

I watched Cliff's steely profile, the way nothing budged in his expression, even though I could see him scanning his options—which weren't plentiful. He adjusted his aim a small amount—scarcely a quarter inch upward—and squeezed the trigger.

BLAM.

The hunters facing us flinched, coiled with tension, but quickly relaxed into relieved laughter. The shot hadn't come close. It had pierced one of the crates on the shipping dock. The advanced lock hanging off the front was smoking, its mechanism frayed. Black wings burst from the lid—there had to be at least five ahools. The bat-like monsters gave piercing cries and descended upon the nearest threats—the trio of hunters standing at the threshold to the main building. Monster and human screams bled together.

"Let's go!" I shouted, waving to Cliff.

As he turned to follow, one of the men managed to shake off an ahool and snap its neck. The creature hadn't even hit the ground before the hunter was lunging at Cliff.

Gwen launched herself at the man, burying one of my blades into his shoulder before he could reach Cliff. The man's howl of pain rivaled the cries of the ahools behind him. He seized Gwen's wrist and gave a brutal kick that connected with her knee. She screamed, staggering.

"Gwen!" Cliff shouted, catching her under the arms before she could fall.

The assailant lurched back unsteadily, the knife still protruding from his shoulder. Gwen struggled against Cliff's grip, trying to take another swing at the hunter with the second blade.

"Forget them," Cliff grunted. "Let's get the hell outta here!"

"My knee's about to give," she gritted out. "I can't run."

Glancing back toward the fast-approaching assailants, Cliff slipped his arms under her legs and threw her over his shoulder, sprinting past me while Gwen loosed a stream of shocked profanities.

We cleared the walkway and dodged through the trees, using them for cover as gunfire rang out behind us. I searched the branches overhead, trying in vain to catch a glimpse of gossamer wings. My mind spun, wondering if she had the energy to make it to the car, wondering if I should be worried about birds of prey in the area.

The goddamn bridge came into view.

Fuck. The golden mist had pooled even thicker, making the fall seem even more endless than before. I forced myself to follow Cliff onto the bridge. The boards rattled like it was about to give, but the thought of our pursuers crowding onto it made me move faster.

"They're coming!" I gasped ahead.

Voices drew nearer, but to my surprise, the rickety boards didn't shake with the weight of the other hunters. The end was in sight. Cliff crossed the last of the boards, setting Gwen carefully on her feet while she batted his arms away with a scowl. I was five feet from solid ground when one side of the bridge gave way with a deafening *crack.*

A scream caught in my throat. I let go of the gun, lashing out both hands to grab the other side of the rail. My boots fought for purchase that couldn't be found. Another *crack.* The bridge was giving out from beneath me—they hadn't boarded the bridge because they were destroying the other side.

"Jon!" Ahead, Cliff threw his arm out to grab me.

Our fingertips fell short of each other's. The boards gave way entirely and swung down. I scrabbled at the planks, trying to launch myself up to solid ground, but the wood was too slippery to catch a firm grip.

Icy pain burst around my wrist. My shoulder smarted as my fall came to an abrupt halt.

Breathing heavily, I craned my neck to find a cluster of ice growing around my hand, pinned to a board. The end of the bridge was frozen in place, crackling with splinters of frost.

Sylvia fluttered above me, her hands aimed at the ice as she grimaced. "Hurry," she croaked. "I can't hold it!"

I swung my other arm up. The ice chunk melted off my skin as Cliff caught my hand and hauled me onto the frozen bit of bridge. The moment we were on solid ground, Sylvia released the spell. The planks fell away, splashing into the water below.

We put distance between ourselves and the steep overhang. I sank to my knees. My lungs burned as I caught my breath, my gaze darting between Cliff and Gwen before finding Sylvia hovering above us. She looked so pale, so exhausted, it was a wonder she could stay on her wings.

"Sylv," I said between heavy breaths. "You need to…" My insistence that she should rest died on my lips. She wouldn't look at me. All at once, the pain from my Pit injuries surged back into focus, stabbing my shoulder, head, and hands. But worse was that I couldn't shake the sound of her horrible, broken gasp as she'd accepted her fate at my hands.

Before I could puzzle out what to say, movement swayed the trees overhead, swiftly approaching us.

"Fuck!" Gwen hissed, shooting her head up in unison with Cliff. "One of those things followed us!"

Sure enough, the shadow broached land, moving with un-natural speed. The skittering of claws against bark sent a chill down my spine. The ahool was small—barely two feet high with a five-foot wingspan—but its bite was just as venomous as a mature adult. It prowled along the branch, watching warily—and *hungrily*.

Cliff raised his gun, but the uncertainty on his face wasn't promising. He had to be low on ammo.

The car was visible at the top of the slope, its weathered green exterior like a beacon. Ahools were difficult to put down without fire, but we didn't have to make it far. A few key shots would slow it down, give us the crucial seconds we needed.

Then I saw Gwen leaning against a tree, clutching her bruised knee, and remembered she couldn't run. She still wielded a blade in her other hand, but that wouldn't do much good if the ahool sank its teeth into her.

A nearby flutter of gossamer wings moved higher.

"Sylv." I jerked my chin uphill, voice low to keep the ahool from startling. "Get back to the car."

She ignored me, lifting her hands with her eyes set over our heads. *No, no, no—*

Sylvia conjured a serpentine line of frost, solidifying into a spear and shooting it into the rustling branches above us. The ahool shrieked as the jagged end clipped its side. Glittering frost settled like snowfall when the creature burst from the foliage overhead. It swung, diving for us. Cliff fired, lodging a shot in its left wing and its chest, forcing it to land.

Click.

His gun's chamber was empty.

Blood seeped from the ahool's injuries, but it kept moving toward us as though spurred by personal vengeance. Its glistening fangs were bared in a cry that carried the rotten stench of carrion. I jolted away from its approach, glancing over my shoulder toward Sylvia, certain she was going to drop out of the air with magic exhaustion at any second—

A targeted line of flames cut through the air like a blade.

Cliff and I staggered back as one, reacting instinctively to the intense heat. We were cleared of its radius, but the ahool howled in agony. It curled in on itself, spasming in the consuming fire. Shrieks turned into whimpers. Finally, it collapsed in a smoldering heap.

The flames petered out.

Rhett lowered the flamethrower in his hands, stepping out from his vantage point between two nearby oaks.

"Well," he said. "That was exciting, wasn't it?"

Though it wouldn't do us any good, Cliff raised his gun while I fought the urge to take my chances in shoving Rhett toward the broken bridge.

Gwen snapped, "Where the fuck did you come from?"

"I know my way around here better than most, lucky for you." But Rhett didn't look at her while he answered. He only had eyes for Sylvia, amazed like a kid in a candy store. He withdrew a pistol from his waistband and drew back the hammer. Though he held it relaxed at his side, the threat settled heavily all the same. A smirk pulled up the corner of his mouth. "Now, what the hell should I make of this?"

To my dismay, Sylvia darted closer, putting herself between us and Rhett. She thrust out her palms and sent Rhett staggering back to dodge a blade of ice through his boot. It embedded itself into the soft earth. Icy mist pooled around her like she couldn't keep it inside, but the spear was brittle and crumbled away. She was exhausted. Her magic wouldn't hold much longer.

"Back away," she snarled. "*Now.*"

"You're looking a little winded, sweetheart. Not your everyday catch, are you?" Rhett lifted his gun, and though I doubted he could land a shot on such a small target, I started toward him with my weapon raised.

"Don't!" I barked. "I told you, she's mine."

He whistled under his breath, giving me a leisurely scan before settling his gaze back on Sylvia. "If I didn't know any better, I'd say you were sweet on her, Nowak. I haven't seen someone so excited to volunteer for something since they invented dick pics."

My mind raced with lies and excuses to explain away Sylvia's vicious protectiveness.

"Don't get it twisted," I said. "She's nothing but a trophy—a useful one. We caught her a couple months back and turned her glamour against her. She'll tear you apart if I tell her to."

"Oh, I don't doubt she's a loyal little thing. But the rest? Bull-shit. You're too high and mighty to be toting around a trophy." Rhett flicked his tongue, smiling as he gestured toward me with the barrel of his pistol. "No… You've got a soft spot for her. Hell, if I'd known how attached you were, I would've called off the fight before it started. You could've just given her leash a little tug."

To my surprise, he lowered the gun and held up his other hand in peace. He shifted his weight, looking up at Sylvia. "Look—for the record, my money was on you, Miss."

Fuck, I wanted to end him for daring to speak to her.

Sylvia didn't budge from her brash stance midair, exhausted or not. "I heard exactly what you wanted," she said, her voice all venom.

Rhett softened like he genuinely meant to console her. "Forgive me for all that talk back there—I didn't think you were a friendly one. Can you blame me? You set a siren loose."

"She was innocent!" Sylvia snapped.

"And you believed her?" He laughed like they were having a chat by the office cooler. "A fairy with rose-colored glasses. You're really something else." His eyes flickered to me, then to Cliff—bearing that same unsettling glint as before. "If you thought being the *Appalachian Reapers* won you admiration before, wait till word gets around that you can tame fairies. My client happens to be *very* interested in her kind."

Sylvia shuddered bodily, but he didn't seem concerned about her magic having a second wind.

"Look, get it through your thick skulls–I'm not your enemy," Rhett went on. "I want the same thing as you guys: less monsters hurting innocent people. You're coming at me for not doing it the way you want, wrapped in a bow? Go fuck yourselves." His jaw ticked, blue eyes flicking from face to face. "We can clear everything up back there as a misunderstanding, so long as you boys start playing nice and come with me."

He reached behind him—not for another weapon, but for a burlap satchel slung over his shoulder. Metal clinked within as he tossed it on the ground between us.

"Silver," he declared. "See? I'm fair. You just need to hold up your end. What do you say?"

"I'll let you guess," Cliff said. "It rhymes with 'get fucked.'"

"You sure you don't wanna at least hear what I could offer you?" Rhett didn't waver, but his grin tightened a fraction. "How's that nest egg treating you, Everett?"

Cliff inhaled sharply. "How the fuck do you know about that?"

Rhett seemed to revel in how Cliff's face drained of color. "My client has eyes and ears everywhere. He can be generous, too. Hey, he might even let you keep your fairy if that sweetens the pot…"

"I'm not a bargaining token!" Sylvia shouted in a strangled voice.

"I don't think you have much of a say in the state you're in, darling."

"Don't fucking talk to her," Cliff spat. "We don't work with psychopaths."

Glancing at me, Rhett smirked. "Could've fooled me."

"Cut the shit and shoot him already!" Gwen interjected, glaring between us.

Uncertainty rippled from her when Rhett shifted his focus to her. His fingers rested loosely on the strap of his flamethrower. "What about you?" he said with feigned concern. "Gwen, right? Surprised you're backing the Reapers after what they did to you. What do they got on you—some dirty photos? Whatever it is, I'm sure we can work it out. I've got people behind me now. They can protect you, too. I mean, now all those folks back there know you're not dead—and that you're a dirty little traitor to boot."

Breathing hard, Gwen sneered. "Bite me. I don't need shit from you."

Rhett groaned, shoulders slumping dramatically as he looked to the sky. "The swear jar around here must be overflowing. Trust me—I'll change your mind eventually. Everyone comes around once I find their soft spot."

He smiled, and that severed the tentative restraint Gwen clung to. I knew that kind of rage—terror not for yourself, but for what you stood before. *Hannah*–just miles away, blissfully unaware of Rhett's vendetta.

"You fucker," Gwen seethed, straightening on her good leg, grip tightening on her blade. She drew back her arm, gaze narrowed on Rhett's chest.

I couldn't move in time—couldn't react as Rhett's arm lifted. Before she had taken two painful steps, a gunshot rang out. Gwen staggered, sprawling onto her side. Blood seeped from a bullet wound in her right thigh, a morbidly black mark blossoming down the dark fabric.

Shock rippled through me.

"No!" Cliff roared. He started to race to her side, but Rhett fired off a warning shot that burst through the wet ground beside Cliff.

Rhett's eyes flicked between Cliff and me. "Don't make this harder than it has to be. Drop the guns and come with me, or the next one goes through her brain."

I couldn't move—couldn't fathom why the hell he wanted us alive so badly. My thoughts staggered with ways to use that against him, but Rhett's sudden cry of pain jolted me back to full attention.

Ice was crawling over the barrel of Rhett's gun, spreading rapidly. In a matter of seconds, frost enveloped his palm and fingers and raced up his arm. The glow of the magic was strange—a shade of lavender I had never seen in Sylvia's magic before. I might have thought there was another fairy present if it weren't for Sylvia's raised hands.

How the hell was she doing that?

"Fuck," Rhett hissed, eyes bugging wide. *"FUCK!"*

But the ice didn't stop. It spread like it was hungry, feasting on his form. He backed away from Sylvia, fear mingling with the pain in his voice. She followed him and rose above his eye level, closing in like a delicate goddess of vengeance. I faltered where I stood, watching with an odd mix of pride and horror as Rhett's movements were forced to halt.

Sylvia's chanting voice was a ragged, unrecognizable cry, growing louder with each verse. The pale purple first completely covered Rhett's body, solidifying around him like a statue. It crackled as clear layers thickened.

A small gasp—and then the spellwork flickered. Sylvia plummeted like a stone, magic exhaustion finally staking its claim on her.

I shouted her name, diving for her, but she hit the ground before I could reach her. She lay unmoving on the mossy earth—but she was breathing. She was alive.

A glint caught my eye. Her amethyst shard lay just short of her fingers.

That was how she'd pushed through the magic exhaustion. She'd finally spent the gem shard her mother had given her. As I scooped up her prone form, I made certain to take the shard too.

I heard Cliff sprinting behind me, helping Gwen sit up. Blood stained both their hands as they applied pressure to the bullet wound. She whimpered through gritted teeth, shaking.

"Deep breaths," he commanded, then glanced toward Rhett. "Is he dead?"

With Sylvia cradled carefully in one hand, I got to my feet and approached Rhett. Faint panting and shifting could be heard within the shell of ice. His eyes followed me as I circled him, vocal cords straining to say something. It was as horrifying as it was impressive, and I stole another glance at Sylvia's unconscious form. Gem magic or not, it never ceased to amaze me that someone so delicate could be capable of such destruction.

The ice was thickest at his hands and feet, but rivets of water were already dribbling down his neck. It was thin enough, and without Sylvia conscious to reinforce the magic, it was only a matter of time before he broke loose.

"Unfortunately, I think he'll live," I called over my shoulder.

A faint sound caught my ear. The rustle of leaves. I turned, my chest tight at the notion of another predator targeting us. Scanning the trees, I spotted movement through the underbrush.

Not a monster. *Humans.* More hunters had found another way across the water, trekking through the mossy woods—directly toward the sound of gunfire.

"Damn it," I muttered, ducking to grab the bag of silver bullets so graciously provided by Rhett.

The car's short distance felt like miles as we bolted, the forest towering over us. I spared a quick glance behind me as it came into view, and I circled for the driver's side.

Cliff had Gwen cradled in his arms, her small frame barely weighing him down despite her injury. I'd never seen her look so *fragile*—her lips pale and her head lolling against Cliff's chest without even so much as a scowl in his direction. Her face was tight with pain, like she was refusing to give in to the urge to weep.

Though I couldn't see the hunters pursuing our trail, I could still hear every distant twig snap under their tread. I vaulted behind the wheel of the car, pausing only to lay Sylvia carefully on the passenger's seat. Cliff helped Gwen into the back seat, barking for me to drive.

I heard him murmuring something assuring to Gwen as I peeled off along the dirt road. The click of the first aid kit.

"Hold on," Cliff urged her. "I've got you."

I didn't have to look back to know—he was cutting through her black jeans skillfully. He pulled off his button-up, twisting the sleeve into a rope. He offered it to her, saying, "Bite down on this."

Gwen did so. A bottle was uncapped and the sharp smell of alcohol filled the vehicle as Cliff sloshed it generously over the wound. Gwen screamed, muffled through the cloth.

"Stay with me," Cliff said, cupping her face and fixing her with a cementing look while he pulled away layers of alcohol and blood-soaked gauze.

He withdrew a pair of tweezers from the kit. "Hard part's next."

14
SYLVIA

Breathe. Just breathe.

The back window of the motel room led directly to the woods stretching behind the building. I ventured deep enough among the trees to hide the motel from sight.

I could almost pretend that there were no humans for miles and miles.

I inhaled deeply, shakily, as though the fresh scent of corn-flower and thyme might heal me from the inside. Peace washed through me with each brush against greenery, clean air filling my lungs. Every forest was sacred. Even this one, with its heavy air, held tranquility like a communal prayer.

My satchel, brimming with the fresh herbs I had foraged, bumped against my hip as I flitted about to keep busy. I carefully arranged cornflower petals in a runic pattern upon a branch—a private offering for the stars to gaze upon. Such formal gifts were typically reserved for Solstice celebrations with the entire village, but a near-death experience felt like a worthy enough occasion.

Wings aching, I was tempted to have a seat on the branch, but perfect stillness would bring me no comfort. The remnants of magic exhaustion and my brush with iron continued to throb through my body and soul. My heart lay in pieces, desperate for commiseration.

Yet, my first instinct was to flee when I awoke in the motel room an hour ago.

I had scrambled off the pillow and sprang into the air, expecting to find myself back in that awful fighting arena with a throng of hunters jeering at me.

But there was only Jon, his expression rising with relief—only to fall again when I flew right past him. He said something—perhaps an apology or a question—but I didn't listen. I stammered an excuse that I was low on rosewater and needed to forage. Even when he offered to put salve on the iron wound I couldn't heal, I fled without another word.

He didn't give chase.

My reasonable excuse was that I couldn't bear to be inside. Couldn't bear to be confined within a structure so damn *human*.

The whole, cruel truth was too tangled in brambles for me to touch. Facing near death at his hands had finally made me realize it.

I *loved* him, and it was too late to save myself from the ache that would come with it. I loved him, and I wanted to howl at the sky for the entire world to hear.

I love him, I love him, I love him.

But what did it matter, if fate seemed determined to keep us apart? We were constantly pushed to the brink, nearly destroying each other as we fought across the tethers that separated us. Love wasn't always beautiful. It was fucking poison when you couldn't have what you wanted.

I didn't even know if he felt the same way. From where I stood, all of our assertions to not get attached felt flimsy. But perhaps he was stronger than me.

One of the petals in my offering was askew. In my haste to fix it, I crumpled its delicate texture. I gritted my teeth, tempted to sweep the entire pattern away in a fury.

Stars, could I not do this one simple thing right?

The tears I'd muscled down threatened to resurface again, but I set the damaged petal back into the arrangement. I supposed that was fitting—one twisted piece in an otherwise perfect collection.

The stars see perfection differently than we do, my love. Mother's voice was calm and certain in my memory.

An ache burrowed through my chest. Embarrassment flashed through me in the same instant. How many times had I brought up my family, my old home, or lost friends in the past months? Each restaurant the hunters introduced me to had me rambling about Mother's cooking and the Elysian kitchens. Each new animal was an excuse to note down every detail for Hazel.

I'd quelled my pathetically redundant mentions in recent weeks, but that didn't mean that the memories haunted me any less. I didn't stop thinking of Mother and Hazel with any amount of space between us. I thought of them every minute.

When I was with the hunters, sometimes that gaping hole in my heart felt less cavernous. Now, it felt bottomless and vast. Unfillable. I just wanted to see my family right now. Just for a moment.

My gaze drifted to the forest floor below me. Before I knew it, I was gliding down to land at the foot of the oak tree. I pushed aside dead leaves, my fingers moving for the soil packed beneath. I could have traced the symbol blindly. My fingers plunged into the soil, my heels burning as I crouched, moving hurriedly—forming the spectral rune.

After stealing a glance around the woods, confirming my solitude from humans and safety from birds of prey, I laid down on the ground and whispered the spell.

I blinked in the dazzling familiar periwinkle. I breathed deeply—not that there was *air* here exactly. No breeze. No earthy scent of the forest. I flexed my hands in front of me, noticing the ache from my strenuous fight absent now. The iron wound marring my shoulder was gone—my skin held no blemishes here, other than the traitor mark I couldn't see.

Home.

The single word gave shape to the rudderless magic in my blood. I didn't care that the nomadic journals warned against it—I willed my memories to resurrect around me. Smoky images of willow fronds danced through the luminous void first, then whirling earthen walls. It was dizzying, like I was flying without spreading my wings.

Home.

My fingers curled, my intention strengthening without reservation. Shadowy, dim surroundings took form around me. I was nestled deep under the earth, with soft moss crawling over parts of the domed ceiling above me. My family's hearth room in Elysia.

The details wavered like trying to peer through a foggy window. Each clicked into place with startling clarity the longer I looked at each spot. The wide stone fireplace was crackling gently. A stove sat beside it, radiating heat I could nearly feel as a dented kettle of herbal tea simmered. The counters were wooden, surfaces worn smooth and gleaming from years of use. Shelves dominated one wall, packed with jars of dried flowers, spices, and berries.

Two arched corridors led off from the hearth room, leading to the two bedrooms. I muscled down the sudden urge to sprint toward the hall that led to my old bedroom, to burst inside and collapse on my quilted bed beside Hazel.

In the center of the kitchen, a round table sat with chairs neatly tucked around. The clay pot I had crafted when I was seven was at the center, stuffed with wilting wildflowers that threatened to overwhelm it. The table was set for tea, with a plate of ginger tarts at the center—all the makings of a quiet Elysian morning, when it was just Mother, Hazel, and me in the comforting solitude of our dormitory.

As the dizziness passed, and I stopped looking for holes in the illusion, my gaze stilled on the table.

It was set for *four*.

Above the fireplace, a family portrait was hung, aged bronze framing the canvas in subtle ivy designs. Frowning, I stepped deeper into the memory, tasting the moment frozen in time. That painting hadn't hung there in years; Mother had long ago tucked it into a spare wardrobe, wrapped in a sheet. Which meant—this was the Elysia from my childhood.

I stood before the painting. I hadn't thought about it or even seen it in years, but my mind conjured it so clearly as though it had never left. The four of us—laughter sparkling in every gaze. Blissfully unknowing of what lay ahead.

Mother's red hair spilled down her shoulders in waves, the way mine did when I'd been little. Father was seated beside her, his strong jaw and flinty blue eyes complementing her regal features. His chin-length tawny blonde hair was exactly how I remembered it. He often joked boastfully how lucky he was that both girls took after their radiant Mother—apart from Hazel, who shared his striking eyes.

He was holding Hazel in the crook of his arm, her cheek resting against his chest. She'd been such a round, giggly toddler back then—a terror even before her wings fully developed.

Stars, I missed her.

And then there was me, standing all of eleven summers, trying to look older than I was and likely fighting the urge to squirm with impatience. An odd mix of compassion and sadness gripped me as I stared into my own face.

Suddenly, everything felt too real. Sensations were supposed to be muted in the spectral realm, but I could practically smell the fragrant steam wafting off the tea. If I closed my eyes and focused, I could picture my family behind that bedroom door. Mother and Father fussing over Hazel.

I took a step toward the door, my mouth dry. I swore that was the dulcet rumble of my father's voice. Would I be able to see them all here? Speak to Father beyond the grave?

My hand trembled as I reached for the doorknob. What would I say to him? The murmured conversation continued. I could hear them clearly now—

From the other side, the doorknob rattled and turned.

I gasped, staggering back. *No,* I couldn't do this. My back slammed into the dining table, sending a chair onto its side and porcelain teacups shattering on the floor. I felt gravity give out beneath me as I whispered the release spell in a panicked, hurried breath.

Back in my body, I wrenched upright, sucking in a deep breath of clean forest air.

"*Fuck!*" I frantically swept my hand through the dirt to break the rune—as though the memory might chase me back into the real world.

I sat with my knees to my chest, grounding myself to the sounds of the woods around me. My breaths labored, heart thudding in my chest like a hummingbird trying to break free of a cage.

Even for a first attempt, the illusion had been vivid. The nomadic journals hadn't been so blinded after all. If I had devoted more energy, perhaps I *would* have seen Father there—Hazel and Mother in the golden light of my memories. It would be enough to make anyone want to stay. Perhaps never leave at all.

Snap.

I flinched at the sound of a twig crunching. My wings flew open, lifting me into a hover—out of reach, at least seven feet in the air. I'd been vigilant for owls and hawks while I wandered, but as I strained my ears against the ambient humming of insects, this rhythm was distinctly human. Slow, deliberate footsteps over fallen leaves.

My mind immediately went to Rhett. After what I'd done to him, *of course* he would hunt me down and strip me for parts like he'd intended for that poor siren.

Though my surface wounds were healed, my graze from the iron still left me shaky as I tried to muster magic to my hands. This time, I had no gem shard to help me. Frost curled up to my elbows. It would have to be enough. No one would thaw him out this time.

The moment the man's shadow emerged from the trees below, I shot a hard line of frost at his head.

The man cursed, his deep voice carrying in the trees as he ducked. The tension in my shoulders went slack.

"Hey, take it easy before you pass the fuck out again," Cliff called, peering up at my tree. He held up his hands in mock surrender before dusting off his long-sleeved tee from remnants of frost. He spotted me and offered a sportive little smile in greeting.

Embarrassment mingled with relief. "I thought you were…" I swallowed, glancing through the forest. No more footsteps. Only him. I shook my head. "What are you doing, anyway? Here to babysit me?" The words came with more bitterness than I'd intended, but I couldn't shake the image of the boys conspiring to take shifts to keep a watchful eye on me after the events at the outpost.

"Stealing your idea. It's nice out here," he said. "Good place to get drunk."

"It's nice over *there*, too." I pointed off in a random direction of the forest.

"Move me."

"If you'd like to stay for target practice, be my guest," I said gamely, summoning particles of ice around my hands.

He clicked his tongue in disapproval. "Light up that magic again, and I won't share any of this." He pulled out his favorite flask and gave it an enticing shake. If there was ever a time to get a little drunk…

No. I needed to stay vigilant.

But a few sips wouldn't hurt.

"This is whiskey," he said, falling to a seat at the base of my tree as I drifted down to meet him. "*Don't* chug it." He poured a bit into the cap for me and handed it off.

I perched on his bent knee and raised the liquor to my lips. "Doesn't stop you."

I thanked him quietly, eyeing him suspiciously over the metallic rim of the cap.

"If you came out to tell me what a dumbass I am, save it. I don't need a lecture," I said before he could open his mouth.

The drink burned my throat, but it was the gentle look in Cliff's eyes that made the tears I had been holding back spill free without my consent.

"You've been through some tough shit today. You came out the other side of it but… I didn't think you should be alone," he said.

I sniffled, wiping my eyes hurriedly though I knew it was too late. I allowed my walls to drop, swallowing as I looked at him, beseeching. The mere extension of kindness made the weight of everything crash down on me with renewed heaviness—fighting Jon for our lives, the car swerving into the water, the dark stares of the elders as I was banished from the only home I had ever known.

"Can you just—can you tell me everything is going to be okay?" I croaked out.

Cliff studied me hard, and I could see a *tough shit, sweetheart* talk on its way. But he surprised me—cupping his hand around me with a solidity that made me feel molten and safe, the way he might've thrown an arm around my shoulders.

"Everything's gonna be okay," Cliff murmured.

I indulged the heat of his touch for a few moments. My exhaustion deepened, beckoned by the delicious comfort that Cliff's presence promised. His familiar features—strong jaw dusted with a faint five o' clock shadow and mossy eyes—were a solace in any storm. No longer a predator hunting me, but my ally. My *friend*.

But I could be stronger than this. I wiped my puffy eyes on my sleeve, pushing him away.

"I'm not convinced," I mumbled.

Cliff rolled his eyes, cracking a wider smile. "Oh my *God*. What do you want, then?"

"A do-over, starting with yesterday," I said, looking down at my distorted reflection in the whiskey. "Maybe all of this would have turned out differently if I could have just kept my shit together in the car with that damn storm. That's when everything started going to hell."

"Sweetheart, things started going wrong when you decided a haunted house was a good place to spend your Friday nights." Cliff chuckled, throwing back another sip from the flask. He sucked on the liquid for a moment, his gaze turning flighty. "On the road during the storm… I shouldn't have shouted at you. I know those panic attacks aren't your fault."

I blinked. *An actual apology?* From him? "Back home, I would take myself straight to the ice caverns if a thunderstorm was brewing. It was a safe outlet for the inevitable magic that burst from the panic." I wiggled my fingers with a bitter smile. *Weak.* Always so weak. "Maybe my magic could've protected me better if it was storming out there today."

"Hey—you handled yourself just fine. Pretty badass, actually," Cliff said. I gave him a flat look that only emboldened him. "Seriously! I swear I saw one guy piss himself when you got the upper hand with that spear. The back and forth was insane. If I wasn't shitting bricks myself, I would've thought to record it."

His voice lifted with fervor that was hard to refute. A smile ghosted my lips at the thought that some of the cruel onlookers had suffered a little indirect misfortune at my hands—much to Cliff's obvious relief.

I took a thoughtful drag of my drink. "Sounds more like you were turned on."

He hesitated for too long before scoffing, "You wish."

My mouth dropped open in surprise, and laughter promptly mingled with my tears. "*Stars*, you were!"

"Don't kink shame me." He nudged my left shoulder lightly, but his eyes widened when I winced at the contact. "Fuck, Sylv. How bad does it hurt?"

I peeked at the angry red mark and shrugged. "More annoying than anything. I think I'm going to have to heal like a… *human*." I shuddered dramatically.

His smile didn't entirely mask the worry in his eyes as he glanced at the gathering clouds overhead. "Looks like rain soon. Will you be okay?"

"Those don't look like thunder clouds. Trust me, when you grow up paranoid about storms, you learn to tell the difference."

His brow furrowed, gaze searching. "What happened with you and storms, anyway?"

"Jon hasn't told you already?"

When he shook his head, my insides stirred with a feeling I couldn't place. When we had first met, Jon shared everything I told him with Cliff. At some point in the last two months, something must have shifted.

"When I was a child, my father and I were training far from the home willow—as far as we were allowed, anyway. He'd chosen the storm by design. He was showing me how to morph heavy rain into icicles without slashing myself to ribbons. And… he'd been experimenting all day, so he used gem magic to keep from tiring out."

I chewed my lip at the memory. His paling face, his fluttering eyelids as I cried for him to get back up. The unpolished ruby glinting dully in the mud.

"The gem magic overtook him," I said. "For hours, I was alone with the thunder bellowing at me."

Cliff sucked in a breath, shaking his head. "What a way to go."

"No—he recovered," I said. "He was lucky. The healers yelled at him when he was back in their ward, though—I'd never heard them do that before. It wasn't until a few years later that his obsession with gemstones finally ended him."

"I'm sorry." Cliff's eyes flickered away from me, resting on a random tree ahead of us. After a measured pause, he asked, "Aren't you worried that'll happen to you?"

"I don't have his ambition," I said.

"Well, that's just bullshit."

"Really," I insisted, chuckling ruefully. "Besides, I'm not having much luck getting my hands on a full gemstone, so what's there to worry about?"

He lifted his eyebrows. "You used that little gem to turn Rhett into an ice sculpture, didn't you? Any power left in that thing?"

I'd glimpsed it on the nightstand before fleeing the motel room. Each day I hadn't used it felt like a victory. And now... "Empty," I said bitterly. "It's nothing more than a worthless stone now." My throat tightened at the knowledge that I'd likely tuck it back amongst my things anyway. "Mother said that Father would have wanted me to have it. I suppose we have them to thank for escaping with our lives."

Cliff tipped the flask to his lips instead, pulling a long swallow. "Gotta say, I envy you."

"Why wouldn't you?" I quipped, rolling my eyes.

He nudged my shoulder for this, giving me a half-smirk that didn't reach his eyes. "I'm serious. I mean—having a father who actually gave a shit. Seems like he was a solid guy before the gemstone stuff." He looked away, jaw tightening. "Can't fathom seeing eye-to-eye with my old man like that. Hell, he made it his personal mission to make sure I knew what a fuck-up I was to him. Every damn day, like I might forget it."

"Your father—" I nearly swallowed down the words, a vice around my heart. "He hit you?"

His eyes dropped, smile so tight it was almost a grimace. "On special occasions."

Horror rippled through me like a silent, seeping wound. The Elders of Elysia left discipline to each family, only involving themselves in extreme cases that surfaced—but it was rare. *So rare.* I'd only once heard that Damian's uncle grew volatile after a particularly festive Solstice feast. It was difficult to imagine Cliff as a soft-faced teenager. He won every fight he entered. I'd seen vampires cower from his advance.

I stirred from my drifting thoughts as Cliff set down his flask, pulling out a set of three tactical throwing knives from his jeans pocket. I hadn't noticed the slight shape jutting against the denim earlier, but I had long since learned to temper my surprise when he pulled weapons from his person. His demeanor was contemplative, almost sullen as he unwound the leather case on his lap and grabbed the first knife in his hand, pinching it by the blade.

"My old man was a hunter—just deer and rabbits. No demonic bastards," Cliff said, more to the blade than to me. "By the time I was eight, he had a Savage Rascal in my hands and dragged me out with him every weekend on his trips. I hated it. Not the noise so much as the killing part, watching the light leave the animal's eyes. First time I landed a shot—lodged right in the buck's neck—" Cliff paused to give a dry chuckle, shaking his head. "I cried, and he smacked me for it. Wouldn't let me look away as it died."

Cliff's wrist twitched in a quick flick. Air rushed as the blade soared across the clearing and embedded itself in the trunk of the tree across from us with a clean thunk. He glanced at me as he reached for the next knife, revealing the guarded glint buried there. My heart ached, but I didn't dare breathe a word. When was the last time someone had offered him comfort, had hugged him?

"See, it was a decent shot but not *good*. I missed the heart because I'd been shaking so bad. I remember begging—*begging* him to kill it for me. Bastard let it suffer until the light went out for good." Cliff sucked through his teeth and threw another knife. It landed directly beneath the first, separated by six inches or so.

"As I got older, he kept bringing me along on those hunting trips, and I kept getting better. Turns out I had a natural aptitude for precision once I stopped shaking like a leaf. He even shelled out five grand to hire some douchey tutor from out of state. The day I outdid *that* guy… Only time I ever caught my father looking proud of me. And for a second, I thought things would be different."

"I'm sorry," I finally croaked. Months of wondering—and now, I didn't know what the hell to say. He was offering me something more valuable than any amount of money or gold—a piece of himself.

Cliff shrugged, offering a humorless smile. "It wasn't all a waste. When things hit the fan with Jon's dad, we were scared shitless and I was the only one who could land a shot on the son of a bitch—besides Tammy of course, when she finally found us."

He threw the last knife, completing the perfect constellation in the tree.

"Your dad was a fucking asshole," I said, after pulling together my thoughts.

This pulled an appreciative chuckle out of him. "Well, maybe he did have a point along the way. Look at me—violence is all I'm good for. At least now I'm killing things that actually deserve it."

My throat felt so tight, I could barely swallow. *Stars,* I wanted to be human if only so I could cup his cheek this very instant, force him to look back at me until he believed what I knew of him.

"Gwen told me you ran from this life once," I ventured.

"I was young. Moment of weakness." Cliff smirked, reaching for the flask. "Don't pity me, Sylv. I've made peace with a hunter's death."

"But what about *living*?" I persisted softly, leaning forward. I thought of how Jon lit up when he allowed himself to contemplate another future. "Jon and I are impeccable company *naturally,* but... Don't you ever think about a family?"

His laugh was deep and full now. "Can you imagine me with a couple of kids and a mortgage? Don't waste your worrying on me. This is my choice, and I'm good with it. Saving people beats the hell out of going to some stuffy Ivy League university to land a job as a corporate tool."

I pursed my lips, sipping at my whiskey. It was nearly drained, to my surprise.

"What about you?" he asked.

"Me?"

Cliff nodded, studying me. "You want that? Family, kids, the whole nine yards?"

My stomach flipped a little, but my head felt buzzy and light. Whiskey was delicious and I couldn't remember why I ever gave Cliff a hard time for nursing a glass.

"You're asking hard questions," I pouted.

Cliff shot me a goading smile. "Are you tipsy already?"

"Duh." I rolled my eyes at him, but I thought hard, trying to picture it—wings heavy and flightless, a baby in my belly. "My mother asked me so much over the last few years, I got used to saying '*no*'. But now... I'm not sure anymore. Maybe with the right partner, someday."

"You miss it? Elysia?"

The sound of my home village on Cliff's lips still sent a shiver down my spine—equal parts pleasant and chilling. "I don't know. I miss parts of it. Probably not as much as I should. Not as much as I miss my family."

He nodded, shadows in his gaze. Another gulp from his flask before it was finished and he let it drop in the grass beside him. "Yeah, I get that. You miss what you wanted it to be."

"I wish I knew for sure if Mother will be waiting at Aelthorin when we finally arrive. I keep imagining arriving after all this effort, all this time… Only for the village to turn me away in disgust because of this thing." I leaned the cap against my knee and drummed my fingers against the traitor mark unfurled over my cheek.

"You remember what you do to the people who fuck with you?" Cliff asked, a little too matter-of-fact for my taste. "You kill them."

He looked like he was kidding, but I knew him well enough to know he wasn't.

"That can't be the only solution," I chuckled.

"But it is the most effective."

I snorted. "A fine introduction—*be nice to me, or I'll kill you.*"

"Works for me," Cliff said.

My answering smile must've betrayed my dread. Something gave in Cliff's expression the way it so rarely did, and his hand shifted, sweeping me up in a sudden embrace to his neck.

"Hey—don't worry right now," he said, his deep voice resonating into my bones. "It'll be fine."

I nearly protested—*you don't know shit that it'll be fine*—but I felt so deliciously safe in his grasp, his body heat radiating into my bones, that I didn't have it in me. I melted against him, letting my wings fold and relax. He smelled familiar, like cedar and whiskey and the cheap shower gel provided by the motel. It all amalgamated into a masculine scent that was uniquely *him*.

I felt pleasantly numb, my head buzzing. My anxieties had been cast across the meadow. I shifted in Cliff's grip, taking him in. Under the hem of his dark tee, tattoos crawled up the strong curve of his neck. Not for the first time, I wondered what it would taste like if I gave that tribal swirl a gentle bite, sinking my teeth into his skin.

Stars, where had *that* thought come from?

While he was still stroking me, he said, "It'll be good for you to be with your own people."

"Trying to get rid of me?" I said into his shirt. "I knew you would ruin the moment."

"Shut up. I mean, I'd be exhausted, too, if our places were swapped and I was the only human for miles. It's not natural to be alone."

"I'm not alone. And if I find a charged gemstone, then you and Jon will be my people, too."

Cliff gave an odd pause. "Unless that spell is janky, or only lasts a day like you've been worried about."

"Then you'll be my people for a day," I scoffed, warmed by the thought. I couldn't see his face, but Cliff's touch became so gentle I wondered if he wasn't secretly pleased by it too. "Didn't you come out here to make me feel *better*?"

"Let's say your family's really at the village," he said, softer caution in his voice. "Say this place welcomes you with open arms. Your first choice *is* to stay there, right?"

"I… Of course."

"Convincing."

"Is it too much to want both?" I blurted, frustrated that I'd allowed liquor to loosen my tongue this much. "To have a home without losing you two?"

He scoffed. "Let's not bullshit each other. You mostly mean *Jon*."

"I care about you, too!"

"Sure, but we're not the ones frolicking in comatose-city every other night."

"The invitation is still open…"

"Yeah, yeah. I heard you the last three times."

I giggled—and it felt *good* to laugh.

"Hey, serious question." I leaned back, catching his eye. "If I was human, would you fuck me?"

Cliff's eyebrows jumped up. As he recovered, I was pleased to see his eyes rake over my body appraisingly—matching the impish glint in my own.

"Yes, but it would be purely carnal," he said, making a sweeping motion with his other hand. "No cuddling afterward."

I grinned at him, dropping my head back onto his shoulder. "That's what I thought, too."

We shared a soft laugh. I felt him turn his gaze back out at the forest, and the rhythm of his stroking continued over my shoulders and side.

I let the quiet stretch for a few moments. I could feel Cliff's mind wandering, his concerns lingering like a fog between us.

"I don't want to hurt Jon," I offered quietly. "He and I shouldn't want anything to do with each other, I *know*. But we were meant to meet. I can feel it in my bones. Why is it so *difficult?*"

"I don't know," Cliff murmured.

"I didn't ask to be like this—some *freak*," I said, my throat closing around the word. It was vile, but utterly resonated.

Cliff scoffed out a dry chuckle, unyielding to my festering self-pity. "We're all freaks, Sylv. Some of us just wear it on our sleeves more than others."

His fingers trailed down my wings comfortingly, lingering on the faint, jagged outline of the bullet scar that marred the elegant swirls. I stilled, feeling how he paused over the irregular membrane again and again.

"I'm sorry," he said, soft and sudden.

I patted his shoulder, glancing up at him. "Ancient history."

"Not to me. Your world wouldn't have been knocked off its axis if I hadn't…" Cliff stopped short, wrestling over his words. He shook his head, brow furrowed deeply. "Sorry doesn't cut it, but I'm *here*. Till the end of the road—whatever that looks like for you."

Warmth rushed through me—along with the startling revelation that Cliff was haunted by that first night. It *had* been his gunshot that had forced our fateful meeting, but sometimes I wondered if the stars hadn't had some plan set into motion long before I had ever flown beyond Elysia's perimeter.

Despite everything, I managed a watery chuckle. "What's with all the petting? Were you *that* worried about me?"

"Nah, I knew you'd be fine." He pointedly continued stroking me, and perhaps just to alleviate my tears a bit more, he added, "Actually, it's starting to make me feel better, too. But if you tell *anyone* I said that, I really *will* chuck you out the car window."

"Consider my lips sealed—*Oh!*"

My giggle seized up when his gentle touch swept under my wings and grazed the base of them at my back. The contact was thoughtless, but it stole the breath from my lungs and made warmth flood me like wildfire.

"Don't touch me there!" I blurted, squirming.

He stopped at once. "Shit—did I hurt you?"

"No, it's…" I snickered, resting my forehead against his neck. "Stars. That spot is *sensitive*, you know what I'm getting at?"

Cliff pulled me away like I'd burned him, gaping at me in horror. "*Ew*, did I just give you a fairy boner?"

My face surged with heat, but I burst into laughter. "Oh, shut up! As if you're not going to fall asleep memorizing what Jon and I looked like pitted against each other."

He *almost* denied it.

When Cliff unlocked the motel room, I pulled to a shocked hover just past the threshold.

"Are we under attack?" I breathed.

The wardrobe door was entirely removed from its hinges and propped against the wall. The supply of silver lay strewn about, bullets and blades half-sorted. The paper they'd lifted from Rhett lay atop it all. I couldn't bring myself to examine the sheet, not with the way Jon sat at the edge of his bed, head in his hands with a half-empty bottle of liquor threatening to spill its meager contents on the sheets beside him.

"Hey, man," Cliff said far too casually as he closed the door behind him. "Dumb question, but you doing okay?"

Jon looked up, blinking hard like he'd only just noticed our presence. He averted his eyes from me and regarded the broken closet door.

"Oh. I was—I was just trying to put away some clothes. Dunno what happened." He started to get up to fix it, but Cliff ushered him back to the bed.

Stars, I'd never seen him so drunk. His high cheekbones were flushed, giving his eyes an unfocused, glossy sheen. His wavy hair was disheveled with a lock falling across his forehead that I longed to reach out and tuck back into place. He sank into the bed, head resting heavily on the pillows as the room no doubt spun around him. Despite everything, my soul tugged at the sight of him—wanting nothing more than to offer some kind of solid comfort.

But as I watched Cliff prop a second pillow under his head, I wasn't sure I could do it like *this*.

"Thanks," Jon mumbled.

"You know the drill. If you puke, you're on your own," Cliff said, clapping him on the shoulder.

Jon scowled at this. "*Jódete.* I'm fine."

I glided over the nightstand, weaving between them. The way Jon's face fell at the sight of me nearly threw my resolve.

"Would you grab the burlap bag in the bottom drawer?" I asked, turning to Cliff. I didn't miss the way his expression clouded for a moment. We both knew what was in that bag.

"Sure that's a good idea?" He gave me a somewhat reproachful look as he moved to pull open the nightstand drawer.

I landed delicately on the pillow and faltered, registering that the concern buried in his gaze was for *me*, too. I offered him a small smile.

"This spell won't drain me like typical magic. I promise. If anything, it recharges me to visit." Although it didn't do the same for Jon… I imagined he would benefit in another way. I worried my lower lip with my teeth, softening my voice as though Jon wasn't lying directly beside us. "I think he needs to see me."

"Sometimes I think you make up these magic rules just to shut me up," Cliff muttered, setting the bag down and loosening the drawstring.

I smirked. "If I'm lying, then I'm learning from the best."

I knelt and gathered fistfuls of the earth we had collected in North Carolina. It had become bone dry from our travels, more difficult to work with as I hurried to form the spectral rune across the taut surface of the pillowcase. Jon watched me intently, but he didn't say a word, either in protest or encouragement.

"Keep an eye on things out here?" I asked, glancing up at Cliff.

"Yeah, I think I can handle five minutes of guard duty." He sat on the neighboring bed, sketchbook and pencil in hand.

I traced the circular rune with the brush of a fingertip and whispered the spell. I met Jon's gaze, searching for a kernel of consent. He placed his hand next to me in answer. Magic roaring in my ears, I touched the side of his hand and pulled us both into the spectral plane.

Our private sanctuary blossomed around us. We were no longer on the motel bed, now standing before each other on ground that seemed smudged with the horizon. Soft and yielding, yet firm under my feet. I felt the dampness of sweat on my brow vanish, my clothes becoming lighter. The colors of the space weren't as sharp as they usually were—perhaps due to my own partial inebriation.

The stark quiet of the plane felt like an embrace, a gentle hum of magic and energy as our minds met.

Jon cut a strong figure before me—little more than a head taller than me here. His cheeks were still flushed and his gaze glassy, but my heart still fluttered at the sight of him. Reachable, touchable, *mine*.

I rushed to close the space between us, taking hold of his arms with a gentle smile. He tensed under my hands, starting to pull away like he'd been scalded.

"Stop wasting your magic on me," Jon said.

"It's not a waste." I let my hands settle on his abdomen, lifting my chin to catch his eyes. "Do you want me to leave?" I asked, barely above a whisper.

Jon studied me. He swallowed and shook his head.

My smile returned, and I allowed my touch to stray with confidence, taking his hands in mine and squeezing. "I just feel like I can talk to you better here sometimes, when we're eye to eye. You know?"

He frowned down at me, the faintest smirk flickering at the corner of his mouth. "That's not happening unless you conjure a stepstool in here."

I snorted. *Stars, he really is drunk.*

But Jon's playful chuckle rapidly faded as he continued to gaze at me, eyes growing wet. My breath caught as he pressed closer, freeing his hands to cup my face. Despite the slight unsteadiness from the alcohol, his hands were still so much bigger than mine, encompassing my cheeks completely. His thumbs brushed over my temples, sending a shiver down my spine. The spectral plane masked some of the sensation, numbing the places where callouses should have been against my smooth skin and stealing his natural warmth.

Jon searched my face like he was looking for an answer. I remembered the man I'd first met in Dottage Mansion—the hulking shadow that captured me without remorse. It felt like that man had died, replaced by *him*, his dark eyes flooding with tears the longer he looked.

"I'm sorry, Sylv," he whispered.

"It's okay," I said, placing my hands over his. "It's alright, Jon."

He frowned, shaking his head. "That look on your face when I had you pinned… It ripped the soul out of me." Jon grimaced around the words. "You thought I was going to kill you."

My breath caught. I tightened my grip on his wrists, glancing down—remembering how it felt to have the air stolen from me in the Pit, the way he'd prowled beneath me.

"Not for a second," I said.

"Then why can't you look at me?"

Fuck. I lifted my chin, forcing my eyes back up. His expression withered at the truth that shone there.

"Jon—" I started.

He shook his head. A tear snaked down his cheek, and he sank down to his knees, hands sliding down to my waist. He looked up at me. "I'm *so* sorry. *No soporto que pienses de mí como una bestia, me mataría.*"

Any other day, I might've been enticed by the sight of Jon on his knees for me. What woman wouldn't be? But he was so shattered, and I couldn't bear it. I sank down with him and pulled him into my arms. His weight nestled heavily against me, anchoring us together.

"It's not your fault—not anyone's fault except those bastards who put us in there," I said. I chewed my lip, hesitating before adding, "I know you'd never be cruel. You'd want to give me mercy."

"No." Jon shuddered in my arms, his head heavy on my shoulder. "You don't understand—I'd let them skin me alive before it came to that, Sylv."

There was something fierce and ground-down in his voice, even when choked by emotion. It made hairs prickle on the back of my neck. I couldn't help but believe him, even as Gwen's aggrieved face flickered through my mind. She claimed Jon had used another hunter—*Luke*—as bait, and I struggled to merge that idea of Jon with *this* one.

I couldn't bring myself to question him. Not when he was like this. Not when I was too laden with exhaustion to bear the knowledge of such a heartless act.

Turning my head, I kissed his temple and murmured, "*Eres un huevón.*"

Jon stilled, pulling back to look at me. His brows were pulled together, a curious glimmer of—was that *laughter* behind his eyes?

"What did you say?" Jon asked.

"Cliff told me it meant 'heroic.' *Stars*, did I pronounce it wrong?"

"A better translation is *dumbass*—but I probably deserve that."

I groaned, embarrassment curling through me.

Jon gave a soft chuckle—my treasured reward. "You should know his priority was to insult people in as many languages as possible. Most of what I taught him are obscenities."

I remembered Cliff calling me *cielito* when he'd offered his advice, and now I puzzled over what harrowing insult had flown over my head. I made a mental note to freeze his flask into a block of ice when we returned to the motel room.

My arms tightened around him, as if holding him could protect him from the darkness preying on his mind. "Let me try again. I've been practicing."

"Practicing?"

"Learning Spanish," I said. "Some from the computer, some from Cliff when he'd help."

This wasn't how I had imagined it—exhausted and half intoxicated. I wanted to give him a piece of his world—something I was learning to hold, too.

His eyes softened in a way that made my breath catch. Jon was so often the honed weapon he had been forced to become—steely and sharp and unyielding. It felt beautiful, *remarkable* that my words could make that steel bend—even a little.

"You'd do that for me?" Jon asked.

I watched the tension in his shoulders ease, his lips parting slightly as though tasting the kindness, unsure whether to trust it. My fingers tangled in his hair, gently combing through the dark strands.

"I know how much it means to you. How it reminds you of home," I said. I pressed my lips to his temple as I worked around the foreign words. "*Tu eres mi vida.*"

Cliff had provided no translation for that phrase—only promised it would drive Jon crazy. I pulled away, searching his face for a sign.

"How did I do?" I asked, uncertain.

For a moment, Jon didn't say a thing, just looking at me like I was something not quite real. His gaze—*stars*, that gaze—turned molten and raw. Jon's arms circled around me, pulling me close. Then, finally, in a rough whisper, he said, "Good. Real good, Sylv."

I let myself melt, surrendering to blossoming warmth in my chest. With our bodies tangled together on the ground, I could feel myself becoming lost to him, my restraint dissolving as his breath curled against my hair. It was dangerous to let this feeling rip through me—how I wouldn't just learn foreign words for Jon. I would follow him into any battle. I would kill for him, to protect what goodness hadn't been stolen from him yet.

I love you.

I tried to cut the thought back, but the sentiment was coursing wildfire in my veins. I was far too late. My greatest gift to Jon would be to keep my silence—even if a part of me cruelly *wanted* him to know. I wanted him to ache with me. To know that we were doomed and to suffer together.

He wouldn't feel the same—he couldn't possibly. I'd always been difficult to love, and we had promised each other...

He pulled back, searching my face before crushing our lips together. I could barely breathe, and I wished I could taste him properly—untethered by the numbing perfection of the spectral realm.

"How do you do that?" Jon murmured between kisses.

"Do what?"

"Make me forget how I was drowning just a moment ago."

His breath curled against a place behind my ear, making shivers shoot down my spine. My back arched as Jon pressed a trail of kisses down my neck. "*Que rica*," he breathed. "You're so *soft*. When I'm here with you, all I can think about is the things I wanna do to you. It's fucking agonizing."

A soft moan escaped me, but the slur in his voice gave me pause. My shoulders slumped. I wanted to give in to the primal urges racing through me, forget everything like we were in the middle of a revel. I could imagine trees rising around us. Soft moonlight. Glittering stars. I could make the illusion rise around us with crisp clarity—I knew I could.

But not like this.

I gently removed his hands from my waist.

"We've both drunk too much," I murmured. My voice tightened, tenderly tracing the strong line of his jaw. "I just need you to be alright before we leave. I... I want you to fall asleep with peace in your heart."

This disarmed him more than any magic or monster I'd seen him encounter. He gave me a long, odd look before leaning in to kiss my forehead. "You're too good. Too fucking good," his voice rasped against me, chilling me. "I'm poison to you."

"Stop it. You're *not*—"

"I *am*," Jon said, leaning back.

His gaze flickered to my cheek–to my traitor mark—and over my body, where a myriad of scars and scrapes were cloaked by the plane's perfection. His eyes, even clouded by whiskey, moved like he had committed the location of each of them to memory.

"You've already been branded and banished because of me," he went on in a low voice. His hand traced along the hem of my cropped blouse, where the outline of a mottled purple mark should have been. "Because we took you. Because you saved me. What if I'm not strong enough to fix what happens next?"

His expression clouded, gaze far away and seeing past me. "There was something off in my dad—something that made him a prime candidate for possession, like it was drawn to him. It's going to catch up with me sooner or later. Maybe there'll come a time when I don't have a choice and I..." He breathed out sharply, and I saw a glimmer reflected in his eyes—a *real* fire. "I'll be the death of you."

From the corner of my vision, I glimpsed a plume of smoke rising in the spectral plane. A house in the distance succumbing to raging flames. I pointedly turned from it and cupped Jon's face to do the same. I brushed his tears away and pressed my forehead to his as though I could bleed tranquility into his mind.

"Jonathan Nowak, you will not frighten me away." I grabbed his face and met his eyes firmly. "If you want me gone, then I swear on the stars themselves that I will leave. But you have to say it."

He trembled. Then he pushed past my hands and buried his face in my hair. "I'm too selfish," he said in a wavering voice. "*Te amo, cariño*—" The last word choked off with a soft sob.

I shushed him gently and held tight around his shoulders. I kissed away the tears on his cheeks until they stopped. When I looked over my shoulder again, the shifting image of the house was gone. Jon's breathing was steadier. I sighed with relief.

I attempted a fragile smile, shifting myself into his lap, looking down into his face. "We're made of stronger stuff than whatever destiny you think is running through your veins."

A glimmer of something familiar struck in his gaze. "Fuck destiny?"

"Yes—fuck destiny," I said, grinning.

Around us, the sky and ground softened in hue. His fingers brushed the wound on my shoulder—where it should have been.

"I can't hurt in here, remember?" I assured him.

Jon frowned deeply, his touch delicate nonetheless. "What does it feel like out there?"

"Jon…"

"Please. Tell me."

Even in this state, the gravity of the situation weighed heavily in his stare. He knew as well as I did that I'd never made direct contact with iron before today.

That moment—when the iron chain had seared against my skin—was the last thing I wanted to think about, but it lived with overwhelming clarity in my mind.

"Like everything about me was stripped away until I didn't exist—only the pain," I said. "I'm lucky it was just a graze. Any longer, and my magic would have been completely snuffed out for who knows how long. Even being near it was horrible—this awful numbness, hot and cold at the same time." I shuddered.

"You can't heal it away?"

"I tried, but it won't budge. I may be rivaling you for nasty scars soon." I found his hands, locking my fingers through his. "Can you put your salve on it?"

Jon's eyes lit up so readily, I nearly melted. He leaned his forehead against mine, sighing. "Promise me you'll actually sleep tonight, too," he whispered. "*Please*. You've been through enough."

My throat tightened. "I promise."

To my relief, we made it back to reality before his telltale nosebleed could make its appearance.

Still seated at the edge of the bed, Cliff looked up from his sketchbook. He eyed Jon with concern as we came to. But when it was clear that Jon was no longer falling apart at the seams—just a little intoxicated—Cliff gave me a grateful nod and came over to sweep the dirt back into the burlap pouch.

I glimpsed what he'd been drawing. The lines were rough and hurried, as though he might lose his memory if he didn't finish it fast enough. It was the alp, partway between avian and reptilian form. A tiny figure hovered above it, delivering the killing blow.

Like something out of a legend.

Meanwhile, Jon rifled through his bag for the salve. He hadn't touched it in weeks, seeing as I had taken over as the resident healer. I settled on the edge of the nightstand and allowed him to apply a fingertip of the salve. I didn't dare complain about the sharp, menthol scent, though I burst into giggles when his sloppy coordination made him smear it up the side of my neck, too.

His medicine brought a coolness to the heat of the burn. Not the instant healing I had known all my life, but far sweeter than any magic because it was *his*.

15

JON

Hannah's living room was a testament to her penchant for local art. Canvases ranging from palm-sized to four feet wide hung on every inch of wall space—eclectic abstracts, colorful nudes, and landscapes of marshes and bayous. The room was a mismatch of decades-old wallpaper and thrifted furniture. Vintage stained glass lamps perched on end tables crowded with picture frames, housing a seemingly endless array of family moments. Many of them were of Gwen and Hannah, but a large portion showcased Hannah's expansive family. I wondered wryly if Hannah kept all these pictures around just to keep track of everyone. To me, having so much family alive and well and speaking to each other was a small miracle.

I barely noticed Hannah's unusually clipped voice as she promised coffee and ushered us to make ourselves comfortable. My mind still raced with the same agonizing thought since waking.

Te amo.

I love you.

Some of the night before was foggy, but I remembered *that* with painful clarity. I'd said it in Spanish, and Sylvia wasn't any wiser to its meaning as far as I could tell. I was spared immediate consequence for that admission, but that didn't change the fact that I'd said it. That I'd meant it.

"How's Gwen?" Cliff asked.

Hannah strode for the kitchen and didn't look back. "Well, she refused to go to the ER. She's in bed, resting." *And not to be disturbed*, her tone implied.

Cliff gave a little scoff, glancing toward the bedroom hall—impressed. "How'd you convince her to do that?"

Hannah met his gaze with tentative levity. "You'd be surprised how convincing I can be."

I stepped toward the couch, squinting a bit as the morning sunlight shone through the green floor-to-ceiling curtains. My head throbbed slightly from the remnants of the bourbon last night. Cliff slouched onto a velvet armchair while I sank into the deep cushions of the sofa. An old, sleepy German Shepherd was curled up on the seat beside me, its tongue lolling eagerly and happy to accept my absent-minded pets.

Most of the other animals were on the move, snuffling around the floor for crumbs. I hadn't noticed until then, but there were various baked goods strewn across several surfaces in the living room, making me wonder if Hannah's garage doubled as a bakery: cookies, muffins, scones, cinnamon rolls.

I stole a glance at Sylvia, whose delicate figure glided across the sunlit room, moving from place to place as she excitedly noted each cat and dog roaming the space. She stole crumbs of pastries here and there. Her smile was radiant as ever, her cheeks flushed with a natural glow as she caught my eye and lifted her eyebrows.

I grinned back, hoping it was enough to quell the lingering worry that surfaced when she looked at me. It was remarkable she could crawl out of bed after the shitshow at the outpost yesterday, but once again, Sylvia proved she was made out of steel, not some damn pixie dust. Somehow, she was still here with me after I'd frightened her—and she still chose to see the light in me anyway. It was simply her nature.

Fuck, I wasn't good enough for her.

How could anyone see the kindness and wildness in her and not want to burn the world to give her anything she wanted? A heaviness settled in my chest—a slow, building panic. What if I wasn't strong enough to let her go at Aelthorin?

If you find a gemstone first, maybe you don't have to. The words were like claws teasing the back of my mind.

There were plenty of reasons not to bank on that—first and foremost, Sylvia's grasp on transformation spellwork was hypothetical at best. No matter how she tried to spin it, we all knew it would be risky without a guideline. A botched spell could mean injury—or far worse.

And if it works?

The voice at the back of my head sounded smug, and I grit my teeth, glancing toward the kitchen. That coffee would be a godsend. *Jesus*, my head was pounding.

At my feet, a small Yorkie wriggled between my boots, tail wagging furiously. I reached down to scratch its head, noting the bone-shaped tag dangling from its collar.

"Theodore? That's your name, huh?" I said to it. "Kind of a weird name for a dog."

"It is," Sylvia agreed. She glided down, letting the dog sniff her outstretched hands. She giggled at the wetness of his cold nose. "*Theodore.* Aren't you sweet?"

I tensed, ready to chuck the dog halfway across the room if it tried to bite her, but to my great relief, the Yorkie was as docile as most of the others that had made a home here. He licked Sylvia's hands and face—much to her audible delight—before nudging my hand for more pets. The dog made no reaction at all as Sylvia landed on his collar and began to stroke the soft fur between his ears.

"I wish I was an animal affinity," Sylvia sighed, shooting me doleful eyes.

"You've mentioned before," I said, unable to mask my fond chuckle. I stroked under the Yorkie's chin.

"I know. But then I'd know what you were feeling, wouldn't I?" She directed her attention back to Theodore, her voice shifting into an affectionate singsong. "I bet you're such a happy boy. Do you like the pets from the scary man?"

"Hey," I objected.

"And he's so *sensitive*," Sylvia went on, pressing three quick kisses to Theodore's fur. "I bet he's just jealous of what you and I have."

I stole another glance at Sylvia's face, relieved to find the sentiments were good-natured, not embittered. Not that I'd have blamed her. The ripple of insecurity was foreign, and I stuffed it down best I could.

The Yorkie shortly lost interest in me, trotting over to where Cliff was flipping through a magazine with disinterest. He'd managed to put distance between himself and the three cats in the living room—staving off another sneezing fit. The dog put its paws on his leg, tail wagging furiously. Cliff lifted an eyebrow, lowering the magazine.

"Little attention whore, aren't you?" he remarked. But when the Yorkie whined, Cliff folded and scooped Theodore into his lap, offering a belly rub with a little sigh of resignation.

Sylvia landed on the sofa's armrest, cooing an audible *"aww"* under her breath. "Who knew you were so good with animals?"

"Well, I've had a lot of practice with annoying little things lately," Cliff said, smirking.

Her expression flattened. "I'm not sure whether I should be more offended for myself or poor Theodore."

"Want me to give you a little scratch behind the ears later ?"

"Consider my question answered."

The Yorkie snapped to attention as raised voices shot from the kitchen.

"You're not supposed to be standing!" Hannah snapped. "Get back to bed!"

"I told you—I've had worse." Gwen's answering voice was weary. "I'm already here, might as well get to the couch."

Gwen entered, leaning on a crutch for mobility. Her expression was tight like she couldn't stand to wince in front of us. The Yorkie scrambled off Cliff's lap and bounded up to meet her.

"Down, Teddy," she grumbled. Cliff was on his feet in an instant to offer help, which she promptly protested. Short of sweeping his legs with her crutch, there was little she could do but allow him to usher her to the couch.

I had to admit that she was handling the injury fairly well. Against all odds, we were indebted to her. She could have driven off the moment she freed herself from Sylvia's ice. Hell, she could have turned on us at any point yesterday at the outpost in order to survive the fight she hadn't asked for. But Gwen had stayed—fighting by our side as though she hadn't once stolen a truck just to put as many miles between us and her as possible.

As Cliff helped Gwen hobble to the armchair, she and Sylvia locked eyes, both of them visibly stiffening. When neither of them said a word, Sylvia caved first, casually retreating to my shoulder. A confusing mix of guilt and warmth surged through my chest at how readily she found comfort in me—even if a small part of her still saw me as a threat.

Hannah strode into the living room with two steaming cups of coffee. Even as she handed them off to Cliff and me, her eyes were glued to Gwen, who was stiffly trying to make herself comfortable in the chair.

"The more you strain yourself, the longer it's going to take us to start packing everything up," Hannah said.

"Pack up?" Cliff echoed.

Gwen wouldn't meet anyone's gaze. "You know I can't afford to stick around after yesterday. Iverson recognized me. He'll smell us out—he's a psycho, you know he won't stop. We're ditching town as soon as I can walk."

The air felt pulled from my lungs. I glanced between Hannah and Gwen, realization crushing in on me. "Shit, I… I'm so sorry."

Gwen's eyes were cold, but there was something else I couldn't read there. "Doesn't change anything," she muttered. "But I suppose it's been a long time coming. Iverson's grip on the outpost was bound to bleed out to us eventually."

I wondered if that was her way of saying *I'm glad you're not dead*. Maybe it was as close as I would ever get after what I had done to Luke.

Hannah smoothed a hand over Gwen's shoulder, her elegant fingers playing with the disheveled strands of her ponytail. "Gwen's been trying to convince me to get out of Cypress Hollow since I met. Maybe this is the Lord's way of setting us on a new path."

Gwen snorted softly, but she shot a grateful look up at her girlfriend—the words a visible balm for the crease between her brows.

"I'm just glad you made it back to me in one piece," Hannah added softer, her touch drifting to cup Gwen's cheek.

The oven timer dinged, and Hannah turned toward Sylvia, brightening a little. "I stocked up on produce at the farmer's market yesterday before Gwen came home. Hope you like strawberry glaze pie. I'll be right back."

"You guys looking to feed the whole town before moving on?" I asked, glancing around at the platters of cookies and sweet rolls laid about the living room.

"She bakes when she's stressed," Gwen explained, giving a sheepish chuckle. "I should see if she needs a hand."

She reached for her crutch to follow Hannah, but Cliff set his coffee aside and rose to his feet to ease her back down.

"She's right, you shouldn't be walking," he grunted. "That gauze is barely holding as it is."

She shoved him twice as hard, but his grip was unyielding. "Too rough, asshole," Gwen grumbled, expression withering as she jerked from his touch.

"Funny, you used to beg me for that," Cliff said under his breath.

"Until you fucked it all up!" Gwen bit out.

Shit, I thought. *Here we go.*

Cliff snapped his head up, lips parted in shock. "Me? You were the one who left! No note, no text."

"Yeah, well, you didn't do much as drop a damn text—even after you knew where I was."

"Sweetheart, I don't beg for scraps. You ran away. You let me think you might be dead for a full month, only to call me from a damn payphone. What did you expect me to do?"

"Follow me!" Gwen's eyes abruptly began to shine with tears. "I wasn't running away from you—I wanted you to choose me, dammit." As her voice cracked, she threw me a sour look, but the venom had gone stale over the past day. She fixed her attention back on Cliff. "But you didn't. Of course you didn't."

Cliff went silent, realization crackling between them. He seemed frozen on one knee beside her. "Well, I didn't know that," he managed after a long stretch.

Gwen's gaze dropped to the armrest, where their hands sat inches apart. Her hand trembled slightly as she brushed her fingers over the back of his, like she was afraid to fully touch him.

"We used to talk about making plans. Adventures and fucking *life* between hunts. Or do you not remember?" It was strange to hear Gwen's usually harsh tone drop away into something quiet. "I got tired of waiting. It was clear to me where your true loyalties lie. You and I would always be second to saving someone else's life."

Cliff moistened his lips, glancing around him and catching my eye for a brief moment. I watched his fingers ease between her slender ones.

"If you'd told me that, we could've worked it out. *All* of us," he said. Another brief glance cut to me.

Gwen balled her fist, moving her hand from his. She hung her head, anger drained as she rubbed her eyes. "Come on, Cliff. We wouldn't have worked out shit—we were so young."

"But not stupid," Cliff said. A smirk lifted the corner of his mouth. "Well, maybe on occasion..."

Gwen's eyes were still wet, nearly sharing his expression. "Don't dwell. Let's be honest, it turned out better this way. I should hate you right now—I should be saying goodbye to Hannah, too, because of the mess you dragged me into. But she refuses to let go."

"Guess she's got that on me, huh?"

"Among other things," Gwen said, though not cruelly.

Cliff hung his head, finally giving a nod of disparaged under-standing. The silence leaching into that bright, colorful room made me want to excuse myself to the car lot with Sylvia in tow. But she was the one who spoke up after a long beat, gently cutting into the heaviness.

"Gwen." Sylvia cleared her throat when Gwen acknowledged her with severity. "Would you like me to heal your leg?"

"No," Gwen said reflexively, and I understood entirely—Cliff and I had grappled with the same resistance. Accepting any form of magic felt like a betrayal against everything we stood for. "I'll go to the hospital today. Soon."

"I promise, it won't hurt." She took to the air and pointed at Gwen's wrapped leg. "Is it riskier to trust a non-human or be limping on one leg while that psycho is gathering support back at the outpost?"

My brows rose—as did Gwen's. Drawing a deep breath, Gwen looked at the ceiling and worried her lip. Finally, she nodded curtly. "Fine. But if you lay a curse on me, I'm getting the flyswatter."

"Naturally," Sylvia said with a tight laugh. "Cliff, can you help her straighten out her leg and remove the bandages?"

Cliff dragged an ottoman over and winced in unison with Gwen as he did as Sylvia ordered, pushing up the pajama shorts and gently tugging away the layers of gauze. As the wound was revealed, it was no wonder Hannah was upset about Gwen not going to the ER. Cliff had done a decent job with the scant resources we'd had, but the skin around the bullet hole was swollen and discolored, ranging from angry red to a deep purple bruise.

As Sylvia hovered over her leg and began the healing incantation, Gwen shut her eyes to block out the view, as if it could be any worse than it already was.

Knowing that a wound like that would take a few minutes to heal thoroughly, I reached into my pocket. "Hey, Gwen—what do you make of this? Rhett was waving it around when he tried to cozy up to us."

The sheet of paper was a little worse for wear after yesterday's chaos, but sections were still crisp and clinical.

Gwen squinted her eyes open, looking relieved for the distraction as she turned the weathered sheet over in her hands. "A fucking monster grocery list?" she scoffed. "Can't say I've seen anything like it before."

"But we have," Cliff said gravely. "There was this little church way out in the boonies. Basement looked like some sort of freak show lab."

I could see how Sylvia bristled at the mention of the place as she recited the healing spellwork. Pulling my phone out, I found the picture I'd taken of the charred sheet in the church basement.

"See that?" I held the screen beside the sheet for Gwen to examine. "Same logo at the top." The corporate, circular *E* emblem.

"What the hell has the outpost gotten itself into?" Gwen muttered, pushing the paper back to me. "Sounds like I'm getting the hell out of dodge at the right time. I don't want anything to do with whatever shit *that* is."

Although I'd scanned the paper dozens of times, I couldn't help but let my eyes trail over it again. The sheet was structured like a purchase order, itemized requests and all. There were columns for *Description, Quantity,* and *Condition Upon Receipt.* The gruesome specificity set my teeth on edge.

A few had been checked off.

Ahools (juvenile). 12. Alive, wings intact.

Vampire. 1. Sedated, breathing.

Basilisk. 1. Taxidermied, no visible scarring.

Werewolf pelts. 3. Fully flayed.

Apparently, Rhett was still short on manticore quills, kelpie hearts, and a live banshee. However, he had penciled something into one of the empty rows at the bottom: *Siren. 1. Alive, hydrated, bronze sedation.*

I tried not to imagine what he would have added to the next row if yesterday had a crueler end: *Fairy. 1. Deceased, fully intact.*

Sylvia finished up the spell, ousting the gentle cerulean glow between her palms. The room seemed darker in its sudden absence.

"How do you feel?" she asked, searching Gwen's face intently.

It was like nothing had ever happened; Gwen's amber skin was smooth and seamless, all traces of the wound erased. Gwen pressed a hand over the area, testing if it was real. Her gaze was wide, lips parted as she met Sylvia's gaze.

"Thank you," she breathed.

Sylvia smiled—and I loved the light in her that surfaced when she healed someone. Softening *Gwen* to that point was a triumph in and of itself.

Sylvia turned back to me, her expression darkening on the paper still clutched in my hand.

"Something's not right out there, Jon. I want to investigate what I sensed by the wreck," she said, brushing her hands on her leggings. "And with those local legends… It sounds like glamour. *Fae* glamour."

I caught her eye, recognizing that look. "You think it could be another village out there?"

"We owe it to ourselves to find out."

The bayou hardly had the same hearty location of the lakeside willow grove that Elysia called home. Unlikely, perhaps—but certainly not impossible.

I glanced at Gwen. "Any chance we keep the Accord on loan for another day?"

"Those fuckers at the outpost will be looking to put your heads on a platter," Gwen said, gingerly touching her healing bullet wound as though she expected the mended skin to be an illusion. "And Rhett's sure to be leading the charge. You saw that back there—they listen to him."

"Yeah, can we talk about that? Who died and put Crazy Eyes in charge?" Cliff asked.

I pursed my lips, stifling a snort at the nomer. "Money talks, I guess. Who knows how much he makes from fulfilling even one of these orders."

"To think his fortune might be from the bones of my people," Sylvia said, shivering a little as though imagining Rhett's hand around her. With the spell complete, she seated herself on the edge of the sofa's armrest with her legs dangling over. "If there is a fairy village nearby, we have to warn them that he's on the hunt for our kind. We have time and general location on our side—the wreck was miles west of the outpost. Even if Rhett did send out scouts to find us, they'd be spread thin."

I let my eyes settle on her, tracing the way the sunlight illuminated her rust-covered wrap top, perfectly contoured to her body with the faintest shimmer embedded where embroidered vinework of the same shade crawled up the sleeves. Why was her discussion of stealth strategy a little *hot*?

That pull surfaced again in my chest. Wanting her to be mine—fighting that burn that I *shouldn't* want her.

"Good thing we're stocked up on iron, then." Cliff lifted a brow at the sour look Sylvia threw at him for the mere mention of the toxic substance. "Sorry, kiddo. Nothing personal."

She sighed, wearily waving a hand. "No, I know Elysia didn't exactly roll out their warmest hospitality when you came to save me."

"What, the entire fleet of guards trying to burn us alive? I barely noticed." Cliff angled his head to catch her eye. "What's the game plan if we find a village out here, then? Assuming they don't try to kill us on sight, you've still got your mark. You said other villages knew its warning."

I tried not to notice how Gwen had fallen unusually quiet, drinking in the fragmented glimpses of our history with bridled curiosity. She observed as Sylvia touched her traitor mark self-consciously, pulling her fingertips across the dark runes.

"That's what I was told," she answered. The stiffness in her voice was a tell—the terrifying frustration of realizing the majority of her worldview had been filtered through people who may not have had her best interests at heart. With the distance between us and Elysia, it was nearly impossible to determine which parts of oral tradition had been true, and which had been fodder to a culture of fear.

"So, we get there," Cliff went on, brows pulling together slightly. "And you're gonna say what exactly? *'Hi, my name's*

Sylvia. I was banished by my last village for allying with humans, but I thought I'd pop in for a social visit?'"

Sylvia met his gaze, her lips quirking. "Well, it'll sound better when I say it," she said airily. She was getting good at that—masking how frightened she really was. She turned to Gwen, all anxiety pushed from her expression replaced by a steely set to her jaw. "That church basement must be where the outpost was keeping that captured fairy. A fire affinity. What were they hoping to gain from... *studying* them?"

Expression unreadable, Gwen stared at the canvas-strewn wall across the room. Sighing, she pulled her leg up on the cushion and brushed her hand over her healed skin.

"Hell if I know," she muttered. "The cleaners were at each other's throats about laying claim to wings and bones before Rhett stepped in and insisted they keep the fairy alive." Her expression somehow became more grim. "Rumor was, he wanted its blood. Not long after the fairy was moved, Rhett was flashing cash and going on about improvements for the outpost."

I swallowed hard and forced myself to look at Sylvia. Her eyes were fixed on the rug, and she made no move to speak.

"There weren't any others after that?" I asked Gwen.

She shrugged. "None that I can tell you about—I wouldn't know. But it's not a stretch to say there's a settlement of fairies out there. Hell, I had nightmares about a swarm of them coming down on the outpost after what happened to their friend."

"*Stars.*" Sylvia buried her face in her hands and shuddered. Cliff offered a soft word of comfort, touching her arm delicately. But when she looked up, it was *my* eyes she found first. She started to push herself off the armrest, started to come to *me* for comfort again.

But that was all wrong. She shouldn't have wanted to be anywhere near someone like me. I stood before she could reach me, pacing toward the other side of the room. The people I haggled and drank with would readily slaughter her and her people on sight. And the worst of it was that I couldn't help but wonder—what if *I* had been there during the fairy's initial capture in the swamp? Could I have been just as eager to be the one to take down strange, new prey?

I wanted to say no, but in the frenzy of bloodlust, I couldn't be sure. My stomach churned at the knowledge that death wasn't even the end of a fairy's abuse at the hands of outpost residents. How many of the renovations had been paid for with that fairy's life?

SMASH!

The shatter of glass sent my hand straight for the gun in my jacket. Cliff and Gwen were on their feet at once, all of us turning to find Hannah in the hallway. Gwen staggered a little—not from pain, but surprise that she could walk so easily.

For a terrible moment, I thought blood was trickling over the shards of glass on the ground in front of her, but it was only strawberries.

Gwen drew in a sharp breath. "Oh, no—honey? Can you hear me?"

Hannah's eyes fluttered. A soft moan escaped her lips, followed by a series of rapid breaths as though she was hyperventilating. Her fluttering gaze became fervent, searching until it found Cliff. She froze, eyes going wide and desperate as she stared at him dead-on. In the next instant, she broke into a toothy smile.

"You're Cliff Everett, aren't you?" Her voice was hoarse, laced with a fragile hope.

Cliff flinched a step back.

"The one from the legends," she went on. Her stare was un-wavering, unblinking. "Are you going to save us?"

"What the fuck is she talking about?" Cliff asked, turning to Gwen, who had her hands over her mouth.

"You're Cliff Everett, aren't you?" Hannah spoke faster, frenzied. "The one from the legends. Are you going to save us? You're Cliff Everett—"

"Enough! Snap out of it!" Cliff shouted, starting toward her.

"No!" Gwen sharply pulled on his arm. "It's alright—let it pass."

I found Sylvia hovering behind my shoulder. I searched her gaze, silently questioning if she knew what the hell was going on, but she looked just as baffled. When I faced Hannah again, she wavered like she might keel over. Rushing forward instinctively, I took her arms to steady her.

She straightened at once, gasping at my touch as though I was wrenching her out of a watery tomb. With a raspy breath, she set her wide eyes on me, hands flying up to clutch the side of my face. Her fingernails dug against my skin. Her smile was gone, replaced by a look of unrelenting horror.

"*You,*" she wheezed. "Her love will ruin you."

Her eyes rolled back, and she slumped. I caught her before she could hit the ground, pulling her away from the broken glass. She was limp for all of three seconds before she blinked in confusion. She jolted when she saw she was in my arms, then scanned her surroundings—each of our faces, and then the shattered dish.

Gwen drew closer, laying a tender hand on her forehead. "It's alright—"

Hannah whimpered, tears filling her eyes. "You shouldn't be standing."

"It's fine—Sylvia healed me. All better now."

A hint of wonder lay buried beneath Hannah's tears as she glanced at Sylvia. Then she gave Gwen a horrified, inquisitive look. "Just now—did I…?"

Pursing her lips, Gwen gave a small nod.

"I—I'm so sorry," Hannah said, looking between each of us.

Flighty with embarrassment, Hannah pushed away from me and mumbled something about getting a broom. She retreated back into the kitchen, shivering.

"Is she okay?" Sylvia asked.

"She's fine." Gwen turned to us and steadied herself. "Load up the car. Go look for your fairies, and try not to die. Alright?"

"Hey." Cliff grabbed her shoulder before she could flee. "What the hell was that?"

"Just a little panic attack. Nothing a hug and a Xanax can't fix. Get going."

"Gwen," Cliff said, his gaze soft despite the *'don't feed me bullshit'* command that lay behind it.

Hannah brushed through the hallway that led to the bedroom, one hand cradling her head—refusing to look at any of us. Gwen hesitated, gaze sweeping over the three of us before settling on Cliff again. Something yielded in her face.

"It's okay, I promise," Gwen said. "We'll talk later. I've got this."

She followed Hannah, disappearing into the bedroom where their voices dropped into hushed decibels.

"It can't be possession, can it?" I asked once we were outside in the early afternoon light. "I didn't feel any cold spots. And retired or not, Gwen wouldn't just stand by while a spirit took the wheel on her girlfriend."

"No, she would've taken care of that ages ago," Cliff muttered, eyes distant.

After being the subject of her frenzy, I couldn't blame him for being shaken. What the *fuck* did that mean? The only legends about me and Cliff that had circulated wide enough in the hunter community was the hunt that earned us the *Appalachian Reapers* nomer, and even then... It just didn't add up. Hannah wasn't a hunter. She wouldn't have known about any of that.

My boots crunched over the gravel of the auto lot, Sylvia's wings a steady hum beside me. She rubbed her arms, as though the slight chill in the damp air was suddenly unbearable.

"It didn't feel malicious," she said. "Not like the spirits I've felt before. Just… *intense*. Like a hive of bees in my mind, out of nowhere."

She screwed up her face, pulling at the roots of her fiery hair—like the energy was something she could claw out of her head.

As we approached the loaner Accord, I stole a sidelong look at Sylvia. She was already looking at me, her gaze flickering with the same haunted glaze as we drank each other in. The more I tried to push Hannah's frenzied words from my mind, the more resonant they became in my memory.

Her love will ruin you.

16
JON

The air was thick with the scent of decaying vegetation and the sharp tang of brackish water. I wiped sweat from my brow, glancing at the murky sky. The forecast hadn't called for rain, but the clouds were darkening with a tell-tale weight. I could only hope it wouldn't pour down on us as we navigated the swamp. At the very least, the Accord was parked at the side of the winding highway where it would be safe from flooding.

Cliff and I pushed into the thicket of waterlogged trees, Sylvia setting our pace as she flew ahead. I wished she would've stayed closer. She glided over the deep water that had nearly been our grave while Cliff and I had to detour a quarter mile until we found a patch of solid ground we could walk on—a narrow island covered in moss and reeds raised above the surrounding water.

Our footfalls grew heavier as we followed, mud sucking at our boots. Glancing back over my shoulder at the tree line, I spotted the path the car had gouged through the damp earth when Cliff had swerved. The crooked lines sloped toward the water perpendicular to a second pair of tracks that must've belonged to the tow truck. I took one last look at the shattered branches drifting in the brackish water—evidence of the incident—before moving on. Sylvia hadn't stopped, so whatever she sensed wasn't there.

Every now and again, a rumble of thunder sounded above the persistent hum of insects. I watched Sylvia carefully—noting the stammer in her flight—but not even a yelp of alarm escaped her.

There was something perturbing about her renewed determination to wrap her anxieties in steel. Her resilience was beautiful, even if it was at the cost of something innocent in her. Something I may have helped suffocate, I thought with a pang.

No sooner had we caught up to Sylvia than she darted ahead again, leaving us to follow the hum of her wings. She navigated to where the water stretched open and deep, and the knobby mangroves dominated the horizon. Our muddy path connected to a dilapidated wooden walkway that jutted into the water. It might've once been a fishing dock, judging by the rotting nets tangled along its edge. The wood creaked under our every step, amplifying the eerie feeling that we were disturbing something.

At the end of the dock, Sylvia was finally rooted in place, hovering in midair just above eye level. She assessed the landscape with intense scrutiny, but I glimpsed awe buried beneath. The distant call of herons, lilies in bloom across the water, and mangroves with their arching roots—all of it was new to her. She had stopped gasping aloud at every unfamiliar terrain on our journey west, but amazement still seized her sometimes, even in the midst of a hunt. It had to be overwhelming—her world exploding in size in a matter of weeks.

I cleared my throat, hating to interrupt her wonder. "Any glamour?"

Her eyes narrowed at the tree line. "I thought it would feel like coming home to Elysia. There's always been a faint buzzing near the glamour bounds. I was hoping it'd feel like a familiar blanket once we came closer, but..." She shook her head. "It's strange here. Cloudy. It doesn't sit well." She folded her arms across her chest, expression darkening.

In the stillness, I fully took in our surroundings—and something odd caught my eye. The dock stretched sideways for several meters, gradually becoming more dilapidated before coming to an abrupt end.

A neat row of objects sat near the edge, looking out of place among the rotting boards.

"Hey—where did that come from?" I started toward the row, then slowed in confusion as the familiarity of the items sent a chill down my spine.

Behind me, Cliff cursed under his breath. "Is that… our stuff?"

The sight looked more akin to a vision from the spectral plane—or a horror movie. Mundane and hunting objects lined the edge of the dock in a perfect row, spaced equally apart from each other. Travel-sized toiletries, single bullets, spare flashlights, a couple of knives and—

"My necklace!" Sylvia cried. She swooped down to grab the snowflake charm before I could stop her.

"Stay back!" I ordered, thinking about how lucky she was that something hadn't leaped up from the water to grab her.

"What the fuck is this?" Cliff demanded.

"They're all from the Pontiac," I murmured. We were at least a quarter mile from the wreck.

Shit. That thing we saw in the water must've gone through our stuff before the tow truck rolled up.

"Sylv?" I prompted, hoping she might have some Fae explanation for why our belongings would be arranged in this way—like something had gone out of its way to be *fucking creepy.*

She brushed grime off the plastic gems of her necklace. Meeting my gaze, she shook her head slowly and held the snowflake out to me. "I can't make any sense of it," she admitted.

I pocketed her necklace for safekeeping, my expression shadowing as I scanned our surroundings—unsure of what I was looking for.

Cliff knelt beside me, reaching to fish something out of the water. It was small, no bigger than his hand. At first, I thought it was a branch or another one of our belongings, but when he angled it in the light, I glimpsed the brittle remains of vertebrae protruding. I looked into the water below us again, finding there were at least ten more fish skeletons in various stages of decay bobbing against the dock.

"Nasty," Cliff muttered, tossing the bone back into the water. "Guess this thing was hungry."

A *splash* sounded across the bayou.

Cliff snapped to his feet, hand flying to his gun while I instinctively did the same. We stood coiled with tension as the disturbed water rippled out—maybe forty feet away from the dock. Slowly, the ripples faded, leaving the swamp eerily quiet. The silence was broken only by the hum of insects and the slosh of water against the old wood beneath our feet.

Inhaling sharply, Sylvia darted between us and the water. Her wide eyes turned to meet mine. "Stars," she gasped. "Move back!"

We didn't question her, backpedaling from the edge of the dock with our weapons raised, searching for whatever threat had set her off.

The distance wasn't enough to quell her. She pointed behind us, her voice pitching into panic. "*Run,*" she gasped. "*Run,* hurry!"

A soft melody crept into the air, silencing all else. Sylvia's voice, the insects, the rustling leaves and lapping water. All gone. I froze, gun pointed stiffly ahead as the sad, soothing lullaby grew steadily in volume. My brow unknitted, a soft breath escaping me in a gust.

Pale hands gripped the edge of the dock. A woman with waves of red hair pulled herself up and sat on the last decaying board. She cocked her head, peering up at me with bright green eyes as her pink lips formed each gentle note.

As her tender gaze met mine, promising that this tune was specially made for me, I remembered one thing—there was no coming back from making eye contact with the siren.

Fuck.

My surroundings dissolved, falling out of focus—Sylvia, Cliff, the oppressive humidity. All my attention was *hers*. As the woman continued to sing, my heart slowed into a calm rhythm. There was nothing to fear now that she had found me. Her ethereal beauty defied the grime of the swamp.

She beckoned me with a delicate hand, and I couldn't work out why I was hesitant.

A dulcet voice filled my mind.

"You don't want to fight anymore."

She was right. I didn't. I hadn't wanted to for a long time.

My grip slackened. I didn't even hear my gun hit the boards below. My hand trembled, itching to pick it back up. But why? For so many years, I had been heavy with weapons and grief.

Something pushed through the peace—a frantic voice millions of miles away. I turned my head, but the melody ensnared my attention back. I lost interest in seeking the other voice when the woman before me whispered again.

"You're so tired. You deserve to rest, my darling."

An observation, not a command. And once again, she was right. A tear leaked down my cheek. I wanted to move forward, but my legs stayed locked in place.

"Come to me. I'll keep you safe—from everything, from yourself. Come."

Her pity was wrapped in love. She saw me as I was and still stared at me with such adoration. Finally, someone understood the exhaustion in my bones. She was going to take all the pain away. She was going to keep me from hurting anyone else.

The swamp water no longer seemed fetid—how could I ever think it was? The depths were a waiting, warm embrace. *Her*. My salvation.

I took a step forward.

The distant, pestering voice made its return.

Sylvia.

Faintly, I could feel her shoving at my neck, pulling at a lock of my hair. A bite of ice made me flinch in anger.

She didn't understand. She was holding me back from the love and peace I deserved. I brushed her away, my eyes never leaving the heavenly woman at the end of the dock.

All I had to do was slide into the cool water and bring an end to the pain that had shadowed me for nearly a decade.

17

SYLVIA

"Jon, stop it!" I flitted between the boys, fighting to steal their attention. "Cliff!" But they wouldn't listen, even when my shards of ice nicked the skin of their hands and necks enough to draw blood.

My injured shoulder throbbed from Jon's shove, dismissive as it had been. If I dared draw within arm's reach again, I could inspire more pointed violence. I turned, raising my hands toward the siren directly.

"You can't have them!" I snarled. Ice swirled in threatening gusts beside me, making the arching branches overhead shiver in the conjured breeze. "Let them go!"

To my surprise, the siren snapped her gaze away from the hunters and focused on me as though she'd only just noticed I was there. The boys' footsteps paused. Perhaps a siren's song took concentration, like any other spell.

The rotting face of the woman was hard to read, but the vicious annoyance was clear—until those milky eyes lit up with recognition. The thinness of the creature was painfully familiar, and I realized with a start that this was the siren I'd freed from the outpost's tank.

"You," I breathed. "You made it home."

"*Are these men yours, Mistress?*" the siren asked.

Hope surged through me, but I didn't dare lower my hands. "Yes, they're mine, so release them!"

Pouting, the siren narrowed her eyes to the fallen weapons on the dock, her tail slapping the water in agitation. "*They are hunters, back to cage me, to strip the flesh from my bones and wear my teeth as trinkets. They deserve to be my first taste of mortal meat.*" Her lips curled, revealing a gruesome smile that set my stomach churning.

"They won't hurt you," I said.

She giggled in disbelief.

"I saved you," I reminded her. "So you'll listen when I say they are *not* to be eaten. They answer to me—just watch. I won't let them attack you."

The siren's voice was petulant in my mind. "*May I have one, at least? Half of one?*"

"None!" The air shimmered with threatened frost, the grimy water beginning to sparkle. "I'll freeze this swamp solid and watch you starve to death—do we understand each other?"

Those glossy eyes shifted in consideration. A soft, clicking purr came from her throat. I remained tense, every muscle ready to unleash the torrent of ice magic waiting at my fingertips.

After another beat, the siren slumped off the dock and back into the water glumly.

I whirled on Jon and Cliff, searching their faces wildly. My heart twisted to see them like this—so disoriented, their minds desperately trying to surface from a choking fog. Sometimes I forgot how fragile even the sharpest human minds could be.

"Don't try to move," I soothed, my voice strained like a wire.

Jon blinked hard. His hands closed around empty air, finding his gun laying on the dock a foot behind him. He scrambled back and seized it. Both men lifted a hand to shield themselves from a second slip of eye contact.

"Fucking siren," Cliff breathed, furious—though there was still something conflicted and dreamy in his wide eyes, like he was still willing to dive in after the creature. His grip tightened on his handgun, gaze darting between the edge of the dock and the algae drifting on the water—as close as he could get to aiming at his target. Behind me, the siren gave a throaty hiss.

My heart raced. I wanted to freeze them all solid, if only to prevent a brief and sudden bloodbath.

"Don't shoot!" I shouted, flying in front of Cliff with my hands raised. "Let me speak to her."

Jon faltered, angling his incredulous gaze carefully to me—*only* me. He kept his weapon raised, finger tensed on the trigger. "You can understand it?"

I nodded, stealing a glance over my shoulder. I could only imagine what she looked like to them, or sounded. According to Cliff's sketches and notes, predatory glamour would cloak her sunken, clammy skin and serrated teeth in radiant beauty. The siren's glossy black eyes protruded over the tide, watching me with a morbid curiosity. I could turn that curiosity into our salvation.

"You have any idea how dangerous sirens are?" Cliff growled. "We're like walking ribeyes to that thing."

"And all non-humans are alike with no exception?" I snapped, lifting my eyebrows.

They both fell silent, and I knew my words had cut deep.

"Five minutes," I pleaded.

I descended to land at the edge of the dock among the items that had been taken from the Pontiac.

The siren bobbed higher in the water, studying Jon and Cliff with a twitch of her lips. *"They do obey you. How intriguing."*

I found myself fighting an odd smile at that. Why did a part of me enjoy the insinuation?

"Do you have a name?" I asked instead.

"Aureline."

My smile was genuine this time. "That's beautiful."

Her soft voice entered my mind again. *"You are not from here, are you, Mistress?"*

"Please, call me Sylvia."

I chewed my lip, measuring out how much information to reveal. I didn't sense any immediate malice from her, but Jon and Cliff were right to be cautious. I didn't miss the way her gaze kept shifting over to them like they were savory herbed pies set out for a feast. She was hungry—and true, gnawing hunger could make even a saint capable of atrocities.

"These items," I said, gesturing at the flashlights and bullets. "How did they get here?"

"For scenting. Pulled from the wreckage to seek the visiting Fae presence." Her eyes brightened knowingly at me.

"You were looking for me," I said, getting the awful feeling that this mission must have led to her capture. I gauged her expression—the way she looked at me like an eccentric friend, not a dangerous outsider. "Your kind couldn't have gotten close enough to search the car. Which means… other fairies are looking for me, too, aren't they?" My throat closed around the words, sudden anxiety shooting through me. "Could you take me to them?"

Aureline cocked her head, falling quiet for a few moments.

"Sylv, what's she saying?" Cliff snapped.

I didn't look back at him, holding up a hand for him to be quiet. He cursed, his stance shifting impatiently. Both hunters' gazes burrowed into me, making my skin crawl—even if it was protective, not predatory.

"The Fae will be most pleased to have found their visitor. You are… different from them." Aureline swam closer, her matted black hair clinging to her skin as she lifted a hand toward me, a single clawed finger extended. *"That mark on your face… Did hunters wound you, too?"*

A clawed finger traced down my side. Gentle, but sinister all the same. I muscled down the instinct to flinch away from her touch. "No, it's—"

I felt air rush behind me. Heavy steps rattling the dock.

"Don't touch her," Jon growled.

"Jon, wait!" I screamed.

He looked down at me, expression blazing. He wouldn't listen—he was going to pull the trigger. Aureline hissed, baring her teeth with a sharp flash of her tail. She slammed her tail into the dock—forcing Jon to stagger to regain his balance. Jon's attention flicked upward only for a second—but a split second was all Aureline needed. Her hiss became a haunting melody.

No, no, no—

This time, I saw the moment his eyes locked with the siren's with excruciating clarity. Horrifying, and yet I couldn't look away. Jon's stare glazed over, expression slackening. Aureline's song surged, and Jon crashed onto his knees like a dog yanked by a chain. I took a staggering flight out of his way. His gun plummeted into the water, vanishing from sight.

"Jon," I breathed, too horrified to scream. It was too fast, too frightening to form anything more coherent.

He gripped the edge of the dock, leaning over the water to peer down at Aureline like she was everything he'd ever wanted. In a sudden, fluid motion, Aureline lunged upward, seizing Jon's jaw in a bony hand. Her voice re-entered my mind like a sigh.

"*I've never seen one like this,*" Aureline said, her expression as dreamy as her distorted features allowed. Her thumb stroked his cheek. "*Look at all the colors in its eyes.*"

"Jon!" Cliff surged forward.

"No, wait!" I shouted, frightening tears blurring my vision. If he shot, the siren might take Jon with her.

If he didn't, she might anyway.

"I'm not fucking waiting," Cliff barked. "Get out of the way."

It had to be nearly impossible to shoot something you couldn't look at directly—but if anyone could do it, it was Cliff Everett.

"She'll *kill* him!" I hissed, turning over my shoulder.

Aureline's clicking purr drew my gaze back forward. She was still smiling at Jon's vacant expression, a cruel game flashing in her gaze.

"Do you want to come with me, my darling?"

"Yes," Jon answered, his deep voice a drone.

My stomach knotted, the single syllable like a blow.

"Let him go. *Now*," I barely recognized the growl of my own voice.

I cast a spell toward the water, creating ice around Aureline's waist in warning. I gave her a steely look, promising that only a flick of my finger could force the ice to close right through her soft skin. She flinched at the cold pressing on her, mouth twisting in what was the closest thing to resemble a pout.

"I won't warn you again," I said in a low voice.

Without taking her dark, iris-less eyes from me, she unfurled her grip from Jon and sank lower into the water. He sagged, gasping and gripping the dock, left staring at his own distorted reflection in the brackish water.

"I will take you, Mistress. If you keep your morsels in line."

I redirected the thread of ice in my palm, letting it coil like a shimmering, frozen serpent. The water around Aureline surged back into motion.

"If they try to hurt you, I'll freeze their hearts," I promised sweetly.

Her willingness to believe me was almost unnerving—what sort of fairies did she normally interact with? She trusted me enough to turn her back on the three of us before disappearing under the water. The tell-tale ripples of movements led along the shore, slow enough to track.

Although I was eager to follow, I darted to Jon first as Cliff helped him to stand.

"Are you alright?" I touched Jon's cheek gently. His eyes were focused now, but I couldn't shake the image of how unreachable he had been, carelessly brushing away my desperation for his attention.

He nodded, catching his breath. "Thanks," he said, looking almost embarrassed.

"I like saving your ass sometimes," I assured him. "It's kind of a turn-on." His instant smile melted the worry gripping my heart.

I pivoted, finding that the siren's movements in the water were quickly vanishing in the distance.

"Hurry," I urged the hunters. "Before she gets too far!"

Although I could hear them following, Cliff scoffed. "Or what—you'll freeze our hearts?"

Wincing, I glanced back, wrestling a playful smile onto my face to diffuse the tension. "If you believed that for a second, I must be getting better at lying, right? How about, '*Thank you, Sylvia. You're as talented as you are ravishing.*'?"

Though Cliff gave me a flat look, Jon gave a small snort of laughter, his eyes warming as he shot me a fond glance.

We cleared past the dock, following along the shore to catch up with the ripples of Aureline's figure. The boys had to take care with the sodden ground along the way, but I didn't need to slow until the trees began to cluster close to the water.

"How do you know you can trust her?" Jon questioned.

I weaved around a pair of branches and kept my eyes forward. "She... I don't know, she speaks to me with such respect. As though fairies have some sort of authority over her." I wondered how often such creatures formed alliances—there were certainly no mentions of it in Cliff's entry on sirens.

"You're sure that's not just her magic working on you?" Jon pressed.

"Unless I'm secretly into skeletal, rotting corpses, I have to say *no.*"

"Hey, you never know," Cliff said. Then he made a noise of disgust. "So you can see what she really looks like? Usually, it takes a blow with a bronze weapon to shake the illusion."

I perched briefly on a jutting bush to let them catch up, suddenly curious now that I recalled how siren illusions were tailor-made for each human. "What did she look like to you?" I asked.

"Hot blonde," Cliff said without hesitation.

"Jon?" I prompted.

He cleared his throat, his gaze pointedly set ahead. "Hard to remember."

"Liar." I took wing and dropped lower, determined to meet his gaze.

Sighing, he finally looked at me. "Reddish hair. Green eyes."

"A traitor mark on her face?" I tacked on. "Stunning blue wings?"

"Her hair was *long*," he said, matter-of-fact.

"I've been thinking of growing it out," I said with equally playful nonchalance. Although he'd called me beautiful plenty of times, pleasant heat flushed through me, knowing that his preference for my features would manifest even in a desirous illusion.

"Can you guys save the horny shit for later?" Cliff groaned. "I'm this close to letting the siren drown me. Hell, I'll do it myself."

Minutes later, something shifted in the air. The light fell differently through the branches and leaves. The humidity wasn't quite so vicious. The vegetation felt lush rather than overbearing.

I pulled to a stop when a stone structure jutting out of the water came into view. Thick layers of moss and lichen covered it so well that I might have thought it was a hill. Vegetation crowded so close to the shore that it practically swallowed the structure, making it blend seamlessly in the rest of the swampland.

Our frantic quest to keep up came to a sudden halt as we took in our surroundings.

Flowers were in passionate bloom in every direction, climbing the trees. From the corner of my eye, I noticed something shifting further away from the water among the trees. Both Jon and Cliff raised their weapons, but they faltered at once.

"Stars," I whispered.

A pair of deer made their careful way through the vibrant bushes. Their coats were white as freshly fallen snow, and pink blossoms had sprouted from their antlers. They avoided us peacefully, disappearing among the brush.

The water seemed clearer here, too. Darting schools of fish were visible, bold with bright colors. I glimpsed a snake with shifting, iridescent patterns shimmering over its scales before it slithered into the water to avoid Jon and Cliff's wandering trek. Butterflies skirted over the swamp, bearing vibrant wings that reminded me of revel nights and the stained glass of the church. A few of them glimmered, twinkling silver and gold like wayward stars above the water.

"Glowing lights," Cliff murmured. "Ring any bells?"

The legend Hannah had recounted came flooding back, but this time, it didn't fill me with uneasiness. The truth behind the story made my heart swell with hope.

"Sylv," Jon murmured, marveling at a glowing blue lily that opened slightly at his touch. He caught my gaze, a breathless grin growing on his face.

We smiled wordlessly at each other, coming to the same conclusion. This was the sign we had been so desperately searching for. All of these creatures and unnatural blooms were signs that a powerful gemstone was nearby—right within reach.

A shadow skirted over the meadow, and we raised our heads to see a hawk circling through the trees. I flinched closer to Jon, certain for a moment that the bird of prey was coming for *me*. Its flight dipped low to the ground, circling around all three of us. When Cliff held up his hands defensively, the regal bird landed on his outstretched arm.

My jaw fell open as it folded its wings, giving Cliff's shoulder a nudge with its head—as docile as one of Hannah's cats. Instead of the typical high-pitched call, the bird emitted a deep, oscillating hum punctuated by unsettling clicks. Cliff straightened his arm like a falconer, exchanging an awestruck look with Jon.

"You guys seeing this?" Cliff breathed.

I swallowed hard, nodding back. The hawk was *translucent*, with glass-like feathers that allowed us to peer directly inside at the sinewy muscles and pulsing veins inside. When it spread its wings, sunlight refracted through each feather like crystal, casting fragmented rainbows over the waterlogged earth.

The stretch of water to our right gave a lurch as Aureline surfaced up to her shoulders, looking wholly out of place in this delicate sanctuary. I darted closer, waiting for further instruction. She dove back down before I could reach her, vanishing somewhere beneath the massive stone structure.

"That's where she wants us to go," I called over my shoulder.

When Cliff set forward, the altered hawk took flight again, soaring through the flowering vines above. I watched it go, committing the beautiful, strange creature to memory.

A narrow path cut across the water, leading toward the mysterious cobbled building. I kept pace with the hunters, searching for an opening in the stone until Cliff pushed away vines and moss to reveal the entrance. The cut of the arched opening had eroded, giving it the appearance of a cave more than a dwelling. The darkness that waited within was a far cry from the gorgeous landscape around us. It gaped like a maw, and I couldn't help but hesitate.

"Maybe you should wait out here," I suggested, beginning to understand how they must have felt when they told me to keep my distance from the outpost.

"No," they both said at once.

I turned to face them, grateful and uncertain. "We don't know how these fairies might take to humans—and if the siren lets on that you're hunters—"

"You're not going in there alone." Jon leveled a firm look at me, then took the first step into the darkness.

18

JON

Sunlight scarcely penetrated the thick canopy of vines draping the mouth of the cave, casting wavering shadows along the walls.

As Cliff and I stepped inside, the air grew cool and damp, the scent of the stone surrounding us. An arched door loomed at the back of the cave, carved directly into the stone wall. There was no handle, and a testing push revealed no give. Intricate carvings bristled beneath my fingertips, and I stepped back to take in the entire door.

Symbols were carved along the arch and in intricate, swirling patterns. *Ancient Fae.* I recognized the character shapes from the spellbooks Sylvia frequently pored over—and from the traitor mark branded across her left cheek. The heart of the door depicted a crescent moon with tears streaming down its grimacing face in lines far too delicate for any human craftsman to carve. Encircling the weeping moon were numerous shooting stars. Their tails dragged across the stone sky with eerie threads dripping from each like fallout plummeting toward the ground beneath our feet.

Cliff shined a penlight over the symbols, expression focused as he brushed a palm over some of the thinnest lines. With his artistic eye, I knew he had to be even more awed than I was. The craftsmanship was bewitching and difficult to look away from—but there was something fucking *creepy* about the moon's face and the way the stars seemed to be draining into the earth.

The focused line of Cliff's light was joined by a wash of cerulean as Sylvia whispered the spell that ignited the ethereal glow beneath her skin. She circled around me.

"This must be nearly a thousand summers old," Sylvia breathed, her delicate fingers outstretched to brush the stone. The reverence in her voice seized the small space, echoing around us.

"What's it say?" Cliff asked. As she flew along the path of the arched doorway, he angled his light to provide her additional illumination to read by.

"Some of it's too eroded to read." Sylvia flew methodically, prioritizing the areas with the most intact etchings. "Passage… exchange… sacred requirement…" She glanced back at us with a frown. "I think it's asking for some kind of payment."

I locked eyes with Cliff, weary resignation stretching between us. Witches and warlocks commonly used security measures like this. I pulled the small bronze knife from my belt, the blade glinting dully in the strange wash of light.

"I think we know what kind of payment it wants," I said.

Sylvia's eyes widened, withering with a mixture of concern and disgust as she glanced between us. She flew out of my way with a muttered, "You've got to be kidding me."

With a quick, practiced motion, I made a small incision on my palm. Blood welled up, dark and glistening, and I pressed it to the rough stone door.

For a moment, nothing happened. The three of us held our breaths, only the unnatural and enchanting birdsong of the clearing outside filtering into the heavy silence. My blood leaked in a thin line from beneath my hand, still pressed to the central carving. A faint, almost imperceptible reaction ignited—the etching flickered briefly, a dim green light pulsing through them before fading again.

After waiting another minute, I pulled my hand back and wiped it on the hem of my shirt.

"It's not enough," Cliff said, rolling up his left sleeve.

He gestured for the knife from me, ignoring Sylvia's flinch as he made a careful cut along his forearm. Blood payments were a fragile art. The incision had to be superficial enough not to kill you but deep enough to draw the amount required—deep enough to be fucking painful.

Cliff grit his teeth, hissing as the blade sliced cleanly through his skin. Blood welled to the surface and spilled, pooling on the ground in morbid droplets. He turned his arm over, letting more trickle onto the base of the doorway.

Sylvia hovered over his shoulder to watch the gaping wound with a healer's scrutiny. I could see her hands flexing, ready to prepare a healing spell—

The blood shivered on the ground—*moving* of its own accord. It trailed in precise lines upward along the stone door, filling in the delicate carvings of stardust. It continued, pulled by unseen magic into the weeping moon until every line was flushed with crimson. The ancient Fae bordering the archway glowed chartreuse, the light intensifying until the entire cave hummed with energy.

With a deep, resonant groan, a door cracked in half along invisible, jigsaw seams and swung inward to reveal a dark passage. The air was colder on the other side, a faint breeze ruffling hair off my face.

"See?" Cliff drawled grimly. "Piece of cake."

That seemed to snap Sylvia's tether. "Give me your arm," she said urgently. She wheeled closer to him and ignited her healing spell. A burst of blue light flooded her hands as she pressed them to his skin on either side of the wound. Within a minute, her magic had knit the wound closed without even a scar.

"Thank you," Cliff muttered, flexing his hand as the last of the pain faded.

"Once again, I loathe to think of what you boys ever did without me."

Cliff shrugged. "Stitches aren't so bad once you get used to them."

Although her answering shudder of disgust was exaggerated, I could see the broader tension lining her posture—it was hard to ignore when she was one of the only sources of light. I couldn't blame her. If there were fairies waiting past the door, there was no telling what sort of welcome we could expect.

But as we followed Sylvia through the opening, darkness was the only thing that lay ahead.

Stone creaked behind us. Cliff swung the light around in time for us to see our only visible exit closing up. Sylvia gasped and made a beeline for the shifting stone, but the opening was completely sealed when she reached it.

There was nothing on the cavern wall. No indication that there had been anything at all.

Her curse echoed off the stone, followed by an incantation. A small volley of icicles shattered against the wall and splintered on the ground uselessly.

"Hey—easy." Cliff felt along the sealed stone, but he could only confirm what I suspected: "There's no getting back through this."

As he pulled away to search the cavern, I nodded for Sylvia to follow. "Deep breath," I murmured to her. "The only way is forward."

She gave a stiff, wordless nod.

With our penlights and Sylvia's illumination, we quickly discovered that the curved chamber didn't run very deep. Sylvia's flight was erratic as she searched our stone surroundings up and down, but evidently, there were no openings big enough to squeeze through.

The cavern ended in another door that looked exactly like the one we'd come through, etched with a weeping moon and shooting stars.

"This is a different constellation," Sylvia murmured, tracing the stars' paths with her fingertip. "The other was the Eternal Chalice. This… this is the Sylph's Path."

"The runes look the same," I said. No need for her to translate what the engraving demanded. "Guess that makes it my turn."

Distress lined her features as I readied the knife over my arm. I offered her a reassuring smile before carefully plunging the blade across. Grimacing, I allowed my blood to spill, stomach churning as the door eagerly soaked up the offering.

Sure enough, the Ancient Fae glowed in acceptance, and the door pulled itself apart to allow us entry.

Sylvia was already halfway through her healing chant by the time she reached my arm, as though she couldn't bear the idea of me being in pain for a moment longer than necessary. In her haste, the faintest pink line stayed behind on my arm, but I gently pulled away when she tried to make a second pass.

"Save your energy," I said. "It doesn't hurt anymore."

As we stepped through, the door behind us sealed once again. Another waited for us at the end of the new chamber, another constellation on display.

"Fuck!" Cliff took the knife from me immediately, eyes beginning to grow wide with alarm. "Three. That has to be it, right? Three's, like, the most significant number in every piece of lore." He turned to Sylvia like she might have an answer to this cryptic cycle of sacrifice.

"I—" She shook her head, lips pressed hard together as she regarded the new door like she might learn something new if she stared hard enough. "I don't know. I've never heard of anything so cruel—to claim the moon and stars want blood…" She darted closer to him when he raised the blade to his arm. "Wait! Maybe we should take a more careful look around. There could be something we missed."

"Where?" Cliff gestured around him with the knife. "There's nothing else, Sylv. All we can do is get through these damn doors. You feel that? There's no air flow in the place."

Rather than watch him grit his teeth from another brush with the blade, I searched along the walls leading up to the door. He was right—it was no use looking for anything else.

When Sylvia healed him, there was a hitch in her words.

The door sealed behind us after we passed through.

And the next one awaited us.

Dread pounded through me as I took the knife again. Even the relief of Sylvia's healing couldn't make me forget the amount of blood I was freely spilling out.

This time, I experimented by hanging back while Cliff and Sylvia passed the new threshold. When it started to close, I hurried to catch up. This place wasn't fooling around—didn't give a shit if we stayed together or not.

"Did we get a good look at how big this place was from the outside?" I asked when we paused at the next door.

No one had an answer.

Cliff sliced his arm with barely a sound, and we kept moving forward.

Two chambers later, we found the first human corpse. The scent hit us before the sight. It was curled against the wall beside the next door. Bits of flesh clung to it and spread onto the stone, stained with bright purples, yellows, and greens that were not natural to rot. Equally vibrant mushrooms sprouted through openings in its skull and ribs—the only living thing in this sealed-up hellscape that could decompose the dead.

In the next chamber, there were three dead. Two in the next, huddled against each other, rainbow decay intertwining.

Sylvia's voice and flight wavered more with each healing incantation. The glow that normally penetrated the light fabric of her clothing was blocked by red stains. Between the magic exhaustion and thinning air, she couldn't hope to replenish our blood fast enough, even if she was closing up the wounds to stop further loss.

"This could be... it," she croaked when my blood opened the twelfth door. "The constellations have been different every time." She paused to chant, to close the self-inflicted wound. "They've only used the major constellations—and there are twelve of those."

She made a distressed noise when she saw the scar she left behind on my skin. Her arms were smeared up to the elbow in crimson. I shushed her soothingly. No point in pristine healing when I would likely just have to open it back up again.

Unless she was right, and we were finally at the end of this sadistic game.

As the door sealed behind us in the next chamber, the utter lack of corpses was the first thing I noticed. A tentative rush of hope filled me—maybe this really was the exit.

But sure enough, my searching light swept over yet another door at the end of the cavern.

In my lightheaded delirium, I prayed that this one would simply swing open.

"*Wait.*" The crack in Sylvia's voice made Cliff and I pause in our stumble to reach the door. She had both hands clamped over her mouth, little sobs escaping through her fingers.

She pointed a shaking hand at the door. "That's the Eternal Chalice." As her hover drew closer to the ground, I spotted droplets of blood near the base of the door.

Fresh.

We were back at the start.

"Fuck this shit!" Cliff might have punched the wall if he had the energy. He leaned against the stone instead, running his hands over the scars on his forearms. "The fuck does it want!"

I couldn't begin to decipher the purpose in any of it. Even the most vicious monsters had a purpose for what they did. But this—this was nothing more than torture. Corpses left to rot *for what?*

Sylvia had slunk all the way to the ground, sitting on her knees and staring up at the door while her glow flickered.

I could picture the next few days as if they were already happening. She'd pass out from magic exhaustion. Her light would go out. Our penlight batteries couldn't last forever. Eventually, we'd be in perfect darkness. Until someone else came along and found a kaleidoscope of mushrooms climbing out of our corpses.

A chill washed over my skin, carried by a breeze. It was fucking cold. Maybe we'd die of that first.

But then, I realized—*a breeze.*

"You feel that?" I uttered, turning my head and blinking hard.

Halfway along the wall across from us, there was an opening that hadn't been there before. A stony threshold crowded with vines, leaves, mushrooms, and light. I swore I could hear a trickle of water. I might have thought I was hallucinating, but Cliff and Sylvia had locked onto it, too.

Stone began to grind together.

The exit was sealing, vegetation pulling itself back into the other side.

We bolted, desperate to reach it in time. Sylvia darted overhead, clearing the threshold just before Cliff and I barely managed to emerge on the other side, stone scraping my shoulder on the way out.

We stumbled forward, and my breath caught in my throat. A vast cavern stretched out before us—far larger than it appeared outside. Craggy ceilings glittered with bioluminescence, towering like a cathedral.

Cliff and I stood on a long strip of earth that jutted above crystal-clear water that churned around us, the surface glowing with the same teal bioluminescence with every ripple. Golden fae lights hovered at fixed points, illuminating small structures built deep along the cave walls like crawling ivy.

The hum of wingbeats flying between these formations filled the air. *Fairies.* Too many to count—not including the two dozen armored fairies that encircled us with spells glowing menacingly at their fingertips.

I exchanged a wide-eyed glance with Cliff, both of us rendered speechless. Hovering between us, Sylvia's cerulean glow faded, casting her in shadow as she clapped a hand over her mouth. Rainbows of color danced over her conflicted expression, refracted by the water.

With a heavy, resonant thud, the stone door sealed shut behind us. The sound hit me like a death toll. I whipped around, cold dread seizing me as I watched the last sliver of the other passage disappear from sight. I could see no other exit—certainly not for humans.

My attention snapped back to the front, where a small battalion of fairies were in formation. Their eyes were sharp, postures coiled and tense.

Cliff and I instinctively pulled our weapons, though I wasn't sure how much good our battered iron hunting knives would do if these fairies coordinated their attack. At the very least, they recognized the metal's poisonous aura; most of them flinched, their flights stammering. Sylvia cringed too, her gaze still fixed forward, never looking back at us.

"Only a precaution," she explained, voice wispy with fatigue.

One fairy in particular glided toward us, drawing my focus. He wore the same armor as the others—a deep, lustrous teal, intricately patterned with scales that seemed to glimmer in the light with every movement. Practical trousers were paired with ankle-high boots caked with mud. His bare arms were deeply tanned and inked with runes, with more favoring the left shoulder.

His presence commanded the attention of the other fairies, who seemed to wait on him for a signal. His gaze rested on Sylvia a moment longer than it did Cliff or me, his expression unreadable.

"On your knees," he commanded, his voice steady and authoritative.

Sylvia balled her fists, summoning a burst of icy air between us—but that was as far as the spellwork blossomed. The threads of frost flickered out, her shoulders sagging. The three of us exchanged resigned looks. We were in no shape to fight, dizzy from blood loss and magic exhaustion.

Muscling down my instincts, I slowly lowered onto my knees beside Cliff. We set our blades down, hands held up in a reluctant sign of surrender. The moment our knees hit, black vines burst through the stone floor like snakes, curling around our ankles with an unyielding grip. A testing pull confirmed it—we were rooted in place.

The commanding fairy met my enraged stare with a toothy smile.

"Welcome to Veloria, hunters."

19

JON

Soft, musical laughter echoed off the walls, making the hair on the back of my neck rise. I squinted in search of the source, new dread unspooling. From the shadows, sirens flitted intermittently through the water—and even more were entering the cavern through a sunken opening in the wall across the way. They didn't pursue us from the depths, but their eyes glinted at us as they surfaced and dove, giggling with a seductive curiosity as their faint, eerie melodies overlapped.

"If you'd kindly discard *all* weapons, please," the commanding fairy went on, jutting his chin toward the iron blades. "We prefer our negotiations to be free of bloodshed, when it can be helped."

Cliff scoffed, his voice a low, bitter murmur. "Sure, that seems like a fair fight, considering you've got two dozen trigger-happy fairies raring to go."

"Would you prefer we carve them out of your hands?"

I hesitated, looking between Sylvia and Cliff. This wasn't *entirely* hostile yet. They could have killed us the second we crossed over that threshold. If we had any chance of proving our goodwill and getting our hands on a gemstone, it was in our best interest to comply.

Cliff glared but reluctantly began to pull at his clothes, stripping away the assortment of weapons he had tucked away. A sheathed bronze blade, two glocks, and a few poison-tipped throwing knives, along with a box of silver bullets. He laid them out with a mixture of resignation and irritation. I did the same, surrendering my favorite knives, a handgun, and the smaller bronze blade we had used for the blood offering, still smeared with fresh crimson.

"Satisfied?" I asked, assessing the faces around us. I felt naked already, the weight of my clothes far too light without the comforting presence of my knives against my chest.

A female fairy with silver, braided hair joined the commander, her eyes narrowed at me.

"You're hiding something," she said. "I can sense it."

The others bristled, spellwork crackling along palms. Sighing, I caught Sylvia's eye. With a reluctant twist, I reached back and dug the ice shiv out of my boot. Sylvia had crafted it for me with reinforced magic, making its razor-sharp point resistant to melt. It was the last weapon I had, and I shot the room a small, sheepish grin as I held it up for them to see before placing it on the pile.

Sylvia lifted her eyebrows, biting down on her lip to stifle a wide smile.

Cliff shot her a questioning look. "Since when are you handing out shivs?" he hissed under his breath.

She shrugged. "You didn't ask."

When the hum of wings approached us, Sylvia's expression hardened. She turned to face the commanding fairy, and although her magic had already failed her, she raised her hands threateningly. I clenched my jaw, certain the vines would come for her next.

"Come any closer, and I'll drive an icicle so far up your ass, you'll choke on it," she said.

But the commander took her hostility without retaliation. The battalion behind him bristled, but he set them at ease with a simple hand gesture before meeting Sylvia's eyes.

"We bear no ill intent," he said. "Our sweet sister Aureline alerted us of your arrival. She returned home yesterday with a miraculous tale of escaping a hunters' fortress thanks to your help.

Even more miraculous was her claim that *you are the outsider who caught our attention the other night*. We were beginning to wonder whether you would find your way here."

Sylvia gestured at us. "Blood sacrifices and restraints are hardly a warm welcome. Why torture us if you knew we helped Aureline?"

The commander's chuckle was surprisingly sheepish. "The ritual is to ensure exhaustion upon a human's arrival. Far preferable to the thought of allowing hunters in our midst at full strength."

"Yeah, those corpses back there looked a little more than *exhausted*," Cliff muttered.

"Hunters and thieves who would have massacred our people," the commander answered matter-of-factly. "Too weak to prevail the price of entry."

"The restraints are unnecessary," Sylvia insisted. "We're not your enemies."

"They retain too much strength despite their sacrifice, thanks to your diligent healing." He quirked a brow at Sylvia. "Surely it brings you some satisfaction to see your captors on their knees?"

Sylvia breathed in sharply. "They're not my—" She glanced back at us and paused, her expression changing thoughtfully. Deception crawled across the features. She squared her shoulders and faced the commander. "You have it mixed up. I'm not a prisoner to them, but I've poured time and magic into taming them for my needs. Killing them would be an offense."

A few fairies exchanged looks with the commander, unsure what to make of her claim. The certainty in her tone was admirable—any worry hidden beneath could be interpreted as fear of losing her investment.

Attagirl, I thought. She'd come a long way from her stressed lies after the capture in Dottage house.

The silver-haired fairy seemed less than convinced, her smile tight. "And have you used these men to raid other villages at your command?"

"Of course not," Sylvia said at once.

"Then, what is your purpose here?"

She hesitated, and I couldn't blame her. There was no telling how these people would react to any shred of the truth. Demanding a gemstone in exchange for rescuing a siren sounded like a stretch, given our current position. That was all the leverage we had.

"I mean no harm here or anywhere," Sylvia said. "This is the first village I've encountered since leaving my own. After witnessing Aureline's familiarity with fairies and sensing your magic from a distance, is it a crime to admit I was curious?"

Interest piqued, the commander drew closer to her. "You claim innocence, yet you bear the mark of a defector. Shall we agree on honesty? You did not *leave* your village. You were cast out." There was no venom or judgment in his voice. His sympathy was startlingly genuine. He glanced toward Cliff and me, then back to Sylvia, gaze alight. "I'm sure there's a magnificent story behind this, isn't there?"

Sylvia was quiet for a moment. Even from behind, I saw how she tilted her head, the way she always did to make her hair fall over her traitor mark. "As I said—I sacrificed much to gain these protectors."

"Clearly." The commander took her chin, tilting her face for a closer look at the rune.

I couldn't help it—I flinched forward on pure instinct to protect her. To pull her away from this smug, powerful stranger. The earth cracked beside me, and more restraints wound around on my wrists in response. I fought back, and when Cliff tried to rip the new vines away from my arms, he was given the same treatment.

"Stop!" Sylvia cried.

In all the commotion, the commander didn't flinch. He looked between the three of us like he was trying to put together a particularly tricky puzzle—and he was thrilled for the challenge.

"Please." Sylvia sounded like she was making a great deal of effort to remain calm. "Let them go before you damage them. They're territorial, that's all."

"You chose volatile protectors, Miss. But quite loyal, aren't they?"

"I could say the same." Sylvia pointed at the water, where the sirens had begun to stir with more interest. "Yet I don't see any leashes on *them*."

"They are an integral part of our home—more than that, they are family. I cannot, in good conscience, release your hunters until I learn more." He raised his hand calmly to halt her argument. "You seem reasonable enough to understand that anomalies such as yours cannot be allowed to roam our community. But rest assured—Veloria is a haven, and you saved one of our own. You and your property will be taken care of as you recover and satiate this… *curiosity* of yours."

"They won't be hurt?" Sylvia demanded.

"So long as they remain docile."

"Swear an oath," she growled.

He gave a startled laugh. "Does the word of a Sentinel-Warrior mean nothing where you come from?"

Sylvia's posture went stiff. "Your rune is real?" she asked, suspicion in her voice. "It isn't just a tribute to the old tales?"

"It's as real as your own marking. Try healing it if you like—it won't vanish."

I swore her hand twitched like she wanted to touch it. Whatever this exchange between them meant, Sylvia stopped arguing as though something had resonated.

Water sloshed sharply to my left—followed by seductive laughter. The bonds on my wrists strained as I tensed, eyeing the flash of silvery tails through the water. The dark, too-large eyes. The sirens weren't glamouring us, revealing glimpses of their true, rotten forms—a sight typically reserved for drowning men.

"They've been asked to leave you be," the commanding fairy's voice cut through my thoughts, reading my face. "Be at ease, child."

My brow furrowed, gaze snapping back to him. Faint lines on his forehead marked him as a few years older than me at most, but he spoke with an authority that rivaled someone far older. His piercing brown eyes sparkled with that infuriating mischief, giving me the sickening sense that he read me far better than I could him.

What the hell have we walked into, Sylvia?

Another inhuman, clicking chirp echoed through the cave, chilling my blood. Though obedient to the order not to harm Cliff and me, the sirens continued to swim with disturbing excitement—unable to tear their eyes from us. They lurked like sharks circling a bloody carcass.

The commander turned back to Sylvia, offering his hand. "Come, get off your wings."

She ignored the aid but followed him down to one of the large, porous rocks that jutted from the ground before us. Several of the other fairies followed while a few of them lingered to circle Cliff and me at a lazy pace, whispering to each other conspiratorially.

The commander introduced himself as Marcellus, lead sentinel of Veloria. When Sylvia gave her name in turn, he kissed her cheek in greeting. Several of the other fairies did the same, pressing in to warmly exchange names. I could see how it disarmed her, stole the confident mask as strangers embraced her. It had to be jarring to be welcomed so warmly when the last fairies she saw banished her from her own home.

Sylvia looked so pale beside Marcellus, so *small.* I wanted her in my grasp, where she was safe. But she was not some naive girl who needed my protection, I reminded myself. The space between us burned nonetheless.

"You must've come such a long way," remarked a female warrior, plucking at Sylvia's torn top with a frown. The iridescent teal fabric was still damp with blood—*my blood*—from her efforts healing us in the passageways.

The tension in the air eased as the warriors pressed in on Sylvia with eager questions and flattering remarks. I heard several more of them voice their concerns about her traitor mark, but none of it was hateful. A willowy woman even kissed it, giving Sylvia a kind look. Another fairy comfortingly remarked that Veloria's alliance with predators like sirens would make them traitors in the eyes of just about every other village—they understood what she'd been through.

"You look hungry," a soft voice drifted past my left ear.

I stiffened, finding a fairy with olive skin and tumbling raven curls eyeing me the way tourists salivated over candy apples being dipped behind glass windows. She looked like she hadn't seen humans in decades, and judging by the corpses we'd passed, that was likely true.

"I'm fine," I said, keeping my gaze forward. I tried to ignore the prickling unease of being watched like an animal.

"Oh, I rather like this one." Another dulcet voice. I glanced to the side—this remark was for Cliff, not me.

A male and female, both adorned in the same lightweight, seafoam-colored armor of the others, hovered closer to Cliff, who was doing his best to block out the attention with a hard clench in his jaw. He seemed to be reserving his energy for staying alert through the blood loss.

"Won't you look at me?" she asked.

When Cliff ignored her, she flexed her hand, whispering under her breath. A thin vine broke from Cliff's other restraints, reaching upward to curl along his jaw. With a pull of her hand, he was forced to face her. *An earth affinity,* I realized. She might be one of the few present who could effortlessly remove these restraints.

"Where did this traveler find a specimen like you? Those lips…"

Cliff's green eyes flashed at her as he leaned against the thin, curling vine. "I almost never say this," he gritted. "But I'm not in the mood to be tied up."

The female giggled. She pouted with focus as she appraised the slope of Cliff's neck, glancing back at the male behind her. "Are you sure he's a hunter?"

"What a waste of a pretty face," the male agreed, clicking his tongue with disappointment.

Cliff offered them a cold smirk. "Oh buddy, if I had a nickel for every time I've been told that."

The male's gray eyes sparked with intrigue. He flew forward, grazing Cliff's jaw with an open palm. He cocked his head to the side. "You have a sharp tongue for your kind. Does it get you in trouble often?"

Cliff jerked away—I didn't blame him. "Touch me again, and I'll bite your arm off."

The female drifted to her partner, clasping his arm and resting her chin on his shoulder. "What if we keep this one, Arthur? If we speak with Marcellus and the others?"

"They would never permit it."

"But perhaps, if we framed it right…"

My breath seized. Temporary holding was a far cry from permanent captivity.

Cliff shared my revulsion, his gaze going stony. "I've got a better idea," he said. "Why don't you two love-fucks get a bunch of your little friends together, and you can all suck my dick?"

The female lifted an eyebrow, less than flattered. A second later, Cliff's bonds had tightened, forcing him nearly prostrate to the floor. His hands braced against the unforgiving stone, his face inches from the ground.

"You wanna kill me or fuck me? I'm getting some real mixed signals here," he panted.

I muscled down every instinct to attempt ripping free of the bonds, knowing I'd end up with my head on the ground too if I tried. My head still spun from lack of blood.

"Hey!" Sylvia swiveled her attention back toward us, glaring daggers at the nearby fairies. "What the hell are you doing to him?"

The dreamy tone in the female fairy's voice had soured. "I didn't injure him. But insults beget punishment," she said, eyes darkening on Cliff. "Don't you prefer him on the ground, dear, where he belongs?"

"He'll stop," Sylvia said evenly. She threw a hard look at Cliff—a promise that she was handling this. Her gaze settled on me for a moment, and my barely contained rage must have been noticeable because her stare pleaded with me.

For a commanding officer, Marcellus seemed utterly unperturbed by the rising tension.

"Disrespect is not tolerated in our territory," he told Sylvia. "Least of all from humans." He cocked his head, regarding her meaningfully. "Honesty is valued with as much ferocity."

We're screwed, I thought, sure that he had figured out she was lying.

"Precisely what drew you here?" he asked. "I find myself doubting that sirens and a shimmer of glamour are to blame."

Sylvia's hesitation said it all, but Marcellus didn't appear upset. "I… I'm a gem scavenger," she admitted. "When I sensed a gemstone and saw its effect on the nearby area…" She chewed her lip, glancing up at him through long lashes with a look that was both fierce and vulnerable. A look that would make him weak in the knees—it always had that effect on me. "I'm in search of a fully-charged gem. I had to come."

Marcellus chuckled. "I fail to see why you are in need of gem magic. You're adept, clearly. Taming hunters, healing such beasts repeatedly, and willing to defend yourself after that ordeal? Surely you have noble blood."

A sudden flush crept over Sylvia's face. "Oh, no—not at all. The noble bloodlines faded from my home over a century ago, if the records are to be believed."

"Powerful lineages find ways to live on." Nonetheless, he let the matter go. "It has been decades since an outsider found their way to Veloria, and is it any wonder? The outside world is not kind to fairies these days." He glanced toward Cliff and me as though we were single-handedly responsible. Reaching behind his neck, he unclasped a pendant and offered it to Sylvia. "I would be honored to show an outsider as tenacious as you what we conceal from the world."

Sylvia didn't move as he looped the pendant around her neck. She touched the charm, too small for me to make out. Her head snapped up to look at Marcellus. "Is this—"

"A mere fraction of what we possess. Please, come."

Sylvia started to follow him without hesitation, then halted and turned to us as if she just remembered we were there. "I can't," she told Marcellus firmly. "Not until my hunters are unbound. I won't leave them to be harassed." She shot a sour look in the fairy couple's direction.

Marcellus raised his eyebrows. "They must stay put."

"And they will," she insisted. She looked between Cliff and me with feigned detachment, cautious about making it appear like she was seeking our approval. I gave her the slightest nod—anything to get us out of here quicker, to give her the chance to find a gemstone.

Even if the thought of having her out of sight set my teeth on edge.

The fragile gleam in her gaze hardened as she read my face, then Cliff's. Sylvia squared her shoulders. "They'll stay put and won't bring harm upon anyone—fairy or siren. But I refuse to leave my protectors open to attack without any mobility to defend themselves."

The demand was a stretch, and I knew it. These fairies held all the cards, and even if Sylvia was firm, there was little she could do if her insistence was shot down.

But to my surprise, Marcellus made a gesture at the earth fairies who controlled our bindings. At once, the vines receded. "They will not be granted mercy if they show any aggression, you understand?"

"So long as you don't provoke them, you needn't worry," Sylvia said sweetly.

Sighing with relief, Cliff sat back up and stretched his neck, but his grateful gaze was all but ignored as Sylvia allowed herself to be led away.

I watched her lift into the air, her familiar form blending in amongst the small crowd. Their flight was graceful and swift, arcing around hanging stalactites dripping with bioluminescence. The room felt even more cavernous when she vanished behind one of the intricate dwellings built into the stone, windows awash with warm light—like some of the oxygen had left with her. An odd twinge tugged on my chest, though not for the first time. I hated that I couldn't always follow where she went; I was human, bound to gravity while she took wing.

"It's polite to accept offerings," said a soft voice beside me.

I snapped my head to the side to see the dark-haired woman from before, this time holding a jug. I hadn't even noticed she'd gone to fetch it. She brought others—three fairies who held covered woven baskets filled with what I could only assume was food.

Although I meant to turn her down again, a steaming scent wafted from the offered food, and I realized I was hungrier than I'd ever been in my life.

20
SYLVIA

Despite instinct telling me to stay on guard, I lost myself searching for familiarity in Veloria. As Marcellus guided me through the cave, I couldn't help but compare my surroundings to Elysia. The space was massive, much like the forest I'd grown up in. The gathering spaces and living quarters built into the stone reminded me of the sprawling underground tunnels of home.

Fairies flew and rushed about, tidying or busying themselves with tasks I couldn't keep track of. Naturally, every single one paused to look at me before hurrying on.

"I hope we didn't send your people into a panic," I told Marcellus, wincing. If our initial welcome was any indication, we were lucky to have not been killed on the spot.

To my surprise, he chuckled. "Not at all. The Celestial Feast is upon us. There is much to be done. Of course, you are invited as a guest of honor. As I said, your presence here is nothing short of extraordinary."

Maybe don't make buckets of blood the price of entry, and you'll have more visitors. I pursed my lips and said, "That's very kind, but I don't think I can stay." My stomach chose that moment to growl. I swore I could smell authentic fairy cuisine already—the herbed bread and berry stews were practically calling my name. I blinked hard. "I would rather not trouble Veloria longer than necessary. My hunters must eat, too, after being so depleted."

Marcellus paused at an elegantly carved archway that appeared to lead into a hub of dwellings. "The feast will easily provide for your hunters," he assured.

I faltered, considering this. Perhaps it wouldn't be the worst thing to have Jon and Cliff taste *my* food for once.

The fairy commander steered our flight through an archway. Behind it lay a two-story building in the popular style of most of the others—carved thresholds yawning over sturdy, polished red wood structures. It was only when we landed on the cool limestone balcony that I could make out signs of weathering at the base of the structure, evidence to decades of withstanding the spray of the water below. I grasped the railing and leaned over the edge.

There were three tiers of dwellings stacked beneath us and two more above, poking out irregularly like cogs on a wheel along the craggy stone. At the very lowest level, the dwelling had sloping ramps to the water instead of railings. A fairy with dark braided hair tinged with blue at the roots was seated outside with her bare legs plunged into the water. Her hands moved skillfully over the flower strand she was weaving—rosebuds and marigolds and peonies all woven into an intricate floral rope that snaked around her.

The task was hypnotizing, inspiring homesickness as I remembered a time when my errands had been to gather berries and scrub the Elysian kitchens before the final meal call—not a tender of bloodshed. I furrowed my brow as the memories flickered in. I pictured Jon and Cliff, surrounded by unknown fairies and waiting for me, and the thought suddenly soured into betrayal. Simpler times didn't mean *better*.

"This way," Marcellus beckoned.

He was holding open the door for me. Folding my wings to my back, I hastened to step inside. There was a quiet hum of energy in the dimly lit dwelling, with only a few women tending to various tasks. They all looked up at me when I entered, the murmur of conversation seizing like an ousted candle.

"They found the wanderer?" a woman voiced, her tone hushed.

"She found us," Marcellus said.

He placed a gentle hand on my lower back to guide me inward. Despite the intensity of their curiosity, I didn't get the sense I was unwelcome. On the contrary, the fairy closest to us scrambled to greet me, kissing my cheeks and clasping my hands tightly, introducing herself as Roslyn.

I barely noticed as she stepped away, enamored by the exquisite furnishings that opened up around us. A pair of crystal chandeliers scattered fae light across the windowless chamber, providing an ethereal wash of bright light. Plump cushions in jewel-tone fabric dominated the floor alongside velvety lounge furniture. End tables were stacked with books, their spines lovingly creased. The walls were polished smooth, dominated by midnight-blue tapestries, where gold and silver threads paid tribute to constellations. Some of the colors were dulled as though ancient hands had woven these long ago. My fingers twitched, fighting the desire to stride over and feel the delicate handiwork for myself.

Roslyn returned with a swath of fabric in her arms, holding it out for my inspection. I frowned, tracing the neckline of what was clearly a dress.

"Something fresh to wear while we launder your things," Roslyn said. There was something maternal in the way she smiled at me, goading. "If you plan to keep them, that is. We can always dispose of them—"

"That's not necessary," I cut in. I stepped away, shooting Marcellus a wary look. I assumed this had been on his orders—which apparently, traveled through Veloria as quickly as wildfire.

"Consider it a favor to me," he replied, taking the gown and pressing it into my hands. "You'll feel better, and you'll attract less attention."

There it was—less a kindness to me and more about protecting this village from distress. Somehow, this softened my resistance.

"You haven't had a new face around here in decades," I scoffed. "A few trailing eyes are the least of my concerns."

"Even still."

His gaze flickered ever so briefly downward—at my hands. Dried blood from both hunters was caked up to my elbows and smeared under my nail beds. Even for a battle-worn warrior, I was a ghastly sight to behold.

I lifted my eyebrows at Marcellus coolly as I snatched the bundle from him. The sand-colored fabric was so soft, it made me ache. Suddenly, my embroidered leggings and wrap top chafed against my skin, worn in at the knees and elbows from constant wear and harsh scrubbing. I held the dress up, measuring. If I tied the waist sashes snugly beneath my wings, it would be a perfect fit.

"You don't like women covered in a little blood?" I asked, sliding my gaze toward him.

Marcellus raked me up and down, smirking. "On the contrary. Sadly, I can't afford to govern based on my personal preferences."

"Tragic," I simpered.

Fuck, I shouldn't speak to him so brazenly. We were vastly outnumbered, and I was exhausted—

No—I wasn't exhausted. Not anymore.

I blinked, briefly glancing at the pendant he'd placed around my neck. The tear-drop sliver of a charged gemstone lay against a gold setting, looking anything but insignificant against my fair skin. The humming of its magic was more pronounced when I focused on it. A beckon, a lullaby—just like the shard Mother had given me.

Marcellus laughed, the sound warm and disarming. He clapped a hand on Roslyn's shoulder. "See that she has what she needs. I'll be waiting, Sylvia."

How strange to hear another fairy speak my name after so many weeks. He strode away, and I waited until I heard the murmur of conversation across the room before stirring from my reverie.

Roslyn led me into a restroom—*washroom*—and I swallowed a contented sigh, knowing that I wouldn't require any assistance with something as mundane as turning on a faucet. Nonetheless, Roslyn stood in the center of the room, watching me expectantly. I'd slowly grown accustomed to waiting for privacy for the boys' sake.

A lax grip on modesty should have been a relief, but Roslyn's stare was far too searching as I stripped my clothes off. She took my leggings and top, her appeasing gaze lingering on my hips more than once. She smiled, polite enough not to ask about the patchwork of bruises that mottled my thighs and below my ribs nor the iron burn on my shoulder.

"You have a rare beauty," she said. "My, you're so breedable."

I coughed on a laugh, uncertain whether *thank you* was the appropriate answer.

"Have you ever been with child?" she asked.

Startled, I could only shake my head. Stepping out of her hold, I said, "Out of the question—at least for now. Gem scavenging isn't a life that can afford nine flightless months—let alone a child to raise."

"Of course," Roslyn said, airily and distracted as she set the bundle of my old clothing on the counter. Her eyes fell to my dagger as I undid the holster from my thigh. Gentle concern—perhaps even hurt—pulled on her expression. "I hope you understand that you have no need for such a crude weapon within the walls of our home, Sylvia."

My grip tightened on the handle. There was no threat or aggression in her tone, but the implication was clear. My instinct to argue wavered. If I didn't relinquish my weapon, perhaps my chances of acquiring a gemstone would be in jeopardy. Hesitantly, I set my dagger among the folds of my clothing.

That seemed to set Roslyn at ease. She drew warm water from the large basin against the wall and assisted me in scrubbing away the remnants of blood from my skin. My hair was soft and dried in no time, leaving me with a sense of freshness that no motel room restroom had ever granted me. I slipped into the gifted gown and put up no protest to Roslyn's offer to fasten the cords that rested below the base of my wings.

While she chattered about the Celestial Feast, I admired the embroidered details along the front of the fabric—an array of constellations that had been adorned with subtle delicate thread. The layered fabric hugged my modest bosom while a slit in the cascading skirt allowed me to move unencumbered. Beautiful *and* practical.

I couldn't help but wonder what my father would make of Veloria with its reverence for the stars. I had no doubt he would be proud of me for making it this far, especially given that this village was marked nowhere on the map.

I am a gem scavenger in my own right.

The thought came bundled with sorrow. I wouldn't know how my father would feel about any of this—not in this life.

While Roslyn busied herself with clearing the basin, my gaze drifted back to my dagger. Before leaving the room, I snatched the sheathed weapon and tucked it into the deep pocket of my gown.

As promised, Marcellus was waiting for me in the main area of the dwelling. I swore his breath caught when he eyed me, but I was distracted as the women hurried to my side to coo over me. In any other situation, I might have been glad to spend leisurely time with them. They were entranced by my presence, suggesting I join them for strolls or chores or the Celestial Feast itself.

I couldn't help but admire how the Velorian women moved with a kind of effortless elegance, their skin a warm, tawny shade that seemed to glow like polished amber, just like Marcellus'. Their dark hair fell in waves or curls, boasting tones of deep turquoise, cerulean, and seafoam green that caught the light. Next to them, my red hair felt like a flare in the sea.

Many of them had gold runes painted on their eyelids, trailing up to their foreheads in beautiful designs. I had only seen Elsyia's Elders wear such runes during the winter Solstice feasts, but their paint had been crude compared to the tapered, intricate strokes these fairies had lovingly painted on each other. I was tempted to indulge their insistence that I join them in weaving garlands of lotus petals; their eyes were kind, promising wine and conversation.

Focus.

The gentle heartbeat of the pendant around my neck sent a shiver of alertness through me. And this was a tiny fraction of what I would attain when I found what I came for.

I smiled politely, glancing at Marcellus for help. He appeared faintly amused, perhaps teasing me by waiting a few more moments before stepping in.

"I'm afraid Sylvia has much to see before she settles in for the feast," he said, taking my arm to lead me away. He kissed Roslyn's cheek on the way to the door. "Thank you, my dear."

Before I could offer my thanks as well, we were out the door.

Smiling breathlessly, I pushed my damp hair back, feeling the soft waves slowly spring back to life. "Your people are certainly friendly."

"You expected a trial? They're enamored." He chuckled and gave me a meaningful look. "Naturally."

My face flushed. I turned away to peer through the archway at the cavern—hoping to catch a glimpse of Jon and Cliff. The path had twisted too much for me to spot them. Concern stirred in my gut as I wondered if I'd really needed to take all that time to clean myself up while they were still essentially captives. Though less than thirty minutes must've passed, worry burrowed in my chest. I wanted to check on them, even for a moment.

Unless it's too late, a sinister voice tickled the back of my mind. Once again, I had to assure myself that this was my own fear—not the Ancients back to collect. *Unless your boys are long dead already.*

No—no, that couldn't be. They were killers themselves; they would have fought. I would have heard them shout.

Marcellus took my shoulder, and I eased the furrow from my brow, cementing a passive expression as I faced him.

"Now, gem scavenger," he said with a roguish grin. "You could sense our stores from afar, but how precise are your instincts?"

I perked up, knowing a challenge when I heard one. He released me and nodded, allowing me to take the lead.

All at once, childhood fantasies came rushing back. I'd spend hours upon hours near the glamour bounds, pretending I was on some great expedition to locate the rarest of gemstones—much to Mother's chagrin. I dodged guard patrols not because I was breaking any rules, but just to see if I could. I dreamt of the beasts I might outwit, the adventures I would conquer.

The thrill of it drove me forward, searching for the exact direction of the gemstones' hum. Marcellus followed, neither confirming nor denying whether I was selecting the correct paths, but I knew in my heart that I was right. *Stars*, I hadn't truly utilized gem magic, but the exhilaration of the chase was intoxicating. It reminded me of how restless Jon and Cliff became when they were *so close* to reaching their target—except there were no monster corpses waiting for me at the end of this journey. Only power and freedom.

Fairies looked up at us as we charged through the air—through windows, from balconies, peering up far below from the water's edge. Seeing so many wings, so much like my own, set me oddly at ease. No one shouted or chased us. Some even smiled curiously, waving.

We were deep in the cavern when I finally paused to gather my thoughts, where dwellings along the walls became scarce and the width of the space narrowed. The idle passing of sirens were left behind us, the rush of crystalline water beneath us too narrow for them to swim. The diamond-like points of bookcases on the jagged ceiling thinned too, making me wonder if perhaps I had misread the pulsing beckon of the gemstones. It looked unfrequented—perhaps forbidden. Had we gone too far?

I felt it in my bones before I saw it—that *pull*. It felt like invisible ropes looping around my insides, tugging me forward with a weightless sensation in my stomach. Directly ahead of us, shadowed in the low light, my flickering gaze set on an entryway.

Like many of the others, the archway was carved out of the stone itself, but this one was different. The stone was carved like a tangle of vines, opals glinting throughout. After catching Marcellus' goading smile, I dove toward the curved balcony. A small set of steep, winding stairs led upward. I lifted the trailing edge of my gown as I ascended, taking them two at a time as I neared the top. My lungs burning, I brushed my palm across an opal embedded in the towering pillar.

No. Not these.

A whisper of air beside me—Marcellus stood before the doors and gestured a spell with his hands. Two spells at once, though he didn't move his lips—and I was watching carefully. A golden orb of light was conjured over his head, while the other spell unlocked the doors with a heavy *shink* of metal and sent them yawning inward.

"After you," he said.

He looked so effortlessly powerful as he gestured for me to enter, his warrior rune glinting in the warm light. My stomach flipped, and I hoped my expression was more collected than I felt. All of my training these past months pushing myself to my limits felt like child's play compared to what this man was clearly capable of.

I was grateful for the conjured illumination as we entered a hallway with lofty ceilings. The path led toward a chamber—the opening ahead wide enough to accommodate over a dozen fairies at once. Statues twice my height lined our path, their faces partially obscured in the bobbing gold light. I couldn't tear my eyes away from the darkness of the chamber—so thick, it seemed to swallow all light. A flicker of fear joined my anticipation. I didn't need Jon and Cliff to protect me, but I still wished they were here. Just to be with me.

But that pulsing rope around my heart roared.

Come, come, come.

It was with a dizzying kind of certainty that I knew what lay ahead in that darkness. Charged gemstones—more than one.

"How did you do that?" I asked, folding my wings to walk beside Marcellus. My hushed voice caught oddly in the hallway. "You didn't speak a word. That takes decades of practice." His amused stare made me suddenly flush, questioning Elysian training yet again. I finished in a smaller voice. "I mean, doesn't it?"

Marcellus held out his left hand to me. His tanned fingers were dripping with rings, and for the first time, I noted the gems in each—emeralds, rubies, topaz. I let my fingers graze the gilded bands reverently. Only then did I notice faint, silvery scars webbing over his palms and the backs of each finger. When my touch strayed to one of the metallic scars, Marcellus pulled away sharply, setting us back at a brisk pace.

"Each of those—they're *charged*," I breathed, looking up at him sharply as I matched his stride.

I frowned, realizing the stone around my own neck may have clouded my ability to sense their individual auras. The entire village felt like a fog of powerful, pulsating magic.

Marcellus' eyes fixed ahead, and he let his hand drop to his side. "I didn't always live in Veloria," he said. "I once belonged to a village many weeks' flight from here. A troubled place—plagued by corruption and predators alike. Warriors were drafted to protect our fragile peace. I didn't have a choice.

"I was only twenty-five summers when I was forced to defend our home from a rabid wolf. It was sick, but that made it all the more difficult to subdue. In the end, I was separated from my attachment in a cavern for days, without food, my wing torn in half. I thought I would join so many of my peers' fate." He paused, giving me a sidelong look. "It was in my darkest moment that I found my first gemstone. My salvation. Deep in the recesses of my prison, there were half a dozen of them, calling out to me. When I answered, everything… *clicked.* Power not only to heal my wings down to their very fibers, but to reinforce them against the elements. Spells flowered at the very thought of my intention—no guiding incantation required."

I shuddered at the very concept, aware of the cool, earthy air biting my exposed skin as we walked side by side. "So, not decades," I said, injecting tentative levity into my voice.

"I spent nearly a dozen years more honing the practice," Marcellus corrected, adjusting a sapphire ring on his left hand. "Power demands discipline and sacrifice."

"I'd say you earned your warrior rune many times over." I shook my head slightly, frowning. "It's funny, I grew up hearing a story like that from my father. The usual old gem scavenger myths—I'm sure you've heard your fair share. Father loved those larger than life figures like Karolyn the Gilded, Cael Firesong, Edin the Valiant…"

Marcellus' gait faltered, his eyes cutting over to me. There was a sparkle of humor there I didn't understand.

"What?" I demanded.

Marcellus coughed, suppressing an undignified laugh. "It's quite a title, isn't it? *The Valiant?* Sounds so pompous. I never cared for it."

I snorted. "Why would the title of a centuries-old warrior bother you?"

But even as I said it, a strange thought scratched at the back of my mind. My smile fell. Those old stories about gem scavengers turned warriors living for centuries…

Was it possible one was still alive today?

The golden orb of light moved forward, pulling my attention with it. I followed. The hallway yawned open into a chamber so vast that the light couldn't touch the walls. The orb split and scattered, illuminating the rest of the room. My breath caught as I scanned my surroundings, nearly too overwhelmed to process what I was seeing.

The chamber reminded me of the blood ritual caverns and the old church combined into one. The stone walls glittered with geodes embedded deep within. Symbols and carvings were too numerous for me to note all at once.

"Welcome to the Starforged Sanctum," Marcellus said, coming to a stop beside me. I felt his eyes on me, watching my reaction.

I forced my gaze to slow, tracing what I could understand. The twelve sacred constellations were the main fixtures on the walls, clusters of geodes tracing the patterns—and each constellation had a gemstone that represented its major star. These were not slivers or even palm-sized chunks—but twelve full, pulsing gemstones that each glowed a different color. Each would have been large enough to cradle in both hands.

My first steps into the Sanctum were tentative, but I soon found myself hurrying to the wall, taking wing to look closer. The gemstones burned brighter as I passed each one, as though they were welcoming me. Upon further inspection, I noted the tiny chunks carved out of them. I was certain I could match the indents to the stones on Marcellus' rings and the gift hanging around my neck.

The air felt different here, too. Whispers of a breeze made the hem of my dress flutter. "This place isn't as contained as the rest of the cavern," I said, squinting up.

"You're perceptive," Marcellus said with unguarded admiration. He waved his hand in an arc, summoning another wordless spell with a flex of his fingers.

The tightly woven vines overhead pulled apart to reveal the clear night sky. I braced my hand against the stone wall, mouth agape as I glimpsed many of the same constellations that were honored in the Sanctum.

I didn't realize I was sinking out of the air until Marcellus was at my side. He guided me down until my feet touched the ground.

"It must be overwhelming," he said kindly, leading me to one of the many benches that circled throughout the Sanctum.

"An understatement if there ever was one," I said with a weak laugh.

As I sat, I tore my eyes away from the constellations and gemstones to scan the other carvings on the wall. Some images were so faded, I could barely make them out. But I could see figures with wings and others with fins. A mixture of them were clustered together, surrounded by constellations.

Marcellus followed my gaze. "Prophecies spoken by the stars," he said in a soft, reverent voice.

I shook my head. "Prophets haven't spoken for the stars in…" I trailed off and turned to face him fully. The longer I looked, the more I allowed my previously impossible thought to surface. Marcellus didn't look all that different from the rare illustration I found of Edin the Valiant in Elysia's archives. Breath catching, I swept my gaze around the constellation stories carved around us. Etched faintly in the dark stone was a solemn profile, a male stern and timeless—the resemblance was vague but unmistakable

Perhaps there were very few things in this world that were actually impossible—I'd just been too sheltered to know it.

I swallowed hard. "*Valiant* may be a pompous title, but Edin is said to have sacrificed himself in the rite that charges empty gemstones. My father always told me that charged gemstones became sparse over the years because fewer warriors were brave enough to offer up their lives to ensure their people had access to potent magic."

Marcellus said nothing for three long breaths. "What would you think of a centuries-old warrior who commanded his underlings to spread a rumor of his sacrifice?" Though his smile was wry, his expression made me suspect he cared very much what I thought.

I broke away from his stare, settling on the ruby that marked the center of *The Fox's Harp*. "My father doubted that he would be willing to perform the rite himself. He said there was too much of the world he hadn't seen enough of yet. So if Edin's sacrifice turned out to be nothing more than a rumor… I don't see the use in shaming him for it."

The chuckle Marcellus breathed was surprisingly humble. Self-conscious. "After a certain number of decades, an unaged face and a new name does wonders. Though, eventually I found no desire to venture far from this place. Not once I gathered others who shared the same vision as I did."

Though I was firmly seated, his confirmation made the room spin around me.

Him?

The mythical warrior I'd read about in old tomes *was* real—and he was seated right beside me. I suddenly realized I could smell the salt and metal on his clothes and was struck by what a privilege it was to know something so intimate as his scent.

"You're centuries old," I whispered. "Impossible."

The corner of his mouth quirked upward, his fierce gaze pinning me. "You have no idea what's possible."

I eyed the many rings on his fingers questioningly, once again considering the faint aura of gemstone magic that clung to each one. He closed his hands on his knees, frowning slightly.

"Do you know why so many fairy communities halted their progress?" he asked. "Isolation. Closed-mindedness. They were unwilling to see the possibilities the world held for them. Even gem magic became ostracized in many places."

I nodded in understanding, my heart pounding. Father had said much the same of Elysia. I remembered his frustration, the arguments with Mother waking me in the middle of the night when Hazel was but an infant. Marcellus wore that same steely look, his eyes glazed with anger.

"No matter the rising odds stacked against us, no matter our dwindling population… Those in power refused to mingle outside of their own kind, certain that no mutual bonds could ever be formed. That no creature besides our own kind could be of use to us."

"The sirens," I realized.

His gaze met mine, certain and bold. "Once a moon cycle," he said. "The population of Veloria gathers here in the Starforged Sanctum, and we drink the sacred gift of our siren brethren. In return, we live in peace together. They are protected within the glamour bounds, safe from rivals and hunters, given plentiful food. *That* is what the stars intended."

Sacred gift?

Then, it connected. *Blood.* Siren blood was said to have healing properties and prolong one's life if ingested. And if someone had an infinite supply of blood…

I should have been repulsed, but all I could focus on was the miracle sitting beside me. *Edin the Valiant.* I was speaking to a living legend, and the defiance of what should have been impossible made my heart flutter. Staring at him, feeling the intense pulse of the gem magic surrounding us, my fantasies felt less impossible, too.

"The gift is not without its drawbacks," Marcellus swept a look around the vast chamber toward the stars winking overhead. "Not every fairy finds eternity palatable. Some choose the inevitable alternative—though I do everything in my power to prevent this. And… It has been many years since the laughter of children has filled these halls."

"*Oh.*" It was all I could utter as this crashed down on me like a wave. I recalled the faces we had passed on our flight here—only now did it dawn on me that not a single child had been among them. No children steering their hummingbird mounts while they waited impatiently for their wings to become rigid enough to carry them.

What the fuck?

He shot me a placating smile, shifting a little. "Procreation is the only drawback of this gift. I hope you don't think I'm some suffering bastard now."

"Of course not," I said, breaking the tension with a laugh. I chewed my lip, selecting my next words with care. "I suppose there are difficult decisions we must make to survive."

I must've chosen wisely—thank the stars. Marcellus' gaze flushed with warmth again.

"Well said," he granted. "In an unkind world, we must protect the longevity of our kind at any cost."

Dozens of questions wavered at the tip of my tongue. Questions that would have revealed how fragile my mask of complacency was. Marcellus did not seem like the type who enjoyed having his way of life challenged—and perhaps I wasn't in any position to poke holes in how someone lived, considering the company I'd kept the last two months.

I cleared my throat and said, "Your camaraderie with the sirens sounds like something out of an unwritten story. A legend to be told in reverent whispers under the stars."

His expression softened. "It *is* written in the stars, for those who are willing to find it." He turned his attention up at the night sky. "I suppose you're familiar with the stories behind the great constellations?"

"Of course." I observed his reverent expression as he stared upward. "Is it strange to say it's a bit surreal to hear that a living legend is so engrossed in the same stories I fawned over?"

"Oh, stories are crucial. Sometimes, they're the best weapons we have in this life. They may seem like simple lessons for younglings, but the truth is always buried beneath." He pointed at *The Eternal Chalice* on the cavern wall. "I've always been partial to that one."

I bit back a laugh. *Can't imagine why.*

"It's about living forever among the stars," I said. "Allyna the Eternal guided her lover's soul to the afterlife."

"A common, though watered-down interpretation." He drew in a slow breath as though he was drinking in the tale. "Ultimately, it's about sacrifice. Just as Allyna sacrificed her lover to earn her title, we must also be willing to exchange what we love most for what is right."

Another uncertain chill ran through me, but I deflected it once more with a chuckle. "My father never went into the grisly details of that story. Even he thought it was too brutal for my young, innocent ears."

Marcellus thoughtfully turned his gaze to me. "May I be direct? It's a bad habit that comes with old age. You speak of your father quite often—no mother, lover, or other can seem to compare. May I ask why?"

"He died nine summers ago." I looked down at my lap. "I miss him, of course."

"Nine years, and yet you speak of him as though he's in the adjoining room."

My heart fluttered at the silly thought that, with every other impossible thing, why couldn't that be true, too?

"I suppose it's hard to let him go," I admitted.

"Why?"

"Because I think he was like me. *Exactly* like me, for better or worse." I hesitated, but now that the floodgates were open, they wouldn't close. "If he were here, maybe… he'd give me his blessing for all my fucking insane decisions. Maybe I'd have fewer sleepless nights if I had one single fairy who didn't make me feel like there was something horribly wrong with me."

I didn't realize tears were welling up until one trickled down my cheek.

Marcellus cupped my face with one hand, wiping the streak away with his thumb. "Who could ever see something wrong in *you?*"

He took my hand and squeezed it, looking at me with intensity that made my stomach flutter. He leaned in, his heat dizzying. This man of legend was here. He was holding me, wanting me—

I shot to my feet. "Thank you for showing me the Sanctum," I said, my voice cracking.

My head spun with the sudden and dizzying possibility that Marcellus might have *kissed me* if I'd stayed still. My heart pounded. I didn't want that, I told myself sternly. Besides, there had to be a line even for him. If he knew how badly I wanted to lay with a hunter someday, he would have been too disgusted to touch me.

"You know why I've come to your village." I wet my lips, summoning my courage. "Tell me plainly—can Veloria stand to part with a gemstone?"

The satin fabric of the sandstone gown lay cool against my body. Suddenly, it felt wrong. I was not like them—I was an imposter infiltrating their home.

For a moment, I worried I'd insulted him with my bluntness. To the contrary, Marcellus leaned back, his posture entirely at ease.

"That depends," he answered.

"On?"

"What would your intention be with such a powerful reward?" He raised his eyebrows at my look of hesitation. Waiting.

"It's a gamble for love," I admitted, each word carefully selected. "And for freedom beyond measure."

"My favorite sort," he drawled, and I nearly collapsed in relief when he didn't demand more detail. He did, however, continue to stare expectantly.

I was *so close*. I couldn't fail now.

"I have items of value I could bargain with. I have historic journals from my village—several of them. Surely your people would be grateful for writings from outside Veloria," I said, trying not to let my urgency creep into my voice. This man was centuries old, and I must've sounded like a rambling child to him as I scrambled to think of what else I could offer. "I… You can keep the weapons my hunters surrendered, as well. Precious metals are difficult to come by."

I winced internally, thinking of the effort Jon and Cliff had taken to garner those weapons.

They'll understand, the pendant around my neck hummed. *A small sacrifice for such formidable magic.*

Marcellus stood, hands raised placatingly as his smile widened. "Enough, please. Don't you understand that your presence is compensation in and of itself?"

He eyed the gems set across the room, as though considering which would suit best to gift me. My heart sank when he strode for the exit without a single spell to dislodge one. He looked back, beckoning with that faint, knowing slant to his lips.

"Dine with us first. You're correct that my people are grateful for stories that come from beyond our walls. Fresh company is more valuable than anything scrawled on parchment."

Biting back impatience, I stole one last look at the gemstones behind me and conceded. As he led me out of the Sanctum, I memorized the path carefully.

21
SYLVIA

I hadn't eaten blackberry tarts in *months.*

The scent of food hit me the moment I set foot over the threshold of the dining hall. Herbed potatoes, savory vegetable stews, spiced apples—and blackberry tarts.

The chamber was cavernous, flushed with the warm light of a dozen fae lights embedded in chandeliers overhead. The dangling teardrop crystals refracted the illumination across the craggy walls, making faint deposits of limestone glitter. I shut my jaw and held my head high to hide that I was salivating.

A pang hit me as we passed a number of long oak tables surrounded by fairies—eating, talking, laughing. It was too much like home, and I found myself taking comfort in the furnishings that were different. Plush cushions lined the walls, inviting after-dinner conversation. A few fairies seemed to have already finished supper and were deep in goblets of wine, speaking nearly nose-to-nose. A male—clearly a fire affinity—flexed his hand absently, playing with a tongue of flame that hovered in a wall niche.

As I scanned the faces around me, my stomach gave a faint twist of discomfort. Now that Marcellus had pointed it out, the lack of children was unsettlingly obvious. Though their bodies were youthful—no doubt the supple effects of drinking siren blood—I couldn't help but wonder at their true ages. Who had been the last among them to enter Veloria before indulging in the longevity of their peers?

When we were guided to sit, I was unsurprised to find myself placed beside Marcellus. A gold platter was placed before me, piled with food and insistence that I help myself to whatever I desired. I was too hungry to put on airs, to pretend that I wasn't ravenous. I was on my second bite of rosemary potatoes when a horrible thought made my throat tight—*what if they've poisoned it?*

A sweeping glance around at the dozens of fairies passing food and eating plentifully set me at ease. Even the most bloodthirsty assassins surely wouldn't kill a whole village simply to end me. Perhaps it was ego talking to even suspect poisoning; what threat was I to them? I was nobody.

"And how long will you be staying with us, Sylvia?" My name spilled so casually from the fairy sat across me—her voluptuous figure accented by her sand-colored dress that cinched with a gold belt at the waist.

"No longer than the evening," I answered. *At most.* It couldn't have been more than an hour or so, but Jon and Cliff were bound to be restless. I doubted they were surrounded by the same ample offerings.

This thought spurred me to my feet abruptly. I offered a weak smile in response to the curious and started looks that fell over those seated around me. Unable to ignore the stab of worry in my chest, I scanned the table and seized a platter of food that was still heaping—a silly gesture, but I wanted to offer my friends *something*.

Marcellus touched my elbow, shooting me an inquisitive look.

"My hunters must be famished," I explained.

Marcellus relaxed into a smirk as if to say, *Oh, is that all?* "You needn't worry. As promised, your hunters are being treated well. They've been given a fair portion of the feast."

I pursed my lips, glancing toward the door. My chest twinged—hoping to hear one of their deep voices carrying off the stone walls.

Why haven't I heard their voices?

"You're sure?" I asked.

"I was told firsthand," Marcellus said, waving a hand to illustrate. "Stuffed mushrooms, pastries, and berry wine."

The pendant around my neck gave a soothing stir—a calm rushing through me. It was a *good* thing I wasn't hearing the hunters cry out. Their silence meant safety, not certain death.

As Marcellus guided me back into my seat, I smiled to myself and set the platter on the table. Maybe this whole debacle wasn't too much of an inconvenience for Cliff, given how he insisted I meticulously describe the taste of berry wine whenever I mentioned revels. Even Jon might appreciate the rare treat.

The thought made me reach for my goblet, hardly touched in my ravenous feasting. I carefully limited myself. The pleasant pulse of the gemstone around my neck alone felt like a touch of intoxication, making me drunk with hope and the idea of a full gemstone's power being hours, perhaps even minutes away.

With that kind of power, my uncertainties about the future would melt away. I could craft my own future. I'd be free.

"Thank you again for the hospitality," I told Marcellus. "I promise we won't stay long enough to trouble you for another meal. Keeping up with the hunters' appetite is a chore, to say the least."

He chuckled. "Sylvia, you needn't keep reminding me that you're in quite the hurry. But I hope you understand that you are welcome in our walls for as long as you like."

A woman in a light green gown hummed in thought. "It must be quite difficult keeping those brutes fed."

A tingle of protectiveness raced up my spine, but I shoved it back down. I smiled tightly. "They sustain themselves just fine."

Even so, I could hear something defensive in my tone, so I quickly added, "In fact, I never worry about my own meals—they bring food to me without prompting anymore. They do whatever I need."

Impressed murmurs swam around me, and I couldn't help but swell a bit at this fantasy—that I had conquered a fairy's worst nightmare. I supposed it wasn't that far from the truth.

"How did you come about these hunters?" a bearded man in a vest asked.

My initial stammering brought heat to my face. I focused on what I'd learned from Jon and Cliff when they lied for information or to stay under the radar—*throw in pieces of the truth and they'll latch onto the honesty without questioning the lies.*

"I intercepted them while they were hunting a *mactir*," I said in a hushed voice, drawing the others to lean closer to hear. "They wounded me, right through the wing." I pointed at the scar, prompting little gasps of sympathy. "But that was the last time they dared hurt me."

My pause, naturally, was met with whispers of, "What did you do?"

"I convinced them I wanted to help end the *mactir* in exchange for my freedom. Of course, I knew they'd never let me go. Unfortunately for them, it was too late. It was all too easy to glamour them into doing my bidding the moment they let their guard down."

A flush crept up my neck and painted my cheeks as I drank in the wide-eyed looks of admiration around me. As I gazed along the table, I wondered if anyone else here was a legendary hero like Marcellus. For all I knew, I was being fawned over by every fabled warrior I looked up to.

When I reached for the platter of blackberry tarts, I realized with a start that they were a raspberry variety instead.

The food rotated too swiftly at this feast that I worried I might not sample it all. When would I have another opportunity?

"What happened then?" the woman in the green dress asked.

I looked up from my plate to find that she was actually in a blood-red gown—or was I looking at the wrong person? I blinked hard. I couldn't have missed such a rich color.

"We completed the hunt," I said slowly. "The *mactir* was unstable and far too close to my home village. From there, I began using the hunters as protection on my gem scavenging journey. But… glamour is easier to maintain when a semblance of their purpose remains intact." I smiled impishly, as though I were describing children who needed to be at play. "I give them a chance to unleash their bloodlust, of course, so they still hunt the beasts that would mean to harm fairies. And I rescue those innocents whom the hunters would kill without a second thought—like Aureline."

The bearded man shook his head in fond disbelief. "My dear, are you certain you don't have noble blood running through your veins? Precious stars…"

I shrugged humbly, hesitating when I noted the color of his tunic seemed lighter than before—and I was sure he'd been wearing a vest. "If I have noble blood, my village certainly didn't appreciate it. I was branded for what I did."

The bearded man stared, then shook his head. "Well, branded or not, it seems that fate has a way of revealing noble hearts. Even if it's much delayed." His eyes twinkled as he lifted his cup, sloshing wine in a toast. The fairies around me murmured their jovial agreement, wings refracting delicate light from the glow of a hundred fae lights flickering around us.

"To Sylvia—the warrior!" the man declared.

Everyone at our table followed suit, making my cheeks flush—not from the wine, but from the overwhelming sense of acceptance. It was dizzying. My free hand grasped at the gemstone pendant around my neck for comfort as I touched my cup to all those I could reach.

As I touched my glass to Marcellus', our eyes caught meaningfully.

"Indeed," he said. "I'd have a hard time finding someone more worthy of the title."

I sipped at my drink, trying to calm my heart because *Edin the Valiant* just called me *a warrior*.

A pair of hands grasped my shoulders. A woman with plaited hair and a sapphire gown smiled down at me as I turned. "Someone like you deserves a rune to match," she crooned, tucking hair behind my ear. "Wouldn't you agree, commander?"

My lips parted as I met Marcellus' honeyed eyes. "Would you like that?" he asked.

I traced the rune gleaming on his bare shoulder with my eyes. *Yes*, I wanted to blurt. Another dream of mine that I had shoved into a drawer long ago and let collect dust. My cheek stung with the memory of the mark I did have. It was sobering, remembering that night. The shattered pottery on the floor. The white-hot, painful stinging. I didn't realize I was clutching my arm until Marcellus' warm hand laid overtop mine.

"It won't hurt," he assured. "I'll make sure of it."

I met his gaze, unable to mask my vulnerability this time. But perhaps I didn't need to. I gave a tremulous nod, emboldened as the fairies around the table cheered and pounded the table.

I thought of the long journey left ahead to Aelthorin. When would I have another opportunity?

Marcellus stood, adjusting the rings on his fingers. He beckoned a fairy sitting halfway down the table, whispering something in her ear. Her eyes widened as she looked from the commander to me. But it was clear whatever he said, it had not been a suggestion. The gossamer cloak cinched beneath her wings billowed out behind her as she urgently cut through the lines of packed tables toward the door.

I had half a mind to pry, but my thoughts flickered out when Marcellus put his hands on me again. He spun me around with a certain grace that made my heart stammer—the kind of grace that came from centuries of practice. His gaze glimmered with that delightful, dangerous mischief as he positioned himself, his hands on my right shoulder—opposite the iron burn. Fairies crowded closer like old friends, anticipation humming in their murmurs.

"Relax," Marcellus said, his voice a purr beside my ear.

His lips didn't move as magic flooded to his hands, white and crackling with energy. Despite his assurances, I braced myself. But when his finger touched my skin, it was *warm*—not blazing hot. A sigh left me as the marking was meticulously traced.

Far from agonizing, the process filled me with a strange, invigorating energy. The gemstone pendant around my neck seemed to pulse in time with my thudding heart. Growing bold, I stole a glance at the blazing mark. Tears filled my vision. It was perfect. It was *mine*.

I turned to face Marcellus with a watery smile. *Thank you* didn't begin to cover the gratitude surging through me, the words catching when I tried to speak them.

"Don't," he said, brushing my tear trails away. He leaned his forehead against mine as I shook with emotion. "It's about time someone understood your worth."

A powerful buzz of energy filled the air, fast approaching. Every head in the room turned toward it, sensing it. I straightened to find that the woman Marcellus had sent off on an errand was returning with a satchel slung over her shoulder. I might have turned and stared at my warrior rune for hours if it weren't for the promise of what was in that bag.

A gemstone.

The woman looked breathless as she handed the satchel off to Marcellus and bowed her head. Hushed whispers flowed around me, brimming with anticipation. My heart pounded with warmth—they knew as well as I did that I deserved this treasure. I could already imagine how it would feel to touch it—how the energy would ripple beneath my skin until the gemstone's power sang through every muscle and nerve of my being.

"I can't believe it," I whispered.

I reached for the bag, every nerve in me singing. Marcellus gently caught my wrist and pulled me into an embrace. Overwhelmed, I hugged him back with as much fervor. I murmured my gratitude—the welcome, the rune, this incredible gift.

"It *will* be yours," he promised.

I stiffened in his arms. "When?"

"I hope you see we're good on our word. We can give you everything you want." He paused, his breath playing a gentle breeze on my hair. "In return for ten years."

His arms were locked around me. The others continued murmuring to each other, and I felt their stares. The noise felt less like the loving hum of family and more like a swarm of bees.

I wriggled out of Marcellus' hold and shook my head, schooling my expression carefully.

"I don't understand," I said, though I knew with mounting horror that I *did*.

"I told you." His smile was patient as ever, hands still clasped firmly on my shoulders. "We must take measures to ensure our people carry on for generations."

The intensity of his stare made me squirm with discomfort—the mixture of desire and desperation burrowed under my skin as the reality of this afternoon crashed around me like a thunderstorm.

"I can't agree to this," I said weakly. Even as my longing eyes traveled to the satchel, sorrow throttled me at the realization that he had never intended to gift me a gemstone simply for being brave and exceptional. I pushed his hands away.

He sighed, hopeful expression withering. "Sylvia, you won't age a single day. Barrenness doesn't take hold for at least a decade. You will still be perfectly intact—as beautiful as you are today." He brushed my cheek tenderly—*reverently*. The graze of his fingertips felt like acid, and I leaned out of his reach. "You will leave Veloria just as you entered, though more powerful than you could have dreamed. It will only feel like weeks have passed."

"I can't—"

Marcellus made a small move to one of the gems on his rings—a painfully familiar gesture. At once, the pendant around my neck pulsed like a comforting heartbeat.

Maybe he's right.

These people were hundreds of years old. What was ten years against that? It would be worth it for a gemstone. And perhaps… I wouldn't *want* to leave in the end.

But what about—

No. I would have my children. My people. I would live among legends until the end of the time.

—my boys?

My breath caught. What would happen to Jon and Cliff? Ten years of captivity? Or would they be released tonight, glamoured into forgetting I ever existed?

The foreign, quelling thoughts tried to roar overtop my worries. Not mine. This *wasn't me.*

Hand shaking, I reached for the pendant and closed my hand around it. I felt as though I were ripping my own heart out as I tore the cord free from my neck, but the moment it snapped, my vision became sharper. My senses surged back to life with overwhelming clarity. The other fairies cried in alarm as I tossed the pendant across the room.

"What did you do?" I whispered, suddenly feeling as though I'd been held underwater for hours. Dread coiled through my stomach. I had underestimated Marcellus. All of them. A foolish mouse in an owl's nest.

Marcellus raised his hands in peace. "The pendant only amplified your true desires."

Liar.

Although my heart was cracking in two, I said, "I don't want it. Not with a price so steep. I'm going to collect my hunters and you *will* let us out of here."

Through the large doorway, I caught glimpses of iridescent wings rushing over the water. Even a few of the nearby fairies pulled away, making me think I'd somehow intimidated them—until I heard the distant call of the sirens growing louder.

"The feast is upon us," Marcellus said to me, stone-faced. "I advise you to accept my bargain, Sylvia. It has been far too long since we've had a proper ceremony. Don't you want to enjoy it the way you're meant to? You have a place here. A family. Haven't you missed feeling at home?"

"Stop talking like you know me."

"I *do* know you, my dear." Marcellus drew closer, his gaze flickering over my traitor mark. "You've been terribly lonely, haven't you? Searching for belonging only to be rejected time and time again. I have lived your life, suffered through your fate."

More sirens were chirping, singing a melody that tempted me to turn in admiration. Fairies joined the tune, their combined voices echoing through the cave. I realized with a jolt that harmonies were coming from the entrance, where I'd left Jon and Cliff.

"This is *not* where I belong," I growled. The delicate gown hugging my hips suddenly felt like a betrayal, the soft fabric chafing everywhere it touched. I wished I could gouge the sacred warrior rune from my skin.

I backed away into the nearby fairies who had stayed behind to form a wall behind me.

Marcellus crowded forward, desperation finally beginning to darken his stoic features. "Don't you see that the stars have fated you to come here? You are a treasure, Sylvia. It's no mere accident that you arrived with the very offering we needed for the Celestial Feast."

I froze. "What offering?"

He chuckled as though I were being facetious. "The stars demand blood, and our sisters must feed on this most sacred of nights. Open your eyes—you know what you've done."

Horror ripped through me so viscerally, all I could do was release a choked sob, covering my mouth with my hands as I felt the cavernous lack of the presences I'd come to know so well.

I've killed them.

Jon and Cliff—I'd left them behind. Abandoned them to these lunatics. Were they already dead? Did I have time to make it back to them before—

Marcellus pulled my hands away from my face, his body like a wall before me. His thumbs brushed away the tears rolling down my cheeks. "Shh, don't be alarmed. Look at me. This isn't a sin—it's a beautiful thing, Sylvia. The stars speak through you. It's an honor."

No—these weren't the celestial forms I'd been raised to revere. The stars asked respect and reverence, but not blood. *Never* blood.

I thrashed, manic and animal. A small, startled circle of space opened around me as the nearest fairies shuffled back.

"You're insane," I snarled, jabbing a finger toward Marcellus before flinging my hand wide, whirling. "*All* of you! Fuck your stars, and fuck *you*. This isn't sacrifice, it's murder."

The crowd began to close in on me again, and my throat became tight. The urge to fight, to *hurt them*, bubbled up in me. But I was vastly outnumbered.

Marcellus closed the distance between us again, and I realized another step backward would have me against the wall. He seized my arm like he was claiming me. My skin felt hot where he touched it as I glowered up at him through my lashes.

"You tricked me," I seethed. Fresh tears—angry and humiliated—spilled down my cheeks.

"I told you many truths," he countered, wrestling back into a calm voice. His unshakeable demeanor had been a comfort—now, it terrified me.

Many truths, I thought bitterly. Notes of honesty that had been velveteen sheets on a bed of bones. How could I have been so fucking stupid?

"If you hurt me," I said in a low voice. "They will kill you."

Marcellus smirked, cocking his head to the side. "Your hunters are a little indisposed at present."

"You don't know them like I do."

Finally, a seed of unease flickered over him. And I might not have gotten a better opportunity than that.

I pulled myself to Marcellus and drove my knee upward into his groin. I felt a sick sense of victory as his breath whooshed out of him in a pained groan—dulled with a pang as I imagined Jon and Cliff cheering me on in my mind's eye.

While he was still doubled over, I lifted my eyes to the ceiling—to the two dozen fae lights glimmering overhead. I shouted my incantation, magic roiling in my veins. I raked my hands downward, ousting both chandeliers and plunging the chamber into darkness.

Fairies cursed and shouted, igniting spellwork to draw new lights. I moved quickly in the chaos. I doubled back, seizing the satchel still slung on Marcellus's shoulder and tearing it into my arms.

"You viper," he growled.

He grabbed my wrist, his grip crushing. I didn't think—I wrapped my hand around his arm and sent a bolt of ice right through his forearm. He staggered back, the shimmering blade protruding through flesh and bone—freeing me to bolt toward the door.

Stealing a look over my shoulder, I saw my ice already cast to the floor, Marcellus healing the wound with extraordinary speed.

Other fairies clawed at me as I fled, their hands tearing at the fabric of my gown, grasping at the ends of my hair, their voices overlapping in a horrible roar. With a burst of adrenaline, I leapt onto the stone balcony and dove off. My wings snapped open to catch the air as I soared into the cavern passageway.

22
SYLVIA

I was relieved for all of two seconds before wings started beating behind me. Not all of the fairies had given chase, perhaps fawning to Marcellus' wound. But enough were at my heels to make my flight panicky.

A woman screamed an incantation—a familiar one I'd heard from Mother many times. Flames grew at her fingertips. Swerving, I sent a burst of frost behind me to deter them. One of my errant spells hit a jar of flowers on a balcony, causing fragments of pottery to rain down on my pursuers.

I set my gaze back ahead, pushing myself harder as I recognized the curve of the dark stone around me. *Almost there.*

The music was growing louder, siren and fairy song piercing the air. The water churned below, a frothing mass of activity as sirens swam toward the village entrance. The guilt threatened to suffocate me.

My thoughts were a jumbled mess of questions and self-reproach, but there was no time to make sense of it now. I flew faster, the weight of the gemstone pressed to my stomach as I careened around sharp corners in the cave, narrowly avoiding collisions with other fairies who were flying in the same direction, ornate flowers woven in their hair and baskets of food in their arms. The eager expressions on their faces made my dread claw deeper.

My heart nearly stopped when I finally reached the entry landing.

Jon and Cliff were there, but not how I had left them. They were seated on the ground, bound back to back against a gnarled vine that jutted out of the rock—crafted by magic for this very purpose. Oppressive weight crushed on my lungs as I drank in the flowered vines that coiled around them, pulsing and moving slowly like living snakes. The flowers were elaborate and beautiful. Some crowned their heads, while others blossomed on the vines that coiled around them and kept their hands bound behind their back. The blossoms glowed gently in the dim light—clearly the work of a talented earth affinity—each dazzling color battling the blueish bioluminescence reflected on the walls around us.

I did a double-take at the jagged ceiling, startled to see a dozen constellations glowing like white-hot runes on the stone above us.

This wasn't just a display. It was a ceremonial offering.

A blood sacrifice.

I could have retched at the violent realization, if not for the battling relief that they were *still alive.*

The hunters' jackets lay discarded in a heap near the water's edge, leaving the bindings to dig in painfully against their bare arms under their t-shirts. Not that they appeared to be in pain—or at least, not aware of it.

I drifted closer. Jon and Cliff's eyes were half-lidded and glazed over, their heads lolled forward and to the side as though they couldn't muster the strength to sit upright. My stomach twisted. They'd been drugged—my brutal warriors now as helpless as rabbits encircled by a snake.

Fairies and sirens crowded near them, singing in the air and in the water. Fairies set food and flowers down around the pyre as they passed, before taking a perch alongside their peers. I froze in midair as I saw one of the fairies break off toward Cliff, dutifully hoisting a bowl of wine. It was dark, a sickly sweet smell wafting from it. She pushed it toward his parted lips, saying something to him. I heard Cliff groan in his throat, his deep voice hoarse. But he was too weak to resist, did not so much as flinch as the fairy tipped the bowl forward.

Panic flared through me, white-hot and desperate. Before the bowl could tip fully, I threw my hand out and shouted a spell. Ice shot across the cavern, shattering the bowl and sending shards of frozen wine scattering over the ground. The fairy jerked back, startled alongside many in the dozens around us.

"Get away from him," I snarled, my voice low and dangerous.

The other fairy's face twisted with such personal, biting hatred that I questioned how I ever could have believed these people were sane. As the fairy charged, lightning crackling between her hands to electrocute me, I shot a spear of ice through her stomach.

Numbness trickled down my spine as she fell to the cavern floor. I had killed monsters—the stuff of nightmares—but never a fairy. As several others darted down to gather around her in worry, I had little time to wonder if there was a healer in their midst to save her.

"Jon, wake up!" I shouted, my voice breaking. He didn't stir as I hovered before him. Hours' worth of enchanted food and wine were pumping through his body, but my dread deepened as I touched the stubble on his slack face. It appeared as though he'd been *days* without a razor, not hours.

The ground rumbled. Several fairies hovered in formation, their hands aimed at the stone floor to make it sink toward the water—to feed the sirens. I thrust my palms out, whispering a spell to send a thick ribbon of frost to the water that splashed against the stone. Ice crackled and took hold, pausing the platform's descent in frozen waves. Sirens clawed to reach over the ice, but they were just out of reach. Still, it would only be a matter of time before their desperation overpowered my magic.

I shot a volley of icicles at the earth fairies, scattering them. The stone floor beneath Jon and Cliff ground to a halt at an unsettling angle, but the descent had been steadied for now. They were safe.

Other fairies approached me from the gathered masses, casting their floral garlands aside to summon defensive magic. I threw spell after spell to keep them at bay. At first, I couldn't believe that they weren't killing me outright. They certainly had the power to slaughter me, but I caught a murmur—*the girl must be kept alive.* And with a sickening lurch, I knew how precious my body was to them.

I needed more time. I couldn't free the hunters while battling an entire village—and Marcellus couldn't be far behind. When he arrived, we'd be *fucked.*

I set my gaze on one earth affinity hovering near the ceiling, who was recovering quicker than the others around her. I shaped another frozen javelin in the air before me, ensuring the point was sharp before hurling it upward with all the force I could muster. The ice grazed the fairy's shoulder and tore directly through her right wing. I turned my gaze away the moment I saw her plummet. The cries of fury and shock from the two others made my ears ring.

This was enough to startle the others, who now gave me a wide berth. I flew to Jon, my heart pounding like a war drum. The sight of him made me freeze for a moment. His handsome face was pale, devoid of its usual flush of sun-kissed color. His brow was slightly furrowed, dark lashes fluttering, and lips slightly parted as though lost in an unreachable dream. The crown of flowers placed on his head made him look almost sacred, like a piece of artistry rather than a warrior.

I had never seen him look so *fragile.*

Closing the distance to him, I screamed his name again and again, shoving his cheek until his eyelids fluttered open.

"Hi, Sylv," Jon mumbled drunkenly, struggling to focus on me before his eyes fell shut again.

"Wake up!" Even a blast of frost to the chest couldn't seem to jolt him. "I can't leave you behind, *please*! I need you both!"

It wasn't enough. I needed *more*.

In my desperation, my hand slid into the satchel, fingertips grazing the gemstone. Without a thought, only will and focus, I placed my other hand on Jon's forehead. I had seen healers rouse unconscious fairies before, but I had never been skilled enough to master the incantation. Nonetheless, I pictured it—the magic pulsing into Jon to counteract what he was fed.

The magic roared in my ears, every hair standing on end. This was more than my own; I was a conduit for something far more powerful. The light pulsed into Jon's skin, webbing out—

He awoke with a violent gasp that made me dart back in alarm.

I laughed shakily, tears trickling from my eyes and relief coursing through me even as panic still clawed for dominance. Alertness saturated Jon's gaze, snapping to the restraints wound around him. I froze the thickest vines around him, turning them brittle and black from the stark cold. With a sudden jerk, Jon tore one arm free, sending frozen shrapnel across the stone.

I hurriedly wheeled around in the air to revive Cliff. My heart clenched at the sight of him, too—soft blossoms trailed over his cropped gold hair, giving him a regal look even in his daze. Anyone might have mistaken him for a fallen prince rather than the brutal fighter he was. The stillness of his body felt so wrong. As I pressed my palm to his cheek and brushed the gemstone with the other, I hoped he would forgive me.

Cliff roused with the same sharpness, his body jerking immediately against the binds.

"What the *fuck*?" Cliff groaned. His voice was hoarse and raw as he struggled against the bonds and squinted to make sense of his surroundings. His green eyes rested on me, breathing heavily as recognition set in. "Wasn't sure you were coming back."

"Me neither," I confessed. I cupped my hands—a well-aimed slice of frost broke through the bindings laced over his chest with a sharp crack. Several of the thinner vines withered and recoiled from the impact, as though fleeing from the taste of winter. From there, Cliff was able to break free. He clawed every flowering vine from his body, letting them fall in a heap.

I backed away as Jon and Cliff both rose to their feet, their movements sluggish at first, disoriented as though fighting through a haze. I watched their posture shift into honed instincts as the frozen waves began to crack under their weight—the one thing separating them from the wailing sirens on the other side.

"Move back!" I shouted.

Jon and Cliff wrenched off the remaining vines and scrambled onto solid ground just in time to avoid plunging into the water as my spell gave way, along with the section of stone they had been offered upon.

The boys dove for their weapons. Handguns, knives, and blades had all been laid in an indent in the stone, scattered with tinder to be set ablaze.

"I'm going to tear that commander fuck in half," Cliff muttered, tossing a silver-hilted knife to Jon, who caught it smoothly.

Their enraged expressions filled me with equal measures of fear and hope—we *would* fight our way out of this, and *fucking stars*, I was glad we were on the same side.

"Aureline!" I cried over the din. She was toward the front of the pack of sirens savagely trying to climb over each other to reach the hunters. "Please—I told you, these hunters are mine! Tell your sisters to stand down!"

The young siren, hauntingly innocent as ever, didn't relent. *"I have yearned all my life for this moment. Tales say human flesh which fights back tastes even more divine!"*

Fairies were circling us again. Perhaps they didn't want to kill *me*, but Jon and Cliff were vast targets. One well-aimed hit could send either of them into the water, and nothing would save them.

While they armed themselves, I countered a blaze of fire and a pair of shooting vines that attempted to restrain the hunters again. When anyone came too close, I drove them back with blasts of frost—but I was quickly becoming overwhelmed by a trio of fairies who were attempting to bind *me* instead. I could pull from the gemstone again—but it was a finite store. If I were too reckless, I would have nothing left.

"Get back, Sylv!" Cliff grunted, stepping in front of me.

I did as he said, watching with wide eyes as he dove for a finely woven net from the scattered belongings and hurled it at the incoming attackers. The fairies hit the ground hard, pinned beneath the fine mesh. Cliff readily tossed iron knives onto either side of the trap to subdue their attempts to break free with spellwork.

"Karma, bitch," he remarked, and I realized one of the struggling earth fairies was the one who'd viciously taunted him upon our arrival.

My breath stuttered. I hadn't seen this mode of attack before from the hunters. Inspiration could only have come from their battle outside of Elysia.

Surrounded, we were forced to move with measured precision. The hunters wielded their iron blades to ward off the bolder fairies who tried to get too close while I took out attackers from afar. Jon and Cliff both held guns in their other hands, but I could tell they were being conservative with spent bullets, taking out only the sirens that managed to throw themselves within grabbing distance.

"We came in through there!" Jon shouted behind us.

As we approached the sealed door, a larger chorus of buzzing wings closed in. Cliff turned and took aim, firing off a single shot. A fairy howled in pain and plummeted, a ragged hole missing from his upper wing. An impossible shot—but not for Cliff. The bullet sent the others fleeing in fear, at least for the moment.

I pulled to a hover and gaped at the fallen, writhing fairy. My breath shuddered, numbness creeping over my senses like poison. Cliff had to shout my name twice before I snapped out of it long enough for us to reach the solid curve of stone.

Jon smoothed his hands over the rock, searching for an opening—for *anything*.

"*Fuck*, there's no getting through," Cliff growled. He raised his blade, ready to slice the back of his hand for a blood offering.

"Don't!" I blurted. "They have control over the sacrificial path—even if it opened, they'd be able to seal us inside." Regardless, I doubted they could survive a second round of blood loss.

We were cornered against the wall—there had been nowhere else for the hunters to run, anyway.

"Any ideas, Sylv?" Jon asked.

Shame flooded through me. The hunters had taught me to always know my exit points when casing an unfamiliar place. That should have been at the top of my mind, but I had been too busy memorizing my path to the gemstone. My mind may have been clouded by Marcellus' gift then, but I was clear now.

"I don't want to use it, but I've got *this*," I said, patting the satchel.

Jon studied me for a moment—then it dawned, and his eyes went wide. "It's—you have a *gemstone*?"

I nodded. "But I think he may kill me for it, fertile or not."

Jon looked fairly confused by that assessment, but his mind was still at work as he considered our surroundings. "There was an opening under the water—the sirens were coming through it."

"There—I see it!" Cliff said.

Cliff grabbed Jon's shoulder and pointed him toward a faint outline of a tunnel passage underwater several meters away.

"We'll need to swim out," Jon breathed.

"Fat fucking chance of that with the sirens," Cliff said. "We don't have enough bronze to take them all out."

"Maybe we won't need to take them all out." I considered the pulse of the gemstone, wondering if I could use the sirens' environmental advantage against them. The thought of being submerged already made me feel like I was drowning, but what choice did we have? "If I can spread the ice further, maybe I can—"

Before I could piece together what to do, a fairy burst from the crowd surrounding us—Marcellus. The others that followed were clearly his reinforcements. The attackers we'd been fending off were mere civilians—a community who perhaps hadn't seen a fight in decades, even centuries. Marcellus was the one who brought control to the chaos. Where the attacks had been emotionally driven and messy before, his warriors approached with precision.

Bursts of lightning, fire, and ice drove Jon and Cliff away from the wall, trying to force them directly into the siren's frothing waters. The boys staggered, and even when Cliff fired off a shot to try scaring the warriors off, they merely shifted formation and continued relentlessly.

"Let us out!" I screamed, surging forward to put myself between the warriors and the hunters. My fingertips brushed the gemstone, and a blast of ice briefly nullified the attacks in the air. I worried over spending the magic within—how fast would this gemstone drain and leave me defenseless?

In the next instant, one siren gripped Cliff's ankle, viciously crawling her hands up his leg to make him stagger. A scream stuck in my throat—it happened so fast. As he fell to his knees, she grabbed either side of his face and pulled him into a fierce kiss, which softened into chilling tenderness as he relaxed.

"Cliff!" I raised my hands and prepared to send an icicle through her skull–unsure if even that would be enough, unsure if I was too late.

But in her fervor to claim him, the siren didn't notice Cliff's eyes were squeezed shut.

With unforgiving speed, he slashed her throat open. Picking himself up, he kicked her back into the water and side-stepped the vengeful hands of the siren's sisters.

Jon swung his iron blade at another approaching formation of warriors to drive them back and make their magic falter. More earth affinities conjured black, twisting vines from the stone. Tendrils laced around his waist and up his leg, forcing his back against the stone.

In my race to free him, I didn't see an assailant beelining toward me until it was too late. He slammed into me at full speed, nearly knocking me from the air. His heavy, muscled body pressed behind mine, wrapping around me.

"Sylv!" Jon bellowed. He reached for me, but the vines renewed their hold on him, forcing him down to his knees while I was dragged higher—far from his grasp.

The fairy restraining me took me roughly by the shoulder and tried to wrench the satchel away. I twisted to face him, my shout of fury dying on my tongue.

Marcellus.

His handsome face was contorted with disgust, wrestling my arms down and pinning my wings against his front. I started to shout an incantation, but his free hand clamped itself over my mouth to silence the spell.

"Words have power," he panted in my ear as I squirmed. "As does their absence."

One of his rings glinted before my eyes. The air shimmered with magic, and agony tore through my mouth as his wordless spellwork took hold. A scream stayed trapped behind my lips, drowning and gurgling beneath the hot liquid filling my mouth.

With a chuckle I could barely hear, Marcellus removed his hand. Noise erupted from me like a dying animal. As I opened my mouth, blood spilled onto my chin, running down my neck until it gathered over the front of my gown. Each rapid pulse of my heart released more and more from the deep laceration that ran along my tongue.

Even as I sagged in his arms, Marcellus wouldn't let me go. My vision turned spotty, his words slipping in and out of focus as he growled in my ear.

"Who are you?" he demanded. "A mere, impulsive child." Agony and unconsciousness writhed within me, battling to hold my attention. He shook me. "You would go against your own people, Sylvia? The will of the very stars that have protected you from your foolish choices—for what?"

I moaned low in my throat, and even that sent a wave of pain so cutting that I forced myself to keep a sob at bay lest I torture myself further. I caught Jon's gaze—so far below on the cave floor now. He was still tracking me, fighting a fruitless battle as he hacked at vines with an iron blade, only for them to regrow and ensnare him once again.

"I certainly hope you aren't begging for death because you will not find it here." His voice was becoming calm again—certain of himself. "You are home, child. You *will* submit eventually when you realize the truth. No one out there will miss you. No one is coming for you. You are nothing more than a pathetic, friendless failed nomad without a family to notice your absence. Without us, you are *alone.*"

Tears streamed down my face as his words stabbed. My heart burned with the memory of my friends and family in Elysia—the people I loved so dearly that I'd lost or had left me, willingly or not. For a moment, the idea of caving into defeat felt like a reprieve.

Alone. I was so *alone.*

Then, new memories flickered through my mind's eye.

Singing off-key to Elton John in the car, the changing landscape blurring outside the windows. The way Jon doubled over laughing, deep and loud, when I'd pranked Cliff by freezing his beer bottle to his hand. The feel of Jon's skin against me when we were entwined in the spectral plane. Watching *Survivor* with Cliff in the motel room over whiskey.

I strained, slipping a shaking hand into my pocket to reach my stashed dagger.

I do have a family. The thought struck through me like lightning, setting a blaze in my heart. A new strength surged in me as my knuckles whitened on the cool metal hilt. I glimpsed Jon far below—fighting his way to stay close to me, his familiar gaze feverish.

I wouldn't let Marcellus take away the people I loved. We wouldn't die at his hands.

With every ounce of strength left in me, I unsheathed the dagger and stabbed Marcellus in the stomach.

No words needed for that, asshole.

His grip grew lax around me, a gasp of agony at my ear. Something savage took hold of me as I twisted, wrapping my legs around his waist and letting my flightless weight rest on him as I plunged my dagger into him again and again. Between the leather plates on his chest, a second incision to his abdomen, his thigh.

The smell of blood choked me as I snagged the satchel back into my arms. I leaned back, letting him see the animal in my eyes. Sorrow and betrayal flickered beneath the outrage in his stare, a sight that gave me pause.

But it was for only a moment. Roaring past the agony in my mouth, I carved the blade across his throat, fresh blood splattering the front of my dress as I watched the light leave his eyes. My stomach churned, but the vicious beast in my chest roared in approval.

He plummeted toward the cavern floor. I started to fall with him until I remembered to snap my wings open and redirect my flight.

Wails echoed off the cavern walls, rising above the chaos as the nearest fairies dove for Marcellus. I glimpsed the glow of healing spellwork from his loyal disciples, but I knew they were surrounding a fallen corpse beyond saving.

The wails swiftly became bloodcurdling screams.

Above it all, Jon's voice boomed. "Sylvia!" He managed to tear free of the binds as the fairies were distracted by the death of their leader. Our eyes locked, and for the briefest second, Jon gaped like he didn't recognize me.

He lunged to reunite with me, but several fairies turned their mourning onto him, forcing him to stagger against the wall as whips of fire lashed in his direction, singeing his skin. Others were darting for me, but they couldn't reach me in time as I dove for Jon. My fingers slipped into the satchel and touched the gemstone—*my* gemstone. Without a single word, I conjured an ice shield to protect us both.

A strange, electric taste entered my mouth as the raw magic surged through me like a conduit. When I opened my mouth, I realized my tongue had been healed through the surge of magic.

"We need to go. *Now!*" I screamed over my shoulder to Jon.

His gaze flooded with astonishment once more at the sight of me. He uttered my name as though he were already in mourning. I couldn't blame him, given how nightmarish I must have looked, blood painting half my face, my neck, and the front of my dress. For all he knew, my throat had been torn as wide open as Marcellus'.

But there was no time to assure him. As enraged fairies began to close in on us, I knew I had to be the one to clear our path. If I didn't act now, we would die.

I placed my hand fully on the gemstone. Power still churned within. Less than before but nonetheless dizzying. The pulse of its force grew to a roar as I readily connected with the magic. I shut my eyes, imagining what I wanted to happen, and all at once, my vision flooded into the reality in time with my wordless scream.

A crystalline serpent erupted from my hands; sparkling fangs bared as it curled and kicked through all the fairies in its path. I wavered for a moment, remembering how I'd witnessed this enchantment on my last day of training in the caverns—just before the night my life changed forever.

The serpent exploded into a shockwave of frosty air, but I took control of the remnants before they could fade, turning my attention to the water. Ice leached into the lapping waves, curving and taking solid shape to herd the sirens away from the hunters. The sirens clawed and shrieked in their fury, denied their promised meal. The wall wouldn't hold forever—especially when fae magic began pummeling it.

Though they were recuperating, the boys still stood at the ready, weapons raised. Their stunned silence made my ears ring.

"The tunnel—it's there." I pointed at what was now an empty pool surrounded by ice—no sirens to speak of.

As they moved toward the edge of the path to survey the water, my courage wavered, and I eased back slightly. I hugged the satchel close, wishing I had any talent with earth magic so I could use the gemstone to burst through the walls themselves.

"What's wrong?" Cliff demanded, noticing my uncertainty.

"I can't swim," I reminded him in a small voice.

Jon stowed his weapons and held his hands out. "I've got you—come on."

The ice was beginning to crack.

"Deep breath," Jon cautioned just before he closed his hands around me.

I squeezed my eyes shut, huddling against him. My stomach dropped as he dived. One moment, I was weightless. The next, freezing water burst around me.

23

JON

The sharp temperature drop threatened to shut my body down. I forgot what to do for a solid three seconds, limbs stiff with shock. But as Sylvia shifted in my grip, rigid from the cold, I forced myself toward the narrow opening in the cavern wall.

At first, the underwater tunnel was wide enough for Cliff and me to swim side by side. The deeper we went, the more it shrank, darkness encroaching until touching the jagged walls was the only way to know which direction to go.

My lungs began to burn. I felt myself falling behind, forced to claw my way forward with only one hand while the other held Sylvia.

Finally, a wink of late afternoon sunlight bobbed ahead.

Gritting my teeth, I strained toward it. Once I was free from the tunnel, reaching the surface seemed like another mile upward. Unnaturally bright fish glowed like lanterns in the filthy depths. Just as my throat was about to give in and swallow a mouthful of water, I burst into the open air and took a deep breath.

Closer to the shore, Cliff coughed heavily, agonized and re-lieved.

I raised my hand to check on Sylvia, but the moment my fingers unfurled, something latched onto my ankle and pulled hard. As I was dragged back under the surface, I lost my hold on her—lost her to the water.

Her name flew past my lips, muted and garbled.

The surface flew out of reach, becoming a mere ripple overhead. I tried to reach out, to grab hold of *anything* to pull me away from my attacker, but there was nothing. Cold hands gripped me feverishly, subduing my thrashing limbs with inhuman strength as I was pulled deeper into the dark and cold.

The siren's melody echoed around me. It rose above the roar of panic in my mind, delicate and beautiful despite the water's distortion. One hand gripped my shoulder, jagged nails piercing my skin like a harpoon sunk into its prey. Another bony hand gripped my jaw. The burning in my lungs was already unbearable, every second excruciating. I needed to *breathe*.

Though I tried to fight, to look anywhere else—our eyes caught.

Immediately, my muscles relaxed. A halo of red hair fanned around her head, eyes bright green beneath long lashes. Recognition surfaced—this was the same siren that had targeted me on the docks, the one Sylvia had freed from the outpost. She was achingly beautiful, otherworldly, *terrifying*.

Her rosy lips spread in a smile, pulling me close enough to kiss me. Her touch became loving, stroking my cheek as though she'd known me forever.

I've got you, darling. You can let go now.

I hardly noticed how frozen her skin was against mine. It didn't matter.

Life is so hard up there. You don't need to fight anymore. We can be together here, forever.

My vision blurred as I tried to glimpse the surface—a faint glow so far away now. The pain in my chest numbed, a distant memory as her sweet voice sang to me. Her promise was a comforting thought. No more pain. No more loss. I'd have given anything to feel whole like that again.

Her mistake was looking too much like Sylvia—because I remembered *she* was up there, and I lost my hold on her, and she could be drowning.

I mirrored the siren's tender grip, cupping her face in my hand like she was a delicate treasure.

Darkness crept into my vision, but I didn't need to see to find the hilt of the bronze knife stowed in my jacket. My hand closed around the weathered handle. I had a promise to uphold.

I am all you need. Urgency laced her lullaby.

I struggled, even as her claws sank deeper into my arm, fighting to hold me in place. I snapped my left hand to grip the siren's hair at the roots, and with the other, I plunged the blade upward through her throat.

Her eyes went wide, the beautiful green flooding with unforgiving black. My mouth opened involuntarily with a shout of effort, water finally flooding in and filling my lungs with frigid pain. Dark blood clouded the water between us. Her ear-shattering screech resounded through the depths as I twisted the knife, vertebrae shattering.

I hoped it fucking hurt.

The siren's bony hands released me. Her true, corpse-like face was revealed as she sank, her screeches weakening and lost to the depths. The sunken eyes and elongated, bony form were eaten by the darkness—a vision that would haunt me.

Air. I needed *air*.

I kicked and clawed my way upward, fueled by a frantic mantra: *Not like this. Just a bit further. Not like this. I can't let her die.*

I broke the surface, gasping and choking. The sweet taste of air burned my lungs. I drank it greedily, whipping my hair out of my face as I looked around. A familiar form caught my eye, standing a short distance away near the shore.

"*Jon!* Hang on!" Cliff crashed through the knee-high water toward me.

I swam desperately, then crawled when my hands and feet hit the soft mud. He grabbed my arm, pulling me the last few feet to shore. I collapsed on the wet earth, breathing raggedly. I couldn't get enough oxygen no matter what I did.

"You okay?" Cliff's gruff voice anchored me. He wrenched up the tattered right sleeve of my tee, scrutinizing the fresh talon wounds that marred my skin.

"Where's Sylvia?" I rasped.

A fresh surge of fear jolted me upright as I scanned the dark water surrounding the moss-covered building—what had nearly become our joint tomb.

"I have her," Cliff said, opening his other hand for me to see.

Sylvia was shivering on hands and knees, coughing up water, but as she caught onto our concern, she flashed us a weak thumbs up. I went dizzy with relief.

"You're bleeding," she croaked, brow knitting at the sight of my arm.

I forced a weak smile. "I'll take this over being fish dinner any day."

Sylvia's frown deepened, etched with fierce resolve. "Let me heal it—"

"Later," Cliff interrupted. "You can't even fucking stand."

Like us, she was drenched to the bone. Her blood-stained gown was plastered to her body, and her wings sagged at her back, heavy and useless. An argument took shape in her expression as she reached for her side—but she went perfectly still when her hands found nothing.

"No," she breathed. "Th-the bag—the gem!" She looked around wildly, pushing her hair back and looking like she would break down into sobs. "It m-must have slipped when—" Her eyes fixed on me.

"When I let you go," I finished. Guilt cascaded onto me in waves colder than the swamp. I glanced back, knowing how deep the water ran. The gemstone had sunk to the bottom by now, lost. My jaw tightened. "It's gone, Sylv. I'm sorry."

A broken little sound rattled through her. It had all been for nothing. She had described the pull of the amethyst shard, the rush of wielding its power. I couldn't imagine what she must have felt like now, a whole gemstone slipping from her grasp. The uncanny environment seemed to mock us now. I glimpsed the snow-white deer again, watching curiously. A glittering snake tail lashed here and there in the muck.

"Hey—how long were we in there?" Cliff sank to the ground next to me, frowning as we surveyed the area. Faint golden light in the trees surrounded us. Sunset—but it came from the wrong direction. I watched the light creep along the unusually flowered branches, realization hitting like a blow to the stomach.

It wasn't dusk, it was *dawn*.

For the first time since waking in the godforsaken cavern, I noticed something *off* about Cliff's appearance. I reached up and touched my own face, finding the scratch of stubble under my fingertips. At least two days' worth. Cliff caught my stare and did the same, eyes widening as he came to the same horrifying conclusion.

We had lost two full days.

"What's the last thing you remember?" I asked.

Cliff shook his head, gaze darkening, and I knew his memory was as foggy as mine after that first sip of wine.

"Those little assholes roofied us," Cliff muttered.

A sudden noise pulled our attention back toward the water, making all three of us freeze up. The moss-covered structure quivered slightly. Ancient vines slithered away from the roof, creating an opening. Fairies began to emerge, iridescent wings flashing golden in the rising sun. In the branches around us, a flock of startled birds flew off as though they could sense the fallout to come.

Cliff and I scrambled to our feet. The deer fled.

"*Ay, coño*," I breathed. My entire body and mind ached—but this wasn't over.

Then, I heard it—the distant wailing rising from beneath the water.

The clamoring voices echoed, hungry and furious. My heart skipped a beat as ripples dotted the water's surface. Sirens—dozens of them. With the protective ice barrier shattered, it would be less than minutes before they flooded the water.

I threw a look to Cliff and Sylvia, scanning them. We were exposed. Sylvia was as pale as a sheet, still trembling as she watched in a horrified daze. Two handguns and a few iron blades remained between Cliff and me. The rest of our arsenal was stowed in the trunk of our borrowed car, over a mile away.

All we could do was run.

We started toward the tree line. Outrunning an angry horde of fairies seemed impossible, but at the very least, we could get out of the sirens' earshot. My heart sank at the realization that the water ran in every possible direction around here. If a siren could escape the outpost and make it here, there was no telling how easily they could catch up with us on the way to the car.

Noise came from within the tree line, making us falter. Engines revved and shouts echoed.

"You hear that?" one of the voices called. "It's coming from over there!"

The familiarity of the voice made my skin crawl.

Rhett.

Normally, a pack of hunters would be a godsend, but with Rhett at their head, any safety would be temporary. We scrambled to the nearest underbrush and found cover behind too-vibrant leaves—affected by the proximity of gemstones. Headlights brighter than the dawn pierced through the trees.

Half a dozen vehicles came into view—pickup trucks and SUVs suited for the soft ground.

"Don't look 'em in the eyes, boys!" one of the hunters called out as he leaped from the passenger's seat of a truck. "Just burn them all."

Others hastened out of their vehicles—familiar faces from the outpost, rushing to meet the onslaught of sirens and fairies.

Cliff huffed. "Had to be a matter of time before they tracked us down."

"Hey—they'll keep each other occupied," I muttered. "Let's go."

We snuck around the back of the vehicles and caught sight of spare weapons ready for the taking. Along the shoreline, I could hear the fight exploding—gunshots and crackling magic, the smell of singed flesh filling the air.

Cliff handed Sylvia to me and reached into the open trunk of a Jeep to grab a sawed-off shotgun. No sooner than Cliff had his hands on the weapon, two figures rounded the corner.

Two hunters, armed to hell.

"Everett!" one of them shouted. "He's here! Over here!"

We had no time to react as a third hunter joined the duo—and they all pounced for Cliff. I would have lunged into the fray at once, but with Sylvia in my grasp, I hesitated a second too long. Cliff was overpowered, pushed against the side of the Jeep as zip ties were lashed around his wrists, binding his arms behind his back.

"Get your fucking hands off me!" he shouted, resisting viciously.

I staggered back behind the pickup truck, frantically looking for a safe place to lay Sylvia before I could rush to Cliff's aid.

"Let me go!" Sylvia, still shivering, tried to elbow her way free of me. "What are they doing to him? Let me help!"

"No," I hissed. "You can't even fly right now! How do you expect to—"

Pain exploded against the back of my head.

The blow sent me to the ground, and past the stars swimming in my vision, I saw Cliff being dragged away. Sylvia tumbled from my hands, landing hard. As she groaned in pain and tried to sit up, everything in my brain told me to get up and fight, but my body wouldn't cooperate.

Once again, I was failing her.

A low whistle came from behind. "You look like shit, Nowak," Rhett said.

I managed to roll over. Anger and shock simmered through me, but I remained cautious, seeing the gun trained on me. He was armed to the teeth beyond that, too—slung with weapons and wielding a long metal rod in his other hand. As he crouched toward Sylvia, I found my voice.

"*Don't*! I'll fucking kill you if you hurt her," I gritted out.

The temperature plummeted. Sylvia was on her knees, summoning ice that rapidly spread across the ground toward Rhett—but he was prepared. With a flick of his wrist, he swung the iron bar outward and pressed it on her stomach, forcing her onto her back. She gave a cry as her ice was snuffed out, crackling along the damp leaves. Only the thin fabric of her bloodied gown kept her skin from burning.

The absolute fear on her face made me fantasize about ripping out Rhett's spine.

His punchably easygoing smile widened as Sylvia lowered her hands in surrender. He tucked the iron bar under his arm, and before she could bolt, he grabbed her by her shredded gown. He stood, gun still trained on me, while Sylvia squirmed to free herself.

"Now, calm down, sweetheart," he crooned. "You'll wear yourself out."

"Go fuck yourself!" she snapped.

He chuckled. "The mouth on you. You sound like *them*." His smirk traveled to me before he regarded her again, eyes bright. "Which means… you're trainable, huh?"

Even from the ground, I could see the sickened look cross her face.

"I'm starting to see why they keep you around," Rhett went on. "Must be useful on a hunt. I gotta say, it ain't easy working solo these days."

"I'm not doing anything for you," she said, voice dripping with venom.

He shrugged as though nothing she said could shake him. "Cooperation or not, I'm getting what I want. I get the feeling I'm about to have a lot of fairy corpses on my hands. Maybe a few surrenders, if we're lucky. You can either work with me and live a little longer—or I can take your blood and wings straight to the bank and win an early retirement. I'm thinking Margaritaville—what do you think?"

"You motherfucker," I growled, trying to force myself up.

Rhett slammed his boot onto my clawed arm.

"No!" Sylvia wailed, her voice fuzzy at the edges as I seized up from the pain. "Leave him alone!"

"Oh, darling, you don't think he's leaving this shithole alive, do you?" He laughed. "First order of business, sweetheart. Put Jon Nowak out of his misery. *Please*."

24
JON

Sylvia's shock stretched out for a painful moment. Chaotic bursts from the surrounding hunt pierced her silence—howls of pain both human and siren, gunshots echoing, the acrid smell of spellwork. For a moment, even Cliff's distant shouts of protests accumulated into a dull, distant roar in my ears.

"No. No, *fuck you*, I'm not doing that," she hissed, her voice wobbling.

"You really want to start our special partnership by insulting me?" Rhett clicked his tongue, shooting her a mockingly reproachful look. "Don't be coy. We don't got all day, if you haven't noticed." He stole a mindful look toward the bank.

Thirty feet away, two hunters were prying the bloodied remains of their teammate away from a siren, her hands and face covered in his entrails. A pair of snapping turtles with iridescent shells sampled the trailing gore, unshaken by the chaos.

Sylvia covered her face with her hands—couldn't bear to look at me. Rhett's arrogant expression flickered. He ground his boot on my injury, the added weight making a shout escape me. Through my red haze of anger, I saw his thumb pulling back the hammer on his semi-automatic. A small metallic click pierced the air—small but certain. All Rhett had to do was twitch, and there would be a bullet in my head.

"Lemme be clear," Rhett said. "Look at me. *LOOK!*" His voice jumped to a roar when Sylvia continued to sob. She flinched her wet eyes up to meet his gaze. "If you don't kill him *right now,* I'll kill you both. I'll have you and his faggot friend watch as I skin him for parts while he's still begging for death. After that, I'll see how long it takes for iron to burn a hole right through that pert little waist of yours."

Rhett stared down at Sylvia, schooling the bloodlust back into something honeyed that didn't meet his eyes.

"Or, you can do what I fucking say," he added, softer. "You can end Nowak's life quickly and painlessly. Doesn't that sound a touch kinder, darling?"

Sylvia stared down at me from Rhett's grasp, locks of her hair sticking to her tear-stained cheeks. Her expression fell with resignation. Mourning me. My pulse pounded as she whispered something—*I'm sorry.*

"Move the iron," Sylvia said, glancing at Rhett. "It's too close."

He balked before letting the rod tucked under his arm drop to the ground. "If even a snowflake touches me, I'll pluck your wings off one by one. See how quick you can heal that."

The world sharpened and blurred around me. As she raised her trembling hands, spellwork shimmering between her palms, my rage fled. There was no time to be angry in these last precious moments.

I watched Sylvia, memorizing her form even as frost blossomed at her palms, forging the weapon that would end me.

I wanted to tell her that I loved her. I wish I'd done it when I had the chance, to tell her how much hope and light she had given me for the first time in so many years. I loved her, and it didn't matter what she was or where she was, I would keep loving her—it was suddenly so simple.

But I didn't dare open my mouth. I wouldn't make this any harder for her. Countless times, I had made my peace that a monster's salivating, fanged muzzle might be my last sight on earth. All things considered, maybe it wouldn't be so bad, dying at her hands, if *she* was the last thing I got to see.

My world narrowed to a point as Sylvia sent the icicle, sharp as a blade, hurtling toward me. I braced.

But instead of blazing pain, the blade embedded itself in the earth just inches from my head. My brow creased with confusion a split second before I caught her eye. This was no missed shot—it was a weapon.

I didn't waste a second.

I wrenched the frozen blade from the earth and plunged it into Rhett's thigh as hard as I could. He seized up in shock, loosing a strangled curse. My arm blazed with pain as I pivoted on the ground—one swift kick, and Rhett's legs buckled, sending him crashing to the ground.

A shriek pierced the air. I whipped my head to the left in time to see Sylvia hit the mud, her drenched wings splayed out around her. The sound of her pain hit me like a jolt, but I couldn't go to her yet. Rhett was scrambling to reach her, to reclaim his leverage.

No—not again. Not while I was still breathing.

I threw my body onto his and wrenched him away from Sylvia. He struggled as I wrestled him onto his back, desperately pawing for his handgun. I knocked it under the pickup truck.

He cursed, trying to buck me off, but I restrained his arms under my knees to keep him from reaching any other weapons he had hidden away. In an instant, it became clear that he was no match for me hand-to-hand. No weapons or leverage at his disposal. So he tried for words instead.

"You'd kill one of your own for that *thing*?" he spat. "I heard whispers that you were fucked up in the head, but I didn't think—"

I clamped my hands around his throat, tightening until not even a wheeze could escape.

My nerves sang with triumph as I glared down at him, waiting for the inevitable fear to enter his eyes. But it didn't. Even as Rhett fought for breath, face purpling, unbridled rage poured from his glare.

A soft gasp made my gaze snap in Sylvia's direction. She flinched as we made eye contact, her hands clamped over her mouth and perfectly still like a deer caught in the headlights.

"Look away," I uttered.

But she wouldn't. She was about to see me kill right in front of her—*again*. I had never killed another human with my bare hands, and she would be here to witness it.

This one's a monster—human or not, I thought viciously.

But why do it myself when there were other options? An animal like him didn't deserve a swift end. My gaze snapped to the churning water. Sylvia wouldn't even have to watch it happen.

I released Rhett's throat long enough to grab the iron bar he'd threatened Sylvia with. Just as he was gasping in his first breath, I swung the bar across his temple, and he was out like a light. Catching sight of the zip ties in his pocket, I knew exactly what to do.

The shoreline whipped about madly. I worked quickly, dragging him to a tree stationed near the water. Thick roots looped in and out of the soft soil, providing the perfect anchor to zip tie his wrists to. His eyelids were beginning to twitch as I finished. A darker part of me roared in satisfaction at the thought of him being awake when the sirens came to collect.

"Cliff!" I called into the din, looking along the shoreline. He had been pulled further away, but between the sirens and fairies attacking, his captors had all but abandoned him to defend themselves.

Screams pierced the air as two of Rhett's buddies were swarmed by sirens. One of them was dragged under, while the other managed to escape—at least for a second. As a fresh melody hit him, he staggered to a stop, face going blank. He drew his gun and pointed it at Cliff, who hurriedly took cover behind a tree, wrists bound behind his back.

The hunter fired his gun until it was empty, then dropped it. He turned and walked calmly into the water. The churning water gushed with red.

I caught a glimpse of Cliff in the foliage. He angled himself forward and gritted his teeth, raising his wrists and bringing them down on the small of his back. The ties didn't break.

As he raised his wrists to try again, I set my sights on finding Sylvia, desperate to ensure she was safe before going to Cliff's aid.

Leaving Rhett behind, I hurried back to find her by the truck. Her bloodied form stood unsteadily by the pickup truck. Relief flooded her face when she saw me.

"Thank the stars you're alright!" she cried when I dropped to my knees before her. "W-where's Cliff? Where—I have to help!" She spread her wings, her voice choking off in a pained whimper. The way she held her arm told me her iron wound must have been flaring from the extra damage. Her wings were still soaked, splattered with mud now, too.

"You have to hide," I ordered breathlessly. "I'll get you to that tree—stay underneath, out of sight."

I reached for her, and she staggered back, hysteria bleeding into her words. "No! I need a higher vantage point for my magic!"

"You're in no shape to fight!" I snapped. "The gemstone's gone, Sylv—you need to lie low!"

Her eyes flashed with anger. "Absolutely not! I have to—"

"*No*—no, you need to listen, Sylv. If you go out there, you'll die! Do you understand me? Cliff needs me too, so you're going to—"

I lashed my hand toward her, but before my fingertips came within inches of her, cerulean burst from her palms. Pain ripped across my forearm—needle-like icicles embedding into the skin. I cursed, reeling back.

"Sylvia," I breathed, knowing full well that she would strike again if needed.

She gave me a dirty look, skittering backward from me. Her wings flitted to shake off moisture, desperately preparing for flight as though she was entirely unconcerned about becoming another corpse on the shoreline. It didn't matter what I said. I refused to go back to the night of the werewolf hunt, when I wasn't sure if she'd ever open her eyes again.

I was *not* going to lose her.

In my mounting panic, I spotted supplies that had been tossed from the bed of another nearby truck, littering the ground. Harpoons, knives, nets… and a couple of small cages. These hunters knew what they were hoping to find by tracking us down. The cages were undoubtedly iron, perhaps originally intended for small reptiles or birds, but perfectly suitable for fairies.

Time whirred to a halt as my plan connected, cruel and *perfect*. I scrambled to the nearest cage, turning it over in my hands. It was a sturdy construction, its wiry bars webbed too close together for even a lizard to wriggle through. The base was a thin metal plate—no bolts. I grabbed hold of the edge and wrenched as hard as I could. The metal groaned, resisting—but it bent. At my third vicious pull, the bottom plate came free, leaving the interior open and exposed.

By then, Sylvia was fully behind the truck, sidestepping stalks of foliage while she attempted to dry her wings and put distance between us. She had less than a second to peer at the cage with glassy, terrified eyes before I slammed it over her, embedding the bars firmly into the soft earth. Her shriek of alarm softened into a groaned *"oh"* like the sound of someone who had just been punched in the gut.

Breathing heavily, I pulled my hands away and cautiously leaned down to watch. Sylvia stood at the center of the darkened space. She gaped at her hands as she swept her frantic gaze around the interior of the cage around her—then to me.

"Jon, what the hell are you doing?" Sylvia's furious shout cracked with terror.

"I'm so sorry," I managed. The wound she'd inflicted on my arm throbbed.

She charged toward me, only to resist the awful aura of the metal webbing separating us like she had run into an invisible wall. Her expression twisted, teeth gritted.

Sylvia paced the perimeter frantically, flexing her hands into casting formations, whispering familiar spells under her breath. Nothing happened. Trying to cast spells surrounded by iron was like trying to light a candle underwater—confirming what we both already knew: she was trapped.

Trapped, but safe. She was well hidden behind the truck, in the shadow of the tree line.

Her flats shuffled on the forest floor as she positioned herself as close to me as she could tolerate. The shock and horror on her face twisted into something else, something that sent chills racing up my bare arms. *Rage*—a raw anger she hadn't fixed on me since our first meeting.

"Let me out. Get this damn thing off—*NOW!*"

"I can't," I panted.

Her breathing was labored and trembling, and the betrayal in her eyes stabbed deeper than any weapon. "You are *not* doing this to me," Sylvia snarled—it was a command. "I am not some helpless trinket you can stow away. Let me out, or I'll—" She tapered off, swallowing a threat.

I reached out, touching the cold iron mesh that separated us. This had to happen. And later, when she was warm and alive and we were far away from this hellscape, she would understand.

I muscled down the emotion in my voice, my gaze hardening. "I can't watch you martyr yourself, Sylv. I won't. I'm sorry. I'll come back with Cliff, and we'll get the fuck out of here."

I forced myself to my feet. I dug Rhett's handgun from beneath the truck nearby, checking its magazine. I glanced across the tangle of multi-colored cypress trees. There was a shotgun abandoned in the mud near a Jeep parked thirty feet away, if I could reach it.

"No, Jon—wait! Don't do this, please. *Please!*" As I stepped away from her, Sylvia's demands broke into begging. I didn't look back at her—couldn't bear to.

"Don't touch the bars," I told her in a tight voice. I knew how horrible she felt now—and how infinitely worse it would be if she made physical contact.

Sylvia's anguished scream tore through the forest—raw and utterly animal. It burned my mind like a brand as I strode back into the hunt.

25

JON

I swallowed a gag when I stepped into the clearing. Body parts bobbed in the foamy black water, a grim mix of human and fairy. The number of attacking sirens had dwindled by half, but I only saw two scaly bodies on the bank, bronze blades protruding from the bony backs. Perhaps the others were beneath the surface in a watery grave. A tiny, iridescent wing, severed from its host, lapped against the shore with every beat of the tide. Fresh bile rose in my throat.

I glanced between the abandoned shotgun up ahead and the foggy shore, desperate to get eyes on Cliff.

Four outpost hunters were left, shouts mingling with measured gunfire and the eerie, melodic hums of remaining sirens. On the slope to my left, movement pulled my eyes—burly, decked head-to-toe in tactical camo—coming straight for me. The hunter's gaze locked onto mine, then shifted to the pickup truck behind me. Recognition flashed over his face, followed by suspicion. I glanced down at the handgun I clutched—*Rhett's gun.*

Resolved, I stepped into his path. He swung first, his serrated bronze hunting knife aimed at my stomach. I dodged, countering with a brutal blow to the ribs. He groaned but didn't buckle. The hunter snarled and pushed forward like a bull—throwing his weight on me, grabbing a fistful of my black tee. The contact sent pain radiating down my wounded shoulder, but I dug my heels into the yielding earth, throwing him off to ensure he had no chance of glimpsing where I'd stashed Sylvia.

He charged at me again—as I knew he would. I caught his free arm and twisted hard enough to make him stagger. I followed with a blow to his throat. The hunter doubled over, his breathing turning to ragged gasps as his windpipe collapsed. I stood over him, considering a targeted kick to the liver to end this quickly.

Then—*rustling*.

The sound came from behind me in the branches, making hair rise on the back of my neck. The muddy earth roiled and gave way beneath my feet like it was opening into hell itself. Vines shot up like vipers as three fairies looped gracefully toward us, their wings glinting an iridescent array of colors in the rising sun.

Fucking earth affinities.

I released the other hunter as the vines slithered toward us with alarming speed. He cried out, gasping as the vines coiled around his legs, up his waist, dragging him down.

"*Help!*" The man lunged, grasping my leg and pulling desperately. Whether he meant to drag himself free or doom us both, I wouldn't let it happen. With a grunt, I shoved him off, tearing free of the fresh vines curling around my mud-caked boots. His eyes bulged with panic as the vines coiled over his neck, clawing him onto the ground with unearthly strength.

A hiss came from above—one of the fairies, hands aglow with spellwork that targeted me. I lifted the handgun and fired off a round into the branches to disorient them, just long enough to sprint out of range.

The man's cries for help became garbled behind me. I stole a look over my shoulder and winced. The vines cocooned his body against the dirt. The fairies were three pricks of light hovering above him, untouchable. With the other hunters occupied at the water, he had no escape.

I didn't wait to watch as the vines pulled into the earth, dragging his body inside like a cruel sacrifice.

I ran through the cypress, the water sparkling ahead of me. A stocky female hunter stood boldly on the water's edge, shielding her eyes with one arm and firing a harpoon into the swamp with the other. One of her shots struck true, hitting a siren—which cried a warbled, watery moan as it vanished beneath the surface.

Don't look them in the eye.

I threw an arm over my face, looking up only sparingly as I navigated through the trees. Even a brief glance could end me—could leave Sylvia trapped and vulnerable—so I moved from one shadow to the next. I dodged the earth affinities' attention, pausing only to scoop up the shotgun from the mud. I checked the safety and tucked the handgun into the waistband of my sodden jeans, letting the familiar weight of the shotgun settle in my palms.

I pressed forward, my focus finally landing on my target: Cliff. He burst out from the foliage, having finally snapped his restraints. He dove for the nearest handgun beside a corpse halfway in the water. He searched around wildly until his eyes found me past the other hunters who still stood between us. They, at least, had their hands full with fighting for their lives.

If I could just get to him, we could turn the tides on this fuckshow and get the hell out of there.

My mind spun with strategy and formation as we raced toward each other. If I could take out the sirens while he kept the fairies at bay, we could push through. With the hunters' numbers dwindling, I doubted they'd be stupid enough to make us a target, no matter how pissed.

To my horror, a siren was bold enough to drag herself past the water. She lunged, digging her talons into Cliff's leg before he could see her coming. Attempting to shake her off, he whirled to shoot her. The siren pulled at him—*hard*. Cliff staggered—and his eyes caught hers.

He went perfectly still.

"Cliff!" I shouted, but it was too late.

His expression went blank, and instead of stumbling toward the water, he gazed along the shoreline. He set his sights on the other hunters and raised his gun. I watched in helpless, abject horror as the most lethal hunter in the country took aim against his own.

I loosed a shaky curse under my breath. There was no fucking chance of dodging a shot if he shot at me—but there were a couple of other hunters between us, too distracted to notice his allegiance had changed.

Keeping my eyes trained away from the water, I surged forward.

Even when he wasn't himself, Cliff's skills were a sight to behold. Incredible. Terrifying.

BLAM—the female hunter hit the ground with a thud.

BLAM—another one cried out and stumbled too close to the water. At once, he was swarmed by sirens, vanishing into the depths.

Cliff's vacant gaze moved to me.

With no one left between us, I raised the shotgun and aimed it at the siren controlling Cliff. I tried to be unpredictable, tried to sidestep as Cliff took aim, but it wasn't enough. He fired first. Pain exploded above my kneecap. The impact made me stumble and sent my own shot wide, missing the siren.

Cliff squeezed the trigger again—*click*.

As he moved to reload, I abandoned my weapon and dove to tackle him. My leg gave out from under me, sending him down, too. Cliff fought viciously—an unsettling sight while his eyes were utterly devoid of emotion. Every muscle in his body tensed with brutal, unrestrained force. An elbow connected with my stomach, inciting a sharp pain that stole my breath.

"Listen!" I hissed. "Cliff, *listen*! You need to—look away!"

As I struggled to keep my arms locked around Cliff, I registered how easy it would be to slam his head down, to knock him out entirely, but I couldn't do that—not to him.

Unless I had no other choice.

I managed to get him in a headlock, forcing his body away from the siren, rolling us into the cover of buttonbush while she desperately sought his attention a few meters away. She couldn't come further onto land, no matter how she snarled at me.

Gradually, Cliff's struggles lessened under my panicked hold. I worried he was losing consciousness. If he went out cold, I'd have *his* body to drag out of here along with Sylvia's—but then I heard his voice.

"Sweet," Cliff rasped. "You remembered I like being the little spoon."

I released him, too relieved to even roll my eyes.

"Thanks," he added more seriously, swiping his gun from the ground. He rubbed one of his wrists, still red from breaking through the zip ties. "Dunno why the fuck Rhett and his band of fuckwads want me so bad, but—"

A haunting song filled the air—the siren's renewed effort to win our eye contact, to pull us back under that dark blanket of comforting numbness. If it went on for much longer, I knew I'd look. I knew I'd cave to that beautiful, tender promise of peace.

As Cliff and I peeled away from each other, he reloaded and raised his gun in the direction of the song.

"Am I good?" he asked.

I flitted my eyes to the side briefly, looking only at the bony, blood-stained hands braced on the ground. The siren's attention was focused on reclaiming Cliff, but I could feel more resolve waver within me, too.

Look, a voice itched. *Just one quick look.*

"A little higher," I forced out.

Cliff adjusted. *BLAM.* The siren shrieked and fell limply on the bank.

We scrambled to our feet, glancing cautiously toward the tangle of hair spread over the ground, concealing her face.

Unmoving.

I leaned heavily on the nearest tree to support my weight. The pain from the bullet lodged in my leg flashed through me with every breath. Cliff's face darkened as he stood beside me, his gaze fixed on the blood soaking through the waterlogged denim.

"Fuck, what happened to you?" Cliff said.

I gave him a tight, shadowed look. It wasn't really *him* who'd shot me. "It's fine," I bit out. "I can get out of here. Just give me a hand."

Cliff's eyes widened, catching the words I wouldn't say. I saw the guilt cross his face as he surveyed the clearing, swallowing as the realization of what he had done clicked into place.

Only two hunters were left alive. One was fleeing for his life with ragged breaths, vanishing through the trees. The other, though, made me falter. It was the same figure Cliff and I had seen through the window of the outpost just the day before—*Cain.*

He was splattered with blood, looking ready to collapse as he staggered along the shore. Although he was facing in our direction, something had caught his eye, and he took no notice of us. He ducked into the shoreline foliage—straight for Rhett.

My heart slammed into my throat. I cursed and tore after him—limping, with every step coursing agony through me. Cliff was right behind me, footsteps steadily pounding the earth.

"Cain!" I shouted. "Cain, leave him!"

He threw a disgusted look over his shoulder, chest heaving from the damage he had taken. We were still yards away when he cursed and turned back to Rhett.

A dead siren was floating on the tide, mere feet away from Rhett's limp legs. She had feasted before death. One of Rhett's limbs was bloody but salvageable. The other looked beyond saving—ravaged to the bone. Swollen, crimson marks marred his symmetrical face—*my marks*, I thought with barely subdued pride.

Rage made my chest tighten as I watched Cain saw through the zip tie with a pocket knife. He clapped his hands on Rhett's face, reviving him. Although Rhett was groggy, he was quick to come to his bearings, those wicked blue eyes darting from point to point. Sheer fucking willpower and adrenaline could be the only explanations for his ability to snap out of the shock of his injuries.

"Up, boy! Get up!" Cain rasped as he helped Rhett lean on him, setting sights on the truck—far too close to where Sylvia was caged.

The buzzing of wings caught my ear.

Cliff heard it too, throwing out an arm to stop me from pushing right into the two enemy fairies as they flew into view. They were angry, grieving—I could see the way they looked at the corpse of the siren before unleashing a torrent of fire and searing lightning toward Rhett and Cain.

Rhett didn't hesitate. With shocking clarity, he leaned hard against the truck and yanked Cain in front of him, using him as a human shield. Cain's screams choked off as he charred, the stench of it cloying the air. His body crumpled, and Rhett sank to the ground, unable to support himself on his ruined leg. The front of his clothing was charred from the attack, skin angry red beneath.

He groped behind him for something—Sylvia was less than a meter away behind the truck, just up the slope. He was dragging himself along the ground, his legs scarcely usable. His roar of agony with each inch gained was raw and animal.

I snapped back into movement. I knew what I had to do. This time, I didn't care if Sylvia watched. I wouldn't hesitate. I would kill Rhett to protect her—to protect all of us. But as I charged,

Rhett finally reached the slightly ajar passenger door. I thought he might try to climb in and peel off in the truck, but he groped inside desperately and withdrew something that froze me in place.

His flamethrower.

"Holy fuck," Cliff breathed beside me, staggering further out of Rhett's path, keeping to the shadows of the trees.

Horror licked up my spine as Rhett squeezed the trigger with a roar. Flames erupted in midair. He was so far gone from the tentative control he had wielded all those years ago in Oregon. Now, Rhett was using no strategy, no aim—just setting everything ablaze. The two fairies who'd killed Cain jolted backward.

Rhett forced himself to stand with a heave of tortured effort, dragging what remained of his ruined leg behind him, squeezing the trigger nonstop to blow the flames further, catching more trees and underbrush in his path. Exposed bone and shredded muscle left a dark trail as he moved—and his scream of agony became a war cry.

Several fairies dove toward the flames—fire affinities, I realized, trying to bend the inferno away from their midair position. For a moment, they were successful—wrangling the fire the way stallions could be broken.

But another shrill cry pierced the air, small and agonized. One of the other fairies was consumed in the blaze and plummeted from the air. This broke the fire affinities' concentration, just for a second. It was enough. Rhett's flames surged forward. More fairies crowded toward him on the offensive, wielding every affinity I'd ever heard about. Lightning singed Rhett's chest, burning him. He sank to the ground, too far away to lean on the truck now.

He kept his weapon aimed upward, unrelenting. Two more winged bodies dropped, and I couldn't watch anymore. The wildness in Rhett's eyes was manic, his face aglow and shining with sweat.

He wouldn't stop. He'd burn this whole fucking place down to get what he wanted—Sylvia, us, the Velorian compound.

Now, a voice in my head barked. *Run, now!*

I exchanged a look with Cliff, his steely resolve mirroring mine. We tore behind the bed of the pickup truck, out of Rhett's line of sight as the heat from his flamethrower burned at our backs. My leg screamed with every step, but it mattered less when Sylvia came into sight.

Relief hit me like a wave. She was still in the cage, her face pallid and her arms caked in dirt. Small rivets were clawed into the earth near the iron bars. She had been trying to dig her way out—to no avail. She was seated in the center, looking sick and paler than I'd ever seen her, but she was *alive*.

"Sylv," I breathed, wrenching the cage off of her, tossing it aside.

I could've sworn color rushed back into her face the moment she was freed. But she wouldn't look at me. Her gaze skirted around us towards the water, and I realized she was still hoping to glimpse the gemstone. My throat closed. I wished I could comb the entire bayou with her to find it. Its loss stung—more collateral damage.

"Come on. We gotta go," Cliff said, scooping Sylvia off the ground.

I was silently grateful for his initiative, unsure if I could bring myself to touch her right now. Not when she bore that vicious look when her eyes skirted toward me—like she was dreaming of driving a knife of ice through my ribs. For a brief, irrational moment, I thought she would; I thought she might conjure spellwork to attack me now that the iron no longer quelled her magic.

Sylvia's wilted silence somehow stabbed even deeper.

Cliff took the wheel of the truck, finding the keys were still in the ignition. Sylvia sat on the dashboard as he peeled out of the clearing, tires grinding on the uneven terrain. The rising sun flashed through the tree line, making my eyes ache. Gradually, branches dripping with iridescent, gemstone-altered flowers and fruit morphed into ordinary leaves, dark and bearded by moss.

"Don't look, Sylv," Cliff said. "Don't look back."

Facing the backseat, her gaze was already vacant. I followed her stare. Through the back window, pinpricks of wavering light glinted in the fire—burning fairies. Her own kind. Bodies of sirens and hunters lay scattered along the shore. Fire caught along the underbrush, clouding the world with smoke.

26

SYLVIA

I wondered if he was coming.

The spectral plane had not felt so cavernous and lonely in a long time. Jon's absence carved out a crucial part of this place. The cape-like sleeves of my ivy-colored top fluttered as I wrapped my arms around myself tightly—as though that might appease the ache in my chest.

I imagined Jon balking out there in the motel room, perhaps even refusing to join me. He could have no misunderstanding. I had made my sentiments clear when I snapped at him, laying down beside the spectral rune on the bedspread. I had whispered the spell without waiting on his hesitation.

Cliff's expression in that moment was cemented in my mind, too, though I wished I could forget how his eyes had lowered, realization clicking uncomfortably between us. Without words, he chose to be an ally to us both. Pissed at Jon, but not nearly as much as he should have been. A selfish part of me wanted Cliff to be *furious,* wanted him to be on my side and mine alone.

I took a tentative, restless step across the horizonless void of the plane, periwinkle mist swirling in my midst. Time was different here, I reminded myself. Hours could be only a few minutes in the real world.

I ground my back teeth. He didn't deserve those minutes—not when his betrayal had come to fruition in a matter of seconds. He owed me this.

Just then, something shifted in the air. It was subtle—not even a sound to mark the change. Perhaps entirely imperceptible to anyone else. I felt *him*, and I couldn't decide if it was romantic or pathetic that I knew the instant when he occupied space near me.

I bolstered my courage before I turned. Jon looked like himself again. The damage from the morning's bloodbath was cleaned and healed—the ice slash, bullet wound, and all. He was in clean clothes that only accentuated how achingly handsome he was. His dark hair was tousled, but it looked like he had combed his fingers through it to push it off his face. The vine restraints in Veloria had left angry bruises along his ribs and neck—but here, his skin was wiped clean, an even olive tone that almost glowed.

"Sylvia," Jon breathed, his stare catching mine.

I craned my neck to hold his stare as he closed the space between us—though there was a primal part of me that wanted to look away, to look anywhere else. He was only a head taller than me here, but this time, it felt like more. My composure was like a thread stretched past its limit.

When Jon reached to pull me into his arms, that thread snapped. Red flashed in my vision, and I tore from his grasp. My hand cracked across his face. He flinched like it hurt, but I roiled at the knowledge that he couldn't feel the physical sting of the contact.

"Fuck you," I said.

He didn't seem at all shocked, but the words stung where the slap could not. The longer I looked up into his face, the more my grief seeped into the anger. Around us, the spectral plane blossomed with deeper hues of pink—scarlet mist that swept in like a heavy fog from my fractured heart.

My voice dwindled into a soft croak. "Jon, how could you do that to me?"

His expression twisted with shame. His eyes swept over me and shuttered. "I'm so sorry, Sylv."

"You trapped me," I said, each word gritted out like poison.

"I know."

"I thought we were in this together—a *team*. No matter our differences."

"We are!"

"But you don't trust me."

"I trust you with my life," Jon said. "I'm not so sure I trust you with *yours*."

He eased closer. I stepped out of reach from his arms—those arms I craved so dearly. "What am I to you, if I'm not an equal?"

Jon's jaw squared. His gaze flicked briefly to the charged mist around us, the luminous colors casting a glow across his skin. "Don't talk like that, Sylv. That's not—"

"Would you have caged Cliff?" I interjected. "Would you have done something like that to *him*?"

"Maybe!" Jon fired back, waving a hand. "If the situation called for it. You were *hurt*. Flightless, wounded… You could barely fucking stand on your own two legs. You were in no shape to fight."

I flinched at the force behind each word—at the truth there. But fire still roared in my chest, aching to burn him. "If the situation called for it," I echoed snidely. "Years ago, did the *situation* call for getting Luke killed? Tell me, did he know he was bait, or did he figure it out when he was being ripped apart?"

"How did you…" He paled, shuddering out a breath that let me know I'd hit my mark. His lips pressed into a thin, bitter line. "Gwen." But instead of anger, regret, and sorrow flooded his expression. "It was a job gone wrong, Sylv. I was younger, stupider. I thought I knew more than everyone around me."

"That hasn't changed one bit," I muttered.

"Maybe," he said softly. "But Luke was a hunter, and hunters go into every job knowing it could be their last. You… you didn't sign up for this life. You've nearly died because of me—because of *us*—too many times. Out there, I saw it was about to happen again."

Jon's gaze softened. He studied me, then took a calculated risk and drew closer again. He cupped my face in one of his large hands, fingertips pushing through my chin-length locks. The slight tremble to his grip made me falter, made me seek his gaze again.

"I know you're as selfless as you are stubborn." His deep voice quavered. "Nothing I or anyone said would've stopped you. I didn't want to grab that iron, but I had to make a choice. An awful choice—to *protect you*."

He made to take my hand, desperate to further the physical bond between us. I was suddenly and acutely aware that he was human and I was not.

But *was* he still fully human, if he could do such inhuman things?

"That's not your job," I hissed, shoving his chest. Jon's hand fell away from my cheek as he let the blow push him back. "You're not indebted to me! Don't act like a caretaker, like I'm some damn child for you to worry over. What's next, a collar?"

Jon's eyes flashed angrily, sending a chill down my spine. He never looked at me like that. Not since he hunted me down in the old Dottage house, suspecting me of bloodshed. The sky around us darkened with plumes of silver and shadow. *His* colors.

"Fuck, it's not that! You really think that's how I see you?" Jon asked roughly.

"You tell me."

His jaw set. "You're *insane* if you think—"

"What the hell would you call *that?*" I all but shrieked, acid in my blood.

He snapped forward, seizing me by the shoulders. Shaking me. Shouting, "I can't lose you!"

My voice was gone. I gaped up into the storm of emotion in his face—still beautiful even when frightening. As his raised voice hit me, the pink-crimson sky of the spectral realm vanished entirely behind the shadows like swirling black clouds had rolled over the sun. Wind gusted around us. I'd never conjured wind here before—it was *him.* My heart raced at the notion of what Jon was doing without so much as a whispered intention.

I felt limp in his grasp. His expression crumpled like he was grieving me right then, like he had grieved me a dozen times already. Though the plane dulled the heat between our bodies, Jon's grip was bruisingly possessive, even as his hands moved from my shoulders to cradle my face.

"I can't make the right call anymore," he said, voice lower. "I would do terrible things to keep you safe. Because I—" He faltered, Adam's apple bobbing in the strong curve of his neck. "Because I love you, Sylv."

My mouth dropped open, but I couldn't form a single word. Had he said this to me any other day, I would have been dizzy with joy. My heart clenched around his words, holding fast. But here, after what had happened—I was terrified.

You can't love me, too.

We can't be together.

Jon's voice dropped to a whisper. "Fuck. I'm sorry. I know it'd be easier if I didn't. I know that you deserve someone better than me." His eyes shuttered like he couldn't stand my stunned expression any longer. "Something's changed in me since we met. I can't ignore it anymore. When I'm with you, I—I'm not drowning."

We can't, we can't, we can't—but the reasons why were harder to remember when Jon held me like this. Like I was the only real thing in a fucked-up world.

There was no regret in his gaze when he dared to look at me again, but a certain resignation surfaced. I had no doubt then that he'd been harboring the same insecurities that burned through me like poison. Perhaps he thought I was coming up with the gentlest way to reject him.

Yes—that's what I had to do. This was my moment, my chance to make the difficult choice to save us both. I would turn him away, tell him to find someone else. *Anyone* else.

My hand balled into a fist against his shirt. The firm wall of muscle pressed against my body had me magnetized.

I couldn't stop myself.

"I love you, too," I whispered. "A lot. Too much." The words left me in a freefall—weightless and terrified. I swallowed hard, peering up into his face. I was broken for him, and he would break himself for me. "Why can't you go find another girl who won't hurt you?"

"I don't want anyone else," Jon said, unwavering.

I swore he could see right through me. It pulled tears into my eyes—happy, terrified tears.

"You're crazy," I scoffed.

His lips curved. "No more than you," he said softly. His eyes kept flicking to my mouth. His grip was no longer desperate but tender.

Still, as my chest roiled with emotions, I resisted. "You can't ignore how doomed we are," I insisted. "Without a gemstone, you know we're only a momentary dream. But you won't admit it, will you?"

"The world is wider than Louisiana. There have to be other gems out there, waiting for you to get your hands on them." Jon pulled a face, grimacing if only to pull a smile out of me. "Maybe a few of them aren't surrounded by psycho warrior-fairies with a power fetish."

Our faces were so close, I felt his breath against mine. "People look at us like we're freaks. Even Cliff. My own mother would be disgusted. She would kill you if she knew—maybe me, too, while she's at it."

Finally, the smallest trickle of uncertainty lined his face. I saw it in the shadows that flickered in his eyes—*yes*, he knew. The way those villagers assumed I was his captive on sight. The way that killing me at the hunters' outpost was the only way those bastards could understand why we'd exist within reach of each other.

"And what if they're right?" I plunged on. I gestured up, though the real stars were a universe away. "What if this is wrong? Like *cosmically* wrong, us being together?"

The wind Jon had conjured became a gentle breeze around us, playfully tousling his hair to frame his dark, tender expression. Jon cupped my cheek in his palm, eyes electric. He brushed a thumb over my lips, delicately tracing. I suppressed a shiver. Where he had once been resistant and cautious, a new steadiness had taken over.

"Then I will gladly spend ages being horrible and wicked with you," he said.

He ducked and kissed me hard, and I lost all resistance because I knew his promises were not made lightly. Just before my eyes fell shut, I saw the spectral plane surge with fresh color—*our* colors—mixing and flourishing into new ones. Radiance with the power to blossom and annihilate all at once. His mouth moved against mine, perfect and drugging. Jon's hands moved slowly from my shoulders to my waist.

Hands that had slammed that fucking cage over me.

I broke the kiss, gripping his square jaw in my hand. I surfaced from my daze to fix him with a blazing look. Tension radiated through my palm as he froze obediently.

"All my life, I've felt trapped. You can't be another person confining me. Not *you*. If you ever turn iron or cages against me again," I said, low and ground-out, "you will never see me again. I won't forgive you a second time."

Wavering pain filled his stare. I was suddenly reminded of the pieces of his past I didn't know. The six years between us felt gaping—years he had spent becoming more lethal while I was cloistered under the willow. I gripped him tighter, fingernails digging into skin as my pleading gaze bore into his.

"Swear you won't ever do that again." I had never heard the commanding growl come out of my own lips, like a vengeful noble.

Finally, Jon nodded in resolute understanding. "On my father's grave."

It was the heaviest whisper I had ever heard. Breaking this promise would shatter the very foundation of who he was—and part of me still wondered if that was enough. I exhaled, uncertain if there was any point in us trying to resist our true natures—a fairy who didn't know when to stop, and a hunter who would do unspeakable things to protect her.

The inches between us suddenly burned, unbearable. I slid my hand down to his chest, savoring the way his eyes hooded. How touch-starved he looked, lips parted and waiting as I lifted onto my tiptoes to crush my mouth to his once more.

Jon's kiss was bruising—like the world was ending and the taste of my lips would be the one thing he could take with him to the afterlife. The weightless feeling was replaced with a sensation of soaring that even my fastest flights couldn't grant me. All our visits to this private sanctuary, and he had never kissed me like *this*. So absolutely. So fiercely.

There was no room for doubt—*he loved me.*

He felt like a storm learning to be still, maybe just so he could better hold onto me.

And I was not alone.

I took hold of his button-up shirt and urged it off, peeling it down his broad shoulders and letting it fall over his toned arms. *Closer.* I needed to be closer.

I felt the bare skin of his arms as they crushed around me again, circling beneath my fanning wings. My fingers slipped over his right shoulder beneath the short sleeve of his tee, seeking the rune-shaped scar I had put there. *My mark.* It did not exist in this realm, my fingers ghosting over smooth skin. Jon knew what I was looking for, lust building behind his soft smirk as he watched me.

He glanced around us contemplatively as though finally noticing the conjured breeze—noticing how it bowed to his emotions. As he breathed me in, his racing pulse slowed—though mine quickened as Jon lifted a cautious hand. He flexed his fingers—cautiously at first, then turning his palm up like he was ruddering an invisible force. The gusts slowed even more, until they were mere whispers of movement circling us.

Tenderness glittered in his gaze as he turned back to me, looking as breathless as I felt. He moved his open palm between us. After a moment of concentration, sparks of light flickered to life at his fingertips—golden, like soft embers.

It was so close to magic, I nearly stopped breathing. My vicious hunter, holding *magic* in his hand.

My awestruck gasp caught in my throat as Jon pressed his hand to my chest, his strong fingers purposefully tracing a pattern over my exposed collarbone. Golden lines were left like scrolling vinework all over the delicate base of my neck, my shoulders. It was a crude recreation of the Fae runes I had left on *him* so many times during our trysts here. Although the mark held no translation, he took evident care to match my style. I let my head tip back as Jon bent down to kiss the places he had marked, leaving golden streaks everywhere his hand roamed.

He roughly spun me around to face the vastness of the special realm before us.

"I want to try something," came his coarse voice in my ear.

One arm wrapped around me from behind, pinning me against his front. The other stretched out, his palm turning upward, beckoning. The whirls of slate-gray and crimson that painted every direction began to brighten and blur. Slowly, shapes took form—walls, windows, and lush fir trees.

"Jon…" I whispered.

Dizziness swept over me as a dwelling slowly took shape before us. It was strikingly similar to how I had created my childhood home from my mind's eye, everything moving and shaping into place without regard for gravity.

Astonished, I observed Jon. The slight furrow between his brows. The determined gleam in his eyes. The set to his perfect jaw. So *human.* He was as intimidating as he was angelic in that moment, with the light of the building shapes and light dancing over us.

Finally, a room paneled in dark wood faced us, sunlight spilling in from a vast floor-to-ceiling window behind a living room. Candles were still lit, like someone had only just left this cozy space. Jon's grip on me slackened when his creation fully solidified before us— spent from the effort. I broke free of him, stepping into the illusion. Though the wall wavered into smoke, the view set in front of us was as crisp as the memory I had conjured of Elysia days before.

Soft carpet sank under my feet. Shelves of books lined a towering wall, with framed photos and personal items littering the spaces in between. I drifted toward the shelves, aware of Jon trailing behind me with soft steps, a matching expression of awe on his face. One of the framed photos bore an image of a family in the snow—smiling parents holding the hands of a scrawny boy with wavy locks and dark eyes. I drifted toward the vast window next, transfixed by the view framed outside.

"Is this a memory?" I asked, reaching out to touch the pane of glass.

Jon came to stand behind me, gazing out at the mountains—*actual mountains*—alongside ribboning rivers and churning waterfalls that cut through glittering quartz. Endless blankets of fir trees stretched out to the horizon. I could practically smell the sharp tinge to the air when I breathed in.

"No. This is where I'm going to take you someday," he said. "A place we can call our own."

He conjured this from nothing? I thought, reeling at the notion.

"You can't keep that promise," I murmured.

"I can make a choice," he said. "I choose *you*. I will not be a victim anymore. Neither of us have to."

My heart lodged in my throat. I knew enough to treasure how a man who only knew violence would lay down his weapons to become something softer. He was choosing me, choosing this life, over a hunter's end.

Even if I was the biggest gamble he'd ever taken. Even if—

"We'll find another gemstone," Jon pressed, as though he could read the crushing emotion on my face.

My throat closed. *That gemstone.* I could still feel the fervent ghost of it, calling to me, making my blood turn electric. It had been full and perfect—raw power cradled in my arms. Lost forever to the hostile forest.

My stomach turned further as I remembered what I had done to have it in reach at all.

"I almost lost you both," I croaked, running a hand over my face.

"They tricked you," Jon cut in firmly.

I shook my head even as I indulged his comforting kiss to the crown of my head. He didn't fully understand how in those moments, nothing else had mattered but that beckoning power. *Nothing.* And that wasn't anything Marcellus had forced on me. That desire was all me.

"I can't be so careless next time. I won't have you spill more blood for me." I sniffed, peering at the room around us. A place Jon had built for us. A place I may only ever carry here, where things were only halfway real.

"I might keep you waiting a while," I said, shooting him a doleful expression.

Jon swept a lock of my hair behind my ear and gently thumbed my traitor mark. "It'll always be you. Wherever I am. Together or apart. So I'll take whatever time I get with you, no matter how it ends."

The thread between us seemed to shiver at his words. I no longer wondered if he felt it, too.

"That's a terribly tragic thing to say, you know that?" I said.

Jon's smile widened. "I've had more than my share of tragedy, and trust me, it's never felt this good."

His kiss was softer when he tugged me back into his embrace. I leaned into him, sinking into the safety of his arms. Here, where we ruled over our own little world, where time stretched and we felt like we could live on forever. We could exist precisely as we wanted with no prying eyes to make us doubt ourselves. Injuries were outlawed, and hope overshadowed dread.

But as I blinked my eyes open and saw blood trickling from Jon's nose, I couldn't help but feel that the two of us were barreling toward heartbreak with our eyes wide open.

: 27

JON

"Where do you want me to put this?" I asked Gwen, hefting a heavy box of books in my arms.

The living room, once warm and cluttered, was nearly empty now. Much of the furniture was gone, and the walls were stripped bare, colorful paintings stacked in the corner by the window. The whole upper floor felt hollow. Even the cats and dogs paced from room to room like they could sense something wasn't right.

I couldn't shake the guilt. Gwen and Hannah wouldn't be uprooting themselves if we hadn't pulled them into our mess. Helping them pack a few boxes was the least we could do.

"Just stack it on top of the others," Gwen said in a low, tired voice. Her raven hair was braided over one shoulder, the strands loose from harried movement all morning.

Cliff walked past, bearing a box haphazardly packed full of DVDs from the bedroom. He dropped it unceremoniously over mine, then fished out a title that had been resting on top.

"*Casablanca?* Really?" He raised his eyebrows, waggling the black-and-white case. "Ten bucks says you've never touched this since you bought it."

"It's a classic." Gwen snatched it from him and tucked it back into place. "I'll get around to it. Soon."

Cliff handed her the roll of shipping tape, his expression skeptical but good-natured. "My sister went on a classics kick once. Insisted she wanted to be more *cultured* than the other middle schoolers. She got over that urge real quick when she realized how many of them were a slog to get through."

Gwen gave him a soft nudge on the arm, a small laugh escaping her. The look on her face was cautious, though surprisingly gentle. "Any word from her lately?"

"Hard for her to reach out when she doesn't have my number, but… I dunno. Sylv was pestering me to call her the other day. I might just do it to get her off my back."

She snorted. "You really have gone soft, haven't you? It's a good look on you."

The front door creaked open, and the three of us turned to see Hannah walk in, wiping her grease-covered hands on her jeans. Her face was sweaty, and her clothes were streaked with oil like she'd been halfway inside a car all morning. All things considered, it wasn't far from the truth.

Sylvia appeared behind her, iridescent wings glinting golden in the midday sunlight streaming in. She'd insisted on keeping Hannah company, though I knew she was hoping to glean some helpful information about the inner workings of an engine.

"So, the car…" Sylvia did a poor job of hiding a wince.

"Don't sugarcoat it." I folded my arms, looking between them as Hannah shut the door.

"Did everything I could, but your Pontiac's dust," Hannah announced. "Transmission's out of commission, not to mention the electrical."

She sauntered into the room, handing Cliff one of the pistons from the engine. The hunk of metal was discolored, damaged from the prolonged stint underwater.

Cliff let out a long sigh, looking at the piston like he had been handed a human skull. "Our luck had to run out somewhere."

Hannah exhaled a shaky laugh as if to question where our luck had begun. But an enthused glint hid beneath her exhausted gaze. "There are plenty of other cars on the lot," she pointed out casually.

She exchanged a smirk with Sylvia when Cliff immediately glanced in the Challenger's direction.

"Why don't you take that one off my hands?" Hannah nodded toward it. "You've been eye-fucking it all week. It'll save you the trouble of jacking it when I'm not looking."

"Oh, come on, I wouldn't—" Cliff's insulted defensiveness took a backseat as he processed what she said. For a second, he looked thrilled, but it quickly melted into suspicion as he narrowed his eyes between Hannah and Gwen. He even threw a glare at me and Sylvia like we were in on a cruel joke. "Don't fuck with me," he said. "We can't afford a tire off of that."

Unfazed, Hannah reached into her pocket and pulled out a set of keys. "Some of the Pontiac parts are workable enough to earn you a couple grand. How's five for the Challenger, plus you move a few more boxes, and we'll call it even?"

"Jesus," I muttered. I wasn't anywhere near as obsessive as Cliff, but even I knew this was beyond a steal; it was a charity case. Then again, maybe that was what we were beginning to look like.

"Consider it a favor for me," Hannah insisted. "My cousin's coming to take over the lot. Love him to death, but he doesn't know shit about maintaining classics. It'll sit around and rust." She tossed the keys, and Cliff snatched them out of the air. Her sweet smile tightened around the edges. "But if this one ends up in a swamp, I suggest you go down with it before I catch wind."

"Noted." Cliff looked down at the keys with disbelief. "Thanks, Hannah," he murmured with surprising sincerity. Then he cleared his throat and glanced at me pointedly, raising his eyebrows. My expression flattened—*thanks a lot*. So, he was dumping it on me to pry.

I tried not to sound like I was interrogating, but there was no way around it. "Are we gonna talk about what the hell that was yesterday—or, Monday?" The lost days were still hard to wrap my head around, but the memory of Hannah slipping into her trance may as well have been from minutes ago.

Hannah's gaze dropped. Her grease-stained fingers wove together, suddenly fidgeting. Gwen put a hand on her arm and shot each of us a warning glare, but she didn't stop Hannah from answering.

"I didn't mean to scare you. I come from a line of mediums on my mom's side," Hannah admitted in a low voice. "Nothing fancy these days; most of us keep it under wraps. My Tante Halle does make a killing with online readings, and my grandma had her own parlor in New Orleans before she passed."

An uncertain shiver ran down my spine. Clairvoyance was typically a short walk from witchcraft, and most covens had a natural medium in their ranks. With how swiftly I was bristling, it was no wonder Gwen was hellbent on keeping Hannah away from hunters.

Sighing, Hannah looked between Cliff and me. "My family calls it *the gift*, though it feels like anything but. My episodes started younger than anyone expected—I was barely nine. I collapsed during recess and spouted off about my friend suffering a great sorrow. I'll never forget how my classmates and the teachers were looking at me when I came to—like I was some sort of freak. Well, it got even worse when my friend's dad died in a car accident a week later."

She swallowed hard. "I could go on about the other incidents, but bottom line, I never wanted anything to do with the gift. My family was so disappointed in me for suppressing my abilities instead of harnessing them. I'm supposed to be *honored* to be blessed, but it scares me." She lowered her gaze, growing melancholy. "And it scares others, too. I'm sorry about whatever I said to you—clearly it put you on edge."

That's putting it lightly, I thought bitterly.

"You really don't remember?" Sylvia asked, wheeling around to take a perch on my shoulder.

A pause drew out—as awkward as it was unsettling. My throat closed at the memory of Hannah's rolling eyes and manic refrain—the words painting my best friend into some kind of messiah.

You're Cliff Everett, aren't you? The one from the legends. Are you going to save us?

Goosebumps prickled on my arms as I recalled the rasped words she had offered to *me*, too.

I side-eyed Cliff's profile. His jaw was squared hard enough to make a vein in his neck visible, but his eyebrows were unknit. He was working hard to school his expression—a dead giveaway to anyone who knew him well. It was an odd comfort that he was just as creeped out by the prophecy as I was.

Gwen took Hannah's hand and squeezed it. Finally, with some obvious embarrassment, Hannah cleared her throat.

"Can't remember a thing. That's how it is with everyone who has the gift in my family." She smirked half-heartedly. "Total client confidentiality. I think Tante Halle records her sessions so she can keep track of her predictions."

"And you didn't know anything supernatural existed beyond that?" Cliff asked skeptically.

"Can't say I wasn't a little curious, but my dad was on my side when he saw how much the gift scared me. He was quick to shut down any talk about visions, prophecies, and the supernatural at family get-togethers when I was in earshot—and I was grateful for it. I guess I never had the chance to cross paths with anything else."

Gwen scoffed. "At least none that you *knew* of. Hell, I don't know how you managed to survive until I came along."

"My *hero*." Hannah nudged Gwen with her hip, eyes sparkling. "When she stuck around after witnessing one of my episodes, I knew she was the one. Obviously, I didn't know she'd seen much worse before."

Gwen glanced at Hannah's lips before looking back at us, momentarily riveted by the memory. "I didn't feel right leaving her alone after the wraith. I couldn't, you know? Not with the outpost right in her backyard. The idea of one of those trigger-happy idiots mistaking her for a coven clairvoyant…"

She looked sharply to the slit of sunlight pouring in through the curtains as a shadow passed over the living room. A passing car—but I couldn't blame her for being jumpy. We were all on a running clock. Rhett's chances of survival didn't seem likely, but any other survivors of the massacre might have us on their radar—especially with how hellbent they had been about targeting Cliff in particular.

"This place became home before I knew it," Gwen finished softly.

A sense of heaviness settled over the room after that—because this wouldn't be *home* for much longer, and it was our fault. I felt Sylvia shift restlessly on my shoulder, no doubt playing with her hair as she waded through the same guilt.

"Have you ever been wrong?" Sylvia asked, her melodic voice strained at the edges like she had been bottling up the question for hours. "About the prophecies?"

Hannah's gaze rested on Sylvia with a sadness that seemed to age her. My stomach twisted as I remembered the haunted way Sylvia had regarded me when we left the garage that day. *Her love will ruin you.* It could have meant *anyone*, it could have been bullshit—but my sweetest assurances couldn't heal Sylvia's worry.

"Honestly, I don't know," Hannah said. "But please—don't let it eat at you. I'm a firm believer that destiny is the wheel of a car. We get to steer it."

She offered us a crooked smile, bearing the weight of grief and hope all at once. A weight I knew well. Hannah bent down to peck Gwen's cheek, and excused herself to pull the *Challenger* around front for us. Cliff looked longingly after the jingle of keys that she had pried from his hands. Despite everything, I smiled. Cliff was going to be insufferable for the next few months on the road, playing with his new toy.

While we transported a few more boxes, Gwen fetched us glasses of lemonade from the dining room. I was surprised when she came back with a thimble for Sylvia, who was too stunned to thank her in more than a stammer.

"Another one of Hannah's recipes?" I asked.

"Mine, actually," Gwen chirped. "If you count thawing a can of concentrate."

Gwen stopped in front of Cliff, reaching a hand inside his jacket. I stopped with my glass halfway to my mouth, watching how he froze up. Her hand grazed over his chest, rooting into the inner pocket—helping herself to his flask. She emptied what was left of the whiskey into her glass and gave him a look through her lashes as if to challenge that *yes,* he owed her this. She took a seat on one of the sealed moving boxes and indulged in a long gulp.

"Where's next for you?" Gwen asked.

"West," Sylvia announced.

"Right, the hitchhiking. You catch wind of something out there?" Gwen asked.

Cliff's eyes cut toward Sylvia, the corner of his mouth lifting. "Something like that," he said.

Gwen glanced between the three of us flatly. "That's all I get?" She scoffed around another sip. "Well, maybe it's better I don't know. Just don't get yourself killed out there."

Cliff gave a strangely knowing chuckle that made Gwen send him a sharp look.

"What are you smirking about?" she snapped, elegant brows furrowing.

Cliff sauntered to her, taking his flask back. He tucked it back out of sight, looking down at her with that insufferable crooked smile. "You're still soft on me," he said, though there was nothing smug in his voice. His broad shoulders pinched in a shrug. "I spent a long time thinking you hated my guts."

Her guarded frown shattered, giving way to a softer gaze as she chewed on her cheek. "I never hated you, Cliff. Even when I tried to."

She set her glass aside and stood, putting them chest-to-chest. She still looked so fragile to him, the top of her head scarcely hitting Cliff's collarbone—though I knew there was nothing *delicate* about what she was capable of.

"It never would've worked between us, anyway," she said, smoothing her hands over his chest. "I need cats. It's a dealbreaker."

Cliff sucked air through his teeth. "Ouch."

Gwen chuckled, cupping his face in one hand. "It shouldn't surprise you that I've always had a thing for strays." She lifted on her tiptoes, brushing a kiss to his cheek. "Thanks for... you know—not leaving me for dead at the outpost," she added, almost shyly.

Cliff's gaze softened on her. "I'd say that evens the score between us."

She chuckled, folding her arms over her chest. "It's a start."

The rumble of the Challenger's engine crossed the front windows. Cliff looked like he wanted to touch Gwen, his hands flexing with restraint.

She was choosing—it just wasn't him.

"I'll see you around," he said.

Cliff stepped away from her, striding toward the door. Sylvia took to the air behind him after setting down her entire thimble and murmuring her thanks to Gwen. She gave the former hunter a reserved look before flitting through the open doorway, asking Cliff something about the new vehicle.

I approached Gwen, hesitating for a moment before awkwardly wrapping my arms around her. Wasn't that the right move? What you're supposed to do when someone saves your ass and you ruin their life in return?

Gwen tensed against me, shoving me off. "Easy, big guy. We're not there yet."

I backpedaled, almost relieved as I shoved my hands into my pockets instead. We studied each other, all veneer of civility dropping now that we were alone. To my surprise, the abject hatred in her honey-brown eyes had cooled somewhat. But the past few days couldn't erase our history—what I had done.

"I owe you an apology about Luke." My words came out gruff and rushed.

"You owe me more than you can offer. Just… don't. I don't want to hear it."

I nodded, pinned by her gaze as she read something in my face. "You've changed, Nowak. Starting to think that little ice princess has you wrapped around her finger." She smirked a little, amused by the notion, but her eyes narrowed at me. "Don't fuck her over."

I smiled—that I could promise. I dug around in my pocket, scrawling my cell number on the back of a crumpled receipt.

"Call if you need anything. Monsters or otherwise," I told her, pressing it into her hands before she could reject the offer.

A German Shepherd and a teacup Yorkie bounded beside me, matching my stride as I crossed the gravel-strewn lot. Up ahead, the *Challenger* idled near the front lot, its burnt-umber body glinting in the sunlight where the towering oaks no longer cast their shade. Despite its vintage year, the car glimmered like it had been dipped in molten metal. The tires were new, made for grip, and the black racing stripes down the center added a certain predatory detail. It was the kind of car that jumped off the pages of a movie poster, and a boyish part of me was itching to get behind the wheel to see what was under the hood.

By the looks of it, I would have to fight Cliff for the chance. I stood beside Hannah at the trunk, watching Cliff circle the car slowly. He moved like a lover admiring every curve, his palms skimming delicately over the paint. He glanced over at me, grinning.

"God, she's perfect, isn't she?" He reached through the driver's window to caress the steering wheel.

Hannah laughed. "I'm glad someone appreciates Brandy. She's a sweet ride."

"*Brandy,*" Cliff echoed, eyes glinting. "I like it."

"I spent a lot of time on her. Not one scratch, you hear me?"

I winced, knowing there was no chance in hell we'd manage that. Cliff knew it, too, because he nodded vaguely and excused himself to pack up the belongings we'd collected from the motel room.

Meanwhile, I had to practically drag Sylvia away from saying goodbye to the animals—even when she insisted that there were more that she had missed inside the house.

"You're taking them all with you?" Sylvia asked Hannah, stroking the German Shepherd's ears while the Yorkie grumbled for attention.

"Can't separate the pack," Hannah said. "It won't happen overnight, but we'll get them over there eventually. Trust me, they'll love it. It's an old family place out in the country with plenty of space for them to run around and get into all sorts of trouble."

"An old place? You'll call us if it's haunted?" Sylvia inquired far too cheerfully as she finally flew up to eye level.

Hannah's eyes widened at the possibility. "I think Gwen's got that in the bag—but I wouldn't mind a non-life-or-death visit sometime. I'll have to see about getting some strawberries to grow out there."

Our future may have been a strained mystery, but Sylvia looked prepared to take whichever path led her back to Hannah's baking.

The trunk slammed shut. Hannah handed off the keys, and we loaded ourselves into the car. The seats were comfortable enough to provide a halfway decent sleep on the nights we needed to camp on the side of the road.

Hannah scooped the Yorkie into her arms and stepped back a good distance to avoid getting sprayed with gravel as Cliff made Brandy take off like a rocket. Cliff hollered with joy while Sylvia clung to me for dear life, but she was screaming with laughter—a beautiful sound that I made sure to memorize.

28

JON

The storm that got us stranded was well and truly gone, leaving behind a landscape that was somehow an even lusher green than before. After being at a standstill for days, long distances seemed to pass us by in a blink.

A mere day on the road had transformed the scenery around us. Much of the land was flat in northeast Texas, but here and there, piney woods rose in the landscape.

"It's so beautiful," Sylvia sighed, her nose pressed to the window.

Cliff ran his hands over the steering wheel wistfully. "Right?"

She snorted but didn't tease him for misunderstanding—this time.

I didn't keep a lot of photos on my phone. There never seemed to be a point when they didn't aid an ongoing case. But as Sylvia gazed outside in wonderment, I figured it wouldn't hurt to have a keepsake. After I snapped the picture, I found myself sending the rolling landscape in a text message.

Sylvia, seeming to sense my hesitance, looked over her shoulder with a frown. "Sending it to my aunt," I explained. "She can show my mom in a couple weeks."

A gentle smile lit up her face. "I'm sure she'll love it."

A few minutes later, my phone chimed. I expected it to be my *tia*, but instead, Tammy's name appeared on the screen like a stop sign to all other thoughts.

I straightened in my seat, immediately tapping the link to a news alert video she had sent.

"*Unprecedented weather has Oklahoma communities puzzled,*" the news broadcast announced.

"Holy shit," I muttered.

"What?" Cliff asked as Sylvia flew in closer for a better look.

I drank in the information, unable to believe what I was hearing.

The past few days, there had been summer-like storms passing through Kentucky, Arkansas, and Missouri. The latest was an abrupt snowfall laced with fog in Oklahoma. The broadcast showed footage of people in downtown Tulsa, confused and delighted by the snowy day. The reporter also noted that cicadas had made an unusual appearance, extremely out of season given the sudden temperature plummet. Each word sent my heart pounding harder, and I sensed Sylvia's rapt stare upon the screen.

Another chime. Tammy had sent a still image from the broadcast, zoomed in on a close-up on the insects. Their wings—usually translucent—were an iridescent red, sending some locals into a fearful rant about an omen of the end of days.

I waited for an explanation from Tammy, but her next message surprised me more than anything.

"*You see this shit? Steer clear. I'm handling it with a crew. Best to keep smaller numbers to avoid much more attention. My gut tells me it's the W.V. coven on the move. Heard whispers of expansion stirring in the west mountain region. We'll intercept them there.*"

"Fuck," I said, grimacing. "She thinks it's the West Virginia coven."

Cliff groaned. "Oh, those guys suck. I swear that the blonde bitch at their head is the one who cursed me."

I smirked. "If we run into her, I'll be sure to ask her why she thought *squirrels* were a fitting punishment."

"Who knows why witches do what they do?" Cliff scoffed. Glancing at me, his frown sobered. "For that matter—what are they doing so far from home?"

"I'm not sure," I admitted, scrutinizing the video again. "Newsworthy chaos isn't their M.O. I mean, usually they're pretty predictable, but this seems more like Veloria."

Heaviness settled in the car at the mere mention of the village, and I knew the three of us were stifling matching sets of vivid, gnawing memories. Sylvia massaged her right shoulder like she could clean away the warrior rune.

"Unprecedented weather, mutated insects…" Cliff gave a ragged sigh. "Yeah, that could be a gem as much as anything else."

I exchanged a tentative look with Sylvia. After the setback we'd experienced, it seemed almost too good to be true.

"The path of weather patterns does seem to be heading toward the west mountains," she breathed, searching my face. "I know Tammy says to steer clear, but… we've been heading in that direction anyway, haven't we?"

"A little backup wouldn't hurt," Cliff said. "I'm offended we're benched on her roster, actually."

"Tammy hates surprises," I reminded him.

"She'll survive. Just keep your head down if we cross paths," Cliff said, directing this to Sylvia.

"Oh, you *don't* want me to introduce myself with a dramatic flourish? Thanks for clarifying," she drawled.

I smiled as they continued, their back-and-forth like a balm to my nerves. I turned back to my phone, tapping out a response.

"*We're headed east anyway,*" I lied through text.

Tammy replied with a thumbs-up emoji and left it at that. I frowned a little. Why *wouldn't* she want backup? Her silence the last few months preyed on me again, raising more questions than I cared to answer. Perhaps she'd been alerted to the trouble we'd caused at the bayou outpost and wanted nothing more to do with us.

"She doesn't have to know we're anywhere near there," I said firmly—though the words tasted like betrayal. Sneaking behind our mentor's back, lying. "If the coven's really heading for the Rockies, we'll look into this shit ourselves."

As silence settled, Sylvia returned to her perch by the window. She was back to her earth-toned form-fitting clothing, having buried the bloodied gown from Veloria behind the motel. She played with her knife as she gazed outside, her thumb running over the jewel in its hilt over and over. Her attempt at a relaxed posture couldn't fool me.

"What are you thinking?" I asked softly.

She turned to me with a subdued smile. Even with a faint glimmer in her eyes, she said, "I don't want us to get our hopes up."

But I had a feeling we both knew it was too late for that. I tried not to think of the supposed prophecy Hannah had rasped, her brown eyes set upon me and bulging with horror.

Her love will ruin you.

It didn't matter. Sylvia was here, and she was *mine*—for now.

If keeping her meant losing myself, I'd pay the price a thousand times over.

MELANIE

Interrogating someone shouldn't have taken this long.

Perhaps this was another way he was stalling our journey—and I knew for a fact he was, to some extent. No doubt he thought I would abandon him once we were in the safety of Aelthorin. I hadn't decided if that fear of his was well-founded or not.

I watched from the car, perched on the passenger's side dashboard for the best view. The windows were rolled halfway down, letting in the cool night breeze. Crickets chirped in the grass, and mossy tree branches groaned in the wind. I saw him standing there, an imposing silhouette next to a slightly stockier man, both of them outlined by the warm glow spilling from the second-floor windows.

Glamour was effective with humans—he had proven that many times over, even with his unusual brand of it. He could convince them to share information, give costly items away at no charge, or even forget recent memories. But *stars*, getting information out of this man would be so much quicker if he were held off the second story of the garage balcony by the back of his shirt.

I whispered a spell—the most familiar words my lips knew apart from the names of my children. I played with a small, crackling orb of flames between my palms, resisting the urge to fly through the window and question the human myself. The threat of being scorched alive usually yielded abrupt honesty.

But that would wake Hazel.

I leaned to peer at the backseat where my child of eleven summers was curled up, sleeping in a nest of white fleece blankets. Her scarlet curls popped against the white belly of the stuffed rabbit she snuggled against. Though it was three times her size, she insisted on sleeping with it each night, enamored. She loved all the gifts that *Mother's friend* lavished her with, too young to understand yet that they were tokens of a guilty conscience.

A soft sigh escaped me. It was a wonder that Hazel was able to sleep so soundly at all, with the chaos of the last two months. *Months*—the thought struck me again like a blow. How had the weeks bled together?

At first, our upended life had been a constant state of frantic movements and frayed nerves—suddenly learning to relocate from place to place like nomads. Hazel had been so petrified, barely speaking for a week. These days, she eagerly peered out the car windows at every opportunity instead of staying plastered against my side. She asked questions of *him* with enthusiasm, hanging on his every word.

I extinguished the fire and rubbed my face in my hands. *She deserves to know.*

Looking back outside, I stiffened at movement edging near our vehicle. One of the roaming dogs sniffed urgently and circled the car. I hissed for it to *shoo*, relieved when I spotted the humans wrapping up their conversation. If Hazel woke up and saw an animal, I'd have no chance of wrestling her excitement back into slumber. The taller man pointed at the stairs, and the stockier one turned and marched up them. *Thank the stars.* The two roaming dogs followed after their owner, bounding past the stranger in their midst.

I braced myself as the driver's door opened and he slid behind the wheel, settling into the seat. My heart ached the way it did every time I looked at him—even when his back was turned to me.

"Under new management," he announced without preamble. "This guy is a cousin of the previous shop owner. He wasn't able to give me more than a vague secondhand description of a couple of men that passed through here two weeks ago, but I'd put money on it—those drifters are who we're after."

"So they survived the accident," I breathed. My stomach still clenched as I remembered the police report I'd skimmed on the laptop. I could only hope Sylvia was still with Jon and Cliff, equally unscathed.

He nodded. "Seems like the car took the worst of it. They scrapped what was left of the last one for a vintage *Challenger*."

I wilted. That stupid car was the only reason we'd been able to tail them this far. Now, Sylvia may as well have vanished into thin air. "So, this was a waste of time."

"You know, it's hurtful how little faith you have in me." He held up his cell phone, which displayed a series of numbers and letters typed into the *Notes* screen. "Our friend was able to provide the new plates. Once I plug this in, we'll be back on track."

He started the car and pulled off the property, leaving the yellowed *Gulf Coast Auto* sign diminishing in the rearview mirror. He was right to move quickly—getting out of sight before the glamour wore off and that human noticed a stranger idling in the lot at half past midnight.

The road was narrow and winding, barely large enough for two vehicles to fit side by side. Tall oaks lined both sides, their spider-like branches blotting out what little moonlight we had. As he drove, he typed quickly into his phone, finger and thumb moving with a practiced ease. I knew the program he used was something very niche, and definitely *illegal*. He'd tried explaining the technology to me more than once, but it still went over my head despite my best efforts. All I understood was that it worked, and that was enough for now.

The app chimed—a cold, unnatural melody breaking the quiet. He slid the phone into the navigation mount on the driver's side, leaning back in his seat.

"We'll have a hit soon, Mel." His eyes darted to the rearview mirror. "She's still asleep?"

I glanced over my shoulder, watching the tiny rise and fall of Hazel's chest in the dim light. "Like a rock," I said quietly.

He laughed—a warm, fond sound that made butterflies stir in my stomach. The way he cared about Hazel and Sylvia was the most attractive thing about him.

"You should get some shut-eye, too," he said, glancing at me.

"*Shut-eye?*" I quirked a brow, smirking. "That's a new one."

"I don't wanna hear it. That's—It's a very common saying."

"It's not the worst I've heard, by far. What was that other one you spouted—'*bite the bullet*'?" I wrinkled my nose, once again picturing the cold taste of metal between my teeth. "It's just nonsensical."

He chuckled again, a bit self-deprecating. When his eyes moved back to the road, I stole another look at him.

In the soft glow of the car's dashboard, his features were illuminated—sharp, but weary, with shadows deepening the lines around his eyes. It suited him somehow. The years had been kind to him, where grief had not. Even the scarred remnants of the burn on his right cheek couldn't dull his good looks. He was still achingly handsome in that way that was both regal and rugged. His tawny blond hair was cut tragically short, tapered on the sides with slightly more length at the top—a common human style that I hated to admire, though it framed his face well. His blue eyes were piercing and intelligent. He still had that broad-shouldered, athletic build that gave off a subtle but commanding presence—something he had always pretended to be unaware of.

And *human*. He was human now.

I stole another look at Hazel. Still asleep.

Squaring my shoulders, I shifted to face the driver's seat fully. "I think it's time we told her, Tristan."

His silence surprised me. Tristan shot me a hard look, studying me. He rubbed his eyes with one hand. "Don't toy with me."

"You think I would throw these words around carelessly?"

Tristan leveled his frown at the road ahead. "What changed your mind?"

The cautious hope and suspicion in his deep voice flayed my heart. He was right to be wary. I wouldn't spare him.

"If we're only weeks behind the hunters now, that means our time together is drawing to a close," I said. "I don't think Hazel would forgive me if she heard the story after your departure. She deserves to have her questions answered by you. Things I can't tell her."

He nodded stiffly, and among everything else, I knew he could focus only on my admission that I intended for us to part ways.

"You know it has to be this way," I said. "No amount of stalling will stop the inevitable."

"She grew up so much," Tristan answered softly. "Can you blame me for wanting more time? Last I saw her, she couldn't even fly."

"And whose fault is that?" I snapped. The pain that washed over him was bone-deep. No matter how I tried to tell myself he deserved to wallow with me in the pain he had caused, I softened slightly. "Hazel has grown fond of you, even as a stranger. She'll be glad to know who you really are. She'll be thrilled you're alive and well. Is that not enough?"

He chuckled humorlessly. "Alive, yes. But I can't say I was *well* until you told me to come find you."

Silence stretched between us. I watched him carefully. Tristan's eyes were far away, perhaps scripting precisely what he would tell Hazel—as if he hadn't already done it in secret for weeks.

"Is your decision final?" he asked after a heavy sigh.

Yes, I wanted to bite out. *Once I have both of my girls, I no longer have to suffer your presence.*

But I couldn't. I was so tired of lying.

"When we find Sylvia, we'll talk again."

ACKNOWLEDGEMENTS

Writing a sequel is never an easy feat. It requires the courage to revisit characters and worlds we've already poured so much of ourselves into—and to do so with the hopes of meeting or exceeding expectations of the first installment. But what made it even more challenging for us was navigating personal struggles and working through difficult publishing circumstances, lessons learned the hard way, and the delays that followed. Still, here we are, and we couldn't be more grateful for the support that's carried us through it all.

First, to all our readers who took a chance on *Shot in the Dark*— your passion, feedback, and unwavering support have been nothing short of a lifeline. You've not only shown us that this story matters, but that our characters have a place in your hearts too. Your kind messages and enthusiasm have proven us wrong after a decade of wondering if this book would ever see the light of day. We're grateful every single day for you!

To our incredible beta readers—Stacy, Allie, Tyesha, Megan, Macey, and Paola—your input and passion was invaluable! You helped us shape this story into something even better than we imagined, and we're forever thankful for your time and energy.

Andrew, thank you for letting Mary spoil the entire series for you. Your willingness to listen, work through ideas, and provide endless support in all areas this adventure has meant the world to her and us. You truly put every book boyfriend to shame.

A massive thank you to our enthusiastic street team—your passion and energy continue to amaze us! To our ARC team, we couldn't have done this without your help in spreading the word, and we're so grateful for your constant encouragement. Our editor, Tabitha (@tabsdoesediting) who rescued us at the last hour with her keen talent!

Thank you to Aimee of @magnolia_mountainsidefl who has been such an avid supporter and worked tirelessly to make a beautiful custom perfume roller scent just for Sylvia! (Check out her page and our Etsy!)

Lastly, we want to acknowledge the unwavering support of our friends and family. Your support and patience with these two chaotic fairies at heart means the world.

To everyone who helped bring *Hunted in the Shadows* to life, we say thank you from the bottom of our hearts. This journey has been one of highs and lows, but it's all been worth it because of YOU. Here's to the adventure continuing!

ABOUT THE AUTHORS

Mary Dublin and Anne Kendsley are a best friend and co-author duo that have been writing and adventuring together for over twelve years.

Anne Kendsley is a writer from South Texas with a passion for weaving stories that explore the fantastical and surreal.

Growing up, she developed a deep appreciation for the power of storytelling and started writing her own tales at a young age. Her love for fantasy and sci-fi has carried into her writing today, blending with darker, grittier themes.

Ultimately, she loves to explore complex characters who stand resilient against societal breakdown while finding beauty in a harsh and unforgiving world. When she's not devouring one book after another or daydreaming about her next story, she's taking a walk in the woods or cozying up with a video game.

Mary Dublin was born and raised in the heart of Florida and has had a passion for storytelling since childhood. Her love for words began at a young age, where she found solace in books that transported her to fantastical worlds and inspired her to begin dreaming of her own stories.

Apart from writing, Mary is a passionate traveler, and her experiences in different parts of the world inspire elements in her novels. When she's not writing, she can be found practicing yoga, trying new hiking trails, or curled up with a good book on a rainy day.

FREEDOM BELONGS TO THE HIGHEST BIDDER IN...

Lured in the Crimson

BOOK III IN THE
SHOT IN THE DARK SERIES

FOLLOW US ON SOCIAL MEDIA OR
OUR NEWSLETTER FOR UPDATES!

ALSO BY

Shot in the Dark
(Pub. 2024)

The Restoration Program
(Pub. 2023)

The Heart Between
Kingdoms
(Pub. 2017)

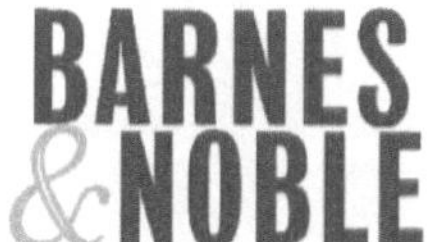

available at **amazon**   kindle unlimited   **BARNES & NOBLE**